Rescue at Pine Ridge

Erich Martin Hicks

Outskirts Press, Inc.
Denver, Colorado

Rescue at Pine Ridge
All Rights Reserved.
Copyright © 2009 Erich Martin Hicks
V4.0 R2.1

Book illustrated cover Rescue at Pine Ridge
by Erich Martin Hicks.

Outskirts Press, Inc.
http://www.outskirtspress.com

ISBN PB: 978-1-4327-2822-9
ISBN HB: 978-1-4327-3683-5

Library of Congress Control Number: 2008934497

Outskirts Press and the "OP" logo are trademarks belonging to Outskirts Press, Inc.

PRINTED IN THE UNITED STATES OF AMERICA

"The story of the heroic rescue of the famed 7th Cavalry, by the 9th Cavalry Buffalo Soldiers."

SOON TO BE AN EPIC MINISERIES

"This is an untapped story that has tremendous potential as a captivating miniseries."

"The author does a great job of capturing the spirit, tenacity and unwavering resolve these soldiers possessed while carrying out their duties and orders as part of the American Army."

To my wife

Through the long hours, days, weeks, months, and years it took to make this epic story possible, this is dedicated to my beautiful wife Portia. This epic story would not have been possible without her friendship, love, understanding, and undivided devotion behind the scenes. To add to this process are our beloved animals.

Acknowledgements

The Buffalo Soldiers—past, present, future

The American Negro Indian Scouts

The America Indians—past, present, future

Eddie Dixon, sculptor, Buffalo Soldier Monument, Fort Leavenworth, Kansas

Debra L. Johnson, attorney at law

Humberto Barga, book cover illustration

The Nebraska State Historical Society for the original negative of the 9th Cavalry, K Troop at Pine Ridge and other photos within this book.

Matt Fletcher, photographer of author's photograph

Embassy Flags - Thanks - Sonora, California

To my very best friend, Tariano (Tito) Jackson

To my friends: Susan Muller-Robb, Frank Lenard,
Gary F. Bentley, John Russell, Walter W. Brady,
Lennister K. Williams, Ernest Ashford, William Harris,
Larry Shipp, Al Adams, Alison Blasko and
Jaclyn Friedlander.
Thank you all for your support...

ANA Special Effects, Van Nuys, California

The 9th Memorial United States Cavalry, Arizona

The National Chapter of the Buffalo Soldiers

The Artifact Tree, Malibu, California

Zuma Jay Surfboards, Malibu, California

The United States Armed Forces

The Ole Mighty Creator

Trooper: Barry Patrick Neal, 1952 – 2004

About the Author

Erich Martin Hicks garners his inspiration from his Grandfather, Buffalo Soldier Captain Lee Jay Hicks, who was the right hand man to General John Joseph "Black Jack" Pershing, during WW-I. He is a fourth-generation Angeleno, "a native to Los Angeles, California." He is the first and currently the only African American to be issued a Special Effects, State Pyrotechnic Operators' 1st Class (Master) License, and this achievement marks a milestone in the motion picture and television industry. Fortunate to have had the support of one of the industry's finest special effects coordinators, Erich attributes much of his success as an apprentice to journeyman and now 1st Class Master to the support of the late Dick Albain, whose industry credits include numerous motion picture and television projects, most notably "The Three Stooges" and "I Dream of Genie." Erich's great love and passion for film and television production captured the late Albain's respect, therefore a professional and personal relationship developed, providing Erich with the mentoring necessary to learn the intricacies of the special effects trade.

Erich's licenses qualify him to plan, lead, coordinate, and determine the safety of every action sequence—from stunts to major explosions—to achieve a realistic scene. Erich is a member of A.F.T.R.A., D.G.A., S.A.G., and IATSE Local 44. Erich descends from a family heritage that includes his grandfather's distinction as a Buffalo Soldier, who served under General John "Black Jack" Pershing. Erich's grandfather was one of the highest-ranking African-American military officers in World War I. As captain in the 317th Armored Train Division, Captain Lee J. Hicks was responsible for moving munitions from the ports of France to the war front.

Erich and his wife Portia, who is also an industry professional, opened a production company, Alpha Wolf Productions, Inc. (AWP). AWP is a conglomerate of sub-production companies geared towards the motion picture industry, special effects, voice-over, and motion-picture productions. Erich and Portia's desires are to further their achievements and expand their company into the realm of producing theatrical and television releases. Through knowledge and ambition, their dream is to develop AWP into one of the largest diverse production companies in the industry, producing feature film and documentary projects in the areas of contemporary action, adventure, and drama, with themes that educate and raise awareness of the African-American contribution to American history.

Because of Erich's passion for America's Buffalo Soldiers, and the gallant rescue of the famed 7th Cavalry by the 9th Cavalry Buffalo Soldiers, he sat down for nine months straight, fourteen hours a day on average, seven days a week, studying the basic history of the 9th Cavalry; and wrote the epic miniseries, *Rescue at Pine Ridge*.

Having made several attempts at marketing to various production houses, and receiving positive accolades such as, "This is an untapped story that has tremendous potential," etc., Erich decided to write the novel, *Rescue at Pine Ridge*.

Erich has written other epic stories: *Stagecoach Mary, Bass Reeves – U.S. Deputy Marshal*, and *Operation "FIREFLY."* Other movies Erich has written include *Choice, Dead Inventors*, and *Lady Liberty*, to name a few. Also in development is Erich's first documentary, "*Soul on a Wave*," a film about the life and styles of the surfers of color and the Black Surfing Association (BSA).

To purchase a photocopy of the 9th Cavalry, K Troop and/or the front cover illustration, please visit: *rescueatpineridge.com*

To stay up to date with Alpha Wolf Productions, please visit: *http://www.alphawolfprods.com*

Table of Contents

Act II   119

Proven Soldiers

Act III   201

To the Rescue

Photos

American flag – 43 stars
General Benjamin O. Davis, Sr
Buffalo Soldier Monument Statue, Fort Leavenworth, Kansas
9th Cavalry Band in Santa Fe, New Mexico, 1880
Native American – Chief Victorio from the Mescalero Apache Nation
Native American – Nana from the Mimbres Apache Nation
Native American – Geronimo from the Chiricahua Apache Nation
Native American – Big Foot from the Mniconjou Sioux Nation
Colonel Edward Hatch
Captain Henry Carroll
Lieutenant Mathias W. Day

Major Guy V. Henry
Lieutenant Henry Ossian Flipper
Chaplain Henry Vinton Plummer
25th Infantry, D Troop
Scout Frank Grouard
Corporal William O. Wilson

Author's Opinion

Wovoka – Nevada Paiute Medicine Man
Ghost Dance
Ghost Shirts
Sioux lay dead with mounted 7th Cavalry soldier
The massacre of Wounded Knee
Big Foot lays dead and frozen
Mass grave, burial of the dead
Sioux Ghost Dance

Quote of Black Elk

Chief Sitting Bull – Tatanka Iyotaka Hunkpapa Sioux

1866 United States flag - 36 stars

The gossip and rumors they experienced were false due to paranoia and racism.

The civilians, their officers, the Indians that gave them their name, who observed their bravery, gallantry and heroism, knew better. For the Buffalo Soldier it was duty and honor!

9th Cavalry, K Troop guidon

Prologue

Rescue at Pine Ridge depicts the true gallantry and spirit of a group of men in the United States Army. These volunteer soldiers endured extreme hardships in their everyday lives, not only from the environment, weather, military personnel, and enemies of the United States, but also from the ones they were sworn to protect.

The mere hearsay and published gossip, "alcoholics, cowards, deserters and even misfits," would be enough to discourage most men; however, these weren't just any men, they were "The Buffalo Soldiers." During the Indian Wars, the colored regiments were nearly one-fourth of the U.S. Cavalry and Infantry, receiving many commendations and honors, as the white regiments did during this period.

For decades in the late nineteenth century, colored regulars were one of the most effective troops on the western frontier. Because of their marvelous feats of gallantry, combating hostile Indians, Comancheros, and outlaws, eighteen enlisted colored, eleven of whom were members of the 9th Cavalry, received the Medal of Honor. In the face of great dangers, the Buffalo Soldiers fought and died to make the United States' western frontier safe for people of all races.

The fictionalized story you are about to read has been dramatically enhanced for your entertainment pleasure; however, most of the stories—and the outcomes within this novel—are historically genuine.

Act I
Introduction

The time period is set from 1866 to 1891. The location is the vast west territory of the United States.

Northeast Texas, fall 1866. It's a clear morning as a bugle call sounds. The smell of thousands and thousands of horse mounts permeates the air in a massive Union Army encampment. Numerous guidons, military tents, and smoldering cooking fires dot the landscape, filling the air with a smoky haze, as over forty-five hundred white Union soldiers move throughout the vast military compound.

This is the reorganizing of the United States Army, after the Civil War. Troopers and infantrymen are carrying on with their everyday activities of soldiering, cooking, marching, drilling, and moving large artillery pieces with cavalry mules.

Outside the encampment, surrounded by trees in a spot of trampled down knee-high grass, is a long makeshift rectangular conference table. There's an assemblage of high-ranking Union Army officers gathered into small conversational groups around the area.

Fifteen officers are present, eight of whom are known. Standing at one end of the table, shoveling through military papers on top, is General Philip Sheridan, who called this gathering, smoking a cigar. Standing to one side of the trampled down grass is Colonel Edward Hatch, Colonel Benjamin H. Grierson, Colonel Abner Doubleday, and several officers talking in their group. Colonel Randall S. MacKenzie, General George Crook, and several other officers are standing yards away, talking in their group. Then there's Lieutenant Colonel George Armstrong Custer, talking with General Nelson A. Miles smoking a cigar at the other end of the trampled grass, away from the other groups.

General Sheridan has placed papers at each chair placement, and then looks to the officers, one by one. General Sheridan is scruffy, standing behind the long end of the table, leaning on the top with both hands, palms down, with his cigar protruding from his mouth, held by his teeth. He is five feet three and thirty-six years old, but he looks fifty. The Civil War days have taken their toll on him, as they have on all of these officers. The war has aged them all, considerably.

General Sheridan takes a puff from his cigar, then removes it with his right hand, exhales, and speaks with a rough raspy voice, "Gentlemen, take your seats."

The officers don't even look to General Sheridan as they begin walking, carrying their individual conversations to the table. However, they remain standing and talking to each other.

General Sheridan looks to the officers with a stern look and then says, "Gentlemen, please take your seats."

The officers walk to their chairs and sit down; however, they continue on with their own personal conversations, as if General Sheridan wasn't even there. General Sheridan looks to the officers, takes a puff from his cigar, exhales, blowing smoke from his nostrils and then shouts, "Gentlemen, gentlemen... GENTLEMEN!"

The officers look to General Sheridan, slowing and stopping their conversations at their own pace as General Sheridan watches patiently with cigar smoke still streaming from his nostrils.

All conversations have ceased as General Sheridan says, "Good morning."

All present return the greeting, saying, "Good morning, General."

General Sheridan then says, "We have a lot of work to complete. Now, I believe everyone knows everyone...in case you don't"—he points to each person sitting at the table—"Custer, Hatch, Grierson, Miles, Doubleday, MacKenzie, Crook...ah, you all know each other. Thank you, gentlemen, for coming. Now..." He looks to the paper in front of him, picks it up, and says, "Now..."

Lt. Colonel Custer interrupts and says, "Phillip, I was ordered to come here last week and—"

General Sheridan interrupts with a stern look. "Yes you were Lieutenant Colonel, and I am going to get down to brass tacks. George...we all know your opposition to accepting command of the 9th Cavalry..." Sheridan looks to the paper he is holding in front of him, and says, "By the Congressional Act of the Thirty-ninth Congress, dated twenty-eight July, eighteen-hundred and sixty-six, section three"—he clears his throat—"there shall be four additional regiments, two of which shall be composed of—"

Lt. Colonel Custer rises from the table in a fit of rage, interrupting General Sheridan speaking. He begins pacing, throwing a well-controlled tantrum, throwing his forearms out in front of him, holding his elbows to his side, clinching his fist tight, then throwing his forearms back down saying, "Damn it Phillip, I already told you...I'm not going to be looked down upon...and have my career jeopardized by trying to get those...'brunettes'...to act like white men in an Army uniform!"

Colonel Doubleday looks to Lt. Colonel Custer and says, "Now George, they fought well in the war. Matter of fact, it was most of them that broke through the southern lines here with Grierson and Hatch, on those midnight raids deep into enemy territory."

Lt. Colonel Custer looks to Colonel Doubleday with an attitude and says, "Abner, you stick to baseball with those 'porch monkeys' and I'll stick to soldiering!"

Colonel Doubleday is exasperated as he stands, slaps his hands on the table and says, "Damn you to death, Custer!"

General Sheridan stands and shouts, "Gentlemen—and you George—sit down!"

Lt. Colonel Custer looks to General Sheridan in a huff and says, "I'm fine where I am, sir!"

Lt. Colonel Custer then turns from the table and walks towards an area of standing tall grass, when something begins moving the grass near a tree in front of him, out of sight of the other officers. Lt. Colonel Custer maneuvers over to get a better look at what's causing the movement, when he spots a little five-year-old boy, Howard J. Mitchell, with long blonde wavy hair, crouching down, trying not to be seen. Howard freezes when Lt. Colonel Custer spots him, and their eyes lock, for this is a tense moment. Howard Mitchell has just seen his first hero, Lt. Colonel George Armstrong Custer.

Lt. Colonel Custer stares at Howard for a couple of moments, then winks and smiles at him. The other officers look to see what Lt. Colonel Custer is staring at, but they can't see the little boy due to the tall grass. The expression on Howard's face shows that he has been taken aback, because his first hero has just acknowledged him.

Lt. Colonel Custer motions for Howard to come to him, but Howard stands and runs off towards a farmhouse in the distance. The commotion in the grass causes all the officers to stand and take notice.

General Sheridan looks to the boy running off and says, "Never mind the boy George, that's the farmer's grandson from Michigan. We have more important matters. We have to decide who's going to take command of the 9th Cavalry. Will you please reconsider, George?"

Lt. Colonel Custer thinks for a moment looking at the boy running away then says, "Hum, my home state, Michigan." Lt. Colonel Custer turns, looks at General Sheridan, and says, "Phillip, give me the 7th Cavalry! Give me the 7th! You can put someone else with those...niggers!"

"...George!" yells General Sheridan reluctantly, "that's unbecoming of an officer. You're lucky I don't court-martial you right here, and now!" General Sheridan looks to Lt. Colonel Custer with a look of reluctant disgust and then says, "All right...you want the 7th Lieutenant, Colonel? I don't know why...the seventh's yours!"

Lt. Colonel Custer looks off in the distance with self-gratification and says, "Thank you, sir. May I be dismissed since all matters relating to me are settled?"

"Yes...dismissed," says General Sheridan disgustedly.

Lt. Colonel Custer snaps to attention and salutes General Sheridan, and then marches back to the Army encampment.

General Sheridan and the others look to Lt. Colonel Custer as they take their seats, some shaking their heads and the others talking amongst themselves.

"H-h-ow...did he ever get his commission?" a somewhat stuttering Colonel Doubleday says.

General Miles, smoking his cigar, exhales, puts both hands on the table, and with a gentlemanly chuckle looks to Colonel Doubleday and says, "My man...he walked into a river-stream...knee-deep to scout for a patrol, and not under fire."

General Sheridan says pointedly, "One should be so lucky." He looks to Colonel Hatch and says, "Hatch, since you did so well with the Colored Second Iowa Regiment, will you take the Ninth?"

Colonel Hatch's face is elongated with a scar on the right side. He has deep blue eyes beaming with intelligence, a Roman nose, thin lips, white hair parted down the middle with a tinge of black that has not been affected by years of war, and a bristly mustache. He is a very good horseman and is tall for a cavalryman, so as he stands he bumps the table with his thighs, almost knocking it over. All the papers on top scatter as everyone holds on to the table.

Colonel Hatch then looks to General Sheridan and says, "Sorry, General," as he is also holding the table while standing.

All the officers at the table have finished straightening out the papers in front of them as Colonel Hatch says, "It will be a pleasure. The colored regiments fought bravely for me. There can be no question about their good soldiering and fighting qualities."

"Thank you Edward," says General Sheridan. "Then gentlemen, our next matter."

The time period is now 1876. The location is the supply depot near the river junction of the Bighorn and Little Bighorn Rivers. It's a peaceful spring June day as big puffy white clouds float across the blue skies, with sounds of birds and the clank and plop of supplies being unloaded from a watercraft barge by three teamsters from a white infantry unit. Suddenly, two army Crow Indian Scouts ride in hard on their mounts. Both are wearing their army blue blouses, with their leather fringed pants, moccasins and a United States Scout insignia pinned on their campaign hats, cross arrows and "USS" lying above the center point of the arrows.

One of the scouts has a bullet wound in his posterior. He is leaning forward in his saddle, and as they come to a hard stop in the middle of the depot, their mounts throw dust. The unwounded Crow Scout jumps from his mount and runs over to help his comrade off his mount.

The wounded scout is almost falling off his mount as most of the depot runs over to investigate where the scouts stopped—including Sam Jones, the barge operator. "Hey, they're from Benteen's group, they're Crow Scouts," Jones says. "They came through here a week ago. I'd remember that corporal's bluecoat he's got on."

The unwounded Crow Scout is tending to his comrade's wound on the ground when he looks up to the crowd that has gathered, gesturing with his hand, and pointing in the direction they rode from. In Crow language, he says somewhat panicked, "Many tepees, many lodges...I need help for my brother...many Indians...many."

"My Crow is a little rusty, but it sounds like he sayin' there's a lot of Injuns upriver," says Sam Jones.

Charlie Taylor, Sam's partner says, "Hey Sam, remember the strong smell of gunpowder in the air the other day?" He points to the scout's wound and says, "I wonder if his gunshot had anythin' to do with the smell? They came from that direction."

"Yeah Charlie, yeah... Now that you mentioned it, that

7

gunpowder smell did come from upriver, more in the direction of the Little Bighorn River Valley," says Sam.

The depot adjutant runs over to Sam and says, "Hey Sam, the teamsters finished unloading. The Far West is coming in. General Terry likes the dock cleared when his Command Boat docks. You got to move the barge."

"Sure thin'. Come on Charlie," says Sam.

Sam and Charlie run down to the dock, board the barge and push off the dock as the steam-paddle boat, The Far West, with its black smokestacks comes into view through the trees.

Charlie spots the steamboat stacks and says, "There she is, through the trees, The Far West, Brigadier General Alfred Terry's Command Boat!"

The steamboat rounds the bend and comes into view, a white, polished, medium-size steamboat. As The Far West paddles towards the depot, it begins to maneuver into docking position as Charlie says, "Boy, ain't she somethin', spit shined and everythin'."

Aboard the Command Boat, standing inside the wheelhouse is Brigadier General Alfred Terry, looking out from the Command Center through the large frame windows that surround the front of the boat, with his Navy captain at the helm.

Standing outside the Command Center are five members of his command, several white infantry soldiers, teamsters, and several civilians, including Howard J. Mitchell, who is now fifteen with the same long, wavy blonde hair. General Terry's command is unaware of the current events as the Command Boat maneuvers in and begins docking.

The unwounded Crow Scout is kneeling next to his comrade, who is being attended to by an Army doctor. Still trying to tell his story, he looks at the crowd, and in Crow language says, "…Many tepees, many lodges…too many!"

Curly, another Crow Indian Scout, comes riding in hard on his mount, stopping, throwing dust, then looks to the crowd that has gathered around his comrades. Curly has been riding for two days straight. He's tired and dusty. His field glasses are twisted behind him, held in place by its leather strap around his neck and arm.

Curly dismounts and walks wearily over to his comrades, walking through the crowd that has now surrounded his comrades. As Curly breaks through, he stops, looks down to his comrades, and speaks in broken English: "How he?"

"Doc said he'd be fine. What happen out there?" said the depot adjutant.

"Food first…then I tell…food first," says Curly.

"Someone get him something to eat!" says the depot adjutant.

A private standing next to Curly hands him his canteen of water. Curly grabs the canteen and begins drinking the water as if there was no more. After quenching his thirst, he pours a little water over his head and then hands the canteen to his comrade, who's tending to the wounded Crow scout. A civilian offers Curly some dried beef. Curly looks at the food as if that was the last meat in the world, grabs the beef intently, and begins stuffing his mouth.

General Terry, his staff, Howard, and the rest of the passengers begin disembarking The Far West and walk towards the crowd. As General Terry reaches the crowd, he begins moving the spectators to each side with his hands, making his way towards the center. When he reaches the opening in the center of the crowd, General Terry stops with his staff, with Howard following, surveying the situation.

General Terry then looks to Curly standing to one side

of his comrades and says, "What happened, Scout?"

Everybody tightens the circle around the area, gathering, awaiting the anticipated answer. Curly looks at General Terry, kneels, and begins drawing a circle in the sand with his finger. After drawing the circle, he then grabs some sticks nearby, breaks them in half making them somewhat even, sticks them within the circle, points to the sticks, and says, "Soldiers."

The depot adjutant quickly says, "Indians. How many Indians?"

"Many lodges...many Sioux...Cheyenne...they thick... they attack all over."

Curly moves his hands in the air above the circle, all around the outside and inside of the perimeter, showing the Sioux and Cheyenne Indians penetrating their skirmish lines. Curly grabs some dead dried leaves nearby, crumbles them in his hands, then sprinkles them all over the outside and inside of the circle of sticks. Then he says, "Sioux...Cheyenne..."

The depot adjutant says, "Then what? Then what?"

Curly looks up to the adjutant and General Terry, wipes the circle clean with both hands, and picks up more leaves, crumbling them all over the entire area.

General Terry says, "What regiment are you with, Scout?"

Looking to General Terry, Curly says, "Seventh," as he stuffs more dry beef in his mouth. With a full mouth of beef he mumbles, "Custer."

General Terry quickly looks to the adjutant and says, "Send a messenger to my regiment. Tell them to meet me at the Little Bighorn." General Terry quickly makes an about-face and marches back to The Far West with his command following behind him. Howard is left standing in the crowd sobbing, talking to the open space in front of him saying,

"No, no...he can't be dead, he can't be." He sobs, "Custer is my hero, I came to see him... He can't be dead!"

General Terry approaches The Far West as the Navy captain stands by the gangplank of the steamboat.

"Captain, fire up the boiler," says General Terry. "Full steam ahead."

The Navy captain says, "Aye, aye sir. Where are we headed?"

"Little Bighorn...to look for survivors. Something happened to Custer's regiment."

Howard, still sobbing, watches General Terry board the steamboat as he begins walking towards the dock. The gangplank is pulled and the tie-lines are tossed aboard while the teamsters on board push the bow off the dock with long poles. The boiler builds steam as smoke billows from the stacks and the paddle begins to turn.

Howard sees the steamboat pulling away as he reaches the dock. He begins running, keeping pace and an eye on the rear of the steamboat as he jumps on the side of the stern near the paddle-wheel just as The Far West pulls away from the dock.

The depot adjutant sees Howard jump aboard, runs down to the dock and yells, "Hey, you, you can't go past this point!"

Too late as the steamboat is already out too far and the noise of the paddle hitting the water at full steam ahead has drowned out the adjutant's shouts to all on board, except for one of the privates in General Terry's command who took notice of the depot adjutant yelling at Howard near the stern of the boat.

The private looks to Howard, walks back to the stern, apprehends him by the arm, and takes him to the side of the wheelhouse. Howard gives no resistance as the private places him against the large frame windows of the wheelhouse and then walks into the Command Center to inform General Terry. General Terry walks out of the Command Center and approaches Howard.

Howard's expression is a little apprehensive and scared as General Terry says, "This is a Military Operation Zone, son! Civilians are not allowed pass the depot."

Howard begins sobbing as General Terry looks at Howard and says, "What's wrong son?"

"Custer is my hero. I saw him when he got his command of the Seventh Cavalry. I can't believe...those savages killed him."

"We don't know what's happened son." General Terry looks to Howard with compassion and says, "Don't worry. What's your name?"

Howard slowly stops sobbing and says, "Howard J. Mitchell."

"Well Howard, if something has happened to Custer, the Army will get its revenge!"

"I want to...I want to join the cavalry...and fight Injuns," says Howard.

The Navy captain is listening to the conversation through one of the open front windows of the wheelhouse and says, "Excuse me sir, I do believe we're goin' to need some extra hands." The Navy captain looks to Howard and says, "You're eighteen, aren't you lad? I mean, sir," as the Navy captain winks at Howard to give him encouragement.

Howard is looking at the Navy captain, hesitates at first, then acknowledges him by slowly nodding his head up and down indicating yes. "Go ahead, General, swear him in, this is your Command Post," says the Navy captain.

General Terry looks from the Navy captain, then to Howard and says, "Howard, do you really want to join the cavalry?"

Howard's face lights up as General Terry says, "Raise

your right hand."

Howard raises his right hand as General Terry begins swearing him into the Army. "Do you Howard..."

The time period is now spring, 1880. The location is a medium-size cavalry depot on the outskirts of Santa Fe, New Mexico. It's early morning, and there's a lot of military activity occurring in preparation for Memorial Day celebrations by various troops. Banners are being hung. Repair work is being conducted. KP duty is in full swing in and around areas of the post. Supplies are coming and going. A United States Cavalry band is heard playing music in the distance, while marching into town, and the sounds of cavalrymen, breaking cavalry mounts are heard coming from the corral.

In the depot stables, two troopers are performing KP duty. One of the soldiers is Trooper Howard J. Mitchell, whom General Terry enlisted into the Army at Little Bighorn. He's taller now, with a short military haircut. His physical body doesn't appear to have had four years of hardened frontier service as that of other troopers of the depot.

Trooper Mitchell is scooping and pitching mount manure out from a stall with his pitchfork. He is with another soldier on KP duty, Trooper David Hartigan, standing outside the stall by the KP duty catcher, the wheelbarrow that's almost full.

Trooper Mitchell is a little upset, but he doesn't show it as he piles on the last manure onto the heap in Trooper Hartigan's wheelbarrow. It's only when he pitches the pitchfork into the ground hard to make it stick that Trooper Mitchell shows his anger. He says, "I'm tired of this...scoopin' manure every day. I didn't sign up for this. I want to kill Injuns...especially them Sioux."

Trooper Hartigan picks up his heavy wheelbarrow and begins pushing it towards the doors of the stables as Trooper Mitchell pulls the pitchfork from the ground. He walks out of the stall, then puts the pitchfork on top of his wheelbarrow—picking up his heavy load full of manure—and begins pushing the wheelbarrow behind Trooper Hartigan.

As Trooper Hartigan strains pushing his wheelbarrow he says, "Well, that's what you get for bein' late for roll call seven times this week."

Troopers Mitchell and Hartigan exit the stables, pushing their wheelbarrows to a large pyramid pile of manure outside the stables. They come to a stop as Trooper Mitchell grabs the pitchfork off the wheelbarrow and begins pitching manure onto the pile while Trooper Hartigan takes a piece of straw out of his pocket and sticks it in his mouth as if it were a toothpick.

Trooper Hartigan then plops one foot up on a log, looks to Trooper Mitchell doing the work and says, "You're lucky you're not cleanin' the shit hole...and, you ain't goin' to find any Injuns around here anymore either...they all mostly been wiped-out...except for the likes of them over there."

A gust of wind blows dust as Trooper Hartigan points to some very sad-looking, nation-lost Apache Indians begging for food and money by the depot store.

"You've only been here a couple of weeks from that military place in Chicago...why you so hell fired bent on killin' Injuns for anyway?"

Trooper Mitchell looks to Trooper Hartigan with a determined look, saying, "They killed General Custer. He was my hero...I was there at the Little Bighorn River Valley when word came in of the massacre. That's where

General Terry enlisted me in the cavalry."

Trooper Hartigan excitedly takes his foot off the log stump, rushes towards Trooper Mitchell and says, "No foolin'...you were there? Did you get to fight any?"

"No...all I did was pick up dead bodies." Trooper Mitchell becomes distraught and says, "They took all their uniforms...their bodies were all cut up, they scalped them...I was the first to find Custer's body. He wasn't cut up and scalped like all the rest, he was only bleedin' from his ears. They punctured his eardrums with sticks...it was horrible." Trooper Mitchell gets mad, throws down his pitchfork and says, "And all I do is sit around this post, and clean shit stalls. I wanna fight Injuns!"

"Well hell, Bighorn was four years ago. You mean to tell me you haven't gotten a chance to fight Injuns?"

"No...after Little Bighorn, General Terry sent me to Chicago. I worked at a desk in a big office for General Sherman, until I transferred here two weeks ago."

"I never seen the Army send out office boys to the cavalry or infantry with little time left. Why they send you out here for anyway? It takes years of this life to get use to."

Trooper Hartigan grabs Trooper Mitchell's hand and looks at his palms as he says, "Why your hands are like a newborn baby's ass, you don't even have harden blisters."

Trooper Mitchell snatches his hand back and says, "What do you expect from sittin' at a desk all day for four years. I just requested frontier duty a month ago, with a promise to reenlist."

"Why would you go do a darn blang thin' like that for...maybe to get yourself killed? Look, my enlistment ends in one year like yours. Don't reenlist. Why don't you get out and go west...like I am?"

"Cause I told you: I want to fight Injuns!" says Trooper Mitchell.

Trooper Mitchell grabs the pitchfork off the ground and continues pitching manure out of both wheelbarrows until they're both almost empty.

Troopers Mitchell and Hartigan then grab the handles of their wheelbarrows and tip them over, dumping out the last of the manure against the pile. They turn them back over and begin pushing their wheelbarrows alongside of the stables towards a fairly large corral, when they begin to hear cheering and yelling coming from the corral pin.

They both look towards the corral pin and see a colored soldier in the corral, saddle-breaking a regimental mount. The saddle-breaking soldier is being cheered on by several of his comrades in the corral that are dressed for the occasion. Some shirts are hanging out over their trousers, suspenders are undone, while others are in their undershirts with their suspenders holding up their trousers. This is a detachment of the 9th Cavalry, K Troop, *Buffalo Soldiers* cheering on their comrade, who is saddle-breaking a beautiful black mount. Five of the colored soldiers are sitting on the corral top fence rail, not far from their saddles, and two colored soldiers are mounted inside the corral to assist their comrade.

One of the mounted soldiers, in his trail uniform, is their sergeant. Sergeant George Jordan—a dark-complexioned man and only five foot four, born in Tennessee a slave—enlisted in 1871 at the age of twenty-one. He completed three years in the infantry then transferred to the 9th Cavalry. He progressed from almost total illiteracy to become quite proficient in grammatical skills.

Sergeant Jordan has nine years of hardened frontier service as he shouts, "Stay on him trooper!"

The other colored soldier mounted next to Sergeant Jordan is Corporal William O. Wilson, who is fairly

educated, flamboyant, and one of the best marksmen in the
9th Cavalry. He wears a wide-brimmed white hat and large
cowboy spurs on his boots.

Corporal Wilson looks to the trooper saddle-breaking
the mount, and humorously says, "Hurry up Temple, we
ain't got all day. We got a parade to go to—and we go back
to Fort Stanton tomorrow. The way you're goin' at it, we'll
be here till next week."

Sergeant Jordan shouts out to the trooper again, "Come
on, stay on him Trooper Temple!"

The cavalry mount that the five foot three ex-slave
Trooper Guy Temple is trying to saddle-break is taking him
for the ride of a lifetime. The mount runs and bucks
Trooper Temple past Sergeant Jordan and Corporal Wilson.
As he flies by his comrades sitting on the corral fence,
Trooper Temple looks back and shouts, "I'm doing my best
Sarggge!"

As the mount runs and bucks, Trooper Temple's cavalry
hat flies off his head. Trooper Temple is being bucked, but
he is sticking with the mount until it finally gives in to the
unmovable soldier on its back.

Corporal Wilson spurs his mount into action, riding
through the corral, bending low to one side out of the
saddle. He scoops-up Trooper Temple's hat off the ground,
sits upright in the saddle, and gallops towards Trooper
Temple.

Corporal Wilson reaches Trooper Temple, handing him
his hat. The colored soldiers are having fun as cowboys;
however, they are very professional soldiers showing their
skills not only in saddle-breaking the cavalry mounts, but
also in the saddle, showing their agility in maneuvers that it
takes to be a good cavalry soldier.

Trooper Hartigan looks to Trooper Mitchell and says,
"I've been watchin' 'em since they first got here a couple

days ago. I found out from the adjutant they're from Fort Stanton, detachment of K Troop, Ninth Cavalry on temporary duty breakin' in regimental mounts. They say the Injuns call them Buffalo Soldiers. They just a bunch of Mud Turtles to me—good for nothin', just a bunch of niggers."

Trooper Mitchell is not truly a racist; however, his comment back to Trooper Hartigan is not a rebuff: "Now, you shouldn't go an' and say that. You must be jealous of 'em boys. I've been watchin' 'em too. Those darkies—they're pretty darn good, you know."

Trooper Mitchell walks over to the corral leaving Trooper Hartigan behind, watching from a distance, folding his arms and chewing on his straw.

As Trooper Mitchell reaches the corral, he lays his pitchfork against the stable and climbs up on the lower rail of the corral fence. He looks to Trooper Temple and Corporal Wilson and says, "That sure is some fancy ridin'. Where all you coloreds learn to ride like that from?"

Corporal Wilson looks to Sergeant Jordan and says, "Hey, Sarge, listen to this." Corporal Wilson looks back, points to Trooper Mitchell, and says, "He wants to know where we learned to ride."

Corporal Wilson spurs his mount towards Trooper Mitchell with Trooper Temple following. Trooper Mitchell appears to be a little nervous and shy at the experience of these colored soldiers spurring their mounts towards him. Sergeant Jordan and the other Buffalo Soldiers also converge upon Trooper Mitchell.

As Corporal Wilson reaches the corral fence, he climbs off his mount onto the fence, looks to Trooper Mitchell and says, "Well, howdy do trooper? What's your name?"

Trooper Mitchell somewhat sheepishly says, "Trooper

Howard J. Mitchell."

"Well I'm Corporal Wilson."

As the other Buffalo Soldiers ride up, they clamor on the corral fence, as if they were going to tell some old-time stories.

Corporal Wilson looks to his comrades then says, "This here is Trooper Guy Temple, the best farrier and saddle bronc in the entire U.S. Cavalry."

All the soldiers agree saying, "Uh huh," and, "Sure enough."

"Corporal Wilson is the best shot in the Ninth," says Trooper Temple.

All the soldiers agree simultaneously, saying uh huh's and sure enough's.

Corporal Wilson then looks to Trooper Temple humorously and says, "Quiet, Temple."

All the soldiers laugh and look to Sergeant Jordan who is riding up. Corporal Wilson looks from Trooper Mitchell, at his comrades, then to Sergeant Jordan and says, "This is Sergeant George Jordan, the best sergeant in the whole U.S. Cavalry."

Again, all the soldiers agree and say, "Sure is," "Uh huh."

Corporal Wilson looks to his comrades indicating with his hand and says, "This is Trooper Irving, Trooper Walley, Trooper Perry, Trooper Chase, and Chief of Scouts John Glass, the best Scout in these parts. Where you from trooper? Not too many white boys wanna know about us."

Trooper Mitchell hesitantly assesses the colored soldiers looking back at him as he says, "I was born in Michigan. But after my parents died, I went to live in Texas with my grandparents."

"Well Trooper Mitchell, we learned to ride, most of us

on plantations, farms...in the South and Midwest, on ranches...as slaves and freemen. Others learned here in the U.S. Cavalry," says Corporal Wilson.

"You pretty darn good. I wanna learn to ride like that—so I can go fight the Sioux and Cheyenne Injuns," says Trooper Mitchell.

"Why do you want to fight Indians for, son?" says Sergeant Jordan.

"For killing General Custer!" says Trooper Mitchell as he becomes sad. He looks to Sergeant Jordan and says, "I was there...I saw what they did to him."

"Trooper, it takes time to learn good cavalry maneuvers. As for fightin' Sioux or any Indian, it sounds like you want revenge, and that's not what we are paid for. We are peacekeepers and that's all," says Sergeant Jordan.

Trooper Mitchell thinks for a moment, then looks to Sergeant Jordan and the Buffalo Soldiers and says, "Hey...there was a large colored boy's body I came across at the massacre...not far from Custers', he wasn't cut-up as bad as the white soldiers...I just remembered..."

All of a sudden, a shot rings out, taking Corporal Wilson's hat off his head, causing him to jump off the corral fence rail and hit the dirt behind the water trough seeking cover. The dirt begins to pop around the Buffalo Soldiers as bullets spray everywhere.

The depot is now under siege by three dozen Comancheros. The depot reacts as all the soldiers begin seeking some kind of cover firing back at the outlaws.

The Buffalo Soldiers begin seeking cover with their Navy service revolvers and Sharps carbine rifles at the ready, except for Sergeant Jordan. He stays mounted low in the saddle, pulls his revolver, and begins calling out orders to his men while taking shots at the Comancheros on the rooftops and on the ground, keeping some of the outlaws at bay.

Sergeant Jordan is acting like the leader he is as he shouts, "Walley, Perry, Glass, get your carbines!" Sergeant Jordan then rears his mount and spins around and shouts, "Flankin' positions! Glass, help seal off the front! Walley, Perry—watch the rear! Chase, Irving, Temple, skirmish line in the corral!"

Scout Glass grabs his carbine and heads towards the front, firing at the outlaws as Troopers Walley and Perry grab their carbines nearby and head towards the back of the depot in different directions.

Corporal Wilson crawls from the water trough and retrieves his hat as several bullets rain down around him. He retreats back behind the water trough with his hat, looking at the bullet hole. He puts his finger through it and says, "My brand new hat!"

Seven Comancheros are taking supplies out the side window of the depot warehouse—rifles, ammunition, and canned goods.

Sergeant Jordan, astride his mount, sees the outlaws. He takes aim and shoots the closest one in the leg, causing him to drop the goods. "They're after the depot's supplies!" shouts Sergeant Jordan as he looks to Corporal Wilson and adds, "Wilson, pick a spot. Halt them from leavin'!"

"Okay Sarge!" shouts Corporal Wilson.

Sergeant Jordan dismounts and joins the skirmish line in the middle of the corral as Corporal Wilson pops his head up and around the water trough to see if the coast is clear. He looks for a safe spot for a pick-off point.

Corporal Wilson spots a good position, across from the supply warehouse and Command Post. He scampers from behind the water trough and retrieves his carbine from his mount through the corral rails, then scrambles to his position across from the supply warehouse with several bullet hits following his tracks.

Once settled into their battle positions, the Buffalo Soldiers begin defending half the post by lying down a withering barrage of lead wherever they see the Comancheros.

Trooper Mitchell had jumped from the corral fence when the shooting began, and is lying on the ground trying to stay out of the way of the lead flying in the air around him. He is weaponless. Several bullets hit the ground near Trooper Mitchell causing him to stand and double-time it towards the barracks for cover.

With all the chaos, the white post commander charges out of the Command Office while pulling up his britches over his long johns. He stops at the edge of the porch, looks around and shouts, "Bugler! Bugler, sound—"

The post commander is violently grabbed around the neck from behind by the Comanchero leader who is holding a knife to his throat, causing the post commander to drop his pants where he stands. He grabs the arm of the Comanchero leader with his hands.

The Comanchero leader looks to the commander and says, "Hey Commander, you're the commander of your men, huh...and I am the leader of my men. Tell your men, to quit shootin'—or I'll cut your throat!"

"Please, please, don't kill me, please," begs the post commander.

Trooper Mitchell does not see his commander under siege while ducking and trying to dodge bullets, running for cover towards the barracks.

A white depot officer, Lieutenant Lawson, takes cover behind several tall telegraph polls when he sees Trooper Mitchell running for cover, weaponless, and shouts to him, "Hey! Soldier!"

Trooper Mitchell stops in his tracks and looks towards

Lieutenant Lawson who then says, "Defend yourself—here."

Lieutenant Lawson tosses a revolver to Trooper Mitchell, who watches the flying weapon in midair flailing towards him. As the weapon reaches Trooper Mitchell, he barely catches the gun, then frantically fumbles with the revolver as bullets hit around him.

Trooper Mitchell cocks the hammer back; however, because of four years of paper pushing in Chicago and inexperience, the hammer falls forward and the gun discharges—BANG! The clang of a bell is heard as the gun recoils upward, startling Trooper Mitchell. "Holy shit!" says Trooper Mitchell as he looks in the direction the revolver fired and sees that he seemingly either struck the post bell, still swinging with its gong rope back and forth, or the Comanchero leader, falling away dead from the post commander.

The Comanchero shooting begins to subside, as the post commander, still standing in the same spot with a silly expression of relief written on his face, says, "Thank God I'm still alive." The post commander's hands are still clutching air from where the Comanchero's arm was around his neck as he then looks to the post bell still swinging somewhat, with a ricochet mark on its brand new brass surface, just a foot from his head. He then looks down at his britches around his ankles while bringing his hands down to his side, slowly. He glances over at the dead Comanchero leader lying beside him with a large caliber hole to the right front side of his head, partially gone.

The post commander looks out to see who shot the Comanchero leader. He first sees Trooper Mitchell standing in the middle of the depot courtyard, still fumbling with the service revolver, looking around, somewhat confused and lost, not quite sure what to do next.

Then, the post commander looks out to the courtyard and sees Corporal Wilson in the background, several degrees to the right of Trooper Mitchell, still pointing his semi-smoking carbine at the Comanchero leader, lying dead on the ground.

One of the outlaw Comancheros sees their leader has fallen dead and yells out, "Vamonos Muchachos, Jason is no more...Vamonos!"

The Comancheros scatter like cockroaches as if a light was turned on in a dark room.

Seeing the outlaws scatter, the post commander bends down, grabs his suspenders, and pulls up his trousers around his waist.

The depot is still firing at the fleeing Comancheros, as the post commander fastens his pants, holds up his hands in the air and shouts, "Cease fire...cease fire!"

Then the post commander steps down off the wood-walk platform of the Command Office, to the courtyard and shouts, "Hold your fire men! Hold your fire!"

The command is given, everyone stops shooting, as the Comancheros disappear.

The post commander takes a few more steps, turns and looks back down at the dead Comanchero leader with the bullet wound to what's left of his head. He then looks up at the post bell with the ricochet mark, then back to Trooper Mitchell. The post commander looks out to Corporal Wilson in the background. He sees Corporal Wilson had a clear standing shot. He watches him, still doing his job as a cavalryman, moving towards the post commander to keep him and the depot safe from the Comancheros by looking for the enemy.

Lieutenant Lawson runs over to the post commander's aid and says, "Are you all right sir?"

"Yeah. I want to thank that young man..." The post

commander points to Trooper Mitchell and adds: "...for saving my life."

"But sir, it was that colored corporal over there," says Lieutenant Lawson as he points to Corporal Wilson, now stopped in the courtyard, checking the dead and wounded. Corporal Wilson is unaware of the current conversation as Lieutenant Lawson says, "He shot the Comanchero. I saw him take the shot, sir."

Lieutenant Lawson walks over and looks at the post bell hanging from the rafter. He then walks onto the wood-walk platform, looking at the head wound on the Comanchero leader. He steps off the porch and walks back to the post commander with several depot personnel and civilians beginning to gather around them. "Please everyone, this is a military matter, please step back," says Lieutenant Lawson. The small crowd walks away, leaving the post commander and Lieutenant Lawson standing alone as Lieutenant Lawson says, "Sir, I don't want to make a scene."

"Then don't!" says the post commander with a stern voice.

"Sir...the ricochet on the post bell is from a small caliber pistol. The head wound on the Comanchero is from a carbine round. The trooper's shot hit the post bell, sir!"

"Lieutenant! There's no way a colored could have ever made that shot! Besides"—the commander looks around to see if anyone is listening, then looks back to Lieutenant Lawson with a pointed look—"you can't have them as officers." The post commander looks to Trooper Mitchell and shouts, "Trooper...trooper...trooper!"

Trooper Mitchell looks to the post commander waving to him.

"Come over here!" says the post commander.

Trooper Mitchell sheepishly looks around, then turns back to the post commander and says, "Who, me sir?"

"Yes, you, son. Come here!"

Still shocked by the firing of the revolver and his apparent killing of the Comanchero or the post bell, Trooper Mitchell slowly begins walking towards his commander, while looking around at the battle aftermath.

In the mean time, Sergeant Jordan looks to Corporal Wilson who's helping tend to the wounded and shouts to him, "Corporal Wilson! Corporal Wilson!"

Corporal Wilson looks to Sergeant Jordan, who says, "Return to the corral."

Sergeant Jordan motions with his hand for Corporal Wilson to come back to the corral, while the other three Buffalo Soldiers that took up flanking positions also return to the corral.

Trooper Mitchell at the same time approaches the post commander with a large crowd now beginning to gather as he sheepishly says, "Yes, sir," while stopping in front of him.

"Trooper, that's the best shot I've seen in a long time...and for saving my life—"

Trooper Mitchell interrupts and says, "Who...me, save your life, sir," as he looks around to see who the post commander could be talking to, then says, "Me, sir." Trooper Mitchell notices that he is the only one the post commander could be talking to as he turns back and says, "Save your life...?"

The post commander interrupts Trooper Mitchell saying, "You have just earned yourself a commission as second lieutenant in the U.S. Cavalry for your actions here today."

Trooper Mitchell's eyes light up, like he just struck gold—commissioned to second lieutenant.

Sergeant Jordan and the other Buffalo Soldiers watch and hear the post commander's jubilant conversation with

Trooper Mitchell as Corporal Wilson joins them.

The expression on Corporal Wilson's face is professional, straightforward.

Sergeant Jordan turns to his men and says, "All right men, go around. Check for dead and wounded."

The soldiers begin walking away, but stop when Trooper Temple grabs onto Corporal Wilson's arm, stopping him from walking away, and softly says, "But Sarge! Corporal Wilson shot that Comanchero...I saw him take the shot from the corral...you saw him too. That's not fair. He should get the commission!"

"Yeah, he sure did take the shot, Sarge," says Trooper Irving.

Corporal Wilson looks to Troopers Irving and Temple saying, "Let it go, troopers..."

"What did I say, Temple and Irving? You too Corporal! Check for dead and wounded. We got a parade to get ready for," says Sergeant Jordan.

Corporal Wilson, Troopers Temple, Irving, and the other Buffalo Soldiers have great respect for their sergeant, as they go to follow his orders.

Later that day at the Memorial Day festivities, the 9th Cavalry Band, an all-colored unit, is smartly marching through the middle of town playing "Rally 'Round the Flag" with a taste of African rhythm, giving the folks of Santa Fe a Sunday afternoon of music pleasure, which is rare in these parts, especially, an all-colored cavalry band.

In the middle of town, there is a park area with a large gazebo. Just outside the gazebo, Sergeant Jordan, Corporal Wilson, and Troopers Temple and Irving with their four other comrades, are standing smartly at attention in their full dress uniforms, along with the rest of the depot command.

Inside the gazebo, a podium is positioned in the middle,

and standing behind the podium is the post commander with so to be, Second Lieutenant Mitchell standing at attention in front of the podium. Lieutenant Mitchell is smartly dressed in his brand new officer's uniform, adorned with his second lieutenant bars and a somewhat arrogant grin.

He is surrounded by numerous United States Army officers, dignitaries, and officials sitting on benches that are built into the large gazebo. Seated are Colonel Edward Hatch and General William Tecumseh Sherman, who is sixty years old, sun-dried, and with a white scruffy beard. He looks like he hardly sleeps, and is chewing on a cigar hanging out of his mouth.

He looks down from his seated position at Sergeant Jordan, to his detachment of men, and then leans over to Colonel Hatch and says, "If I were compelled to choose 5,000 men to go into battle with, Colonel, I would rather take 5,000 white men. The colored is too docile...lack muscle, endurance, will, and most of all, courage, especially in combat."

Colonel Hatch just looks to General Sherman with a look of disbelief and says, "Hummm."

The 9th Cavalry Band marches into the park area still playing "Rally 'Round the Flag." After the band is fully in the park, the bandleader brings them to a halt and stops the music with hand and baton signals.

The post commander looks to the band, clears his throat, smiles, then looks to Lieutenant Mitchell and says, "In recognition of your bravery and gallantry today, you have earned a commission in the United States Cavalry. General Sherman will issue your commission now."

The post commander steps back from the podium as General Sherman stands, clears his raspy cigar-chewing voice and approaches the lectern.

As he approaches the podium, he reaches into his jacket pocket and brings out a wad of papers and begins shifting and shuffling through the mess.

He quickly finds the paper he is looking for, clears his throat, and begins reading from the piece of paper. "Son, it's always a pleasure to see fine young men like you...who display the courage and gallantry in the face of danger. Because of your bravery in saving your commander's life, I hereby commission you to, second lieutenant...Seventh Cavalry!"

The look on the Buffalo Soldiers faces' varies. For Corporal Wilson, Scout Glass, and Troopers Irving and Temple, this is normal routine, while the others—their faces tell it all. Troopers Chase, Perry, and Walley, they believe they would never have a chance of a commission, even if the marksman were known.

Sergeant Jordan's expression is brief. He knows the wrong, but he still has to be a leader of his men.

Lieutenant Mitchell, on the other hand, had no idea that he would ever be in the 7th Cavalry, much less an officer!

This is all too much for Lieutenant Mitchell to handle. Excitedly, he turns, and walks away towards the stairs, with General Sherman shouting at him, "Lieutenant...!" General Sherman forgot Lieutenant Mitchell's name, as he snaps his fingers together then looks to Colonel Hatch.

"Mitchell," says Colonel Hatch.

General Sherman turns back to Lieutenant Mitchell stopped in his tracks and says, "Lieutenant Mitchell! Get back here!"

Lieutenant Mitchell snaps back to his position at attention in front of the podium.

General Sherman looks at Lieutenant Mitchell with a stern look and says, "The first thing you need to learn as an officer, son, is protocol. If you want to remain a lieutenant—Lieutenant! You don't move from attention until told to do so by a higher-ranking officer! Is that understood?"

"Yes sir," says Lieutenant Mitchell sheepishly.

"Now," says General Sherman, as he looks around to the crowd with a smile, "for the main reason why I came to your beautiful town."

General Sherman looks past Lieutenant Mitchell like he is not even there and says, "Ladies and gentlemen, as of next month, Santa Fe, New Mexico, will be the Ninth Cavalry's Regimental Headquarters."

Some of the crowd stands and cheers their approval with jubilation, while other townsfolk have blank stares on their faces. General Sherman waits for a subsidence in the cheering. "And Colonel Hatch," he continues, indicating with his hand to the colonel, "will be the commander."

The 9th Cavalry Band strikes up "Battle Hymn of the Republic," and now most of the crowd stands and cheers.

The next day - it's a beautiful spring morning in Santa Fe, New Mexico. The detachment, K Troop, 9th Cavalry, is making final adjustments to their mounts, preparing to leave Santa Fe Depot on the trail going back to their post, Fort Stanton.

Sergeant Jordan is standing in front of his men with their mounts facing him. They are lined up, left to right, Corporal Wilson, Trooper Temple, Scout Glass, and Troopers Irving, Chase, Walley, and Perry.

Most the depot is watching as Sergeant Jordan finishes making adjustments to his saddle. He puts his left foot in his stirrup, mounts, looks to Corporal Wilson, then says, "Ready Corporal?"

Corporal Wilson turns to Trooper Temple and hands him the reins from his mount. He walks over to Sergeant

Jordan, already mounted, and says, "Ready Sarge, but I don't know about Trooper Temple."

"Why's that, Corporal?"

Corporal Wilson laughs a little, and is not really serious as he says, "That black mare gave him a hard ride yesterday. He'll be sittin' in the saddle mighty tall this mornin'."

They both chuckle as Sergeant Jordan says, "Yeah, and it's a good thing he saddle-broke that mare before the Comancheros attacked or else he would of been like a duck in a pond, bobbin' up and down all by himself."

They chuckle as Sergeant Jordan looks around and becomes serious as he bends down, looks to Corporal Wilson, and says, "By the way, Corporal...that was a very good shot. Sergeant Shaw will be proud when he hears the news about one of his students."

"Thanks Sarge. Sergeant Shaw is a good teacher."

"I heard...you're getting the best. He's the best marksman in the whole entire cavalry."

"I hope to follow his footsteps, Sarge."

"You picked a good man to follow, Corporal." With a smile, Sergeant Jordan sits upright in the saddle.

"Sarge," says Corporal Wilson, looking around the depot, "They're watchin'."

"I know," says Sergeant Jordan as he turns to his men. "Ready men."

The detachment simultaneously says, "Yes, Sarge."

"Stand by your mounts," says Sergeant Jordan.

The Buffalo Soldiers hurry to the left side of their mounts, standing by their saddles with the reins in their right hand, facing Sergeant Jordan at attention.

Corporal Wilson returns to his mount, takes the reins from Trooper Temple, and makes an about-face by his saddle—assuming the position of attention facing Sergeant Jordan.

"Prepare to mount," says Sergeant Jordan.

The Buffalo Soldiers make a right-face, transferring the reins from their right hand to their left. They then grab onto their saddles, putting their left foot in their stirrups, looking straight ahead, and await their next orders. Their mounts are well trained; they don't move during this military procedure.

"Mount," says Sergeant Jordan.

The soldiers mount their mounts simultaneously, giving a performance of cavalrymen. They are smartly seated upon their mounts, facing Sergeant Jordan, awaiting their next orders.

"Right-face...by a column of twos."

The single line of Buffalo Soldiers turn their mounts to their right and every other soldier from the second soldier to the rear rides to the right of the soldier in front of them. Corporal Wilson rides to the lead of the right column as Sergeant Jordan rides to the lead of the left column, holding up his right hand to signal the next order saying, "Forward *hooo.*"

Sergeant Jordan's hand falls forward, and by a column of twos, Sergeant Jordan and his men begin riding out of Santa Fe Supply Depot, leaving the blank stares behind. Lieutenant Mitchell and Trooper Hartigan are also standing by the barracks staring to the colored soldiers riding away.

Lieutenant Lawson and two other white troopers are standing by the garrison flagpole. Out of protocol, the two troopers and Lieutenant Lawson salute the colored soldiers passing by them as Sergeant Jordan and his men return their salute. Then Sergeant Jordan raises his right hand in the air and brings it forward, spurring his mount to a trot with his men smartly following behind their Sarge.

The soldiers cross the imaginary line of the depot, riding into Santa Fe, in military fashion, by a column of twos.

Santa Fe is coming alive. People are going to and fro, with wagons lined on both sides of the road from Memorial Day festivities. Some of the townspeople wave good-bye as the soldiers pass while the rest just stare.

As the soldiers near the end of town, Sergeant Jordan calls his orders: "Troop at a gallop, ho."

The soldiers spur their mounts from a trot to a gallop as they begin to see the 9th Cavalry Band and their wagons, just outside of town, preparing to depart.

The bandleader, Sergeant Major Sammy Brown, is sitting on the lead wagon's bench seat when he hears the hoofs of cavalry mounts galloping towards him. Sergeant Brown turns and sees Sergeant Jordan and his men headed towards him. He then turns, reaches into the wagon, and grabs a guitar from inside. He turns back, looking to the approaching soldiers and shouts, "Trooper Irving!"

Trooper Irving looks ahead to Sergeant Brown standing on the wagon's foot box, holding a guitar out, past the side of the wagon at arm's length. As the right column gallops by the wagons and begins to pass the lead wagon, Trooper Irving reaches for the guitar, grabbing it as if it were an egg, without missing a beat. As the soldiers ride several yards past the wagons, Trooper Irving looks back to Sergeant Brown and shouts, "Thanks Sergeant Major...take good care of our dress uniforms, they's expensive."

"Don't worry, they're well taken care of," shouts Sergeant Brown to Trooper Irving riding away.

Sergeant Brown pats a trunk that is sitting on the seat bench next to him as the Buffalo Soldiers ride out of town, into the wide-open prairie of the New Mexico desert.

Later that day, the sky is crystal blue in the New Mexico desert, with a spring rainstorm over a distant mountain range. Lightning flashes inside the dark clouds, highlighting their towering plumes, with rumblings of thunder audible for miles.

The terrain is rough: dust, wind, tumbleweeds, scrub, cactus, scorpions, and snakes—the New Mexico desert, 1880.

The Buffalo Soldiers are astride their mounts, riding along the Pecos Desert Trail towards Fort Stanton to the south. Trooper Irving, riding third in the right column, with the guitar strapped to his back, takes off his campaign trail-hat and slaps the trooper riding to his left on his arm, playfully, then says, "Now why you go say a thin' like that?"

"Cause it's true," says Trooper Henry Chase. He's twenty years old, small stature. Enlisted two years ago, Trooper Chase is somewhat educated, still a raw recruit. Trooper Chase then says, "They'll never give us dignity. Look what happened when we chased that outlaw who escaped from the jail in Lincoln last year..." Trooper Chase looks to Trooper Temple and says, "Guy, what was his name?"

Trooper Temple turns to Trooper Chase and says, "You're talkin' about William Bonney, and he's still on the loose, last heard."

Scout Glass looks back to the troops and says, "That was one of his false names. His born name is Henry McCarty. We now know him as...Billy the Kid."

"Yeah him," says Trooper Chase, "We chased him for a good month or so, and the white soldiers took the credit for us doing all the chasin'...and the same thing just happened to Corporal Wilson. He should of got that commission!"

The trooper riding in back of Trooper Chase is Trooper Charles Perry. A native of South America, he's a twenty-five-year-old second-term enlistee, saving his money for the future. With a South American accent, he says, "Makes no difference to me, thirteen dollars a month—room, board, medical, clothing—you can't do better than that. I don't care if they ever gave me a commission."

Trooper Irving turns in his saddle, looks to Trooper Perry and says, "What are you goin' to do with all that money, boy? You never spend it. You must have at least five hundred dollars by now."

Trooper Irving sits back in his saddle with a satisfied expression and says, "Shoot, a man could retire off that and live mighty good for the rest of his life...done right."

Everyone agrees, chuckles and laughs with Trooper Irving, except Sergeant Jordan and Corporal Wilson; their expressions are basically straightforward as Sergeant Jordan looks to Corporal Wilson and says, "Corporal, lead on."

Sergeant Jordan spurs his mount forward several yards, stops, and turns his mount left until he is facing the columns, letting the columns approach him. The soldiers look to Sergeant Jordan facing them, and then slow their individual conversations, except Trooper Perry.

Trooper Perry is talking with Trooper Irving, saying, "I'm savin' for the future, goin' to buy me one of those farms here in New Mexico when I get out and..." Trooper Perry slows and stops his conversation as he looks at Sergeant Jordan while they ride by him.

Sergeant Jordan looks to the columns with a sergeant's smile on his face as he says, "You're at at-ease gentlemen. You don't have to quit talkin' on my account."

Everyone looks to Sergeant Jordan with respect as they ride by him, then turn back in their saddles and slowly begin to converse with each other again, riding over a small hill. The trooper, counter right of Trooper Chase, is Trooper Augustus Walley, basically 100 percent colored, a first-term enlistee, and educated. He enlisted in Baltimore.

Trooper Walley says, "I think Chase is right. No matter

what we do, we'll never be recognized. Besides, no white man gonna take orders from no colored!"

All of his comrades agree with that statement, with a little laughter, chuckles, and serious Amens.

Trooper Chase, turning right in his saddle, says to Trooper Irving, "You see, I'm not the only one."

The columns have ridden over the hill as Sergeant Jordan has turned his mount back in the direction the columns are headed, and is riding oblique left of the columns and within hearing distance.

Trooper Chase, not seeing Sergeant Jordan yet, turns a little to the right in his saddle, looks back over his shoulder and looks at Trooper Perry. "You better take that money and go back east before they find you hung from a—"

Trooper Chase slows, stops his conversation when he hears, then sees Sergeant Jordan spurring his mount at a gallop towards the rear center of the columns, eyes fixed on Trooper Chase. Trooper Chase quickly turns back facing forward as do the other soldiers. Sergeant Jordan rides in between the columns, slowing his mount in between Troopers Perry and Walley's position, riding at their pace.

Sergeant Jordan looks around to his men. His facial expression, and his approach to his men, is stern. However, he understands their feelings as young colored men.

Sergeant Jordan then looks at Trooper Chase ahead of him and says, "Trooper Chase! You don't like the way the Army is ran?"

Trooper Chase turns, looks back and says, "No Sarge, that's not what I mean. That boy, Sarge...he was handlin' that sidearm like it was a hot potato, like he didn't know what to do."

All the soldiers chuckle as Trooper Irving turns in his saddle, looks at Sergeant Jordan and says, "Sarge, the commander saw who shot that Comanchero, he looked right at Corporal Wilson. It even looked like that white officer was even tryin' to tell him so."

"Yeah, Sarge," says Trooper Walley, "And the word I heard cleanin' up before 'Taps'—is the bullet wound on the Comanchero was a carbine shot."

"Gentlemen," says Sergeant Jordan, "There's a lot of wrongs in this world, and we as colored people know it full well. However, because we're U.S. Cavalrymen, we have to look past the wrongs, towards the future! There's a lot of colored peoples' countin' on us to uphold a good standard...to show a good light...to hopefully make things' better one day for us."

Trooper Chase says, "Sarge, I'll eat my hat the day I see a colored officer!"

Sergeant Jordan spurs his mount forward, staying between the columns. He slows, keeping pace in between Troopers Chase and Irving as he looks at Trooper Chase, smiles, and says, "You just might one day, trooper. I'm goin' to be holden' to you on that 'hat' issue."

Sergeant Jordan then looks at Scout Glass up ahead and says, "John Glass! Scout out ahead, if nothin's out there, meet us at Arroyo del Macho."

"All right, Sarge," says Scout Glass.

Scout Glass spurs his mount and takes off at a fast run from his position, leaving dust in his tracks. Scout Glass is twenty-eight, five foot six and somewhat educated. He's three-quarter colored, one-quarter Apache, and brown-complexioned. He wears buckskin fringe clothing, cowboy boots, a wide-brim brown hat with a U.S. Scout insignia pinned on the front—not the typical cavalry uniform. Strapped to his waist, on his left side, a curve-handled pistol, held from a brown leather sheath on its own ammunition belt, facing out for his right hand. On his right side is a large Bowie knife in a buckskin sheath, held by its own belt.

Corporal Wilson looks at Scout Glass riding off and shouts, "See what you can find for supper!"

Scout Glass turns in his saddle riding away and shouts back, "I'll see what I can find!"

Troopers Chase and Perry move up one position in their column, filling the void left by Scout Glass. Corporal Wilson turns to Sergeant Jordan, riding back to his lead position in the column and says, "Glass is one of the most flamboyant Scouts I've ever seen."

"He sure is," says Sergeant Jordan, "I hope he can find some flamboyant food for supper tonight too."

Sergeant Jordan turns to the columns and says, "Prepare to dismount and walk. Troop...hooo, dismount!"

Early that evening, at the Arroyo del Macho campsite, it's a starlit night with the lightning storm in the distance still rumbling. The flashes highlight the towering clouds in the now darkened sky, along with the desert and mountains in the background.

Corporal Wilson is standing by a campfire with speared meat on eight fresh long sticks made from tree branches, which lay across two large logs, setting aside of the fire, and a small coffee pot suspended in the air from a tripod made of tree limbs. Corporal Wilson sips from his coffee cup as Sergeant Jordan and the detachment ride into camp, single file.

Sergeant Jordan heads to the left side of the picket-line, already strung by Corporal Wilson, with the detachment following in suit. Sergeant Jordan stops at the left end of the picket-line, turns his mount right, looks to his right, sees everyone has arrived and stopped in a signal line facing him as he calls out his orders: "Right-face, dismount."

All the soldiers turn their mounts towards the picket-line, dismounting simultaneously as Sergeant Jordan gives his next orders. "You know your duties. After you groom, feed and watered your mounts, prepare for supper. Temple, Perry, take first guard duty. Chase and Walley will relieve you for supper."

Supper is smelling mighty good. Everyone smells the air, hurrying in a orderly fashion to their duties, taking off their McClellan saddles, saddle blankets, and equipment from their mounts. Sergeant Jordan ties his mount to the picket-line. He looks at the detachment and says, "Irving, take care of my mount."

"Yes Sarge," says Trooper Irving.

Sergeant Jordan walks over to the fire as Trooper Temple takes his saddle and saddle blanket off his mount, walks over and lays the blanket across a log and sets the saddle upon the blanket as if it were his mount. All the soldiers do mostly the same. If not a log, they sit their saddles on the ground as their pillow.

As Trooper Temple walks back to his mount to prepare for guard duty, he looks to the fire pit, then to Scout Glass and says, "Scout Glass, we could smell that meat for miles back. Lucky there aren't any breakouts, or else they would of been here before us."

"The last I heard," says Scout Glass, "the Apaches have been stayin' put mostly—except for Victorio and Nana. Word is Grierson and the Tenth have been chasin' 'em all over Texas."

"God bless the Tenth. They're goin' to need it. Chasin' those two," says Corporal Wilson.

Sergeant Jordan reaches down to the fire pit, and Corporal Wilson follows suit. They both bring out a stick with some very large chunks of juicy, tasty-looking meat speared in the middle. Sergeant Jordan holds the stick to his mouth, blows on the meat to cool it, grabs a piece with his teeth and pulls it off the stick into his mouth with some juice running down the side of his cheek.

Sergeant Jordan reaches in his back pocket and brings out his paisley handkerchief to wipe his mouth as he says, "Mmm, this is the best fire-cooked meat I've had in a long time. Glass, how did you get this meat tender and juicy?"

"After I skinned them, I beat the meat against a rock, cut it in chunks, then speared the meat on those wood sticks...put the meat in the fire. I had some bacon fat in my saddlebags and I melted it over the meat. That's their skins right over there"—Scout Glass points to five large diamondback rattlesnake skins, pinned, stretched, and drying out for his future clothing items on a piece of wood plank that was once a large tree bark. "They'll make real nice belts and hat bands. Diamondbacks. There was a whole pit of them about a mile back. They were curlin' in, gettin' out of the night air. I'll leave the skins here, come back in a week or so, they should be dry."

The rest of the soldiers now join Sergeant Jordan and Corporal Wilson at the campfire, grabbing their own sticks of rattlesnake meat and begin scarfing down the juicy morsels. Their looks, the sounds and talk, tell it all: "Mmm.... Mmm.... This is good," say the soldiers simultaneously.

Later that night, Trooper Irving is off guard duty playing his guitar in the background with Trooper Temple playing his harmonica. Standing by them, also off guard duty, is Trooper Perry humming while Scout Glass sings, "Them Old Cotton Fields Back Home."

Troopers Chase and Walley are standing guard duty, opposite sides of camp, Trooper Chase to the north and Trooper Walley to the south in the far background.

Sergeant Jordan and Corporal Wilson are standing by the fire, enjoying the music and song, and drinking coffee.

Both have one foot propped up on a log with their towering, fire-lit, shadowy figures standing tall in the background.

"We should hit Stanton, day after tomorrow goin' along the Pecos Trail," says Sergeant Jordan.

"Sarge," says Corporal Wilson.

"Yeah, Corporal."

"That was pretty good...what you said to Chase and Walley, but why did you wait?"

"I needed to hear what was on their minds, and they had to get it out...get it off their chests. Corporal, we both know what it feels like, not to receive dignity or to be recognized. Like I said today, we have a duty to uphold. If we do a good job here, keeping the peace and not makin' judgment calls, then our people who are countin' on us...perhaps, their hopes will not be in vain."

An owl hoots in a tree nearby as they both look out into the wide-open desert.

"Sarge," says Corporal Wilson, "do you ever think...we'll ever have a chance to be officers one day?"

"It's hard to say Corporal. I wish I knew."

Sergeant Jordan and Corporal Wilson then look to Scout Glass, Troopers Temple, Irving, and Perry filling the night air with song, as the storm rages and rumbles in the distance. The soldiers know the wrongs, but they won't let it stop their moral and brotherly camaraderie. They are happy from the break of dawn till late at night, cracking jokes with laughter and singing songs.

The next morning, it's quiet, except for a few birds audible from some scattered trees. The sun is just peeking its crest above the horizon, with remnants of the storm highlighting the beautiful sunrise.

The Buffalo Soldiers are atop their mounts in their same formation. Trooper Chase is holding Scout Glass's reins to his mount, as Scout Glass throws water on the remaining campfire, extinguishing it in a puff of smoke and steam, before kicking dirt on top of the smoldering wood.

He walks to his mount as Trooper Chase hands him his reins. He mounts, as Sergeant Jordan calls his orders, "Forward...*hooo*."

The columns head out towards Fort Stanton by a column of twos, as Sergeant Jordan turns and calls to his men, "You're at-ease, gentlemen."

The Buffalo Soldiers settle into their own relaxed positions astride their mounts. As the columns ride a few paces, Trooper Walley turns to Trooper Irving looking out at the morning desert and says, "Irving. Irving."

"Yeah what?" Trooper Irving replies.

"Who do you think our new commander is goin' to be?"

"Can't quite rightly say, Sergeant Shaw told me he thought it was goin' to be Captain Henry Carroll from F Troop."

"Anythin' will be better than Colonel Dudley," says Trooper Temple. "After that big shootout in Lincoln, that Billy the Kid outlaw we were talkin' about yesterday...they say Colonel Dudley took sides, went to the McSween house, where he thought that Billy the Kid was hidin' out, burnt the house down. McSween, the old man, was killed."

Corporal Wilson turns and looks back to Trooper Temple and says, "He did, that's why he's no longer our commander. The military charged him with arson of the McSween house and he was in violation of General Order number forty-nine, which forbids us from interfering in civil matters."

"I heard he got command of Fort Union," says Trooper

Chase, "he must know some good legal tricks."

"It's not always what you know trooper; it's who you know," says Corporal Wilson.

Sergeant Jordan looks to Corporal Wilson and says, "It's who you know...hum Corporal," as Sergeant Jordan with a smile says, "Lead on."

Sergeant Jordan angles his mount right, riding diagonal towards the center of the columns, then back in the direction the columns are riding, stopping, letting the columns ride past his position on both sides.

As Troopers Chase and Irving pass Sergeant Jordan, Sergeant Jordan spurs his mount forward, just off their tail ends, keeping pace. He looks at the entire detachment as he says, "Gentlemen, let me have your attention." Everyone turns in their saddles as they ride along, looking at Sergeant Jordan as he says, "It's about time you knew this, so you all can quit guessin'. Here's what I know. Captain Henry Carroll may be your new commander by the time we return to Stanton." They all look to each other with approval, as if they could change it if they didn't approve, as Sergeant Jordan says, "He enlisted and was commissioned in the Civil War, worked his way up in ranks to captain. He is a harsh disciplinarian, conscientiously looks to his military work, an untirin' campaigner, and will relentlessly weed out soldiers who fail to meet his military standards. Any other questions...gentlemen?"

They don't say anything, but they all look at each other with a sense of, "No that was enough and we'll be on our toes."

"Glass, scout out, meet us at Salt Creek. We'll take the Pecos River Trail," says Sergeant Jordan.

"Yes, Sarge," says Scout Glass, taking off south as Troopers Chase and Perry move up to fill the hole he's left in the column.

Trooper Temple looks back at Sergeant Jordan and says, "Hey, Sarge, isn't that dance tomorrow night?"

"Sure is Temple, and the New Commander's Welcome," says Sergeant Jordan. Sergeant Jordan spurs his mount up to Trooper Chase, riding parallel alongside of him as he says, "Trooper Chase, when we get back to the garrison tomorrow, take care of your duties, then take a couple of men to the garden and pick some fresh vegetables for the gala."

"Yes Sarge," says Trooper Chase.

Sergeant Jordan rides back to his position alongside of Corporal Wilson, then looks to Corporal Wilson and says, "I sure hope the band is back in time with our dress uniforms."

"Yeah, and in one piece, I hope," says Corporal Wilson jokingly. He adds: "Ever since Colonel Hatch has been trainin' the band to go out on patrol, they've started actin' like cowboys—instead of musicians."

With a smile, Sergeant Jordan says, "You mean actin' like cavalrymen, don't you Corporal?"

Corporal Wilson raises his eyebrows to Sergeant Jordan. Trooper Irving looks to his comrades and says, "Sure glad we is headed towards the river, so I can take a good bath. I goin' to smell mighty nice for them ladies."

"You need a bath even if the ladies weren't there," says Trooper Chase, jokingly.

Sergeant Jordan and the detachment all begin to laugh and say their Amens to the statement as they ride on.

Later that day is beautiful and sunny in the Pecos River Valley. Trees, birds, and assorted wild animals abound, as the sound of rushing water, running at a good pace from the spring thaw, is heard. Sergeant Jordan and his men are paralleling the river, about fifty-five miles out from Fort Stanton.

As the Buffalo Soldiers ride along, they enter into a watery meadow, where some wild deer are spooked and scatter away as the columns approach.

Sergeant Jordan stands in his stirrups, turns to his men, and says, "Here you are gentlemen, now you all can smell nice for the ladies."

Sergeant Jordan turns back, facing forward, still standing in his stirrups looking around the area, as Trooper Chase looks to the river and says, "Wee-oo, that water looks cold, and look at that river, boy, is she bank-full."

Corporal Wilson turns to Trooper Chase and says, "You're lucky it's been warm lately trooper, and when you get in, make sure you don't get carried away, cause she's runnin' fast."

As the columns ride into the meadow, Sergeant Jordan sits back down in the saddle, raises his right hand and calls his orders: "Company ho." The columns come to a stop as Sergeant Jordan calls his next order, "Prepare to dismount, and—" Sergeant Jordan's attention is distracted by a rider yelling and waving to the columns in the far distance, riding hard and fast towards them.

Corporal Wilson stands in his stirrups, looks to the rider through a few scattered trees, and says, "Hey, that's Glass. Why is he in such a rush?"

"Probably trouble. Corporal keep an eye peeled, pass the word," says Sergeant Jordan as he holds up his right hand, adding: "Company, at a gallop, *hooo*." Sergeant Jordan's hand falls forward and the columns command to a gallop towards Scout Glass.

Scout Glass sees the columns galloping towards him as he spurs his mount even faster over earth's natural obstacle course—ditches, logs, fallen trees—plowing through small-to medium-size streams to reach his comrades. As Scout Glass comes within shouting distance, he begins yelling to the columns, "Wagon in river, wagon stuck in river! Wagon stuck in river! Wagon in river!" Wagon in river! Wagon in river!"

As Scout Glass and the columns near each other, Sergeant Jordan raises his right hand and calls his orders, "Troop, *hooo*."

The columns come to a stop as Scout Glass rides up fast, splashing water everywhere, then stops with urgency written in his eyes. Almost out of breath he says, "Sarge...Sergeant Johnson, from G Troop...is tryin' to save some people in a supply wagon...they're stuck in the river...about three miles back."

"Lead the way Glass," says Sergeant Jordan.

Scout Glass turns his mount around and spurs his steed back into action.

"Troop at a gallop, then a run, *hooo*," says Sergeant Jordan. Sergeant Jordan and the columns begin to gallop, in military fashion, their mounts splashing water through the wetlands, as Sergeant Jordan raises his right hand and calls his next order: "*Hooo*."

Sergeant Jordan's right hand falls forward, and they take their mounts from a gallop up to a full stride in the direction Scout Glass is headed downstream.

Downstream, there is a large, uncovered, strapped-down crate-filled supply wagon, leaning perpendicular, on the upstream side of the trail-path that cuts across the rapids of the Pecos River.

The passengers, one man and three women, are leaning away from the river, sitting on the wagon seat, on the high side, as the river splashes and laps at the low side of the wagon. The wagon is in danger of being swept away over the trail-path by the current with its four passengers and team of mules in the middle of the rushing Pecos River.

On shore, facing the team of mules, is Sergeant Robert T. Johnson, who is preparing for the rescue by first securing the wagon with a rope. However, Mr. Bernstein, the driver of the supply wagon, wearing a long black coat, is not convinced that Sergeant Johnson, or any colored person for that fact, is capable of the task.

Mr. Bernstein is furiously whipping the driving reins and yelling at the mules: "Yah. Yah, yah!"

Mr. Bernstein is trying to drive the mules to pull the wagon, him, and his family out of danger; however, the mules are not up to the task by themselves. The mules are tugging at the wagon tongue, splashing water everywhere, trying to pull the wagon out of the hole, as Sergeant Johnson shouts to Mr. Bernstein over the roaring Pecos River.

"Mr. Bernstein, I said please hold on, you're endangerin' yourself and your family! Help is comin'. We will rescue you! Please catch this rope."

Mr. Bernstein stops, looks to Sergeant Johnson, and yells back, "You colored boys, you don't know nothing! I'll rescue my own family!"

Mr. Bernstein ignores Sergeant Johnson's plea, and continues whipping the wagon reins with determination and yelling, "YAH. YAH...YAH!"

Sergeant Johnson shouts to Mr. Bernstein, over Mr. Bernstein's yelling at the mules and the river noise, "Mr. Bernstein, I assure you, I do know what I am doin'! Please take this rope!"

The three women on board the wagon are holding onto the crates, to each other, and the wagon for dear life as the wagon jerks back and forth from Mr. Bernstein's unsuccessful attempts. The river is rising and lapping more and more at the wagon. Unless they are rescued soon, the wagon with passengers, mules and goods will be swept away.

Mr. Bernstein is still trying to get the mules to pull the wagon out of the river as Sergeant Johnson shouts, "Mr. Bernstein! Mr. Bernstein...!"

Sergeant Johnson is interrupted as Scout Glass rides in fast up to the riverbank, stops, and shouts to Mr. Bernstein as Sergeant Johnson looks on: "Help is on the way...help is on the way! You'll be alright!"

Scout Glass then rides over to where Sergeant Johnson is standing and dismounts, side saddle slide—right leg over saddle dismounting—without the use of his hands as the mount stops. Scout Glass grabs his rope and then looks to Sergeant Johnson.

Sergeant Johnson looks to a tree and then to the wagon, with Mr. Bernstein still persisting to do it himself as Sergeant Johnson shouts, "Mr. Bernstein...Mr. Bernstein, please quit what you're doin' and catch this rope."

Mr. Bernstein stops exhaustively and realizes that his actions are futile. He then looks to Sergeant Johnson throwing the rope to him as Sergeant Johnson shouts, "Here, tie this end to the wagon seat."

Sergeant Johnson's first toss to Mr. Bernstein is successful as he catches the rope, with Sergeant Johnson retaining the other end. He points to the wagon seat, shouting, "As low as you can, Mr. Bernstein." Mr. Bernstein begins tying the rope to the wagon seat as Sergeant Johnson turns to Scout Glass and says, "Scout, take your rope, tie it to this one, then take your end over to that tree. You should have enough rope."

Scout Glass ties the two ends together, then takes the rope and runs over to the tree. He begins pulling the rope towards the large tree trunk. Mr. Bernstein has finished tying his end to the wagon's seat as he shouts to Sergeant Johnson, "It's tied!"

Scout Glass hears Mr. Bernstein say the rope is tied, and begins pulling the rope taut, around the tree, as Sergeant Jordan and the rest of the Buffalo Soldiers ride into the rescue area, looking to the wagon. Scout Glass looks to Sergeant Johnson and shouts, "There's my unit Sergeant!" Scout Glass turns to the Bernsteins and shouts, "You'll be alright now!"

The Bernstein women now have hope written on their faces as they see this group of colored soldiers, their rescuers coming to their aid. As for Mr. Bernstein, he has a little fear, some hatred, and a lot of shock written on his face as he sees this gallant unit of Buffalo Soldiers coming to their rescue stopping their mounts.

Sergeant Johnson looks to Sergeant Jordan and the detachment with relief, because he knows it's going to take more than two people.

Sergeant Jordan looks at Scout Glass with the rope in his hands, and then calls out to the detachment, "Temple, help Glass."

Trooper Temple turns and spurs his mount towards Scout Glass. As he reaches the tree near Scout Glass, he dismounts, side saddle slide, and runs over to assist.

Trooper Temple grabs the rope along with Scout Glass, as both soldiers begin pulling the rope taut, hoping the wagon won't be swept away. Once Scout Glass and Trooper Temple achieve tension on the rope, they walk the rope around the tree trunk, wrapping it several more times, after which they tie the rope, securing the wagon.

"Sergeant," says Scout Glass, "that should hold them."

Scout Glass looks to Trooper Temple and says, "Temporarily!"

Sergeant Jordan looks to the river, then looks at

Corporal Wilson and shouts, "Corporal, take two men, go downstream, find a place to cross with a safety line."

"Yes, Sarge. Walley, Irving, lets go!"

Corporal Wilson, Troopers Walley and Irving race downstream on their mounts as Sergeant Jordan looks to Troopers Chase and Perry then says, "Dismount troopers, stay with me." The three dismount and rush over to assist Sergeant Johnson. Sergeant Jordan looks to Sergeant Johnson and says, "I just sent three of my men downriver to tether a safety line. How did you get into this?"

"I was on my way to Fort Bascom to deliver a message when I heard Mr. Bernstein's yells to the mules. Came to see what the yellin' was about. That's when your scout showed up." Sergeant Johnson then looks to Sergeant Jordan with seriousness and says, "Sergeant, the day is warm, and the river is risin'."

"What do you want to do Sergeant," says Sergeant Jordan.

Mr. Bernstein interrupts their strategy planning and thinking by shouting. "You sure you know what you're doing? I didn't know they let you boys be soldiers? You coloreds need to go back and pick—"

Sergeant Johnson, interrupting says, "Mr. Bernstein, please. You're frighten' the ladies."

Sergeants Jordan and Johnson's faces seem to express it all, as if to say: "What are you saying, when we are risking our lives for you?" But their thoughts are for a brief second, for they are soldiers and have a duty to perform.

Mr. Bernstein looks to his wife and two daughters and sees how scared they are. He calms himself and sits down on the wagon seat to comfort his family, watching the soldiers do their duty.

Sergeant Johnson looks at Sergeant Jordan, then to the wagon and says, "The wagon seems to have slipped or sunk into a ditch off the path...the way the mules are standin' on higher ground." He then looks back to Sergeant Jordan and says, "He told me, he's a saloonkeeper; the wagon is full of liquor. That's what's holdin' it from bein' carried away."

"That's what's holdin' it down...good thin' they went off upriver, instead of down," says Sergeant Jordan, as he looks to the river. "The river is too rocky, and runnin' too fast here for a mount rescue."

"I know...we'll have to go swimmin'," says Sergeant Johnson.

Sergeant Jordan looks to Sergeant Johnson with a quizzical smile.

Downstream, moments later, Corporal Wilson, Troopers Irving and Walley gallop on their mounts into an area where the river widens and slows its pace from the fast-moving currents back upriver. They slow their mounts as they begin passing trees that border the riverbank on both sides.

"This is a good spot, Trooper Irving," says Corporal Wilson, as he points across the river. "On your mount go across the river. It will carry you downstream. When you reach the other side, double back to that spot"—he points again—"across from us to that tree."

Trooper Irving takes off on his mount towards the river as Corporal Wilson looks to Trooper Irving splashing into the river shouting, "And be careful!"

Corporal Wilson and Trooper Walley watch Trooper Irving on his mount making their way across the river. Trooper Irving's mount is kicking its way across with little difficulty as the current carries the mount with Trooper Irving on board downstream. As Trooper Irving reaches the other side of the river, he spurs his mount out of the river shouting, "yah", "yah" "get-up"- "get-up"! .

Trooper Irving is dripping wet and feeling good, spurring his mount back upriver to the spot directly across from Corporal Wilson and Trooper Walley. He looks at his comrades stopping his mount and shouts, "Wooo-ee, that sure does feel good."

"Trooper Irving, Trooper Walley is going to throw one end of this rope to you!" shouts Corporal Wilson, as he points across the river. "Tie it low on that tree when you get it."

Trooper Irving jumps off his mount as Trooper Walley tosses the rope across the river. Like clockwork, Trooper Irving catches the rope, wraps and ties it low on the tree trunk with precision. Trooper Irving then looks across the river to Corporal Wilson and shouts, "Corporal Wilson, she's tied."

Corporal Wilson looks to Trooper Walley and gives his orders, "Trooper Walley, take your end and lay it upriver side of that tree stump."

Corporal Wilson points to a large tree stump as Trooper Walley dismounts, walks over and pulls tension on the rope. He then stands back and whips the rope in the air so it falls to the upstream side of the stump. Trooper Walley holds the rope with little tension, letting it fall. It somewhat drags in the water to serve as their rescue line.

Trooper Irving shouts to Corporal Wilson from across the river: "Now what, Corporal Wilson?"

"Trooper Irving, stay by the riverbank on your mount. We'll wait—and hopefully we won't have to jump in and rescue anyone," says Corporal Wilson.

Back at the wagon, Sergeants Jordan and Johnson have been preparing for the rescue by taking off their hats, gloves, shirts, boots, and pants. The only thing they have left on is their long underwear, which is causing some blushing in the wagon. Sergeant Johnson looks to the wagon and shouts to Mr. Bernstein, "Sergeant Jordan and I are goin' to wade our way to your wagon, and carry the ladies and you to safety on our shoulders to lighten the load...then we're gonna drive your wagon out. Do you understand?"

"You, you, you put back on your clothes. You're embarrassing my wife and daughters!" shouts Mr. Bernstein.

The ladies are turning a little red in the face as Sergeant Jordan looks and shouts to Mr. Bernstein, "Sorry we can't do that Mr. Bernstein. You see, the water would have somethin' to grab onto, makin' it hard for us."

Troopers Chase and Perry run up to Sergeants Jordan and Johnson with four ropes, two each, as Scout Glass and Trooper Temple join them. Each holds a backup rope.

"Here's the ropes you asked for Sarge," says Trooper Chase.

Sergeant Jordan takes both ropes from Trooper Chase, hands one to Sergeant Johnson, then both begin tying them around their waists as Sergeant Jordan looks to Trooper Chase and Perry and says, "Chase, Perry, you gonna hold our lifelines. We gonna have to go downstream side of the mules and wagon where the trail-path is so we can get a firm foothold. You'll have to follow us with our safety lines till we get in front of the mules. That's where you'll have to use the trees or dig footholds for leverage in case we're swept away."

Sergeant Jordan then hands his line to Trooper Chase as Sergeant Johnson hands his to Trooper Perry. Sergeant Jordan looks to Scout Glass and Trooper Temple, saying, "Glass, Temple, you help Chase and Perry until we get the Bernsteins to safety. Then prepare to mount your mounts after Sergeant Johnson." Indicating the ropes, he says, "Tie those ropes to the wagon tongue. He then will throw you each one end, which you will tie around your mounts to assist pulling the wagon. Any questions?"

"No, Sarge," says Scout Glass.

Sergeants Jordan and Johnson, Scout Glass, and Troopers Chase, Perry and Temple head down to the riverbank, upriver of the wagon, as Sergeant Johnson looks to Sergeant Jordan. "The river should carry us close to the mules or the wagon on the trail-path to where we can grab onto them and stand," Sergeant Johnson says.

"If we miss, Sergeant...we're goin' for a ride," says Sergeant Jordan as he looks back to his men, especially looking to Troopers Chase and Perry shouting, "Troopers Chase and Perry, you make sure you watch us. When we get close to the mules, that's where the path should be. If we miss, the current is goin' to take us and it's goin' to be a hard jerk on these lines."

"We got you Sarge," say Troopers Chase and Perry simultaneously.

Sergeants Jordan and Johnson enter the water as Troopers Chase and Perry begin letting out safety lines from around their waists, letting Sergeant Jordan and Johnson pull at their own pace. As their torsos submerge into the river, Sergeants Jordan and Johnson shutter and grunt simultaneously, "Burrr...!" "Urrr...!" "Urrr...!" Burrr..." pulling their safety lines at their own pace, wading their way across the river, letting the current take them towards the Bernsteins.

The looks on Sergeants Jordan and Johnson's faces tell it all. The water is cold; however, they have a job to accomplish. Scout Glass and Trooper Temple automatically begin digging small holes in the ground, in front of Troopers Chase and Perry with the sergeants' safety lines. As the sergeants approach the wagon, the current takes them in front of the mules where they attempt to stand.

Sergeant Johnson begins to stand in the thigh-high water, grabbing onto the reins of the mules, getting a firm foothold. As Sergeant Jordan nears the mules, he reaches for the reins, then attempts to stand several feet away from Sergeant Johnson. However, the strong current pushes his legs out from under him, causing him to lose his footing.

Sergeant Jordan is now swept over the waterfall created by the trail-path and carried away by the river as his safety line tightens and yanks Trooper Chase, standing his ground with Scout Glass and Trooper Temple also holding onto the rope in back of him.

"We got you, Sarge!" shouts Trooper Chase.

Thank God for Sergeant Jordan's safety line, for it stopped him from being swept away. The river current and the tension on the line cause Sergeant Jordan to pendulum into the riverbank downstream. Scout Glass and Trooper Temple rush over to help their sergeant, as he begins climbing out of the water.

Trooper Chase is winding up Sergeant Jordan's safety line as Trooper Temple and Scout Glass reach their sergeant.

"You alright, Sarge?" shouts Scout Glass.

"Yeah...I'm alright...I'm alright," says Sergeant Jordan. He's a little out of breath as he says, "Let's get back at it."

The water is pushing Sergeant Johnson's legs downstream, away from the mules and wagon, as he pulls himself towards the wagon and the Bernstein's, looking to Sergeant Jordan shouting, "You alright, Sergeant?"

"Yeah! Go ahead, keep going, keep going," shouts Sergeant Jordan as he looks to Trooper Chase with a smile and says, "Thanks, Trooper. All right, let's get back to it."

Sergeant Jordan stands, turns, and runs back upriver of the wagon, trailing his safety line behind him with Trooper

Chase feeding out the line. As Sergeant Jordan enters the water, Sergeant Johnson has reached the Bernsteins, pulling his legs down into the water, standing, with the current trying to pull him away from the wagon, and with the water splashing off the wagon into his face.

Sergeant Johnson looks up to the women Bernsteins and shouts, "Which lady first?"

Mr. Bernstein says, "Aren't you worried about being carried away?"

Sergeant Johnson wiping the splashing water from his face with his forearm shouts, "The extra weight on our shoulders should help hold us down."

Mr. Bernstein pauses a few moments then says, "Take my daughters first."

One of the Bernstein daughters maneuvers over to where Sergeant Johnson is standing in the river holding onto the wagon. She then steps off the wagon and slips down onto Sergeant Johnson's broad shoulders. Sergeant Johnson turns and begins walking back along the trail-path towards Trooper Perry, who's keeping slight tension on his lifeline, pulling as Sergeant Johnson walks towards the riverbank with the Bernstein daughter astride his shoulders.

Sergeant Jordan is now wading his way back to the wagon as Sergeant Johnson reaches the riverbank with one happy Bernstein daughter on his shoulders. Sergeant Johnson looks up to the Bernstein daughter as he lifts her off his shoulders, putting her down on the ground and says, "Excuse me, ma'am."

The daughter smiles at Sergeant Johnson as he quickly turns and runs back into the water, upriver of the wagon as Sergeant Jordan has just taken the second daughter astride his shoulders and heads for the riverbank. Sergeant Jordan walks along the trail-path carefully as Trooper Chase keeps tension on his lifeline, holding his ground.

Moments later Sergeant Jordan reaches the riverbank and deposits the second daughter on the shore. Sergeant Johnson has just taken Mrs. Bernstein astride his shoulders and is heading back towards the riverbank.

Meanwhile, Sergeant Jordan is already back in the water, wading his way back to the wagon for Mr. Bernstein, as Sergeant Johnson deposits Mrs. Bernstein on firm ground. Mrs. Bernstein looks to Sergeant Johnson with a worried look as she says, "My husband, my husband."

"No problem, ma'am. Sergeant Jordan is goin' to get him right now."

Scout Glass runs to Sergeant Johnson and hands him several coiled ropes as Sergeant Johnson looks to Scout Glass and says, "Thanks, Scout."

Sergeant Johnson takes the ropes and puts his left arm and head through the coiled ropes as he runs back upriver to their entry point. The river is rising. Sergeant Johnson enters the river as Sergeant Jordan arrives back at the wagon to take Mr. Bernstein to safety.

Mr. Bernstein looks down from the wagon seat at Sergeant Jordan and yells, "I'm not leaving...I'm not leaving. I don't trust you!"

Water splashes in Sergeant Jordan's face as he stands in the river holding onto the wagon, shouting, "Mr. Bernstein...Sergeant Johnson is a very good wagoner and besides, we need your weight off the wagon and you should leave for your safety."

Sergeant Johnson nears the wagon, as Sergeant Jordan stands in the river, shouting to Mr. Bernstein. The current almost carries him away as he grabs onto the front part of the wagon. Sergeant Johnson then looks to Sergeant Jordan with water splashing in their faces and shouts, "Why's Mr. Bernstein still on the wagon?"

"He doesn't want to leave!" shouts Sergeant Jordan.

Sergeant Johnson moves around Sergeant Jordan, grabs the wagon sides with both hands, pulls his cold wet body on board without difficulty and plops down next to Mr. Bernstein. Sergeant Johnson begins untying his safety line with Mr. Bernstein still clutching the wagon reins, and now his waist.

Mr. Bernstein glares at Sergeant Johnson with contempt; however, he knows he does not have what it takes to put up a fight and gives the reins to Sergeant Johnson. Sergeant Johnson then ties them and his safety line to the brake handle, looks to Mr. Bernstein, and says, "Mr. Bernstein, please go with Sergeant Jordan. He'll carry you to safety. We need as much weight off of here as possible."

"I'm not leaving my wagon!" yells Mr. Bernstein.

Sergeant Johnson knows the river is rising. There is no time to argue so he removes both coiled ropes from over his head looking to Sergeant Jordan, saying, "Sergeant, can you tie these ropes' ends to the tongue of the wagon?"

"Sure thing, Sergeant," says Sergeant Jordan. Sergeant Johnson tosses both ends of the rope to Sergeant Jordan as he is being pulled away from the wagon by the strong current with water splashing in his face. Sergeant Jordan catches the ropes and begins pulling his way towards the front of the mules and the tongue of the wagon.

When Sergeant Jordan reaches the tongue of the wagon, he takes several deep breaths, dives under the water, and begins tying the ropes as a sudden surge of water hits the mules and almost dislodges the wagon. Trooper Chase is holding his ground with his sergeant's safety line taut.

The wagon is lifted up by the surge, and as the surge passes, the wagon falls back into its same position. The only thing keeping the wagon from being carried away was the heavy weight of the cargo and the mule team. The only thing keeping Sergeant Jordan from being carried away as he surfaces was the ropes he just tied to the wagon tongue, and Trooper Chase holding his ground with his sergeant's safety line pulling on him.

Sergeant Jordan is wading and holding onto the ropes that he has already tied to the wagon tongue several feet away from the mules. Sergeant Johnson looks to Sergeant Jordan and shouts, "Sergeant Jordan, swim, swim—get on a mule! Swim!"

Sergeant Jordan swims to a mule and pulls himself astride.

Sergeant Johnson, standing on the foot box, throws and lets go of the two rope ends headed for shore. Scout Glass and Trooper Temple, standing on the riverbank, catch the two rope ends, then tie them to two other ropes. They then run to their mounts pulling the ropes, as another wave hits the stranded wagon, causing Sergeant Johnson and Mr. Bernstein to hold on tightly.

The two soldiers reach their mounts, grabbing their bedrolls with Trooper Perry's help. They wrap their bedrolls over the ropes, and hold them across their mounts' chests, protecting their mounts from the pulling rope. They mount and tie the ropes in back of them making a loop, then turn their mounts and begin pulling tension on the wagon.

Sergeant Johnson unties the reins and his safety rope from the brake handle, letting loose of the safety line, holding onto the reins as he looks to Mr. Bernstein with a very serious look, and says, "I told you to get off!" Then Sergeant Johnson looks to Sergeant Jordan and shouts, "Ready Sergeant!"

"Ready!" shouts Sergeant Jordan.

Mr. Bernstein looks to Sergeant Johnson with a look of, "Help, I surely hope you know what you're doing, let me off!"

Too late, as Sergeant Johnson stands on the foot box, looks to Mr. Bernstein and shouts, "Hold on Mr. Bernstein!"

Sergeant Johnson then whips the drive reins, and with a mighty shout, yells, "HUH! YAH!'

The mules begin pulling and tugging with Sergeant Jordan spurring the mule he's sitting on.

Scout Glass and Trooper Temple begin spurring their mounts, pulling tension on the ropes, while Trooper Chase steadies Sergeant Jordan's safety line. Mr. Bernstein's eyes widen at the shear tenacity of these soldiers and their action.

At first, nothing happens, with water splashing everywhere, and the wagon rocking back and forth. Sergeant Jordan is spurring the mule, and Sergeant Johnson is whipping the drive reins. Both are shouting simultaneously, "YAH... YAH, yah... HAH, yah!"

Suddenly, the mules, Sergeants Jordan and Johnson break the wagon lose out of its entrapment, pulling the wagon back onto to the trail-path. They drive the wagon along the path, splashing water as they go, until they reach the riverbank and dry land out of harm's way.

In the wagon, frozen in place, shaking, a little wet, and holding on for dear life, sits Mr. Bernstein, safe and sound, sitting on the wagon seat next to Sergeant Johnson.

The Bernstein women run over to the wagon, climb up, and help Mr. Bernstein down with very shaky legs. Sergeant Jordan dismounts the mule. He is dripping wet as Trooper Chase and Scout Glass assist him, bringing his towel and uniform.

Troopers Perry and Temple walk to Sergeant Johnson

with his uniform and towel as he jumps down from the wagon.

Trooper Chase looks to Sergeant Jordan and says, "You alright, Sarge?"

"All in a day's work, Trooper."

"I thought the water had you," says Scout Glass.

"Now, we couldn't let that happen, now could we Glass," says Sergeant Jordan, as they all smile and kind of laugh.

Sergeant Johnson finishes checking underneath the wagon, stands, then takes his pants from Trooper Perry and begins putting them on, buttoning the opening. He then walks over to Sergeant Jordan, with Troopers Perry and Temple following, still holding his shirt and boots.

Sergeant Jordan is halfway dressed, with his pants and boots, as Sergeant Johnson walks towards him and says, "Wagon's alright. That was some pretty good ridin' Sergeant."

"Learned a few tricks here," says Sergeant Jordan, looking to Trooper Temple, "from my farrier, Trooper Temple."

Moments later, Sergeants Jordan and Johnson are almost dressed as Mr. Bernstein approaches with the Bernstein women following. He begins shaking all of the soldiers' hands and saying, "Thank you." Mr. Bernstein then looks to both sergeants and says, "Gentlemen, ah, ah...I don't know what to say...but, thank you, thank you. How can I ever thank you gentlemen...here..."

Mr. Bernstein reaches into his money belt around his waist and brings out a wad of cash.

The Buffalo Soldiers expressions are "holy smokes," except for the sergeants. Mr. Bernstein then looks to both sergeants and says, "Please, let me give you something to show my appreciation and gratitude."

Sergeant Jordan says, "Mr. Bernstein, we are soldiers. This is our job," then with a smile, he says, "Thanks, but no thanks."

Mr. Bernstein says, "H-h-owww about some...good old Jewish brandy?"

"Sorry Mr. Bernstein, we can't accept," says Sergeant Jordan.

Sergeant Jordan finishes buttoning his shirt as Mr. Bernstein whispers something in his wife's ear.

Mr. Bernstein and the women then walk off quickly as Sergeant Jordan looks to Scout Glass and says, "Glass, head downriver, tell Corporal Wilson the rescue is over. Everyone is safe. As soon as we are done here, we'll come to you."

"Yes, Sarge," says Scout Glass as he looks to Sergeant Johnson and says, "See ya, Sergeant Johnson.

"Good-bye Scout," says Sergeant Johnson.

Scout Glass turns and runs towards his mount, mounts from behind, hands on the mount's exterior—up and over the hump into the saddle. Scout Glass grabs his reins, turns, and spurs his mount downriver.

Sergeant Johnson has finished putting on his boots as he approaches Sergeant Jordan and his men with his mount and says, "I better get goin', Fort Bascom is a another day's ride. It was good meetin' you Sergeant."

"Same here Sergeant. It's a shame you got to be at Fort Bascom, we're gonna have a pretty nice dance tomorrow night at the garrison," says Sergeant Jordan.

"I've heard about the Diamond Club and the galas you put on. I hope to have the pleasure one day Sergeant, but now, duty calls."

With a kind look to each other, Sergeant Johnson shakes Sergeant Jordan's hand, and then shakes the rest of K Troop's hands.

Sergeant Johnson turns to his mount and mounts, as Sergeant Jordan turns to his men and says, "Mount up, K Troop."

Sergeant Jordan, Troopers Chase, Perry, and Temple head towards their mounts, wrapping up their ropes, as the two Bernstein daughters run towards their wagon from Sergeant Jordan's mount. The Bernstein daughters climb aboard with Mr. and Mrs. Bernstein already seated in the wagon.

Sergeant Jordan and his men mount their mounts as Sergeant Jordan looks to his men and says, "Say good-bye to the ladies, gentlemen." The Buffalo Soldiers tip their trail hats to the ladies, who begin blushing—especially the daughters looking at the sergeants—as Sergeant Jordan calls his orders to his men: "Forward...ho."

Sergeant Jordan and his men ride out into the afternoon sun as Sergeant Johnson rides out one way, and the Bernsteins ride out another way waving back to the soldiers.

The next day is a beautiful bright spring early afternoon as Sergeant Jordan and his detachment ride past an encampment of Apache Indians, going about their business on the outskirts of Fort Stanton. The Buffalo Soldiers cross over the garrison's imaginary boundary and enter the adobe and wood fort from the New Mexico desert, with their uniforms a little tattered.

There's more garrison life than there was at Santa Fe Supply Depot. Townspeople from the town of Lincoln come and go. Fort Stanton's officers and their wives go to and fro, with garrison chickens running about. One hundred and fifty enlisted cavalrymen and infantrymen drill march, perform KP duties in and around the garrison, including the garrison garden, while their wives, girlfriends, and the laundress wash clothes on suds row. Other women of the garrison and from the town of Lincoln are helping with final touches and preparations for tonight's dance at the assembly hall.

One thing is slightly different about this garrison. Virtually all the troopers are colored, except for their white officers and the officers' wives. Several of the colored women on suds row wave to Sergeant Jordan and his men as they pass, and a very pretty young colored lady winks at Trooper Perry. Trooper Perry looks back to his comrades, then at the young lady and says, "Boy oh boy, I'll see you tonight, won't I Cherry Blossom?"

She shakes her head yes with a shy smile as Sergeant Jordan and his detachment ride past suds row, towards the center of the garrison where they see the 9th Cavalry Band's wagons.

Trooper Temple looks to the wagons in shock. He then looks to his comrades and says, "How did they get back here so fast? They must of been back hours, the wagons are almost unloaded...they weren't suppose to be back until this evenin' in time for the dance?"

Corporal Wilson looks at the wagons with a concerned look and says, "I hope our uniforms are alright?" Then he turns to Sergeant Jordan and says, "I told you they were turnin' into cowboys."

With a smile Sergeant Jordan says, "Not cowboys, Corporal. Cavalrymen. Corporal, take the detachment to the stables. When they are finished with their mounts, send a man over to the Command Office to get my mount."

"Yes, Sarge, see you later," says Corporal Wilson.

As Sergeant Jordan and the detachment split up, Corporal Wilson shouts to Sergeant Jordan, "Hey Sarge, let us know if Captain Carroll is our new commander when you find out."

Sergeant Jordan, riding towards the Command Office, waves his hand in acknowledgment to Corporal Wilson, who is leading the detachment to the stables.

As Sergeant Jordan reaches the Command Office, he dismounts, ties his mount to the hitching rail, takes off his trail hat, and slaps it against his body, removing the dust from his uniform before approaching his commander's office. Sergeant Jordan puts back on his hat, walks up the steps of the wood-platform porch, then to the open front door, where a sentry stands at attention with his carbine.

Sergeant Jordan stops, knocks on the door jam and stands at attention as a voice from inside says, "Enter."

Sergeant Jordan removes his hat with his right hand, puts it underneath his left armpit, and walks into the office away from the bright sunlight and into a semi-lit office.

As Sergeant Jordan enters, he cannot see inside with any detail as he walks halfway to the center, comes to a stop at attention and salutes. A voice says, "At-ease, Sergeant."

Sergeant Jordan drops his salute, takes the position of at-ease as his vision adjusts and returns. He first sees Colonel Hatch seated in front of him. Colonel Hatch is forty-nine years old now, and walks with a swaggered step. He never asks more of his men then he does from himself. Colonel Hatch has been consistently overlooked for promotion as many officers are in colored regiments. Colonel Hatch finds the loyalty of his men a deeper reward than any promotion.

Colonel Hatch is seated at First Sergeant Shaw's desk in front of him, and seated to the right of him is the garrison adjutant, who has a horrible scar around the front of his neck. He is seated at his desk doing paperwork. Further to his right is First Sergeant Thomas Shaw.

Sergeant Shaw is thirty-four years old. Born in Kentucky a slave, he ran away to join the Union Army at the age of eighteen. He worked his way up the ladder in rank. He's a sharpshooter, the best marksman in the U.S. Cavalry and, like Sergeant Jordan; Sergeant Shaw is hardened by years of frontier service. He is seated at an empty desk and smiling with accomplishment, looking to Sergeant Jordan.

Sergeant Jordan then looks back to his left, past Colonel Hatch, when he sees his new commander: Captain Henry Carroll—the one who said "enter"—seated at the commander's desk.

Captain Carroll has a semi-round face. His eyes are almond shaped and sit upon his soft rounded cheekbones, in between a sharp protruding nose. He has medium-length hair combed back and a long, well-trimmed mustache, which protrudes down both sides of his mouth to the bottom of his chin.

Captain Carroll looks to Sergeant Jordan and says, "Report."

"Sir, welcome to Fort Stanton... Sir, we completed breaking in regimental mounts, per orders, just as the depot was attacked by Comancheros."

"Yes, I got the telegram that night when I arrived, and Colonel Hatch filled me in on what he knew. He said you and your men performed excellently."

Sergeant Jordan looks to Colonel Hatch and says, "Thank you, sir. Sir, we were surprised to see you back here so soon."

"I know Sergeant, the Ninth's band took a shortcut they said they knew." He then looks to Captain Carroll and says, "Henry, do you know since I gave orders for the Ninth's band to begin cavalry training, they have become quite proficient at it. They made it back to Stanton—in wagons, record time. Their training is working quite well I must say. They're turning into some good cavalrymen." He chuckles and smiles, then says, "cowboys."

Sergeant Jordan is surprised by Colonel Hatch's word, "cowboys," and double takes his expression from Captain Carroll to Colonel Hatch and then, back to Captain Carroll with a puzzled look.

"Anything wrong, Sergeant?" says Captain Carroll.

"Ah, no sir," says Sergeant Jordan as he regains his military posture, then says, "Sir, there is another incident I need to report."

"Yes, go ahead Sergeant," says Captain Carroll.

"My Scout came across Sergeant Johnson from G Troop, trying to rescue a saloonkeeper and his family in their supply wagon. They were stranded in the Pecos. The wagon was weighted with liquor, about fifty-five miles out. My Scout backtracked to our position, alerting us to the family's circumstances. We then followed him back to the family and performed the rescue, along with Sergeant Johnson, successfully I may say, sir."

"Excellent report, Sergeant," says Captain Carroll as he then says, "anything else?"

"No, sir. Nothing else to report."

"I expect a full written report by tomorrow morning, Sergeant."

"Yes, sir. Anything else, sir?"

"Yes Sergeant, yes there is," says Captain Carroll.

Captain Carroll closes a Military Record Book in front of him. On the cover is written, "9th Regiment, K Troop." Captain Carroll stands and begins pacing in back of his desk, stopping at the window behind his desk and looking out to the garrison. He says, "Colonel Hatch has told me a lot about you and your troopers, Sergeant."

Captain Carroll then turns from the window, looks to

Sergeant Jordan, and says, "He informed me, K Troop is one of the top regiments in the U.S. Cavalry". "And looking at the regiment's service record..." Captain Carroll then walks to his desk, looking at the closed book on top, then looks to Sergeants Jordan and Shaw saying, "Quite remarkable accomplishments, Sergeants."

"Thank you, sir," says Sergeants Jordan and Shaw simultaneously.

Captain Carroll then walks from behind his desk, walking to the front. He sits on the front edge of the desk and looks at both sergeants as he says, "Sergeants, I'm looking forward to the Diamond Club's dance tonight. I hear your galas are always quite the affair, right to the last details."

"Yes, sir, Sergeant Shaw and I take pride in our garrison. There's not much else out here, so we try to brin' about as much pleasantries as possible for officers and enlisted, sir."

"Then keep up the good work Sergeant. Dismissed," says Captain Carroll.

"Thank you, sir, and please, enjoy yourself at the supper and dance tonight," says Sergeant Jordan. He snaps to attention and salutes Colonel Hatch and Captain Carroll, who return his salute.

Sergeant Jordan makes a smart about-face towards the front door, as Sergeant Shaw says, "Sergeant Jordan, I'll come and see ya after I finish preparing these orders, and fill you in on the details."

"I'm going over to the stables and get my saddlebag first...clean-up...meet me at the assembly hall later Sergeant."

"See ya their Sergeant, and good job," says Sergeant Shaw.

Sergeant Shaw nods and smiles to Sergeant Jordan,

who marches out of the Command Office in smart military fashion.

Later that night, "The Blue Danube" emanates from the assembly hall as torches, mounted in their holders throughout the garrison, highlight the elegant night. Red, white, and blue banners hang from the rafters protruding from the hall.

Cigar smoke rises in the night air from townsmen dressed in their Sunday best. Colored soldiers and their white officers dressed in their splendid dress uniforms converse and mingle outside the hall.

The townswomen, colored soldiers' girlfriends, and officers' wives are dressed in their fabulous flowing gowns, conversing with the men, white to white and colored to colored. The illusion of brotherhood is only on the surface when in these formal situations. Only a few white officers care to admit to these soldiers' gallantry and honor. Sergeants Jordan and Shaw, and Trooper Chase are talking with each other as Corporal Wilson approaches.

Sergeant Jordan looks to Corporal Wilson approaching and says, "Corporal, I see your dress uniform made it back in one piece."

Corporal Wilson, looking to his uniform, proudly says, "Yeah, no tears, and not even dusty. The band is turnin' into some good cow—I mean cavalrymen, Sarge."

Sergeant Jordan looks to Corporal Wilson with a confused expression on his face, "Cavalrymen, or cowboys." Colonel Hatch, Mrs. Evelyn Hatch, Captain Carroll and his date approach, attracting Sergeant Jordan's attention. The officers look to both sergeants, Corporal Wilson and to Trooper Chase as they all salute.

Colonel Hatch and Captain Carroll return the salute as Colonel Hatch looks to Sergeants Jordan and Shaw saying,

"Sergeants, again an exquisite night. Supper was superb."

"Yes Sergeants, an elegant night, I must say, I have to teach my daughter these fine techniques of a gala," says Mrs. Hatch.

Sergeant Jordan and Sergeant Shaw bow their heads in respect to Colonel Hatch and Mrs. Hatch. Sergeants Jordan and Shaw then look to the Hatch's, and say simultaneously, "Thank you Colonel, thank you Mrs. Hatch."

Captain Carroll looks to both sergeants and says, "Sergeants, the squash and turnips we had for dinner were excellent...fresh. Did they come from the garrison's garden?"

"Yes sir. Sir, Trooper Chase here." Sergeant Jordan puts his arm around Trooper Chase's shoulders and says, "He manages the garrison's garden with help from KP duty and volunteers. It's been warm lately, and the vegetables ripened fast for this time of year."

"I must say Trooper, not having vegetables for weeks, that was quite a treat," says Captain Carroll.

"Thank you, sir," says Trooper Chase.

Sergeant Jordan removes his arm from Trooper Chase's shoulders, as Trooper Chase looks to his sergeants and says, "Anything else Sarge?"

"No, Trooper. Go with Corporal Wilson," says Sergeant Shaw, as he looks to Corporal Wilson and says, "Corporal Wilson, let Sergeant Major Brown know we'll be in shortly."

"Yes sir," says Corporal Wilson. Corporal Wilson and Trooper Chase salute the officers, who return their salute. They make an about-face and walk smartly into the assembly hall.

Captain Carroll looks to both sergeants with amazement and says, "How are you able to put on such an event?"

Mrs. Hatch does not hesitate to take center stage at this

question as she says, "Ah, Captain its all quite simple. Sergeant Jordan and Sergeant Shaw formed the Diamond Club and started group committees to hold these fabulous galas—finance, invitations, decorations, food, refreshments, and the bar." Mrs. Hatch very proudly says, "Which I am head of that committee."

"Well, I must say then Mrs. Hatch, we should go and try some of your committee's treats," says Captain Carroll.

Captain Carroll smiles to Mrs. Hatch as she giggles at the invitation. Sergeant Jordan extends his hand in the direction of the front door of the assembly hall as Sergeant Shaw leads the way. Mrs. Hatch and Captain Carroll's date proceed as Captain Carroll and Colonel Hatch follow with Sergeant Jordan bringing up the rear.

Moments later, Sergeant Shaw walks through the front doors of the assembly hall, into a large lavish foyer, and then proceeds to the entrance of the hall with the ladies, officers, and Sergeant Jordan following. The ladies and officers stop and marvel at the sights of American, Haitian and Liberian flags, hanging on poles and stationed on both sides of the foyer, tilting towards the center.

They then look towards the hall and see mounted above the entryway two arched crossed sabers, with the troop letter "K" wreathed and mounted below the center point of the sabers. Above the center point—also wreathed—is the number "9" and above that, the word "WELCOME" in gilt lettering.

To Colonel Hatch and Mrs. Hatch, this is nothing new. However, it's all new to Captain Carroll and his date, who stare with amazement and doubt. The group then proceeds under the crossed sabers and into the assembly hall only to find a more elegant festive gala.

Women are waltzing with their men to the 9th Cavalries Band's beautiful song, "The Blue Danube," in their lavish gowns that flow with their every movement in the middle of the New Mexico desert.

This is the Buffalo Soldiers' time to shine, and to show another side of their hardened frontiersmen character. Other members of K Troop are on the dance floor. Still others are standing at the bar, which is well attended by other regiments, colored soldiers, and white officers, indulging in wines, whisky, old cognac, and extra-fine cigars.

Captain Carroll and his date marvel at the extravaganza as Sergeant Shaw escorts them to the bar. When they reach the bar through the crowd, Sergeant Jordan reaches into a box on the bar and brings out four cigars, the best of that time. Sergeant Jordan then hands one each to Colonel Hatch, Captain Carroll, and Sergeant Shaw, keeping one for himself.

He lights Colonel Hatch's cigar, as Mrs. Hatch looks to Captain Carroll and says, "Brandy Captain, for you and the lady?"

"Why yes, thank you Mrs. Hatch," says Captain Carroll.

Captain Carroll bows his head to Mrs. Hatch, as she then looks to the bartender to place her order. Sergeant Jordan has finished lighting Captain Carroll's cigar, and then lights his own. After lighting his cigar, Sergeant Jordan looks up and sees Corporal Wilson in the background waving respectfully for him and Sergeant Shaw to come to his locality near the band. Sergeant Jordan taps Sergeant Shaw on the shoulder and points to Corporal Wilson signaling to them.

Sergeant Shaw looks at Corporal Wilson then Colonel Hatch, his wife, to Captain Carroll, and to his date and says, "Sirs, madams, please excuse us, we need to attend to affairs."

"Certainly Sergeant, go ahead," says Colonel Hatch.

Sergeants Jordan and Shaw bow their heads to the ladies and walk towards Corporal Wilson, who is standing near Sergeant Major Brown.

Captain Carroll takes his brandy glass off the bar, toasts the ladies, then with a bewildered expression, looks to the flags in the foyer, then to Colonel Hatch and says, "Colonel, what are those two other flags the soldiers have standing alongside the United States flag?"

"Captain, the black and red flag with the palm tree in the center is Haitian, and the other flag, the one that looks like ours except for the eleven stripes, and the one large white star in the blue pattern is Liberian. They use these flags at all their gatherings. It symbolizes parts of their African ancestry."

"I see Colonel...is this proper and respectful? I've heard many stories about these men that bring into question their capabilities and loyalties."

"Captain, for the Buffalo Soldier—proper and respect have *never* crossed their path. Having pride in their ancestry, and of the slave issue, there is nothing wrong with that Captain. As for their capabilities and loyalties, they're impeccable. Tomorrow morning, Captain, I'll share a letter with you that I'm sending to General Pope regarding the latest travesties that happened to these marvelous soldiers."

After Colonel Hatch's comment, Captain Carroll looks out into the assembly hall towards the Buffalo Soldiers, to the 9th Cavalry Band, to the extravaganza. He begins to realize that there is something special about these men.

As the gala continues, Sergeants Jordan and Shaw stand near the band, as Sergeant Shaw whispers into the adjutant's ear. The adjutant then makes an about-face and walks through the foyer towards the outside. As the waltzing continues, the guests outside begin to file inside as the band starts to wind down the music.

Dancers and non-dancers applaud the delightful evening of music, as Sergeant Shaw approaches the podium. He looks out to the crowd, raises his arms to quiet the hall, and says, "Welcome, welcome everyone. I trust that you are having a good time."

The entire assembly hall that was quieting down erupts with applause again. Sergeant Shaw holds his hands up to settle the ovations.

The crowd settles as Sergeant Shaw looks to the gathering and says, "Sergeant Jordan has a few words before we introduce our new Garrison Commander."

The festive crowd applauds again, as Sergeant Shaw steps back. Sergeant Jordan steps up to the podium, holding up his hands to settle the crowd.

The crowd quiets down as Sergeant Jordan says, "Thank you everyone for comin' and celebratin' with us Spring Days, and Fort Stantons' new commander."

Again everyone applauds, as Sergeant Jordan awaits the crowd's ovations to subside. The crowd applause settles, as Sergeant Jordan says, "It is my pleasure to introduce Captain Henry Carroll...Fort Stanton's new commander."

Again, everyone applauds Sergeant Jordan as he steps back from the podium to make room for Captain Carroll. Captain Carroll approaches the podium, with the crowd still applauding as he tries to greet the guests over their ovations.

"Good evening. Good evening ladies and gentlemen," says Captain Carroll.

The crowd slows their applause and responds back to Captain Carroll with, "Good evening."

Captain Carroll looks to the hall and says, "Thank you. First, I want to thank Sergeant Jordan and Sergeant Shaw for this elegant evening." The crowd applauds Sergeants Jordan and Shaw as Captain Carroll holds up his hands to settle the ovations. The noise dies down as Captain Carroll surveys the assembly hall, pauses for a few moments, then says, "Second, a salute to Colonel Hatch for his new Command at Santa Fe."

Immediately all the soldiers set down anything they have in their hands, turn, and salute Colonel Hatch, then they join the townspeople in applauding.

Captain Carroll waits for the ovations to subside as he looks to the crowd somewhat seriously, clears his throat and says, "I've been a tough disciplinarian...a very conscientious and an untiring soldier. I will kick out any soldier who fails to meet my standards. And I came here...prepared to do exactly that...based upon what I've heard..."

Troopers Chase and his comrades look to Sergeant Jordan, with a look of, "Sarge knew."

"I've been here for just over a week. I've been watching and I must say, I am amazed at what I've seen. Also—" Captain Carroll looks to Colonel Hatch, then looks back to the crowd. "...Colonel Hatch has offered his opinions. Thus I've come to my own conclusion. You the 'Buffalo Soldiers...'" Captain Carroll hesitates, looks around the room then begins to smile, and says, "They must have been talking about some other regiment."

All the Buffalo Soldiers look to each other and then join the entire hall in applauding Captain Carroll. Captain Carroll holds up his hands trying to subdue the crowd as he says, "Please, please, please," shouting.

However, the Buffalo Soldiers now know they have made another friend, and give a second round of applause and ovations to Captain Carroll, as he shouts to the band over the crowd's ovations, "Without further ado, let the band play on!"

The 9th Cavalry Band strikes up "The Battle Cry of Freedom" as the crowd settles, and proceeds to their business of enjoyment. Trooper Perry and the young lady he spoke to earlier begin their dance routine, along with Colonel Hatch and Mrs. Hatch, Captain Carroll and his date, the regiment and townspeople.

Sergeant Major Brown and some of the band members demonstrate their extraordinary talents by playing with either hand, as Sergeants Jordan and Shaw, Corporal Wilson and Trooper Chase exit the band area, walking towards the bar.

When they reach the bar, Sergeant Jordan looks to Sergeant Shaw as the bartender automatically serves both sergeants, Corporal Wilson and Trooper Chase, a dark brown-colored drink in brandy glasses.

Sergeant Jordan looks to Sergeant Shaw and says, "Well, what do you think?"

"I think...we've got a good commander, Sergeant," says Sergeant Shaw.

Sergeant Jordan then says, "I think you're right, Sergeant. Anything beats Lieutenant Colonel Dudley, or the likes of that commander back at Santa Fe I told you about...where Wilson here shot that Comanchero, saving the post commander's life."

Sergeant Shaw looks to Corporal Wilson, raises his glass, and says, "Here's to Corporal Wilson...you learn good."

The group then raises their glasses to salute Corporal Wilson, as Corporal Wilson raises his glass.

Trooper Chase looks to the group and says, "Cheers to the best marksman in the whole entire U.S. Cavalry." He then looks to Sergeant Shaw with the expression of "oops!" and says, "I mean—second-best marksman."

"That's all right, Trooper, he'll be there one day," says Sergeant Shaw.

"Here, here," says Sergeant Jordan.

The group clangs their glasses together and sips their drinks.

Sergeant Shaw's expression to Sergeant Jordan is "wow, that is the best drink I've ever had," as he says, "Is that the brandy you said the saloonkeeper hid in your saddlebag?"

"Yeah," says Sergeant Jordan as he looks to Corporal Wilson. "When I brought my saddlebag back to the barracks, went to clean my bag, this fell out."

Sergeant Jordan picks up the bottle of Jewish brandy the bartender left for them on the bar, and shows it to the group. Then Sergeant Jordan shows the bottle to Corporal Wilson and says, "Mr. Bernstein must have slipped it into my saddlebag when we weren't lookin'. I gave the bartender the bottle before supper to serve for this special occasion."

Sergeant Jordan looks to Trooper Chase, who downed his drink in one swallow, not realizing this is brandy. Furthermore, not having had the finer liquors in his life, his eyes begin to bulge as he tries to talk with a raspy voice, "What's…in that!"

Corporal Wilson holds on to Trooper Chase in case he passes out as Sergeants Jordan and Shaw and Corporal Wilson begin laughing. Trooper Chase begins regaining his composure as Troopers Irving, Temple, and Walley join the group with other members of K Troop at the bar.

Trooper Temple looks to Trooper Chase and says, "What's wrong with Chase?"

"I think he thought this was like drinkin' sarsaparilla," says Sergeant Jordan, showing them the bottle.

Trooper Walley looks to Trooper Chase and says, "I

didn't know a colored man could change shades of colors."

Everyone laughs as Trooper Temple looks to the group and says, "Is he goin' to be able to give Tone tonight?"

With a somewhat raspy voice, Trooper Chase looks to everyone and says, "I'll...be alright."

Again, the group chuckles and laughs as some pat Trooper Chase on the head to let him know he'll be all right. He's a soldier as the bartender serves the other soldiers.

Later that night, torches light the garrison as the air is filled with soothing music from K Troop's barracks as sentries walk their post. The Buffalo Soldiers are well versed in plantation songs; their voices are so rich and full of their African ancestral melodies. Their voices are not loud, but just loud enough so a soothing tone of melody is felt throughout the garrison.

A sentry stands guard just off the porch of the Command Office as Mrs. Hatch and Captain Carroll's date sit on a bench swing on the wood platform on the left side of the porch facing the garrison. Colonel Hatch and Captain Carroll are also on the platform, standing at the porch rail, facing the garrison.

They are enjoying the music and song when Captain Carroll looks to Colonel Hatch and says, "Colonel, how did they get the name Buffalo Soldier?"

Colonel Hatch looks to Captain Carroll and says, "Word has it Captain, I believe about twelve years ago, Captain George Washington Graham, Tenth Regiment, I Troop, were cornered in the Missouri Territory by an overwhelming number of hostile Cheyenne...'Dog Soldiers'. I don't know if you've ever seen a buffalo cornered Captain, it's an animal that doesn't take well to the threat, and will fight with every ounce of tenacity to find its way out. Well, the colored soldiers, they were cornered and fought their way out, only losing one man and killing many Cheyenne."

Captain Carroll says, "That's how they got their name, Colonel?"

"Yes, after the Cheyenne took one look at them, with their dark skin and curly hair, and knowing their sacred animal, they named the colored soldier after them."

"Remarkable story, Colonel."

Captain Carroll's date gets up from the swing and walks over to him. He puts his arm around his date and looks to Colonel Hatch and says, "It's amazing Colonel, they seem to never tire of music."

"They call it 'Tone', Captain. It's one of their ways of maintaining their high spirits and morale."

Mrs. Hatch stands up from the swing, walks over to Colonel Hatch, standing by his side, as she looks out into the garrison courtyard, then to the stars. "The melodies are so beautiful," she says, looking to Captain Carroll. "I look forward to my visits to the darkies' post, Captain...it's such a pleasure. I actually can fall asleep listening to their songs."

Colonel Hatch and Mrs. Hatch, Captain Carroll and his date look to the stars, listening to the melodies.

Inside K Troop's barracks, Sergeant Jordan is enjoying the music with four dozen troopers of K Troop. Trooper Chase is finishing his song with several other troopers singing backup, along with Trooper Irving playing guitar and Trooper Temple on harmonica. Among the troopers in the barracks are two corporals, one guidon trooper, and one bugler trooper. Some troopers are getting ready for bed by fluffing the straw under their blanket, which covers the wood slats that lay over the iron bunk-frame they sleep on, while others sit on their bunks and enjoy the camaraderie of their comrades.

After playing his last note, Trooper Temple wipes off his harmonica on his nightshirt as the little singing group prepares for their next song.

Trooper Walley looks at Trooper Chase and says, "Give us another Tone, Chase."

"Last one before 'Taps' gentlemen," says Sergeant Jordan.

"All right Sarge. Hey Sarge, where's John Glass? Haven't seen him all night. He surely can harmonize with me on this next one," says Trooper Chase.

Trooper Irving says, "You were down at the creek when word came in that the Tenth chased Victorio back into New Mexico. Glass got cleaned up a bit. Took off like a jackrabbit with its tail on fire...said he be back tonight or mornin'."

"All right, got it by myself," says Trooper Chase.

Trooper Chase takes in a couple of deep breaths, extends his arms and hands out into the open air of the barracks and looks skyward. Trooper Chase then begins to hum, as Trooper Temple melts in, playing his harmonica, and as Trooper Irving begins picking the strings on his guitar, while the other members fill in the background by also humming.

Trooper Chase begins singing, "Swing lo...sweet chariot...comin' forth to carry me home...swing lo...sweet chariot...comin' forth to carry me home. Now a band of angels, comin' after me...comin' forth to carry me home...swing lo...sweet chariot...comin' forth to carry me home..."

The sound of coyotes yakking in the far distance is barely heard.

At 5:30 a.m. the next morning, it's just turning light as a rooster begins to "COCK-A-DOODLE-DOO," but then quiets as Fort Stanton's bugler sounds "Reveille" with an improvised, semi-jazzy unorthodox sound.

The American flag begins to rise along the flagpole, by a trooper hoisting it aloft smartly into the crystal blue morning air. The trooper hoisting is standing with two other troopers in a triangular-shaped pattern beneath the pole.

While the trooper pulls the flag a aloft, another one is holding the flag while it unfurls out of his hands, and when the flag leaves his hands, he snaps to attention, salutes while the other soldier, the guard, stands at attention with his carbine.

Inside the barracks, K Troop is stirring in the early morning. The last soldier is climbing out of his bunk as Sergeant Jordan finishes buttoning his cavalry shirt. He looks out to his men and gives his morning orders. "Good mornin' gentlemen. You know your duties. Lets get those bunks made, get cleaned up and you know the rest: assembly, stable call, breakfast, sick call. Let's get to it! Corporal Wilson."

"Yes, Sarge."

"Corporal, when you're dressed, see if John Glass is back and inform Sergeant Shaw and myself."

"Yes, Sarge."

K Troop is performing their first duty, getting dressed, and following their Sergeant's orders, but also having a little morning camaraderie.

Trooper Temple looks to Trooper Walley making his bunk and says, "Augustus, did you see that pretty little thin' Charles was dancin' with last night?"

"Sure did. He kept callin' her Cherry Blossom...all night," says Trooper Walley.

81

Sergeant Jordan sees the morning camaraderie getting ready to take place and quietly whispers to Corporal Wilson to get his attention, "pssst, pssst...pssst."

Corporal Wilson looks to Sergeant Jordan, just as Sergeant Shaw walks through the front door of the barracks and sees Sergeant Jordan nodding his head, nonchalantly, pointing his finger in the direction of the conversation.

Corporal Wilson and Sergeant Shaw also look in that direction, with most of the barracks' attention now diverted to Trooper Perry and the conversation. Trooper Chase looks to his comrades and says, "That's one of those new laundress. Came in on that stagecoach just as we left for Santa Fe."

Another corporal in K Troop, Corporal Dorch, enters into the conversation. "Yeah, she is one of the prettiest things we seen in a long time. Everyone tried to court her while you were gone. She just ignored everyone, it seems"—he carries his look from his comrades to Trooper Perry—"until she saw Charles yesterday."

Everyone jokingly hoots at Trooper Perry making his bunk, trying to ignore his comrades. When the hoots and laughs settle, Corporal Dorch says, "Shoot, when Charles called her Cherry Blossom, she took to him like a pig would take to a new patch of mud."

Everyone hoots again at Trooper Perry as he finishes tightening the corners on his bunk. Looking to his comrades with a semi-serious expression, he stands, saying, "You all jealous, when I get out in two years, I gonna have me a good wife. Those laundresses, they take good care of a man..."

Trooper Perry looks to Corporal Dorch and says, "You gotta know what kind of mud to mix, to get the right pig."

Trooper Chase looks to Trooper Perry and pulls the trigger on the morning barracks' joke by saying, "You mix the wrong mud Charles, you might get a warthog."

The entire barracks laughs, including Sergeants Jordan and Shaw, as well as Corporal Wilson as Trooper Perry throws his towel at Trooper Chase. The laughter continues as Sergeant Shaw slows his laughter, looks to Sergeant Jordan and says, "John back yet?"

"No, I just told Corporal Wilson to check and let us know as soon as he gets back."

Corporal Wilson has just finished making his bunk as he says, "On my way Sarge." Corporal Wilson grabs his towel, toothbrush, hairbrush and exits out the front door of the barracks with Troopers Chase, Irving, Perry, Temple, Walley, and other members of K Troop following with their hygiene gear.

Troopers are exiting their barracks with towels and hygiene gear, walking to the garrison's water well. At the well, the soldiers retrieve buckets of water and carry them over to several wood-plank troughs and earthen-dug washbasins, where they pour the clean water into the basins, flushing out the old water.

Some laughter, joke telling, and singing emanates from the garrison's barracks and compound as Colonel Hatch, carrying his saddlebag, walks towards the Command Office with several soldiers stopping and saluting him smartly as he walks by.

Just outside the Command Office, a sentry stands on the raised wood-platform porch at attention with his carbine. Captain Carroll stands just in front of the sentry, looking out to the garrison as Colonel Hatch approaches. Captain Carroll salutes the colonel as he reaches the porch with Colonel Hatch returning the salute, and Captain Carroll saying, "Good morning Colonel."

"Good morning, Captain."

Colonel Hatch walks up the steps up onto the porch as Captain Carroll looks to Colonel Hatch and says, "Quite a festive night, Colonel."

"Yes, yes it was Captain."

Captain Carroll walks to the edge of the porch, stops, looks out at the garrison, and says, "Colonel Hatch, since I arrived, before your return yesterday, each and every morning has also been full of song and laughter. I'm still astounded over their cheer…are these men this cheerful?"

"Yes Captain."

Colonel Hatch walks to the edge of the porch, then stands next to Captain Carroll proudly, looking out to his regiment and says, "At every permissible moment you will hear music and song...from 'Reveille' till 'Taps.' You'll never see them moping, sad or isolated, but always in crowds of their peers, bad or good weather alike, they are always cheerful."

"Remarkable Colonel. They seem to have a more cheerful morale...than most of the white troop companies I've commanded."

"Captain, they are very proud men and they consider the U.S. Cavalry their home. Our country, Captain, views these colored soldiers either as misfits or dangerous. They joined the cavalry to escape those indignities of civilian life, only to find the same people they have been sworn to protect, distrusting them, and just plain darn right disrespectful, calling them...niggers and spitting in their faces."

Captain Carroll looks to Colonel Hatch with a more astounded expression than last night and says, "I had no idea, Colonel...even after what I said last night and from what you have told me. I mean, from what I heard throughout my career—alcoholics, cowards, deserters and misfits—it's just the opposite."

Colonel Hatch looks from the garrison compound to Captain Carroll and says, "Captain, we've had a few problems, no one is perfect. However, the colored regiments have had far less desertions and drunken payday sprees than the white regiments, you saw their record, Captain." Colonel Hatch sighs as he then says, "I took the liberty and asked the adjutant to bring our breakfast to your office. I want you to read about the latest travesties that took place in Lincoln before the mail goes out with the Twenty-fourth this morning."

"Fine Colonel, I made some fresh hot coffee," says Captain Carroll.

Captain Carroll motions with his hand to the front door of the Command Office; however, Colonel Hatch has turned back, looking to the compound. He stands proudly looking out to the garrison, at his soldiers and their officers as the bugler sounds assembly. The soldiers begin to assemble in the middle of the garrison compound for roll call as Colonel Hatch turns with a smile on his face and walks into the Command Office with Captain Carroll following behind him.

The sentry moves from attention to parade-rest, closing the door behind them.

Moments later in the Command Office, Captain Carroll walks over to a book cabinet and picks up two coffee cups, then walks over to a potbelly wood heater with a flat stovetop, where a coffeepot sits, with steam coming from its spout. Captain Carroll walks over to Colonel Hatch standing by Sergeant Shaw's desk. He hands Colonel Hatch a cup, picks up the coffeepot off the stove and begins pouring the coffee. As he finishes pouring Colonel Hatch's, he pours his, and then returns the coffeepot back to the stove.

Captain Carroll then walks around his desk to his chair and sits down as Colonel Hatch sits on the corner of Sergeant Shaw's desk facing Captain Carroll. Colonel Hatch reaches in his saddlebag, which is lying on the desk, and brings out the letter, as the sounds of roll call from Sergeant Shaw and Fort Stanton's command is heard in the distance.

Colonel Hatch looks to Captain Carroll with military matters and says, "Any word yet from Chief of Scouts, Captain."

"Nothing yet Colonel. When he rode out, he said he be back late night or morning. I sent Sergeant Shaw to check with Sergeant Jordan. He said when he heard any information, he would inform me directly, but until then, he would perform roll call."

There's a knock at the door.

"Enter," says Captain Carroll.

The sentry opens the door and the adjutant enters with their frontier breakfast: hardtack, molasses, beans, bacon, and eggs. He sits one breakfast in front of Captain Carroll and the other on Sergeant Shaw's desk for Colonel Hatch.

Colonel Hatch looks to the adjutant and says, "Thank you, Adjutant."

The adjutant salutes as Colonel Hatch and Captain Carroll return his salute. The adjutant makes a smart about-face, and exits, with the sentry closing the door behind him.

Colonel Hatch hands Captain Carroll the letter. He turns and walks to Sergeant Shaw's desk, sits, and begins to eat his breakfast when he looks to Captain Carroll and says, "Captain, here it is in the short. Three weeks ago, two soldiers from G Troop were arrested in Lincoln—just for having their Army issue revolvers and carbines."

Captain Carroll looks up from eating and says, "What did they do?"

"What do you mean, what did they do! Nothing, Captain—except be colored. They went before the circuit judge of Lincoln and were fined the money in their pockets, and their weapons...that had no other purpose, Captain, other than robbery under the Color of the Law! That's why I am sending that letter to General Pope."

As Captain Carroll reads the letter, he looks up and says, "Very impressive information, Colonel."

Captain Carroll finishes the letter, re-folds it and inserts it into the envelope, then looks to Colonel Hatch and says, "What do you think General Pope will do, Colonel?"

"Nothing, Captain. He's powerless with these civilian politicians. It's just a matter of record."

In the distance, the sound of men and wagons in a hurry are heard coming into the garrison. Colonel Hatch and Captain Carroll stop eating and talking, look to the sound, then stand and rush to the front door, opening it and rushing out to investigate.

As Colonel Hatch and Captain Carroll come to a stop on the porch, they see three military supply wagons coming to a stop by the garrison's warehouse and stables. The 24th Infantry, B Troop guidon is flying from the first wagon. The garrison command is still in formation, standing at 'parade -rest', for roll call, as Sergeants Jordan and Shaw are talking with the lead wagon's infantry sergeant, who is pointing his finger in a westerly direction.

The other teamsters who came with the wagons are beginning to load bales of wire from the garrison's warehouse onto their wagons as Colonel Hatch looks at Captain Carroll then to the wagons and says, "They're here early, Captain. I wonder why they rode in hard?"

"Colonel, by the records I've reviewed when I arrived, this should be the last leg of telegraph wire they're stringing from Santa Fe to El Paso."

Colonel Hatch looks to Captain Carroll and says, "Yes, Captain—and on time..."

He then looks back to his sergeants and wagons with a concerned look and says, "It looks like something happened."

Just then, Sergeant Jordan leaves Sergeant Shaw talking with the 24th's Infantry sergeant, double-timing towards Colonel Hatch and Captain Carroll standing on the Command Office porch. Sergeant Jordan reaches the office, stops in front of Colonel Hatch and Captain Carroll, and salutes. They return his salute as Sergeant Jordan says, "Sirs, Sergeant Harris from the Twenty-fourth, B Troop reported...Scout Glass found their camp about fifty miles out towards the San Mateos, told them to bring the information, Victorio is back in the territory...he found signs of depravation, to meet him, this side of the San Mateos."

"Sergeant, tell the bugler to call 'Boots and Saddles', then tell Sergeant Shaw to mount up the garrison, only sentries remain behind," says Captain Carroll as he looks to Colonel Hatch. "Even though we're shorthanded Colonel, we'll find them."

Sergeant Jordan salutes and is prepared to drop his salute and carry out his commander's orders.

Captain Carroll turns back to Sergeant Jordan, returning the salute, while Colonel Hatch holds his salute. Looking to Sergeant Jordan, he says, "Hold on Sergeant."

Colonel Hatch drops his salute and looks to Captain Carroll and says, "Sergeant Jordan can take K Troop to meet up with Scout Glass and keep us posted, instead of tracing all across the territory with the entire regiment and supply wagons, Captain."

"But Colonel, we can pick up his trail," says Captain Carroll.

"Captain, you're dealing with the world's best Lightweight Cavalryman ever to have lived. While their main unit is going in one direction, the rear guard is covering the main tracks and creating a false trail in another direction. The last thing you want to do Captain, is go tracing off with the entire regiment, that's what he wants you to do."

Captain Carroll looks to Colonel Hatch and says, "What should we do then, Colonel?"

Colonel Hatch turns to Sergeant Jordan and says, "Sergeant Jordan, take a detachment of K Troop, provisions for five days, each trooper as much carbine ammunition they can carry—at least two-hundred fifty rounds—and fifty rounds of pistol ammunition. That means only the clothes on their backs, Sergeant. Once you meet up with Scout Glass, see if you can pick up a good trail. When you find Victorio's trail, send a messenger back with your location."

"Yes, sir," says Sergeant Jordan.

Sergeant Jordan salutes his officers as Colonel Hatch and Captain Carroll return the salute. Sergeant Jordan then makes a smart about-face, and double-times back to the wagons, as Colonel Hatch shouts to him, "Sergeant!"

Sergeant Jordan stops in his tracks and turns back to Colonel Hatch and says, "Yes, sir."

"Tell Sergeant Shaw he'll remain with me and the rest of the garrison, until you pick up Victorio's trail."

"Yes, sir."

Sergeant Jordan again salutes his officers as Colonel Hatch and Captain Carroll return his salute. Sergeant Jordan then turns and double-times back to Sergeant Shaw with Colonel Hatch's orders.

The next afternoon, Sergeant Jordan sits astride his mount as the guidon of the 9th Cavalry, K Troop blows from its staff in the desert wind behind him. Twenty-four of his men sit astride their mounts in a column of twos, with the detachment in the same order, just behind the guidon trooper and bugler. Sergeant Jordan looks down to Corporal Wilson, who's kneeling down on one knee, looking at a strand of barbwire cattle fencing that has been severed.

Corporal Wilson looks to Sergeant Jordan and says, "Fresh cut, Sarge, no rusts." Corporal Wilson then stands, walks over to where there are many tracks in the dirt. A fence pole is lying on the ground with other cut strands of barbwire.

He bends down to examine the tracks and pole, then looks to Sergeant Jordan and says, "Unshod pony tracks, Sarge, and these poles were pulled out by rope. Someone drove cattle through here, recently, then scattered in all directions."

"All right Corporal, mount up," says Sergeant Jordan. "We'll follow these tracks," he says, indicating with his finger. Corporal Wilson stands, walks back to his mount, takes his reins from the bugler, and ascends his mount as Sergeant Jordan looks to Corporal Wilson and says, "Corporal, pass the word, keep your eyes opened." Sergeant Jordan takes off his campaign hat and raises it above his head, as Corporal Wilson turns and spurs his mount to the rear, passing Sergeant Jordan's orders on. Sergeant Jordan turns and looks to the columns as he calls his orders, "Forwarrrd, *hooo'*!"

Sergeant Jordan turns back in his saddle. His hand falls forward as the columns move out in military fashion, smartly, by a column of twos. Sergeant Jordan puts his hat back on as the columns begin following the tracks. However, as Corporal Wilson rides back to his position in the column, he sees two riders in the distance, riding hard and fast towards them. Corporal Wilson points to the riders and says, "Sarge."

Sergeant Jordan looks at Corporal Wilson, then in the direction Corporal Wilson is pointing and sees the two riders. As the riders approach, Sergeant Jordan recognizes one of the riders and says, "Glass."

Corporal Wilson looks to the riders and says, "Ya...who's that with him?"

"I don't know," says Sergeant Jordan. Sergeant Jordan turns in his saddle and calls his orders: "Pass the word, at a trot." Sergeant Jordan stands in his stirrups as the orders are passed. He then takes off his campaign hat, holds it above his head, and shouts his orders. "Columns at a trot...trot!" Sergeant Jordan's arm falls forward from the extended position as he sits back in the saddle with the columns taking their mounts from a walk to a trot.

Scout Glass and the other rider are approaching at full stride as Trooper Chase looks to his left and sees the beginning puffs of smoke from a mountaintop. Pointing to the smoke, he shouts, "Sarge, smoke signals!"

Sergeant Jordan and his men look to the smoke signals as Scout Glass and his companion come to a stop as the columns near. Sergeant Jordan—looking at the smoke signals—turns forward, takes off his hat, raises it in the air and calls his orders: "Troop...*hooolt!*"

The columns slow and come to a smart stop just in front of Scout Glass and his companion.

Sergeant Jordan puts back on his hat, looks to Scout Glass, and says, "Glass, glad to see you alright." Then Sergeant Jordan looks to the smoke signals and says, "Apache looks to be, saw some cut wire, and unshod pony tracks a little back."

"Sarge, that's the least of our problems," says Scout Glass.

Sergeant Jordan turns back to Scout Glass and then looks to his companion, a Mexican rancher who begins crying and then sobbing. Sergeant Jordan looks to Scout Glass and says, "What's the other problem Glass? Who's your companion?"

"Sarge...this here is Mr. Salinas. He was tendin' his herd last night when he saw fire comin' from the direction of his house. He went back to his house—and saw what looked to be Victorio, from his description, and about one hundred hostiles. He said he hid, and saw his whole family bein' tortured...butchered...raped. Sarge, he said after they left, he just took off on—"

Scout Glass stops his report as Mr. Salinas begins sobbing and talking aloud, looking to Sergeant Jordan, saying in Spanish, "My wife, and little girls, they raped...my boy they tortured, then they...killed them, they took all my cattle. My wife...my children..."

Mr. Salinas is really sobbing now as Scout Glass looks to Sergeant Jordan and continues telling his report. "I followed a large pony trail to the cut fence wire. I rode back to where I saw the Twenty-fourth's encamped and told them of my find. I then rode back to see if I could pick up their trail. That's when I came across Mr. Salinas, about twenty miles out, on his horse riding full stride. I had to spur my mount to catch him, his horse was well lathered."

"Main trail," says Sergeant Jordan.

"Lot's of tracks Sarge, like you saw back at the cut wire. They took the herd and scattered out in all directions. No main trail."

Sergeant Jordan looks to the smoke signals and says, "They know we're here, that's what those signals are about.

All right Glass, lead the way back to Mr. Salinas's ranch." Sergeant Jordan turns to the columns and calls his orders, "Pass the word. Keep your eyes peeled." Sergeant Jordan then looks back to Scout Glass and says, "Glass, tell Mr. Salinas, we are very sorry."

Scout Glass nods his head to Sergeant Jordan, then looks at Mr. Salinas still sobbing and says in Spanish, "Vamonos Señor Salinas, the sergeant says he's sorry for you and your family...we go back to your house and bury them now."

Mr. Salinas, still sobbing, turns his horse along with Scout Glass and heads back to his house as Sergeant Jordan looks to the bugler and says, "Bugler, lets let 'em know we're here. Sound forward!"

The bugler sounds his call, adding some rhythm, as Sergeant Jordan holds up his right arm and calls his orders: "Forward...*hooo*." Sergeant Jordan's arm falls forward and the columns head out, looking to the smoke signals, going to take care of a grim task, riding in back of Scout Glass and Mr. Salinas.

The sun is setting as Scout Glass and Mr. Salinas arrive and stop at what's left of the Salinas property, with Sergeant Jordan and the detachment of K Troop following in columns of twos.

Sergeant Jordan holds up his arm and calls his orders: "Troop, halt."

The columns come to a stop amongst the charred ruins of what used to be the Salinas house and barn. The troops gaze and look at the smoldering wood structures, then to the livestock strewn across the ground with arrows protruding from their bodies.

The bodies of Mr. Salinas's wife and children also lie about the property, butchered. Mrs. Salinas's body is charred, with no clothes, tied to what's left of the charred corral fence. She was apparently raped, and then burned.

The boy, scalped, used as target practice, staked to a post, looks like a pincushion with many arrows protruding from his chest.

The girls, also scalped, are staked to the ground and apparently were also raped.

Sergeant Jordan and most of the men are seasoned; they are used to the sights. However, several of the troopers have not had the experience, and begin to upchuck their last meal, including Trooper Chase.

Sergeant Jordan turns his eyes in the direction of the sounds of regurgitation. He compresses his lips together, with eyes of pity, as he says, "Corporal Wilson, we'll make camp here tonight. Tell Corporal Dorch to set out sentries and a picket-line. Tell Corporal Scott to get a fire goin' and put together some grub, and if we use any of Mr. Salinas's supplies of what's left, write him a government receipt for what we use."

"Yes, Sarge."

Corporal Wilson turns and spurs his mount to the rear, calling out Sergeant Jordan's orders. "Corporal Dorch, set out sentries, picket-line, Corporal Scott, find..."

The two corporals begin calling out their orders, as Sergeant Jordan looks to his men and calls his orders: "Dismount."

The columns dismount and begin going about their duties.

Mr. Salinas is still seated in his saddle staring out at what use to be his happy home, as Trooper Temple along with three other troopers begin wrangling the mounts from their comrades for the picket-line.

Corporal Wilson returns mounted, then dismounts, giving his mount's reins to one of the trooper wranglers, as

Sergeant Jordan calls his orders. "Corporal Wilson, take Troopers Chase, Irving, Perry and Walley. Set about a burial detail. After supper tonight—" Sergeant Jordan looks to the sky, then says, "It's half moon tonight. Take Troopers Perry and Temple, see what you can find, trail-wise. Also, have the messenger's mount saddled, standin' by with Mr. Salinas's horse."

"Yes Sarge."

Corporal Wilson, Troopers Chase, Irving, Perry, and Walley head to perform the grim task of burying the Salinas family.

Sergeant Jordan looks to Mr. Salinas, then to Scout Glass and says, "Glass, I kept you here to stay with Mr. Salinas. See what you can do for him?"

"Yes Sarge."

Scout Glass approaches and helps Mr. Salinas off his horse as the detachment go about performing their duties.

Later that night a campfire crackles and throws sparks high into the night air, as coyotes yak in the distance. Sentries cross paths, walking their post with their carbines at the ready, watching for any movement in the surrounding brush. Most the detachment is lying, sitting, or standing, huddled around the fire's warmth, relaxed, not talking, just staring into the fire with their carbines standing nearby, in stacked pyramid formations.

Mr. Salinas charges over to Sergeant Jordan with urgency written on his face, with Scout Glass following. Mr. Salinas looks to Sergeant Jordan, then to Scout Glass walking up and says in Spanish, "The fire brin' 'em back...tell your sergeant."

Scout Glass looks to Sergeant Jordan, already knowing his sergeant's plans, and says, "Mr. Salinas says the fire will bring 'em back."

Sergeant Jordan looks to Mr. Salinas with a determined look and says, "I hope so, Mr. Salinas." Sergeant Jordan pats his carbine lying near him, no need to translate his feelings or intentions to Mr. Salinas. Mr. Salinas then bows his head and almost collapses as Scout Glass grabs him. A trooper puts a crate down near Mr. Salinas so he can sit down.

Mr. Salinas sits down, staring at the ground, as Sergeant Jordan surveys his men and says, "Gentlemen, let me have your attention." All the soldiers look from Mr. Salinas to Sergeant Jordan, who says, "Some of you got a little sick this evenin'...your stomachs didn't like what your eyes saw. As soldiers, you have a duty to perform, and not to make judgment calls, but to follow orders. Our orders as soldiers are to keep the peace in the territory. However, under these circumstances gentlemen, you should know what would make a people do what you saw this afternoon."

A trooper throws several more logs onto the fire as Sergeant Jordan looks to Scout Glass and says, "Glass here...will tell you an Indian's view of what you saw today."

Scout Glass looks at Sergeant Jordan with the expression of, "Do I have to, Sarge?" Sergeant Jordan nods his head yes, as Scout Glass turns, looks out to his comrades, and says, "The Indians are between a hard rock and a bed of cactuses. First, they have been removed from their land, dismounted, disarmed and put on reservations, their way of life taken from them. The Indian agents assigned to help them, help themselves, and cheat the Indians of their government substances, causin' 'em to go hungry. The Indian has two choices: leave the reservation in search of food, be labeled a hostile, sought out and killed, or—stay on the reservation and starve to death."

Trooper Chase says, "Why didn't they just take the

food? Why they have to kill them like that? Take their skin off their heads, rape the women, then burn them?"

"Trooper, when the white man came to this land, he taught the Indian scalpin', it was his way to show the number of dead they've killed. The Spaniards, they were the first to try to take the Indians' land, and in doin' so in their warfare, taught them those fine arts of torture and mutilations you saw—"

Scout Glass is interrupted, as Corporal Dorch, one of the sentries, shouts, "Sarge, rider...comin' fast!"

Scout Glass grabs his pistol from his holster along with the entire detachment reaching for their carbines in the pyramid stacks and taking defensive positions, smartly.

Corporal Dorch shouts, "It's Temple."

Sergeant Jordan and the detachment relax their posture as Trooper Temple comes riding in hard and fast, stopping as a trooper grabs the head-harness of Trooper Temple's mount. Trooper Temple dismounts and runs over to Sergeant Jordan. Out of breath, he says, "Sarge...we found the main trail...just the other side of the Black Range...headed for Old Tularosa. From what we could tell...there's about ninety in the main force driving about fifty head of cattle...and another twenty or so that we saw as the rear guard."

Sergeant Jordan looks to his men with urgency, and shouts, "Messenger!" Then Sergeant Jordan looks back to Trooper Temple and says, "Corporal Wilson and Trooper Perry trailin' 'em?"

"Yes Sarge. Corporal Wilson said you would try to make Tularosa before them."

Sergeant Jordan smiles with an expression of intuition as the messenger runs over to Sergeant Jordan. He stops at attention and looks to his sergeant, as Sergeant Jordan says, "Go back to Stanton as fast as you can with Mr. Salinas.

Tell Colonel Hatch and Captain Carroll, come at once. Victorio possible attackin' Old Tularosa, already killed and pillaged Mr. Salinas' family. We'll ride all night, go around their main force, arrive Tularosa mornin'."

The messenger just kind of stands there, awaiting more instructions from Sergeant Jordan. Sergeant Jordan looks at him, slaps him on his butt, and says, "Get!"

The messenger snaps to and runs to his mount already waiting for him as another trooper holds the reins. The messenger runs and plummets over his mount's rear end, as the trooper hands him his reins. The messenger then looks to Mr. Salinas sitting in his saddle. He grabs Mr. Salinas reins, spurring his mount shouting, "YAH, yah...yah!"

The messenger and Mr. Salinas ride off in a cloud of dust to Fort Stanton as Sergeant Jordan looks around his detachment and says, "All right gentlemen, we're goin' to mount up, ride all night to Tularosa as you heard. Get to it!"

Sergeant Jordan and the detachment move as if they were ants in an orderly hive, breaking camp, packing up gear, saddling their mounts, putting out the campfire.

The next day, the sun has risen on the small settlement on the outskirts of the abandoned post, Fort Tularosa.

The settlement looks untouched with sagebrush filling most of the open areas of the town's road and perimeter. Weeds are growing through broken windows and through cracks in the rickety buildings. There are no signs of being attacked, no movement either. It's very quiet, almost too quiet.

Sergeant Jordan and K Troop are approaching from a wooded forest into cleared land by a column of twos as Sergeant Jordan turns and looks to his men and says, "Be alert, pass the word."

The detachment begins passing the word as a single rifle shot echoes over their heads from the settlement, causing the detachment's soldiers to crouch in their saddles with Sergeant Jordan shouting orders to his men with urgency: "*Hooo*, dismount! Take cover behind your mounts! Draw your weapons!"

The detachment jumps to their sergeant's orders. The soldiers begin dismounting, positioning their mounts between them and the settlement, in a semi-skirmish-line. They draw their carbines and service revolvers, pointing them in the air, but not at the town—yet. Sergeant Jordan, still mounted, steadies his mount, then looks and shouts to his men. "Everyone alright?"

The soldiers all say simultaneously, "Yeah, we're alright."

Sergeant Jordan then looks to the settlement with military determination and shouts, "This is a United States Cavalry troop you've just fired upon! Do not fire again. Repeat, do not fire again, or I will be forced to return fire!"

A male voice emanates from the settlement shouting, "State your business!"

"We are a United States Cavalry troop. A band of renegade Apache Indians are headed this way. You are in possible danger. We're here to protect you."

"You sure you soldiers? We ain't never seen nigger bluecoat soldier boys before," shouts the male voice from the town.

Sergeant Jordan looks to Scout Glass who shrugs his shoulders and somewhat smiles. Sergeant Jordan rolls his eyes and looks back to the town with military business and shouts, "We're from Fort Stanton, Ninth Cavalry, K Troop. Renegade Apaches are headed this way."

"Some Injuns took shots at us early mornin'," shouts the voice.

Scout Glass looks to Sergeant Jordan with concern and says, "That means..."

"I know. We're being watched by their lead scouts," says Sergeant Jordan as he looks to the settlement and shouts, "We're comin' in, do not shoot!"

Sergeant Jordan looks to the detachment and says, "Mount up...column of twos, keep your weapons at the ready!"

The detachment mounts up, as Sergeant Jordan raises his right hand, with his carbine, calling his orders. "Forward, *hooo*."

Sergeant Jordan's arm falls forward and the columns move out with military precision riding towards the settlement while covering their fronts, and their rears.

Sergeant Jordan and the detachment enter the settlement as eight men walk out of what's left of the rickety town's buildings with the few weapons they have: pitchforks, old rifles, pistols, and a shotgun.

The men begin walking backwards along the squeaky porches of the buildings, backing away from the oncoming soldiers riding through the town's street. The townsmen stop as they reach their women and children staring out from open doors and broken windows, who are also holding old farm tools as weapons.

As Sergeant Jordan and his soldiers proceed into town, their eyes are fixed forward, except for Sergeant Jordan's. He is looking to the townspeople, as the townspeople stare back with apprehension at these dark-skin bluecoats.

Sergeant Jordan turns in his saddle, looks to his men and says, "Troop, halt. Corporals Dorch, Scott, front and center! Trooper Temple, take care of the mounts. Troop, dismount! Bugler, sound assembly."

The Bugler sounds his call as the guidon trooper

dismounts and stands next to Sergeant Jordan, who remains mounted. The detachment dismounts except for Sergeant Jordan, who turns his mount to face the townspeople. Corporals Dorch and Scott ride up to meet their sergeant, as Trooper Temple and the other troopers begin wrangling K Troop's mounts. The detachment begins to assemble around the guidon trooper and bugler.

Sergeant Jordan is still sitting on his mount with his carbine pointing in the air, the butt end of the carbine resting on his leg. Sergeant Jordan looks to the townspeople from his mount with determination and says, "Who's the sheriff or mayor?"

The townspeople look to an older man, who walks out in front of his peers with his long double-barrel shotgun in hand, looking to Sergeant Jordan with an unkind look and says, "I'm the mayor...nigger!"

Sergeant Jordan takes his disgusted looks from the mayor, looking to Scout Glass and Trooper Irving, saying, "Glass, Trooper Irving, relieve the mayor of his weapon, and the rest of the nice townspeople's, then see if you can find any other weapons."

Scout Glass and Trooper Irving turn to the mayor and respectfully relieve him of his shotgun, along with the rest of the townspeople's weapons, taking rifles, pistols, and farm tools. The townspeople give no resistance. However, if looks could kill, they would try.

Sergeant Jordan, sitting on his mount, looks to Corporal Dorch with his carbine in hand and says, "Corporal Dorch, take your men and set out sentries. Find some high places." Corporal Dorch turns and begins calling to his men, as Sergeant Jordan then looks to Corporal Scott with his carbine in hand and says, "Corporal Scott, see what you and your men can find for barricade material." He looks to the fort, then the

Erich Martin Hicks

settlement, saying, "The town is more defendable than the post. I want strong barricades at all open points, we don't have much time."

"Yes Sarge."

Corporal Scott turns and begins calling to his men as Sergeant Jordan looks to his remaining men and says, "Glass, help both corporals with what they need. And keep an eye out for Corporal Wilson and Trooper Perry."

"Yes Sarge."

Scout Glass goes to follow his sergeant's orders as Sergeant Jordan looks to his other men and says, "Trooper Chase, Irving Temple, Walley, stay with me." Sergeant Jordan then turns in his saddle, looks to the mayor and says, "Thank you for your patience, mayor..."

The mayor interrupts Sergeant Jordan, saying, "Where is your officers, nigger? If you're a U.S. Cavalry soldier, where's your officers—NIGGER!"

Sergeant Jordan looks to his men with a more disgusted look, then looks back to the mayor and says, "I'm a sergeant in the U.S. Cavalry, sir, in charge of this here detachment." Sergeant Jordan looks to the rising sun and pointedly says, "About mid-afternoon...there will be about one hundred hostile Apache Indians comin' through those trees." Then Sergeant Jordan looks back to the mayor, with a very serious expression on his face. "...Lookin' for you! I don't have time to tell you where my officer's location is, sir." Sergeant Jordan looks to his troopers and says, "Troopers, secure these people at the end of town."

The troopers simultaneously say, "Yes, Sarge."

The troopers begin following their sergeant's orders, corralling the townspeople towards the end of town. Sergeant Jordan, still disgusted by the mayor's comment, spurs his mount over to Corporal Scott who is building the

102

main barricade. As Sergeant Jordan arrives at the barricade, he stops, dismounts, and begins helping his men.

Later that afternoon, the barricades are finished. All areas that were open to the frontier, are now blocked. The 9th Cavalry, K Troop guidon is affixed to the top of the main barricade, casting a long shadow, flying high above barrels, crates, wagons, and parts of wagons. Pieces of furniture, buildings, and anything they could find that wasn't hard-nailed down, is now part of the settlement's barricades.

Sergeant Jordan and his twenty-two Buffalo Soldiers are positioned at every point within the settlement, awaiting the attack. The townspeople are sitting near a small shed towards the rear of town, near the garrison, guarded by two soldiers. Scout Glass is on top of the main barricade, looking through his field glasses, looking out to the open land between the settlement and the forest. He takes the field glasses from his eyes and looks down to Sergeant Jordan, who is climbing up on the barricade towards him. Sergeant Jordan looks to Scout Glass and says, "We've done all we can do Glass. If the messenger got through, Colonel Hatch should be here mornin'. Any sign of movement out there?"

"Nothing yet, Sarge." Scout Glass looks back to the settlement and sees the mayor and some of the townspeople walking towards them with one of their guards. Scout Glass looks to the mayor, then nudges Sergeant Jordan to get his attention and says, "You've got company."

Sergeant Jordan turns and looks down to the mayor, as the mayor looks up to Sergeant Jordan and says, "Sergeant, our herdsmen went out early this mornin' to tend to the few cattle we have before the Injuns took shots at us. He should of been back early noon."

"Where's your cattle?" says Sergeant Jordan.

The mayor points to a grove of trees in the far distance and says, "Over to the west, just on the other side of those trees." The mayor points in the direction as Scout Glass looks back through his field glasses, looking to the trees that the mayor pointed to, as does Sergeant Jordan. Sergeant Jordan then turns, looks to his men and says, "Trooper Walley, Trooper Irving, front and center." Troopers Irving and Walley look to Sergeant Jordan, then run to the barricade, climbing up. Sergeant Jordan looks to the soldiers climbing up as he points to the grove of trees in the distance and says, "There's a herdsman with cattle on the other side of those trees. See if he's alright, then have him drive the cattle to the garrison so we can keep an eye on 'em."

"Yes Sarge," reply both troopers simultaneously. They climb down from the barricade, run and jump on their mounts as part of the barricade is removed for them to ride out. They spur their mounts, with carbines in hand, and ride out of the settlement towards the grove of trees.

The barricade is being rebuilt as the mayor eyes Sergeant Jordan looking out to his soldiers riding off. "Sergeant," the mayor says. Sergeant Jordan turns, looks down to the mayor, as the mayor says, "You sure you know what you're doin'? With one hundred Injuns headed this way, as you say...you've only got twenty-two men."

Sergeant Jordan looks to the mayor with confidence and says, "No mayor, I have twenty-four men, and I assure you, we are well up to the task."

Scout Glass, looking through his field glasses, shouts, "Sarge, two soldiers, comin' in the clearing from the east, riding fast this way."

Sergeant Jordan quickly turns back and looks to the soldiers spurring their mounts across the cleared land as

Scout Glass shouts, "It's Corporal Wilson and Trooper Perry—and they got company!"

Behind the troopers, the forest comes alive with Apache Indians firing their Winchester rifles and arrows at Corporal Wilson and Trooper Perry, spurring their mounts towards the garrison and settlement.

Sergeant Jordan shouts, "Man your positions!"

All the soldiers hurry to their positions, as the Apaches give chase. Corporal Wilson and Trooper Perry return fire with their service revolvers at the ensuing Apaches. The chase glides across the clearing as Sergeant Jordan calls to his men, "All right gentlemen, get ready. Wait till Corporal Wilson and Trooper Perry flank off, then open fire on my command!"

The soldiers settle into their positions, aiming and steadying their carbines, watching Corporal Wilson and Trooper Perry race towards them, firing back at the wave of Apaches on their tail, knocking a few off their ponies. The townspeople stand and try to peer through some of the cracks and holes made into the barricade, as Sergeant Jordan calls his orders, "Hold your fire men..."

As Corporal Wilson and Trooper Perry close within yards of the settlement, they split apart in opposite directions, towards the rear of the town, opening up the advancing Apaches for clear shots from Sergeant Jordan and K Troop.

As lines of Apaches follow each soldier, Sergeant Jordan calls his orders, "Hold your fire. Wait till they're in the open. Follow your man. Lead them. Lead them...FIRE!"

The townspeople watch Sergeant Jordan giving orders, and gaze at this military machine working as the entire detachment lays down a withering blanket of lead, dropping or wounding at least as many Apaches as there are soldiers. The remaining Apaches stop their ponies in their tracks, hopping off, picking up the dead and whatever wounded they can hastily help or carry to their ponies, and then ride back to their positions in the distance.

Sergeant Jordan calls to his men, "reload," then points to the rear of the settlement and says, "Let Corporal Wilson and Trooper Perry in through the back." He looks to his men with military professionalism and says, "Good shootin' gentlemen."

Sergeant Jordan and the detachment are reloading as Scout Glass looks through his field glasses and watches the Apaches reassemble by the tree line. The Apaches are gathering around two other Apaches, as Scout Glass takes the field glasses from his eyes. Then with urgency he looks at Sergeant Jordan and says, "Victorio and Nana."

Sergeant Jordan quickly turns and looks to the Apaches gathering in the distance as Corporal Wilson and Trooper Perry ride through the back of the cleared barricade.

Corporal Wilson spurs his mount towards Sergeant Jordan, who stands at the top of the main barricade. He stops his mount at the bottom, looks to Sergeant Jordan, and says, "Victorio and Nana are out there!"

"I know, we're lookin' at 'em right now, they're out of carbine range," says Sergeant Jordan, looking to the Apaches.

"Hey Sarge, they're pointing to that grove of trees where Irving and Walley went," says Scout Glass, looking through his field glasses.

Sergeant Jordan looks to the Apaches, sees them pointing in the direction of Troopers Irving and Walley.

Trooper Chase then looks over to Sergeant Jordan, and says, "Sarge, you think the Apaches know Irving and Walley are out there?"

Sergeant Jordan looks at Trooper Chase with a pointed look, and says, "They do!" Sergeant Jordan climbs down off the barricade, walks over to Corporal Wilson, stops and calls to his men, "Trooper Chase, Perry, Temple, Corporals Dorch and Scott, front and center." Sergeant Jordan then looks to Corporal Wilson mounted and says, "I know you just got in. I'm gonna need you on this one."

"No problem Sarge."

Troopers Chase, Perry, and Temple, and Corporals Dorch and Scott assemble in front of Sergeant Jordan as he looks to his men and says, "Corporal Scott, you will remain here with your men and defend the settlement. If the hostiles come in range, fire at will. I, Corporals Wilson, Dorch and their men, will engage the enemy." Then with a resolved look on his face, he says, "If you need to, give the townspeople their weapons."

Then he looks to Scout Glass on the barricade and says, "Glass, you're with us."

Scout Glass climbs down off the barricade as Corporal Scott climbs up the barricade and begins positioning his men. The Buffalo Soldiers hurry to their task and make quick adjustments to their military mount equipment as Sergeant Jordan calls his orders: "Mount up!"

The detachment mount their mounts as the mayor walks towards Sergeant Jordan with his escort guard. Sergeant Jordan and his men sit astride their mounts as he calls to them: "Check your carbines and side arms. We may be at this a while." The soldiers begin checking their weapons as the mayor stops on the side of Sergeant Jordan's mount, looks up to him and says, "You goin' out there Sergeant? There must be at least three times your number."

"Mayor, to answer your question, yes—and there's five times my number."

"That's insane," says the mayor.

"No, that's my job!" says Sergeant Jordan pointedly.

Corporal Scott, standing near the top of the main

barricade, calls to Sergeant Jordan with urgency. "Sarge, looks like they're splitting up, Victorio and a large group are headed south through the forest...Nana is still there, probably his rear guard." Then, Corporal Scott shouts, "Sarge! Nana is chargin' towards Irving and Walley!"

Sergeant Jordan quickly smiles to the mayor as he and the detachment, the bugler, Scout Glass, Troopers Chase, Perry and Temple, and the rest of Corporal Wilson's men, Corporal Dorch and seven of his men, sit astride their mounts checking and loading their weapons.

On the other side of the group of trees, in a clearing, Troopers Irving and Walley sit astride their mounts, peering through a group of trees, watching and pointing their carbines at the Apaches, now charging their position, only minutes away.

Trooper Walley looks to Trooper Irving and says, "Don't worry Lee, it's only about thirty of them—and two of us."

"Who's worried? I'm not, and he diffidently isn't," says Trooper Irving, looking down from his mount to the dead herdsmen, scalped and looking like a pincushion with arrows protruding out of his torso. "At least he doesn't see what's a comin'."

Moments later at the settlement, Sergeant Jordan and his men have finished checking their equipment and loading their weapons as Sergeant Jordan looks to them with military determination and says, "Ready men!"

All the soldiers shout, "Ready!"

"Bugler! Sound, cha'aaarge!" says Sergeant Jordan.

As the Bugler sounds his call, the troopers on the ground remove a part of the barricade.

Sergeant Jordan and his men begin shouting, "Hah!"

"Yah! Yah hah...!" "Yah!"

Their mounts begin dancing in place, ready for action, as Sergeant Jordan shouts his orders: "CHARGE!"

Sergeant Jordan and his men still shouting, charge towards the barricade at full stride.

At the same time, Troopers Irving and Walley look to the settlement as they hear the bugler's call and shouts coming from their comrades. Trooper Irving looks to Trooper Walley excitedly and says, "You hear that, you hear that...here comes Sarge!" Troopers Irving and Walley see Sergeant Jordan and their comrades spurring their mounts through the opening of the barricade, charging the Apaches from their flank side with the bugler sounding the Cavalry Charge.

As the Buffalo Soldiers exit the settlement, the columns form a "V" shape, to meet their foe, with Sergeant Jordan at the point.

The Apaches hear the bugle charge-call, and look to Sergeant Jordan and his men charging towards them; however, they keep surging towards Troopers Irving and Walley.

Seeing their comrades coming to their rescue, Trooper Walley looks at Trooper Irving and says, "Let's get 'em." Trooper Irving returns the glance with an expression of, "I sure hope you know what you're doing." Trooper Irving nods his head up and down, and then they both spur their mounts out of the trees, into action with carbines in hand, charging the Apaches head-on.

As they spur their mounts, Troopers Irving and Walley hoot and shout simultaneously, "Yah! Yah! Yah! Huh! Huh! Yah...!"

The Apaches see Troopers Irving and Walley riding at them and open fire with their Winchester rifles, causing the troopers to ride sidesaddle, letting the Apaches' shots fly by them.

They return upright in the saddle, riding full stride, taking aim with their carbines and return fire, knocking two Apaches off their ponies. They holster their carbines in their carbine saddle mounts and pull their service revolvers from their holsters and begin firing at the Apaches.

The Apaches, still hearing the bugler's charge-call, look away from Troopers Irving and Walley, to Sergeant Jordan and his men charging them from their flank side. It's all too much for Victorio's lieutenant, Nana, who leads this band of thirty-plus hostile Apaches. Nana signals to his band and they turn their ponies into the forest to evade the soldiers.

Troopers Irving and Walley see the Apaches turn their ponies into the forest, stop their mounts, and then look to Sergeant Jordan and their comrades charging towards them.

Sergeant Jordan begins waving his arm in the direction of the Apaches and yells to the troopers, "Get at 'em. Get at 'em!"

Troopers Irving and Walley spur their mounts back into action and pursue the marauding Apaches into the forest. A running battle ensues as Nana's band has slowed their ponies, taking cover behind trees, and begins shooting at Troopers Irving and Walley riding fast through the forest. The bullets hit several trees around them as Troopers Irving and Walley slow before halting their mounts behind some trees.

Sergeant Jordan and their comrades ride up fast, see the troopers hiding behind trees, as they stop behind other trees. Sergeant Jordan, sitting astride his mount with carbine in hand, surveys the situation and calls to Corporal Dorch, "Corporal Dorch, send two men to the right flank and two to the left. Flush 'em out."

Corporal Dorch signals his men with his hand, two to

the left flank and two to the right flank. The flankers spur their mounts into action as an Apache that is dismounted appears from behind a tree, shoots one of the right-flanking soldiers through the shoulder. The shot knocks him off his mount to the ground like a sack of potatoes.

The two soldiers on the left flank see the Apache who just shot their comrade. They fire several pistol rounds, killing him. As the Apache falls dead, his comrades further away hop on their ponies and take off in the direction of their band. Sergeant Jordan and his men search the area with their eyes, weapons at the ready, looking for any more ambushers.

A trooper is checking the Apache ambusher on the ground as two other troopers dismount and tend to their comrade, propping him up against a tree as Trooper Walley looks to Sergeant Jordan and says, "Sarge, the herdsman's dead, shot by Apache arrows, and no cattle."

"Good report, Trooper," says Sergeant Jordan. He looks to both troopers and says, "Good job back there. I'll make sure your records reflect your gallantry."

Sergeant Jordan looks to his wounded man, then to the two troopers assisting him and says, "You two men, take the trooper back to the settlement." Sergeant Jordan looks to the rest of his men and says, "All right gentlemen, let's get at 'em before they get to Mexico." Sergeant Jordan then looks to Corporal Wilson and says, "Victorio is miles away by now, but they can't move 'em cattle that fast."

"Looks like Nana is his rear guard pushing 'em cattle," says Corporal Wilson.

Sergeant Jordan nods his head in agreement with Corporal Wilson as he holds his carbine in the air, looks to his men, and signals forward.

Sergeant Jordan and his detachment spur their mounts back into action, going after the cattle. Moments later, as the soldiers ride over a hill at a trot by a column of twos, Corporal Wilson sees through some trees, in a distant clearing, Victorio's rear guard Nana hurrying the stolen cattle along.

Corporal Wilson looks to Sergeant Jordan. Quietly, he says, "Sarge, look...cattle ahead, Nana and the rear guard."

Sergeant Jordan raises his carbine in the air, slowing the trotting soldiers. He looks to Corporal Wilson and quietly says, "Pass the word, Corporal, 'line on me' on my signal...hold your fire until fired upon."

Corporal Wilson turns to the columns and quietly passes the word as Sergeant Jordan turns to the bugler and says, "Bugler, on my command."

Nana has not seen the Buffalo Soldiers yet, as Sergeant Jordan raises his carbine above his head, causing both columns to fan out quickly, left to left and right to right—coming parallel with Sergeant Jordan as he looks to the bugler and says, "Now!"

The bugler sounds the charge-call as Sergeant Jordan's arm falls forward with his carbine in hand. Then with a mighty shout: "Charge!" Sergeant Jordan spurs his mount from a walk to a full stride with the bugler sounding the charge-call as the single line of soldiers also spurs their mounts towards the Apaches.

As the Apaches hear the bugle, they turn and see the soldiers charging their position. They quickly look to each other, and decide to live and fight another day. They heel their ponies to a full run, into a tree thicket, away from the soldiers, headed south, leaving most their plunder behind.

Sergeant Jordan and his men begin overtaking the cattle, with brand "T" on some and "S" on others, burnt into their hides. Sergeant Jordan slows his mount, turns to his left, and shouts to Scout Glass, "Glass, take Troopers Chase and Walley, continue on, see if they left the area and search for cattle."

Sergeant Jordan looks at the rest of his men and calls his orders, "Troop *hooolt.*"

Scout Glass, Troopers Chase and Walley continue on as Sergeant Jordan and his men come to a stop. Sergeant Jordan looks to his other men and says, "Corporal Wilson, take your men, check the left flank. Corporal Dorch, take your men, search the right flank."

Corporals Wilson and Dorch and their men spur their mounts to their flanks in search of cattle and Apaches as Sergeant Jordan sits on his mount, holding his carbine, butt end on his leg, barrel pointing in the air. Sergeant Jordan is looking out at his men searching and herding cattle to a central location.

The next morning, two long cavalry columns pass by a dozen Apache graves that dot the landscape outside the settlement. Colonel Hatch is riding center, ahead of the columns, followed by Captain Carroll, who is leading the left column as Sergeant Shaw leads the right column.

Directly behind them is the American flag with thirty-eight stars, followed by Apache scouts, officers, sergeants, corporals, and seven 9th Regimental troop flags dispersed throughout the 298 Buffalo Soldiers that follow. Two Colored Infantry regiments are driving nine supply wagons positioned in the middle of the columns.

As Colonel Hatch leads the columns past the open main barricade, riding into the settlement, he sees about thirty head of cattle in a temporary stockade within the garrison ahead of him. Then he looks to Sergeant Jordan and his detachment, which stands at parade-rest on both sides of the settlement road that leads to the garrison. That's where the townspeople sit or stand in front of a building near the soldiers as their guards stand by them.

As Colonel Hatch begins to pass in front of Sergeant Jordan and his men, Sergeant Jordan calls his orders: "Attention."

All the soldiers in Sergeant Jordan's detachment snap to attention as Colonel Hatch takes off his campaign hat, raises it in the air, and calls his orders to the columns: "Troop, *haaalt...*"

The command is passed back with rhythm, via Sergeant Shaw, and the other officers and sergeants. The columns come to a stop on a twenty-dollar gold piece, as Colonel Hatch and Captain Carroll dismount.

Two troopers that know their job, near the front of the columns, also dismount quickly and hurry to relieve their officers of their mounts' reins. Colonel Hatch and Captain Carroll approach Sergeant Jordan with urgency leaving the regiment mounted.

As the officers approach, Sergeant Jordan salutes Colonel Hatch and Captain Carroll. Colonel Hatch returns the salute, then looks to Sergeant Jordan and says, "At-ease, Sergeant. I see everything is still in one piece." He looks to the stockade, where the cattle are held, and says, "And you recovered Mr. Salinas's cattle."

"No sir, only nineteen head of Mr. Salinas's cattle and all the settlements...I wish to report, sir."

"Yes, go ahead, Sergeant," says Colonel Hatch.

"On word from Trooper Temple, that Corporal Wilson and Trooper Perry were trailin' the hostiles to Tularosa, I sent the messenger to inform you with Mr. Salinas. We left the Salinas Ranch, goin' around Victorio's main-force, arrivin' here yesterday mornin'. After we barricaded the garrison, the mayor of the settlement told me their herdsman had not returned after the settlement was shot at earlier by a few renegades, most likely Victorio's scouts. I sent out two troopers to check on the herdsman, when Victorio attacked the settlement and post. We repulsed the attack, causing Victorio to give up the assault."

"Are those the graves we saw, Sergeant," says Captain Carroll.

"Yes sir. May I continue, sir."

"Yes, go ahead Sergeant."

"Victorio took two-thirds of his band and headed south, leavin' Nana as his rear-guard. Nana charged towards my two troopers that I sent out to check on the herdsman. I took fourteen men, charged the hostiles from the settlement. My two troopers set out from their position, facin' the hostiles, killin' two, causin' 'em to give up the fight and retreat to the south. We gave chase. One of my men was wounded in the shoulder. I sent Scout Glass to follow their trail. He reported back they were headed southwest."

"Excellent report Sergeant," says Colonel Hatch as he looks to Captain Carroll and says, "Captain Carroll, send scouts out, south, southwest, we will leave immediately."

"Yes, sir," says Captain Carroll. Captain Carroll salutes Colonel Hatch, makes an about-face and walks back to the regiment with military urgency, calling orders to the Apache scouts.

As Captain Carroll calls out orders, Colonel Hatch looks to the townspeople, then to Sergeant Jordan and says, "Very good job, Sergeant. Any problems with the...townspeople?"

"Nothin' I couldn't handle, sir."

Colonel Hatch proudly looks to Sergeant Jordan and says, "Bully Sergeant, take your men. Return to Stanton."

"Yes, sir. Sir how many weeks' rations you carryin'?"

"Nine weeks' rations Sergeant, so mind things till we're back."

"Yes, sir," says Sergeant Jordan.

"Oh, one other matter, Sergeant. There's a new officer coming to Stanton in three months around the time of the regimental fights. His name is Major Guy V. Henry. He'll be alternating from troop to troop. He's a good officer, Sergeant."

"Yes, sir."

With a smile, Sergeant Jordan salutes Colonel Hatch, makes an about-face and calls orders to his men.

Colonel Hatch walks to his mount as the mayor approaches with his guard and says, "Excuse me Colonel..."

Colonel Hatch stops and looks to the mayor as he says, "I'm the mayor of this settlement. We've never seen nigger soldiers before. I mean...at first, they scared us. Your sergeant there, saved us, Colonel...I never thought that a nig—colored would stand and fight against the odds they faced, much less, fight at all."

Colonel Hatch looks to the mayor proudly and says, "Mayor, these are the finest soldiers in the U.S. Cavalry. I wouldn't trade them for any soldier." Colonel Hatch turns to the trooper holding his mount's reins. The trooper hands them to him, salutes Colonel Hatch, then makes an about-face, returning to his mount.

Colonel Hatch mounts his mount and calls to the regiment, "Bugler, sound...forward." The bugler sounds his call as Colonel Hatch stands in his stirrups, takes off his campaign hat, raises it in the air, and signals forward to the columns.

The regiment begins riding out of the settlement as Colonel Hatch looks to the stunned mayor and says, "Good day, Mayor." Colonel Hatch heels his mount as he reaches into his saddlebag. He brings out his journal and begins writing as the regiment passes the townspeople.

The mayor and townspeople stare with amazement at the sight that's before them. As far as they can see, Buffalo Soldiers are riding by them proudly.

Moments later, Colonel Hatch and the columns ride past the boundary of the settlement as he finishes writing in his military journal:

"...Sergeant Jordan against insurmountable odds defended the settlement and abandoned garrison of Tularosa, then took half his men, numbering about fourteen, and committed to a running battle, killing several hostile Apaches and only having one wounded. Sergeant Jordan displayed gallantry and courage against the enemy. I highly recommend Sergeant Jordan for the Medal of Honor."

As Colonel Hatch finishes, he puts the journal back into his saddlebag and looks to Captain Carroll and says, "Captain, remain with the supply wagons, then continue on to Gila River. Sergeant Shaw and I will meet you there."

Captain Carroll salutes Colonel Hatch, turns his mount to the rear, spurs his mount towards the wagons calling out to them as Colonel Hatch calls to the bugler, "Bugler, sound at a gallop."

The bugler sounds his call as the 9th Cavalry takes their mounts from a walk to a gallop.

Act II
Proven Soldiers

Three months later, four colored cavalry soldiers escort a military stagecoach over Fort Stanton's imaginary boundary. The coach is driven by a colored infantry trooper, with his colored comrade sitting next to him holding a carbine. A shotgun lies between them.

The coach rolls under a large banner hanging between two garrison buildings. Written on the banner in large letters are the words: "U.S. Cavalry, Regimental Fights, 6th Cavalry, 'Fighting Irish' vs. 9th Cavalry Buffalo Soldiers, 'We Can, We Will.'"

Cheers and roars emanate from the boxing arena as the coach rolls towards the Command Office. Sergeant Shaw and the garrison adjutant are standing at attention outside the Command Office as the stage rolls to a stop in front of them.

A colored trooper by the name of John Brown sticks his head out the open window and looks to the outside latch of the coach door. He reaches out and grabs the latch, opening the door from outside, letting the open window swing past his arm. He steps out, stands at attention, holding the door open as a seven-year-old boy, his mother and father, an Army officer, step out of the coach.

The officer is Major Guy V. Henry. He is a West Point graduate, forty-one years old, born in Arkansas. Five foot seven, he has a long torso, light eyes, and a thin face. His hair is shorter than medium length, parted on the left side, and he has a dashing bushy mustache.

Major Henry is not wearing his gauntlets, revealing that his left hand is stiff, as if it had a slight permanent cramp, and he is missing a finger from frostbite. He also has two distinctive marks just under both eyes.

Sergeant Shaw and the adjutant salute Major Henry as he looks to Sergeant Shaw and says, "Good afternoon Sergeant."

"Good afternoon, sir, I'm Sergeant Shaw and this is the garrison adjutant, Corporal Smith. Colonel Hatch has Corporal Smith act as the garrison adjutant. He's mute, sir"

Major Henry looks to Corporal Smith with curiosity and says, "From that scar around his neck, Sergeant?"

"Yes sir. A southern lynching rope. Corporal Smith here was studyin' to be a lawyer in the North before the war. He joined the Union Army and was captured. The Southerners didn't take kindly to colored men wearin' blue uniforms, especially smart ones—so they hung him. By the faith of God, the rope didn't break his neck. His outfit found him hangin' there, cut him down; was fixin' to bury him when he started breathin'."

Major Henry shakes Corporal Smith's hand, then looks to him with favor and says, "Corporal, thank God for faith."

Corporal Smith looks to Major Henry with appreciation and recognition, as Major Henry looks to both soldiers and says, "I'm Major Guy Henry, this is my wife, Julia, my son,

120

Guy Henry Junior, and this is Trooper John Brown, my personal assistant for Henry Junior."

Sergeant Shaw tips his hat to Mrs. Henry, shakes Henry Junior's hand and Trooper Brown's, then he looks to Major Henry and says, "It's a pleasure to meet you, sir. We've been expectin' you."

A big roar from the crowd emanates again from the boxing arena as Major Henry looks to Sergeant Shaw and says, "Who's winning, Sergeant?"

"It's tied, sir."

"Sergeant, can you see to my wife's needs, and the unloading of our luggage? The coach has to return to Santa Fe right away. Trooper Brown will assist. I would like to see the fight with my son."

"Yes, sir. Adjutant, show Mrs. Henry to their quarters and take care of the family needs, also help the soldiers unload the major's luggage from the coach."

"Why thank you, Sergeant," says Mrs. Henry.

The adjutant and Trooper Brown begin taking luggage from the troopers on top of the coach as Sergeant Shaw motions with his hand to Major Henry towards the boxing arena and says, "After you, sir."

Major Henry, Henry Junior, and Sergeant Shaw walk towards the boxing arena. As they approach, the mood becomes more festive. Refreshment stands, games, and salesmen of all kinds—especially the salesman on his carnival wagon selling the cure-all medicine—surround the arena.

Once Major Henry enters the arena, he stops and looks to the regimental flags blowing slightly in the breeze from each boxer's corner. He then looks to the hundreds upon hundreds of soldiers, civilians, and dignitaries from the town of Lincoln who are cheering and watching the fight.

Most of the 6th Cavalry Regiment, and the entire 9th Cavalry Regiment—except for sentries—are sitting or standing in the bleachers, all cheering for their man. Whites are cheering for the white heavyweight fighter; however, most of the white officers from the Buffalo Soldier regiments and all their colored troopers are cheering for the colored heavyweight fighter.

Major Henry looks to the chalkboard sitting on a platform behind the judges' table showing the scores: "6th Cavalry, '1', lightweight division, 9th Cavalry, '1', middleweight division." The heavyweight division space is blank.

The crowd yells as Major Henry looks to the colored fighter being hit hard by body shots from the Irish fighter just as the bell sounds, ending the round. The referee steps between the fighters, breaks up the fight, and the men return to their corners.

A crudely painted wood placard is turned from the number fourteen, to number fifteen, as Major Henry looks to Sergeant Shaw and says, "Sergeant, where's Colonel Hatch?"

"He's at the top of the bleachers, sir." Sergeant Shaw points to the top bleacher through the spectators behind them at Colonel Hatch, who is sitting with most of the 9th Cavalry, K Troop. Sergeant Jordan, Corporal Wilson, Troopers Chase, Temple, Irving, Perry, and Walley, and also Captain Carroll, Corporals Dorch and Scott are sitting with the group.

K Troop does not see Sergeant Shaw or Major Henry because of the numerous spectators standing in front of them.

Scout Glass is watching the fight on the other side of the boxing ring, standing with several Apache scouts as the bell sounds, beginning the last and final round. The entire boxing crowd stands and begins cheering for their favorite boxer.

Major Henry looks to the colored fighter and begins moving his shoulders a little, throwing a couple of short uppercuts and jabs, mimicking the Buffalo Soldier fighter saying: "Watch him, throw that jab, there you go, keep him off of you."

Sergeant Shaw looks to Major Henry and says, "Sir, would you and your son like to sit down?"

Major Henry nods his head in acknowledgment to Sergeant Shaw, as Sergeant Shaw begins looking for a place to sit in the bleachers. Sergeant Shaw sees two empty seats in the bleachers, and then motions with his hand to Major Henry.

Major Henry and his son walk to the seats as Major Henry lets his son sit first, then he sits, with Sergeant Shaw standing next to them as the fight continues.

The Irish fighter throws a right hook to the body, then a hard left hook, hitting the colored fighter on the jaw, knocking him into the Irish fighter's corner. The Irish fighter follows the colored fighter to his corner, throwing a couple of hard body shots into his torso. The colored fighter has his guard up. He appears dazed and hurt; however, out of nowhere he begins throwing left jabs and right jabs, all connecting, backing up his opponent.

The 9th Cavalry is exhilarated over their comrade's sudden surge. He throws a right right jab, then a left left jab, and then a right uppercut connecting with his opponent's lower jaw, sending him back like a giant pine tree to the canvas. He's out cold.

Major Henry and his son are jubilant over the knockdown as the referee counts to ten and the entire 9th Cavalry throws their hats into the air in triumphant victory. Major Henry is overjoyed and also throws his hat straight up into the air, and when the hat comes back down, he catches it.

Sergeant Shaw looks to Major Henry and shouts over the loud celebration around them, saying, "Sir, would you like to head to the Command Office now? Colonel Hatch will meet us there."

Major Henry smiles, nods his head yes, then puts his hand on top of Henry Junior's head to guide him off the bleachers as Sergeant Shaw leads the way.

Sergeant Shaw, Major Henry, and his son are walking to the Command Office as they see Scout Glass taking a picture with two Apache scouts. Major Henry stops and looks at them posing in front of a garrison building surrounded by medium bushes in the background, small cactuses and rocks in the foreground.

One Apache scout sits left on a rock wearing a traditional Apache turban headband, a light-colored shirt, with a medallion hanging from his neck. His pistol is in its brown leather sheath, positioned inside of his right leg, against his thigh from its gun belt, which is strapped around his waist.

The other Apache scout is center, seated lower, holding a Winchester rifle, wearing a Apache headband, a light shirt with a vest and a feather bead necklace. Both scouts are wearing linen pants and moccasin boots. Scout Glass stands to the right in his usual attire, brown hat, buckskin fringed suit, with his knife and sidearm.

Sergeant Shaw and Major Henry begin walking towards the Command Office as Major Henry glances back. Sergeant Shaw looks to Major Henry and says, "Sir, those are some of our scouts. The one Apache scout on the left is Bonito, center is Sergeant Jim...the colored scout is Chief of Scouts, John Glass."

Major Henry stops with a surprised expression on his

face and looks to Sergeant Shaw saying, "A 'colored' Chief of Scouts?"

From left to right, Bonito, Sergeant Jim,
and Chief of Scouts John Glass
Arizona Historical Society

"Yes, sir, part half-breed."

"Part half-breed, Sergeant?"

"Yes, sir, his father is part colored...and I believe Seminole Indian. His mother is colored."

"I take it he's a very good scout, Sergeant?"

"A very good scout, sir."

Major Henry turns, puts his hand on Henry Junior's head, and continues walking to the Command Office with Sergeant Shaw at his side.

As they reach the Command Office, Trooper Brown walks up to Major Henry, salutes, hands him his leather satchel, then says, "Anything else, sir?"

"No, that's it for now, Trooper Brown. Take Henry Junior and continue helping Mrs. Henry."

"Yes, sir," says Trooper Brown.

Trooper Brown salutes Major Henry, makes an about-face, and walks towards the officer's quarters with Henry Junior following. Sergeant Shaw looks to Colonel Hatch, Captain Carroll, and Sergeant Jordan approaching through the dispersing fight crowd and says, "Sir, here comes the colonel now. We can wait inside if you like, sir."

"Yes, thanks, Sergeant," says Major Henry.

The Command Office sentry snaps to attention and salutes Major Henry, who is walking up the steps of the porch. Major Henry returns the salute, with the sentry dropping his. He moves from attention, to open the door for Major Henry and Sergeant Shaw to enter.

Several minutes later, Major Henry and Sergeant Shaw are standing in front of Sergeant Shaw's desk facing the front of the office as the sentry opens the door.

Colonel Hatch, Captain Carroll, and Sergeant Jordan walk through the front door as Colonel Hatch looks to Major Henry with elation and says, "Uh, good afternoon Major. I see you made it okay. Did you arrive in time to see the regimental fights?"

"Yes Colonel, last of the fourteenth round. A very good match I must say."

Colonel Hatch looks to Major Henry with pride and says, "That's our ninth victory, Major, the best record in the

U.S. Service."

"I know Colonel, I've been keeping track of the regiment's success in the Army and Navy Journal." Then, Major Henry looks to Colonel Hatch with a kind look and says, "Edward, it's been a long time."

"Yes, yes it has, Guy."

Major Henry and Colonel Hatch walk towards each other, hug and pat each other on the back as old friends would who haven't seen one another in years. Colonel Hatch looks to Major Henry and says, "I'm sorry Major, let me introduce you." Colonel Hatch looks to the others in the room while motioning with his hand, then says, "This is Captain Carroll and Sergeant Jordan..." He looks back to Major Henry and says, "This is Major Guy V. Henry."

Major Henry walks up to Captain Carroll, stops, shakes his hand and says, "It's a pleasure Captain, I'm looking forward to serving with you."

"I the same Major, I've heard a lot of good things about you from Colonel Hatch."

"Thank you, Captain."

Major Henry then turns to Sergeant Jordan, who snaps to attention and salutes. Major Henry returns the salute, then shakes his hand and says, "It's a pleasure, Sergeant Jordan, I'm also looking forward to serving with you."

"Thank you, sir," says Sergeant Jordan.

Colonel Hatch looks to Major Henry and says, "I see you've met First Sergeant Shaw."

"Yes Colonel, Sergeant Shaw escorted me and my son to the fight upon my arrival. He also saw to my wife's needs, settling in."

Colonel Hatch looks to Major Henry with pride and says, "Major, these are the finest sergeants in the U.S. Army."

Sergeants Jordan and Shaw show no signs of being

conceited as they stand at parade-rest. They are very proud military men, doing their job for a fantastic colonel, as Major Henry looks to Colonel Hatch and says, "Yes I know Colonel, I've reviewed both sergeants' records while at the Department. Sergeant Shaw is the best marksman in the U.S. Cavalry and I read your recommendation for Sergeant Jordan, for his services at Tularosa."

Colonel Hatch looks to Major Henry with a surprised expression and says, "My report made it to the Department already...amazing. I hope the Army moves as fast on the recommendation. You know the military, Guy. It'll be years before they take action."

"All too well Colonel," says Major Henry.

Colonel Hatch looks around and says, "Guy, please have a seat."

Colonel Hatch motions with his hand to Sergeant Shaw's desk as Sergeant Shaw pulls back his chair for Major Henry. Major Henry turns to the desk, lays his satchel on top and sits in the chair. Colonel Hatch then looks to Major Henry and says, "I trust your trip was satisfactory, Major?"

"Yes Colonel, very pleasant. My wife and son marveled at the land, and are looking forward to frontier life."

Major Henry looks to Colonel Hatch with a serious look and says, "Colonel...I brought news from Military Headquarters."

Everyone in the room looks to one another with curiosity. Is it bad news, or good news? They look to Major Henry as he reaches into his satchel and brings out military-type papers. He stands, hands one each to Colonel Hatch and Captain Carroll, then he looks to everyone with resolution and says, "You'll notice the date, October, twenty-one, eighteen-eighty...Victorio is dead."

The officers stop reading. Sergeants Jordan and Shaw

look to the officers, and all almost stop breathing. Their looks are straightforward, and their expressions show shock, and somewhat disbelief, as they look to each other.

Colonel Hatch looks to Major Henry and says, "How did he die?"

"Mexican Federal troops caught him and his Warm Springs Tribe, and his Chiricahua' band near Tres Castillos in Mexico last week."

Sergeant Shaw, with a stunned look, turns to Colonel Hatch and says, "Colonel, then he never came back to U.S. Territory."

Colonel Hatch looks to Major Henry and says, "Major, we were hot on Victorio's tail for the last three months. Why, we ran several skirmishes with his rear guard and his main force all the way to the Rio Grande. We must of rode nine hundred miles." Colonel Hatch becomes frustrated and says, "And if it won't for those damn darn bureaucrats in Washington, we could of pursued Victorio across the border, but as you know Henry, we can't pursue into Mexico, until the United States makes a treaty with the Mexican government."

"I don't know if the United States will ever make a neutrality treaty with Mexico, Edward, but as you'll read further down, they are taking credit for hunting down Victorio," says Major Henry.

Captain Carroll looks at the paper then says, "No mention of the 9th and 10th U.S. Cavalry." With outrage, he adds, "How is it that the Mexican Army gets all the credit." Then he looks to everyone and says, "They act like they did it all. Victorio was a sitting duck because of us. They would of never had a chance against Victorio if he was at full strength. It was the Ninth Cavalry that deprived him of the will to fight. We killed a third of his men, destroyed his supplies, we out-fought them on their best ground, and the

Mexican Army gets the credit—damn them!"

There's a knock at the door as Colonel Hatch calls to the knocker, "Enter."

The sentry opens the door as Scout Glass walks in and looks to everyone, then to Colonel Hatch. He salutes and says, "Colonel, Sergeant Jim and Scout Bonito just got word, Victorio is dead, killed by the Mexican Army."

Everyone conveys a look of "how fast news travels" as Colonel Hatch turns to Scout Glass and says, "Scout Glass, I want you to meet Major Henry. Major, this is Chief of Scouts, John Glass. Major Henry will be alternating between troops and will be acting as my liaison in my absence."

"It's a pleasure, sir," says Scout Glass.

Scout Glass walks to Major Henry, salutes as Colonel Hatch looks to Scout Glass and says, "Glass, Major Henry just brought the news regarding Victorio."

Scout Glass looks to everyone and says, "News travels fast."

Sergeant Jordan looks to Colonel Hatch and says, "Sir, permission to speak."

"Yes Sergeant, of course," says Colonel Hatch.

"When Victorio left the reservation he pillaged and plundered travelers, ranchers, miners and railroad-men. As you know sir, he was forced out...because of the conditions on the reservations. Is there somethin' that can be done to halt the corrupt Indian agents, which causes the Apache to leave, and be termed hostile, sir?"

"Sergeant, even General Pope has written about his dislikes for the reservation policies. He's received reports regarding Indian agents stealing government supplies meant for the Indians...and the whole idea of this Concentration System is a damn mistake, but because they were termed to be hostile, Sergeant, the Army has no choice, but to follow orders, return the Indians to the reservations and keep the peace."

Sergeant Jordan looks to Colonel Hatch with respect and says, "Understood sir."

Captain Carroll looks to Scout Glass and says, "Any news of Nana?"

"He's also in Mexico now sir, Scout Bonito thinks Nana will come back—to avenge the death of Victorio."

"Why? We didn't kill him," says Captain Carroll.

Scout Glass looks to Captain Carroll and says, "No, we chased him to his death. I'll know when Nana is back, I'll have scouts in and around the reservations. He'll most likely try to get other Chiricahuas off the reservation to join him in the White Mountains of Mexico where he is now."

"Well gentlemen, until then," says Colonel Hatch, as he walks to the empty desk. He points to the bottom drawer while looking to Sergeant Shaw. Sergeant Shaw nods his head yes, as Colonel Hatch opens the drawer.

He brings out a bottle of whiskey, six glasses, and pours each glass with the liquor. Then, looking to everyone in the room, he says, "Gentlemen, please join me in a toast."

Everyone walks to the empty desk and picks up a shot glass of whiskey as Colonel Hatch looks to everyone and says, "You have just witnessed...the last greatest Lightweight Cavalryman, ever to walk the face of the earth."

Colonel Hatch holds up his glass to the center of the room, as everyone else holds theirs up as Colonel Hatch says, "Victorio."

Everyone in the room says, "Victorio," simultaneously.

In one swallow, their drinks are gone. They put their glasses down, and then salute the center of the room.

Fort Stanton—eleven months later. It's a beautiful day as several soldiers come and go from the garrison library with books in hand. Trooper Chase is sitting in a chair on the porch outside the library reading the local newspaper when Sergeant Jordan and Scout Glass ride up fast and stop. Sergeant Jordan looks to Trooper Chase with urgency and says, "Trooper Chase, find Corporal Wilson. Tell him to meet me in the Command Office at once."

"Yes Sarge." Trooper Chase rises, throws the newspaper on the chair revealing the date and the headlines, as he double-times away.

Scout Glass looks at the newspaper, then taps Sergeant Jordan on the shoulder preparing to ride off. Sergeant Jordan turns and looks, as Scout Glass points to the newspaper with his finger and says, "Look at the headlines."

Sergeant Jordan looks at the newspaper and reads it aloud saying, "President Garfield still in critical condition, from assassin's bullet."

"No, the next one."

"Sitting Bull returns to U.S., at Fort Buford, with one hundred eighty-six tribesmen; arrested, held at Fort Randall." Sergeant Jordan looks to Scout Glass, nods his head in acknowledgment, then turns and spurs his mount towards the Command Office with Scout Glass following.

Moments later, Sergeant Jordan and Scout Glass are standing at parade-rest in the Command Office in front of Major Henry sitting at the empty desk. Captain Carroll, Sergeant Shaw, and the garrison adjutant, are sitting at their desk.

Major Henry looks to Sergeant Jordan and says, "Yes, Sergeant."

"Sir, scouts spotted smoke signals outside of Sabinal."
Captain Carroll says, "It's been quiet, Sergeant. We haven't heard anything across the telegraph wire." Then he looks to both men and says, "How long ago?"

"This mornin' Captain. Sergeant Jim believes this could be Nana," says Scout Glass.

Sergeant Jordan looks to Captain Carroll and says, "Sir, as reported yesterday, there were several breakouts."

"Nana may be back in U.S. Territory, trying to recruit young braves from the reservations as Scout Glass has been mentioning," says Major Henry. Major Henry stands, walks to the territorial map, looks to the military markers, then says, "There was pillaging south of there last week, no killings, and as you said Sergeant, several breakouts yesterday. The news regarding Sitting Bull could incite more breakouts, and if Nana is back in U.S. Territory, this could encourage him to pick up where Victorio left off..." He looks to Sergeant Jordan and says, "Sergeant, assemble a detachment at once, rations for nineteen days."

"Already in the works, sir," says Sergeant Jordan.

There's a knock at the door as Sergeant Shaw calls to the knocker, "Enter."

The sentry opens the door as Corporal Wilson walks into the office and stops, looks to Sergeant Jordan, then to Major Henry and Captain Carroll; Corporal Wilson then salutes.

"At-ease, Corporal," says Major Henry. "Yes."

"Sir, Sergeant Jordan requested I report to the Command Office."

Sergeant Jordan looks to Corporal Wilson and says, "Yes Corporal, 'Boots and Saddles,' K Troop, rations for nineteen days."

Corporal Wilson says, "We only got eighteen men, Sarge. Trooper Walley is temporary with I Troop and—"

Sergeant Jordan, interrupting, says, "Eighteen it is, Corporal."

"Yes, Sarge."

Corporal Wilson salutes both officers, makes an about-face, and exits the Command Office as Sergeant Shaw looks to Sergeant Jordan and says, "Count me in, Sergeant—with the major's and captain's approval."

Major Henry says, "Of course, Sergeant." Then he looks to Sergeant Jordan and says, "Sergeant Jordan, that new lieutenant...Lieutenant Parker, take him along, so he can get some field experience."

"Yes, sir."

Sergeant Shaw says, "Adjutant, inform Lieutenant Parker he will lead K Troop in search of hostiles per Major Henry's request, then go to the stables, have Corporal Wilson saddle my, and Lieutenant Parker's, mount to accompany K Troop."

The adjutant snaps to, and begins to leave as Major Henry calls to him saying, "Adjutant, one moment please." Major Henry tears a piece of paper from a pad on Sergeant Shaw's desk and begins writing a message on the paper as he says, "After you finish Sergeant Shaw's task...take...this...message." Major Henry finishes writing on the paper, folds the message, and says, "...to the telegraph office. Have it sent right away to Colonel Hatch in Santa Fe." Major Henry hands the message to the adjutant, who salutes and hurries out the door.

Major Henry walks back to the territorial map and says, "Sergeants, please come here."

Sergeants Jordan and Shaw walk to the territorial map, as Major Henry points to the map and says, "Proceed south of the Sacramentos, look for any signs of hostiles, if you find the renegades, send a messenger back, on your path. After the regiment is saddled, Captain Carroll and I will be directly behind you, by a day or so. Gentlemen, I just sent word to Colonel Hatch to be prepared to send as many troops as possible, upon your findings."

Sergeants Jordan and Shaw simultaneously say, "Yes, sir."

Major Henry looks to Captain Carroll and says, "Captain Carroll, 'Boots and Saddles', provisions for nine weeks. I want every man available, mounted."

Captain Carroll says, "Yes, sir," as he puts on his Capi, walks outside of the Command Office and calls to the bugler, "Bugler, 'Boots and Saddles',"

The bugler sounds the call as Sergeant Jordan and Scout Glass salute Major Henry, then make an about-face and walk to the front door. Sergeant Jordan looks to Sergeant Shaw finishing his work and says, "See ya at the stables, Sergeant."

"As soon as I finish this last document, Sergeant."

Sergeant Jordan and Scout Glass open the door and exit the Command Office.

Several days later, smoke wafts in the air from a charred and smoldering covered wagon. Several Apache Indians rifled through what's left of the contents that lay strewn on the ground as several more spirit away the wagon's horse-team.

The Apaches are painted with war paint. They're a wounded animal, angry and darn right mean looking. Their whole society has vanished, their people dead and gone, the reservation system has failed them, they have nothing to live for—except to fight and pillage for survival.

Fifty more Apaches ride up to the wagon, with a little old man Apache at the lead. This is Nana. He's been fighting intruders confiscating his land since before he can remember. Nana speaks broken English at times. He is only four feet ten inches tall, over eighty years old, scarred and wrinkled, partly crippled, and just about blind. His pony is medium in height, and it still looks too big for him. A white man traveler moans, lying on the ground in front of his wagon. Nana looks to one of his young warriors, then points to the white man and says in Apache language, "Quiet him...take hair."

The young warrior fires an arrow dead center into the man's chest, exhausting any life left in him. The warrior then rides over to the traveler, dismounts, pulls his knife, and begins cutting the man's scalp from his head.

Other warriors hop off their ponies and begin picking the traveler's pockets as Nana looks to his warriors around him, and says in broken English, "White man kill, take land...Apache take hair."

His warriors hoot and laugh, as one of Nana's scouts on a nearby hill shouts down in Apache language, "Nana, bluecoat soldiers...come."

Nana looks to his scout, motions with his hand to leave, and then he looks to his warriors and says, "Quick, quick, quick." The warriors that were picking the traveler's pockets quickly mount their ponies as Nana heels his pony with his entire band following, leaving their depredation behind.

Sergeants Jordan and Shaw are leading two columns of eighteen troopers and a messenger, with Scout Glass and the original soldiers in the same order in front. A white officer is riding to Sergeant Jordan's left: Lieutenant Charles Parker—young, ambitious, and with no frontier experience. Lieutenant Parker wipes his nose with his paisley, as Scout Glass sniffs the air and says, "Lieutenant, Sarge, you smell that?" He sniffs the air again. "Canvas, wood burnin', comin' from up ahead."

Sergeant Jordan now also sniffs the air and says, "Yeah...canvas, wood alright."

Lieutenant Parker also tries to smell the air. "I don't smell anything, Scout," he says.

"Sir, you ain't goin' to smell anythin' till that hay fever clears up," says Sergeant Jordan. Lieutenant Parker sneezes as Sergeant Jordan looks to him respectfully and says, "Sir, please try and hold your sneezin', we don't want to give ourselves away."

"You're right Sergeant, you call the orders. It seems every time I...speak..." He sniffles then adds, "I sneeze."

Lieutenant Parker sniffles again, then sneezes, as Sergeant Jordan turns to Scout Glass and says, "Glass, see what's up ahead...Corporal Wilson, Trooper Chase, go with Glass."

Corporal Wilson and Trooper Chase simultaneously say, "Yes Sarge."

Scout Glass, Corporal Wilson, and Trooper Chase spur their mounts ahead, causing the columns to move up to fill their void, as Sergeant Jordan looks to Lieutenant Parker and Sergeant Shaw and says, "I'll be right back."

Sergeant Jordan turns his mount around, facing the detachment. He stops his mount, looks to the columns riding by him and says, "All right you dusty soldiers, keep your eyes, ears open, and mouths shut. There may be hostiles up ahead. Pass the word."

With military precision, the word is passed back through the columns trooper by trooper as Sergeant Jordan turns his mount around and rides back to his position in the column. Lieutenant Parker looks to Sergeant Jordan settling his mount back into the column. He is a little nervous, and sniffles as he says, "Sergeant, do you think there's hostiles up ahead?"

"Yes, sir. Any Indian outside the reservation is

considered a hostile. The smoke signals, that cut telegraph line we saw awhile back, and now whatever is up ahead is considered off the reservation."

Lieutenant Parker looks around and realizes this is for real. This is no longer the Academy. He's confident, but still is a little nervous.

Sergeant Shaw stands in his stirrups and looks to a rider, riding fast towards the columns, as he says, "Rider comin'...Trooper Chase."

"Yeah, where's Glass and Corporal Wilson," says Sergeant Jordan.

As Trooper Chase nears, Sergeant Jordan calls his orders to his men, "Troop, *hooo*." The columns come to a stop as Sergeant Jordan waits for Trooper Chase to stop in front of them.

As Trooper Chase reaches the columns, he stops his mount fast and looks to Lieutenant Parker, Sergeants Jordan and Shaw saying, "Sirs, Sarge, there's a burnt-out wagon about a mile up the road. One man dead, by arrow, gunshot and scalped. Glass said the trail is fresh—no more than maybe, half an hour old. Glass and Corporal Wilson are following their trail now."

"Good report trooper. Lead the way," says Sergeant Jordan.

Trooper Chase turns and spurs his mount back in the direction he came from as Sergeant Jordan looks to Lieutenant Parker and says, "Sir." Lieutenant Parker nods his head yes and then sniffles, as Sergeant Jordan stands in his stirrups, takes off his campaign hat, turns to his men and calls his orders, "Forward *hooo*." Sergeant Jordan's hand falls downward and the entire columns move out at a walk. Sergeant Jordan raises his hand in the air again to signal the next command. His hand falls forward and the columns go from a walk to a gallop at Sergeant Jordan's pace. Sergeant Jordan sits back in his saddle, draws his service revolver, and then holds it up in the air to signal to his men to draw their weapons. Each soldier draws his carbine or revolver, as K Troop gallops following Trooper Chase.

At the same time, Scout Glass and Corporal Wilson are galloping their mounts, following the hostiles' trail, when Scout Glass spots them moving across the lower desert plains below them. "Corporal, look," he says. Scout Glass points to Nana and his band galloping across the plains, towards a canyon in a group of mountains in the distance.

"Yeah, they're headed for Carrizo Canyon. Glass, stay on their trail, I'm goin' back and get Sarge."

"No problem Corporal. Just make sure you get Sarge fast. I'm goin' to try to slow 'em down." Corporal Wilson spurs his mount back towards Sergeant Jordan as Scout Glass trots his mount towards the Apache Indians, drawing his carbine from his saddle holster, keeping low in the saddle, so he won't be seen.

Moments later, Trooper Chase, Sergeants Jordan and Shaw, and Lieutenant Parker with the rest of K Troop, arrive at the burnt-out wagon as Sergeant Jordan calls his orders, "Troop...*hooo.*" The columns come to a stop as Lieutenant Parker and Sergeant Jordan ride around the wagon surveying the scene. Lieutenant Parker rides over to where Trooper Chase stopped by the dead traveler, with Sergeant Jordan following. When Lieutenant Parker sees the dead man, he begins to turn pale in the face. Sergeant Jordan then looks to Trooper Irving in the columns and says, "Trooper Irving." Trooper Irving spurs his mount from the column, towards Sergeant Jordan, as Sergeant Jordan looks to Trooper Chase and says, "Trooper Chase, pull that arrow."

Trooper Chase dismounts, bends down, and begins pulling the arrow from the dead man's chest, as Trooper Irving rides up and stops alongside of Sergeant Jordan.

"Trooper Irving, help Trooper Chase carry him over to the wagon, then cover him."

"Yes Sarge," says Trooper Irving dismounting, as Sergeant Shaw looks to Sergeant Jordan and says, "Sergeant, rider, ridin' fast, looks like Corporal Wilson."

Sergeant Jordan looks to the rider, then to Troopers Chase and Irving, saying, "Trooper Chase, Trooper Irving, fall back in ranks." Troopers Chase and Irving mount their mounts, then spur them back into the columns, as Sergeant Jordan looks to his men and shouts, "Messenger! Messenger!" The messenger leaves his position in the columns, riding towards Sergeant Jordan, as Corporal Wilson rides in fast, stopping in front of the columns.

Corporal Wilson, slightly out of breath, looks to Lieutenant Parker, then to Sergeant Jordan and says, "Lieutenant, Sarge…Nana is headed towards Carrizo Canyon with at least fifty hostiles, no cattle. Glass is going to try and slow them down."

The messenger rides up, as Sergeant Jordan looks to him with urgency and says, "Return on our trail…Major Henry is followin', tell him Nana is headed towards Carrizo Canyon…we'll try to hold 'em, and await his arrival, that's all trooper." The messenger spurs his mount back on their trail as Sergeant Jordan looks to Lieutenant Parker and says, "Lieutenant, if Nana gets up into that canyon, he'll be well entrenched."

Lieutenant Parker sniffles, then says, "Sergeant, carry on."

Sergeant Jordan salutes Lieutenant Parker, then looks to his men and calls his orders, "All right gentlemen, pass the word, make sure your equipment is tight and right."

Quickly, the soldiers check their equipment. Sergeant Jordan, Lieutenant Parker, and Corporal Wilson trot their mounts towards the front of the columns as Sergeant Jordan calls his orders, "Troop...at a trot then a gallop..." Sergeant Jordan passes the front of the columns, with Lieutenant Parker and Corporal Wilson following as Sergeant Jordan shouts the order, "Ho...Corporal Wilson. Take the lead."

Sergeant Shaw leads the columns off at a trot, then to a gallop, behind Sergeant Jordan and Lieutenant Parker, with Corporal Wilson taking the lead, racing to help their comrade.

At the same time, Nana and his band are galloping on their ponies across the desert, towards Carrizo Canyon, situated in a large string of Sandstone Mountains jetting out of the desert floor several miles away. As they scurry along, Nana's scout turns on his pony and sees Scout Glass riding fast towards them from a flank rear angle. Nana's scout points to Scout Glass, then looks to Nana and says in broken English, "Soldier scout—"

BANG! A rifle shot echoes as one of Nana's warriors is hit by Scout Glass's carbine shot, falling to the ground from his pony. Nana and his band slow and stop their ponies, as Nana looks from his wounded warrior on the ground, then to Scout Glass riding at them, now slowing and stopping his mount. Scott Glass reloads his carbine, then holds his mount's reins in his teeth as he aims his carbine in their direction, taking another shot, wounding another warrior in the shoulder.

Nana looks to Scout Glass as if he is crazy. Then he looks to his warriors pointing to Scout Glass, as he shouts angrily to a group of his warriors in Apache language,

"Get him! Get Him!"

A large group of worriers turn and heel their ponies towards Scout Glass with Nana and the rest of his band galloping behind them. Scout Glass, seeing the hostiles charging at him, holsters his carbine, turns his mount back in the direction he came, pulls his service revolver, and begins spurring his mount, carrying him out of harm's way.

The Apaches begin firing at Scout Glass, as he starts riding to the side of his saddle, low, turning and firing back at the hostiles with his revolver. It's a mad chase across the desert as the Apaches try to shoot Scout Glass off his mount. Scout Glass turns and fires at a warrior, hitting him, knocking him off his pony. He cocks his revolver again, aims, pulls the trigger—click, he had just fired his last round. He sits back upright, low in the saddle and spurs his mount across the desert as the Apaches give chase.

Moments later, Corporal Wilson is galloping on his mount, looking for his comrade in the far distance, ahead of him, as the columns follow. As he looks out into the desert, he sees his comrade, riding fast towards him, being chased by the hostiles. Corporal Wilson turns with urgency in his saddle, looks to Sergeant Jordan and shouts, "Sarge, they're after Glass!"

Sergeant Jordan looks at the hostiles chasing Scout Glass in the distance as he then turns in his saddle calling to his men, "K Troop, are you ready!"

K Troop yells, "Yes Sarge!"

"V Formation...left column, wheel left...right column, wheel right."

Like clockwork, the columns pan out, forming a "V" shape, with Corporal Wilson at the lead.

Sergeant Jordan looks to his right, then to his left and shouts, "Let's get at 'em." He turns back in the saddle, facing the hostiles and shouts, "Charge!" The two columns go from a gallop to full stride towards the hostiles chasing Scout Glass.

At the same time, Scout Glass is keeping his distance between himself and the hostiles, as Nana squints to see the Buffalo Soldiers charging towards them in the distance. Nana slows and stops his pony, with most of his main-force also stopping, except for Nana's scout and a few other warriors, who are still chasing after Scout Glass. They slow their ponies while looking back to Nana. Nana points to the canyon and yells to his warriors chasing Scout Glass, "Quick, quick...hide, canyon, hide, canyon!"

Nana's warriors stop their ponies and watch Scout Glass ride away towards the oncoming charging soldiers in the distance. They turn and look back to Nana, as does Nana's scout, shouting in broken English, "No...more of us!"

Nana points to the mountains and shouts in broken English, "Better to fight in mountains...soldiers not white man."

"No...stay, fight," shouts Nana's scout.

Nana spits on the ground, and then heels his pony towards the mountains drawing the rest of his band to follow him, including his scout.

At the same time, Scout Glass is riding full stride towards his comrades, looking back over his shoulder, seeing the hostiles retreating. He then slows, and brings his mount to a stop, takes off his hat, and waves it to his oncoming comrades.

Sergeant Jordan begins waving his arm forward at

Scout Glass, indicating to him to pursue the hostiles. Scout Glass turns his mount back in the direction of the hostiles, reloading his service revolver then spurring his mount back into action.

Corporal Wilson, Lieutenant Parker, Sergeants Jordan and Shaw lead K Troop spurring their mounts towards the hostiles at full stride, as Sergeant Jordan calls his orders, "Left flank, fire!"

The soldiers on Sergeant Jordan's left fire their carbines at the retreating Apaches, dropping a few from their ponies as Sergeant Jordan again calls to his men, "Reload." The soldiers reload at a run as some of the Apaches turn on their ponies and return fire, causing the soldiers to veer out of the path of bullets. It becomes a running battle across the desert until the Apaches scamper into Carrizo Canyon.

As Nana and his band ride into the canyon, disappearing from the soldiers, Nana quickly looks to his warriors and says in Apache language, "Quick, quick, quick, climb high, take bullets." Most of Nana's warriors dismount, while others spirit away their fellow warriors' ponies through the canyon. Nana and his scout move through the canyon as his warriors scramble up into the crevasses of the canyon, carrying their weaponry and extra bullets in their hide pouches.

Moments later, Sergeant Jordan and K Troop approach at a trot, on the far left side of Carrizo Canyon as several shots ricochet off the multi-colored layered sandstone wall in front of them. The soldiers quickly crouch down low in their saddles, as Sergeant Jordan calls his orders raising his right hand: "Troop, *hooo*."

Sergeant Jordan and the soldiers come to a stop with several more shots ricocheting off the rocks in front of them. Sergeant Jordan then looks to his men and says,

"Gentlemen, ride yourselves out of rifle shot...Troopers Temple, Perry, climb up, keep a look out."

The soldiers spur their mounts in close to the left side of the escarpment as several more shots ricochet off the rocks. The soldiers crouch close to their mounts again, as Troopers Temple and Perry dismount, with carbines, ammunition belts and begin climbing, with their comrades looking after them. Some of their comrades automatically point their carbines towards the top of the bluffs and cliffs guarding their comrades' ascent as Sergeant Jordan looks to Lieutenant Parker and says, "Sir, you feelin' better?"

"Yes Sergeant. Thank you."

Lieutenant Parker looks around and says, "What do you suggest, Sergeant?"

"Sir, we don't have enough men to go around and outflank them. I suggest a frontal attack, on foot, using the crevasses of the canyon as cover. Try and hold 'em, till Major Henry arrives. We should get their attention from both sides of the canyon. Sir, I'll take the right flank?"

"All right Sergeant, take half the men...I'll take the left flank."

"Yes, sir. I only need six men sir."

Lieutenant Parker glances at Sergeant Jordan with a look of, "That's all you'll need?" as several more rounds ricochet off the canyon walls, causing everyone to crouch lower. Sergeant Jordan shouts to his men, "Glass, Corporals Wilson, Scott, Troopers Chase, Irving, stay mounted. Everyone else, dismount, you're with the Lieutenant!" Sergeant Jordan then looks to Sergeant Shaw and says, "Sergeant, I'm goin' to need your cover."

"No problem, Sergeant."

Sergeant Shaw dismounts with his carbine and ammunition belt in hand, works his way along the edge of the canyon wall, then climbs up through a fissure, and around some crevasses, looking for a good advantage point. Lieutenant Parker surveys his men and says, "Troops, dismount, take weapons, ammunition...begin climbing, take positions..."

Lieutenant Parker stops giving orders when a hail of bullets ricochet off the sandstone, causing everyone to grab their weapons and ammunition quickly, as Trooper Temple cries out from above, "Sarge, they're attackin'!"

Lieutenant Parker quickly looks to Sergeant Jordan and shouts, "Sergeant Jordan, go as soon as you can!"

Troopers Temple and Perry take cover, then return fire as Lieutenant Parker and his men begin climbing and firing at the hostiles, temporarily slowing their advance.

Sergeant Shaw is in his position, in a notch within the canyon walls, waving his hand to Sergeant Jordan below. Sergeant Jordan looks to him and then looks to his selected group of men and says, "If we're goin', we better get at it. Get! Get! Get! Yah! Yah! Yah...!"

Sergeant Jordan and his group spur their mounts into action, arcing wide across the mouth of the canyon with rifle fire trailing behind them. They fire back into the canyon, when, midway across, Corporal Scott's and Trooper Irving's mounts are shot, and fall from under them.

The soldiers tumble to the ground hard as Corporal Scott yells to Sergeant Jordan, "Sarge, Sarge...Sarge!"

Sergeant Jordan looks over his shoulder to Corporal Scott and Trooper Irving, crouching behind their dead mounts. Sergeant Jordan then stops his mount, looks to his other men headed for the other side of the canyon, and shouts, "Trooper Chase! Trooper Chase!"

Trooper Chase stops his mount, turns his mount around and sees his comrades in danger, with bullets hitting all around them. Sergeant Jordan is now spurring his mount back to rescue his men as Trooper Chase turns and spurs his mount back towards his comrades for the second rescue. Corporal Wilson and Scout Glass have made it to the other side of the canyon and are now giving cover fire.

Sergeant Shaw on the other side of the canyon is also giving cover fire, keeping some of the hostiles at bay, protecting Sergeant Jordan and his men.

Sergeant Jordan stops his mount in front of Corporal Scott, giving him cover from the canyon. He removes his foot from his stirrup, giving Corporal Scott a firm mounting-place. Corporal Scott quickly stands from his dead mount, and puts his left foot into the stirrup, as Sergeant Jordan grabs his arm, pulling him up onto his mount. Just as Corporal Scott sits on the back of the mount, he is hit in the shoulder, causing him to swing around from the gunshot, falling to the ground hard.

Trooper Irving then runs to Corporal Scott's aid, as Sergeant Jordan looks to Trooper Irving from his mount and shouts, "Help him up!"

Sergeant Jordan reaches down to Corporal Scott again as Trooper Irving picks Corporal Scott up by his good arm, and helps him over to Sergeant Jordan. Corporal Scott puts his foot into the stirrup again as Sergeant Jordan pulls him onto the rear of his mount. Trooper Chase now arrives, and quickly picks up Trooper Irving by the arm, pulling him up onto the rear of his mount.

Sergeant Jordan and Trooper Chase then spur their mounts to safety, carrying their comrades out of harm's way towards Scout Glass and Corporal Wilson, giving cover fire on the right side of the canyon.

As they dismount, a terrific gun battle erupts. The Apaches, commanding the highest advantage point on both sides, cut loose with a hail of bullets, which rain down on the soldiers. Other Apache groups, on the left side of the canyon, begin moving down towards the soldiers.

Sergeant Jordan sees the enemy surge and shouts to his group, "They're tryin' to encircle 'em. Pick your targets gentlemen. Hold 'em back."

Sergeant Jordan and his group, except for Corporal Scott who is lying against a rock with his shoulder wound, defend K Troop by putting up a wall of lead, keeping the hostiles at bay.

The soldiers are out-numbered three to one as a fierce fight ensues. Lieutenant Parker and his men are trying to get better positions with which to fight the hostiles less than thirty yards away as Trooper Temple looks to Trooper Perry and shouts, "Perry, Perry!"

Trooper Perry looks to Trooper Temple as Trooper Temple says, "Perry, see if you can move up?"

Trooper Perry fires a round at the Apaches, reloads and makes his way towards the hostiles as several bullets ricochet of the rock in front of him. Trooper Perry looks too, and fires his carbine at the Apache, who just fired at him, hitting the Apache in the chest just as Trooper Perry is hit in the head.

Trooper Perry falls dead as Trooper Temple anxiously yells to his comrade, "Perry! Perry! Perry!" Trooper Temple, seeing his comrade, dead, angrily drops his carbine, takes out his revolver and lets loose, pulling the hammer back, each time, firing at every Apache he sees, hitting several. He pulls the hammer back again—click, it's empty. He then looks for cover and ducks behind a boulder, reloads frantically as Lieutenant Parker looks to his men and yells, "Charge!" Lieutenant Parker and his men begin surging up towards the hostiles. Bullets are hitting everywhere.

Trooper Temple finishes loading his revolver, comes from behind his cover, and begins firing at the Apaches. Nana's scout sees Trooper Temple, aims his Winchester rifle and fires, hitting Trooper Temple dead in the forehead. Trooper Temple falls like a sack of potatoes to his knees, and then his upper torso falls to the ground hard.

Nana's scout holds his rifle in the air to celebrate his kill, when all of a sudden he jerks, drops his rifle, and then grabs his throat with both hands as blood begins pouring through his fingers. Nana's scout looks in the direction the bullet came from and sees Sergeant Shaw firing again, hitting him dead in the forehead. Nana's scout falls to the ground like a felled redwood tree.

Nana looks at his dead scout, then to the advancing soldiers as he yells to his warriors in broken English, "We go. We go." Then, pointing randomly at some, he says in Apache language, "Stay. Keep shootin'. Keep shootin'." While some Apaches keep firing at the soldiers, keeping them pinned behind crevasses, Nana looks to another warrior and says in broken English, "Geronimo, send warriors stronghold. Take son. Go. Go. Go!"

Geronimo stops shooting, taps the shoulder at what looks to be his Apache son, and then shoulders of other Apaches as he stoops down low avoiding the flying bullets, hurrying away with other Apache warriors. Geronimo's son stops firing at the soldiers and follows his father, as do many other Apaches who are carrying away their wounded.

The next day, Major Henry is mounted with several officers, non-commissioned officers, and 149 troopers of the 9th Cavalry Regiment. The American flag blows in the wind, along with seven Troop flags: D, F, B, I, G, E, and H. Nine supply wagons stand at the mouth of the canyon.

K Troop is dusty, dirty, tattered, tired, but in the best spirits possible, standing at parade–rest next to their mounts, with Trooper Perry's and Trooper Temple's bodies laying on tarpaulins. Corporal Scott and the other wounded sit on their mounts as Major Henry talks with Lieutenant Parker, Sergeants Jordan and Shaw, "...Just those two dead, Lieutenant?"

Lieutenant Parker sniffles and says, "Yes, sir, shot through the head...three troopers wounded and nine mounts dead. We found five dead hostiles..." Lieutenant Parker sniffles again. "No wounded. Sergeant Jordan said they took their wounded with them. By the time we climbed the bluffs, they had slipped away...almost like they melted into the territory." After another sniffle, he adds: "Scout Glass followed their trail and reported back. They were headed southwest. Towards Mexico."

Lieutenant Parker sniffles again. "Good report Lieutenant," says Major Henry, "We have extra mounts for your return to the garrison."

"Thank you, sir. I'll submit a full report."

Major Henry looks to the south and says, "I don't know how that little old Apache is able to keep up this pace? Maybe Colonel Hatch will run into the hostiles west of here."

"Sir," says Lieutenant Parker.

"Yes Lieutenant."

Lieutenant Parker sniffles then says, "Sir, Sergeant Jordan and Sergeant Shaw saved K Troop. We were being overran by the hostiles...under heavy rifle fire."

Major Henry looks to the sergeants, proudly, and says, "Good job Sergeants."

Sergeants Jordan and Shaw say simultaneously, "Thank you, sir."

Major Henry then looks to K Troop and says, "Gentlemen, after you left the garrison, the adjutant brought a telegraph from General Pope, Department of the Missouri. In November, Colonel Hatch and Regimental

Headquarters will transfer to Fort Riley, Kansas. Troops D, F, K, and I under my command, will transfer to Fort Sill, Indian Territory..." Major Henry becomes elated and says, "Gentlemen, you're finally getting the rest you deserve."

K Troop cheers with joy at the news as Major Henry looks respectfully to Lieutenant Parker, Sergeants Jordan and Shaw, saying, "Take your dead back to the garrison for burial gentlemen. The regiment should be back in six to nine weeks. Captain Carroll is acting post commander until my return." Major Henry then looks to the bugler and says, "Bugler, sound forward."

The bugler sounds his call as Major Henry reaches into his saddlebag and pulls out his military journal and begins writing: "Sergeant Jordan and Sergeant Shaw against insurmountable odds..." The regiment rides to the south in pursuit of Nana, as Lieutenant Parker, Sergeants Jordan and Shaw, and their troop look to their regiment on the move.

Fort Stanton, four months later. It's a cool overcast fall morning as Captain Carroll and Lieutenant Parker stand alongside Major Henry mounted, talking with him, while Scout Glass talks with Sergeants Jordan and Shaw mounted, standing next to them.

The 9th Cavalry is mounted, and dispersed throughout the columns, troop flags wave in the breeze, designating each troop: K, D, I, and F.

Major Henry, Sergeants Jordan and Shaw are positioned at the head of the 9th Cavalry regiment. There are 138 Buffalo Soldiers, mounted behind their sergeants and corporals, in a column of twos, all wearing their yellow-lined blue overcoats, with five supply wagons dispersed between the troops.

Mounted side-by-side, behind Sergeants Jordan and Shaw, is the guidon trooper from K Troop, and across from him is Corporal Wilson, followed by the adjutant, another trooper, the bugler, Trooper Irving, then Troopers Chase and Walley. Next in the column is Corporal Dorch and Corporal Scott, who has recovered from his shoulder wound, their men, and the rest of the 9th Cavalry.

Scout Glass looks to Sergeants Jordan and Shaw. Somewhat tearfully, he says, "I'm gonna miss you guys."

"Me too, Glass...me too," says Sergeant Jordan.

"Thanks, Sarge...you'll be in good hands. Scout Robinson is Scout of Indian Territory in those parts. He's pretty good from what I hear."

Sergeant Jordan smiles and says, "I'm sure he's not as good as you Glass."

Scout Glass smiles as Major Henry talks with Captain Carroll and Lieutenant Parker saying, "Captain, it's been a pleasure serving with you during my short assignment."

"Thank you, Major. I'm sure your new assignment will be just as pleasurable," says Captain Carroll as he looks to his pocket watch then says, "Your wife and son's stagecoach should almost be at Fort Sill by now, Major."

Major Henry chuckles as he says, "My son wanted to ride with us Captain, but his mother said a seven-year-old is not up to the nine day ride. Speaking of a nine day ride, we better get started." Major Henry looks to Sergeant Jordan and says, "Regiment ready, Sergeant?"

"Yes, sir."

Sergeant Shaw, Corporal Wilson, and Troopers Chase, Irving and Walley look to Scout Glass, as Sergeant Shaw says, "See ya, Scout."

"Good-bye my friend," says Scout Glass.

"See ya, Glass," says Trooper Chase.

"Bye Glass," says Trooper Irving.

"Adios Glass," says Trooper Walley. Then all of K Troop says, "Bye Glass."

As K Troop says its good-byes, Sergeant Jordan bends down and shakes Scout Glass's hand and says, "Stay safe Glass, maybe we'll see each other after we retire?" After Sergeant Jordan and Scout Glass shake hands, Captain Carroll and Lieutenant Parker salute Major Henry as he calls to the bugler, "Bugler, sound forward."

The bugler sounds his call as the regiment moves out on their trip to their new garrison. Captain Carroll and Lieutenant Parker also salute the soldiers departing the garrison for the last time. When the regiment reaches the boundary of the garrison, they begin to pass the garrison's cemetery as Sergeant Jordan calls an order to his men, "Eyes, left...salute."

All the soldiers turn their heads to the left, and then salute as they look at the two fresh graves and headstones with heavy hearts.

The words inscribed into the headstones are, "Trooper Charles Perry, 1855 to 1881, Killed in Action."

"Trooper Guy Temple 1853 to 1881, Killed in Action."

Several hours later, the two long columns of the 9th Cavalry regiment wind their way through the desert towards Indian Territory. Trooper Chase looks across to his right at Trooper Walley who just returned to the regiment and says, "Augustus, you feelin' all right? You haven't said a word since you got back to the regiment this mornin'?"

Corporal Scott looks to Trooper Walley and says, "Yeah, Walley, we haven't seen ya in four months."

"Um...I'm all right," says Trooper Walley.

"Well be that way," says Trooper Chase. Trooper Chase then looks to Trooper Irving, one man ahead of

Trooper Walley and says, "Lee, Lee."

"Yeah Chase," says Trooper Irving.

"Did you see the headlines in the newspaper? Why would a white man kill President Garfield?"

"I don't know Chase, maybe, some white men are just...plain crazy."

"It's a shame. He was only in office four months. He didn't even get a chance to try to be President," says Trooper Chase.

Then, Trooper Walley, a little mournful, looks to his comrades and says, "It's a shame Perry and Temple had to die! What the hell happened out there? They were damn good soldiers!"

"After you went to I Troop, there was a report that Nana was recruiting renegades from the reservation...so the major sent us to scout the territory," says Trooper Chase.

"Yeah, and when we found Nana, we chased him and his band into Carrizo Canyon," says Trooper Irving. Mournfully he adds, "Where Perry and Temple died."

Trooper Walley thinks for a second, then says, "That must of just been before I Troop ran across him at Cuchillo Negro."

"Yeah," says Corporal Dorch, "We heard you saved a soldier whose mount was shot from under him. Sarge and Chase did the same thin'...came back and rescued Corporal Scott and Irving here—shoot, bullets were just about settin' their britches on fire almost."

"Hey, Augustus, tell us what happened with you," says Trooper Chase.

"Shoot, it was nothin'. We were out-numbered almost two to one. One of the troopers' mounts was shot from under him, like you said. Hell, he started callin' for help, forty or so yards from the hostiles. I just couldn't let him be used as target practice, so I spurred my mount back to get him. When I got to him, I got 'em onto the back of my mount with bullets flying everywhere." Then with a happy look, Trooper Walley looks to his comrades and says, "Boy, it's good to be back with K Troop."

"All I can say is, at least we won't be chasin' Comancheros, outlaws, and hostile Indians anymore. We just gotta keep white land-grabbers off Indian land now—ain't nothin'," says Trooper Irving.

Trooper Chase says, "They don't call them land-grabbers Lee, I read in the newspaper—they call them Boomers."

Corporal Scott looks to his comrades and says, "I don't care what they call 'em, I'm just lookin' forward to some good old rest. Nothing to do, except sit back and enjoy life."

"I don't know about all that sittin' back stuff Corporal, I got a feelin', there's not goin' to be that much sittin'," says Corporal Dorch.

As Corporal Dorch finishes his statement, Major Henry calls to the bugler, "Bugler, sound dismount at a walk." The bugler sounds his call as Major Henry calls his orders to his men, "Troop *hooo*...dismount." The regiment comes to a stop and dismounts as Major Henry looks to his men, then calls his orders: "Forward, at a walk, *hooo*."

The regiment members begin walking with their reins in their right hand as Sergeant Jordan looks to Major Henry and says, "Sir, mind if I ask you a question?"

"No, Sergeant, not at all. What's the question?"

Sergeant Shaw listens to the conversation as Sergeant Jordan says, "Sir, you told us about how you lost your finger, but how did you get those two scars below your eyes? They look like bullet wounds, sir."

"You're right, Sergeant. In seventy-six, I was shot in

the face during General Crook's expedition against the Lakota Sioux." Major Henry points to the bullet wound on his left cheek and says, "The bullet went from the left side, through my mouth, and exited out the right side."

"You're blessed, sir, that the bullet didn't hit you an inch higher," says Sergeant Shaw.

"'It is nothing, Sergeant, for this aren't we soldiers'?"

Nine days later: It's a cold gray day in Indian Territory as the 9th Cavalry is within eyesight of Fort Sill. Many stone and several wooden structures, with log roofs, draw the imaginary boundary defining the garrison in the distance.

To the east, the 9th Cavalry looks at a long procession of troop flags of the 10th Cavalry Regiment, and their supply-wagons, riding away from the garrison, several miles out to the southeast.

As the 9th Cavalry approaches the garrison, two soldiers ride out from the garrison towards the 9th. Major Henry, Sergeants Jordan and Shaw are looking to the entire 10th regiment, when their attention diverts to the two soldiers riding towards them. Sergeant Shaw looks hard and long at one of the approaching riders, then says, "Are my eyes goin' bad on me?"

Sergeant Jordan is also looking hard and long at the approaching riders and says, "Uh...naw...naw..." as he then smiles a little, then says, "I believe your eyes are pretty darn good, Sergeant..." Sergeant Jordan turns, looks to the columns and calls his orders, "Trooper Chase, front and center!"

Trooper Chase spurs his mount towards the front of the columns as some of the soldiers also look to the approaching riders, and begin talking among themselves with excitement. As Trooper Chase reaches the front of the

156

columns, he slows his mount, keeping pace in between Major Henry and Sergeant Jordan, then looks to Sergeant Jordan and says, "Yes Sarge."

"Trooper, remember that promise you made over a year ago about eating your hat?"

"Uh...uh...uh...yes, Sarge," says Trooper Chase.

"Well Trooper...I'm goin' to beholden' you to that statement—do you prefer pepper or salt? Take a look." Sergeant Jordan points to the soldiers approaching the regiment, and now Trooper Chase looks to the soldiers, especially looking at the officer.

As the soldiers near, Major Henry calls his orders, "Troop *hooo*."

The regiment comes to a stop as the two soldiers ride up to the columns, stopping their mounts in front of the 9th Cavalry regiment.

Sergeants Jordan and Shaw, Major Henry, and the rest of the 9th Cavalry, including Trooper Chase, are amazed. Their eyes are wide open, and they are speechless as is the entire regiment. The expressions on their faces are as if a miracle transformed in front of them, with colored, First Lieutenant Henry Ossian Flipper sitting on his mount. Lieutenant Flipper is five foot seven, twenty-five years old, born of slave parents. He's mulatto, with black curly, wavy hair, parted on the left side. Lieutenant Flipper is intelligent, handsome, and respectful. He knows who he is.

Lieutenant Flipper salutes Major Henry, then says, "Sir, I'm First Lieutenant Flipper, carrier, 10th Cavalry, and this is Scout Robinson, scout and messenger for Forts Sill, Reno and Supply, sir."

Major Henry looks from Scout Robinson, back to Lieutenant Flipper, and even with the admiration he has for his colored soldiers, he is also finding this hard to believe—a colored officer on his mount before him as he says, "I'm...Major Henry, this is Sergeants Jordan and Shaw...Ninth Cavalry."

"Sir, your wife and son arrived last week with Trooper Brown. Your wife and son are settled in your quarters and Trooper Brown is in K Troop's barracks, sir."

"Thank you Lieutenant," says Major Henry.

"Sir, Colonel Grierson sends his regards, sir."

"Did the colonel already leave Lieutenant?"

"Yes, sir, Colonel Grierson left early this morning for Fort Davis, our new garrison. Colonel Grierson had me stay behind. He wants me to show you the mechanics of a drainage ditch in the garrison, before my departure, sir."

"Very good Lieutenant," says Major Henry. He proudly adds, "You are the first colored officer I've ever seen...or my men have seen, Lieutenant."

They both turn and look back to the 9th Cavalry, to Sergeants Jordan and Shaw, then around to the rest of the regiment. There are many big speechless smiles among the regiment. Heads are moving in and around the columns, trying to get a good look at Lieutenant Flipper.

The regiment is enthused, as is Major Henry, who is looking back to Lieutenant Flipper, before saying, "This is a real pleasure, Lieutenant. Not only for myself, but for my men."

"Thank you, sir. I am the first colored to graduate from West Point, class of seventy-seven...fifty out of seventy-six, School of Mining and Engineering, sir."

"Lieutenant, you can call me Major or Major Henry."

"Yes, sir...I mean, yes Major Henry."

They both smile, as Major Henry looks to Lieutenant Flipper and says, "Lead the way Lieutenant Flipper."

Lieutenant Flipper and Scout Robinson turn their mounts back towards the garrison as Major Henry calls his orders, "Bugler, sound forward."

The bugler sounds his call as the 9th Cavalry regiment spurs their mounts towards their new garrison. Sergeant Jordan looks to Trooper Chase and says, "Trooper Chase, let Lieutenant Flipper in that spot. You ride behind the Lieutenant."

"Ye...ye...yes Sarge," says Trooper Chase as he barely swallows with his eyes wide open looking to Lieutenant Flipper.

Scout Robinson leads the way as Lieutenant Flipper slows his mount and rides between Major Henry and Sergeant Jordan, keeping pace with them. Sergeant Jordan is giving Trooper Chase a lesson, and a treat at the same time, by not ordering him to go back in ranks, but instead letting him ride behind Lieutenant Flipper.

Major Henry looks to Lieutenant Flipper and says, "So what's this drainage ditch, Lieutenant?"

"There is a low area of the garrison that won't drain. We had a severe problem with malaria from mosquitoes. I designed a channel system through a series of ditches in which the stagnated swamp water will drain."

"How long have you been with the Tenth, Lieutenant?"

"Three years, Major."

"I'm sure Colonel Grierson is very happy to have you in his command, Lieutenant," says Major Henry.

"I hope so, Major."

They smile to each other again as the long columns of the 9th Cavalry ride tall in their saddles, approaching Fort Sill, their new home.

Later that day, Lieutenant Flipper, Scout Robinson, Major Henry, and Sergeants Jordan and Shaw are standing on high ground of the swampy area inside the garrison near the barracks.

Lieutenant Flipper is pointing out the swamp area and

the drainage system as he says, "...That area over there sits lower than the rest of the garrison, causing water to collect." Lieutenant Flipper points to an open channel and says, "That's an open feeder channel you see, it cuts north, to a higher point up to the river. When the water gate is lifted, it feeds and fills this area with water." He points to a hill. "Then I had other channels cut south, over that hill, from the bottom of the swamp area to a lower point than the swamp."

Sergeant Shaw says, "I don't see the channels running south, sir, except for that flat rock lying in straight lines goin' over the hill...looks like fingers of slate. How did you get water to run uphill, sir?"

"You're right Sergeant. The channels are lined and covered with cut slate from the surrounding hills—protection for the channels from being undermined by the moving water. To answer your other question on getting water to move uphill, you have to create a siphon system, a closed tunnel. The channels running south are buried several feet under, covered with slate and available clay, which creates a good seal for the channels. The slate you see on top protects the clay seal below the cover from erosion, protecting the channels below them. Then once the water level reaches the top of the hill, gravity takes over and does the rest, sucking the water out of this area."

Major Henry says, "Very impressive, Lieutenant. You designed this yourself?"

"Yes Major. Colonel Grierson calls it, 'Flippers Ditch.'"

Sergeant Jordan then looks to Major Henry and says, "Sir, with your permission."

"Of course, Sergeant."

Sergeant Jordan looks to Lieutenant Flipper and says, "Sir, I'm sure your regiment, the Tenth, and the other colored regiments, the Twenty-fourth and Twenty-fifth

Infantry, are equally proud of you, but we wanted you to know...the Ninth Cavalry is just as proud."

Sergeant Jordan takes off his hat and raises it in the air as the 9th Cavalry, K, I, D, and F Troops—over one hundred soldiers—double-time towards Sergeant Jordan, stopping just below them, gathering as they shout, "Hip, hip, hurrah! Hip, hip, hurrah! Hip, hip, hurrah!" Then the soldiers give a round of applause, drawing in Major Henry and Sergeants Jordan and Shaw.

Lieutenant Flipper looks to Sergeant Jordan with appreciation and says, "Thank you Sergeant." He turns to the 9th Cavalry then says, "Thank you, thank you men."

While the applauding continues, Lieutenant Flipper turns and shakes Sergeant Jordan's hand as Sergeant Shaw looks to Lieutenant Flipper and says, "Lieutenant, sir, it's a true pleasure."

"Thank you, Sergeant," says Lieutenant Flipper.

The troops that ran over and cheered Lieutenant Flipper now settle in their excitement, and talk amongst themselves, looking to the colored officer as he moves over and shakes Sergeant Shaw's hand.

Lieutenant Flipper looks to Major Henry and says, "Major, to make the system work"—he points uphill—"follow the open fill ditch to the river. There, you'll find a divert cut into the river. Pull the water door up, and gravity will do the rest. Once the swamp is full, return the water door and the swamp will drain its self. The only maintenance required is to keep the top of the channels well covered and it should work fine...Major, if you will excuse me, I must catch up to my regiment."

"Sure, Lieutenant. It was truly a pleasure meeting you...and I'll make sure your drainage system is well maintained and keeps your name," says Major Henry.

Lieutenant Flipper salutes Major Henry, then turns to

Sergeants Jordan and Shaw, saying, "Sergeants, it was a pleasure meeting you both." He turns to the 9th Cavalry and says, "I'll always remember this, men...thank you."

Sergeants Jordan and Shaw, Major Henry and the entire 9th Cavalry snaps to attention and salutes Lieutenant Flipper. Lieutenant Flipper returns the salute, then walks down to his mount, mounts, waves good-bye with his campaign hat, and spurs his mount after his regiment as Major Henry looks to his sergeants and says, "Well, Sergeants...how about that."

"I had a feelin' one day, sir, that a colored would be able to be an officer, truly somethin'," says Sergeant Jordan, as he looks to his men watching Lieutenant Flipper ride away. He adds: "All right, back to your duties. Let's get settled in. Trooper Chase, front and center."

The soldiers go back to their duties, still glancing at Lieutenant Flipper riding away, as Scout Robinson walks towards Major Henry, Sergeants Jordan and Shaw, stopping in front of them.

Indian Scout Wash Robinson is in his forties. A colored half-breed born in Mexico, he was kidnapped by Navajos as a child, then sold as a teenager to the Pueblos. Later, he lived with Indians in the Wichita Mountains, and was captured in a battle with the U.S. Army. He speaks Spanish and several Indian languages, learned to speak English while incarcerated as a prisoner of war, then was paroled. He joined the Army and was given the position of messenger and scout.

Scout Robinson looks to his new comrades—Major Henry, Sergeants Jordan and Shaw—and says, just as Trooper Chase arrives, "Seventh Cavalry challenged you to race. This mornin' they say, colored soldiers no match for white soldiers."

Major Henry chuckles a little as he looks to Scout

Robinson and says, "What's the race Scout Robinson, and when?"

"Hare and Hound, spring, every year," says Scout Robinson.

"What's a Hare and—" says Sergeant Jordan as he looks to Major Henry, Sergeant Shaw, and Trooper Chase. "You ever heard of a...what's that, Hare and...?"

They all shake their heads no and shrug their shoulders as Scout Robinson looks to Sergeant Jordan and says, "Hound."

"Naw, never heard of it," says Sergeant Shaw.

Major Henry laughs a little as he says, "Scout Robinson, what is this Hare and Hound race?"

"Eighteen-mile race, start here, Fort Sill, on foot, go through Wichita Mountains, to Medicine Bluff Gorge, then back here."

"That's easy enough, eighteen miles," says Trooper Chase.

"There's more," says Scout Robinson.

Major Henry says, "More, Robinson?"

"You have fifteen-minute head start, three of you are the Hares."

"That makes it better," says Trooper Chase.

"More," says Scout Robinson.

Sergeant Shaw says, "More?"

"After they start, seven Hounds track you down," says Scout Robinson.

"With a fifteen-minute head start, they'll never see us—just like the slave days, Master chasing us runaway slaves," says Trooper Chase.

"Something like that Trooper, you, Hare, must stay on trail, but Hounds, take shortcut when they see you, but, must return to nearest trail when you are no longer in sight of you. First one back wins."

"How do you keep someone from cheating, Robinson?" says Major Henry.

"Both regiments have troops as lookouts, on the race trail. To keep everyone honest," says Scout Robinson.

Next spring, 1882, it's a beautiful festive day at Fort Sill as soldiers, colored and white, move around the garrison. A banner blows in the breeze, strung between two trees near the center of the garrison.

Written on the banner: "Tenth Annual Hare and Hound Race, 7th Cavalry vs. 9th Cavalry."

At the starting point, Scout Robinson is stringing the start-line across from tree to tree. Close by, Major Henry is lying on a blanket, looking to Mrs. Henry massaging his legs. Several feet away from them is Sergeant Jordan, stretching on the ground, and Trooper Chase, running in place. The Hares are in uniform only, no weapons. They are being coached by Sergeant Shaw and assisted by their comrades, Corporal Wilson, Troopers Irving and Walley. Corporals Dorch and Scott, little Henry Junior, Trooper Brown, several women, colored and white, and the rest of Fort Sill's 9th Cavalry are standing by to cheer on their comrades.

On the other side of the 9th's cheering section is the 7th's cheering section: local townspeople, miners, ranchers and a ragtime band holding their instruments.

Several troopers throw logs into large earthen pits, and then set the logs on fire, as some of the crowd begins cheering. The Ragtime band begins playing "The Swallowtail" for the 7th Cavalry detachment of thirty cavalrymen, riding into the garrison carrying their regimental flag.

Sergeant Jordan looks to the 7th Cavalry, and the longhair Lieutenant leading them. Then he looks to Corporal Wilson, saying, "Corporal Wilson, look at the lieutenant leading."

Major Henry, Sergeant Shaw, and the 9th Cavalry are looking at the 7th Cavalry riding in, as Corporal Wilson looks to the Lieutenant, then looks back to Sergeant Jordan and says, "Yeah Sarge, what about him?"

"Don't he look like someone you seen before?"

Sergeant Jordan motions with his hand to the lieutenant, then looks to Corporal Wilson and says, "Look real good."

Corporal Wilson and some of the group look back to the lieutenant, as Corporal Wilson turns back to Sergeant Jordan and says, "Yeah...a little Sarge."

"That's the soldier who got commissioned a couple of years ago in Santa Fe for killing that Comanchero you killed."

Major Henry turns to Sergeant Jordan with a surprised expression and says, "Corporal Wilson 'killed' a Comanchero, and that soldier got a commission?"

"Yes, sir. The depot was attacked by Comancheros. One of the bandits had the Commander by the throat with a knife. Corporal Wilson picked him off with his carbine." Sergeant Jordan looks, then points to Lieutenant Mitchell and says, "That soldier, at that time, was only an enlistee, not an officer. Durin' the attack, he was fumblin' with his service revolver." He looks back to Major Henry and says, "The commander knew who took the shot, sir. He looked at the Comanchero with the large hole in his head, then to Corporal Wilson, but gave the commission to that lieutenant."

Major Henry says, "Did you tell the Commander of the Post about your observations, Sergeant?"

"No, sir. It wouldn't of done any good," says Sergeant

Jordan as he looks to Major Henry with an expression of resolve.

Major Henry shakes his head in agreement as Sergeant Jordan, Corporal Wilson, and the group go back to preparing for the race, while periodically looking to Lieutenant Mitchell with some displeasure.

As the 7th approaches their area, Lieutenant Mitchell gives orders to his men: "Troop, ho. Dismount." The 7th Cavalry detachment comes to a stop and dismounts, with some of the crowd gathering around them, as Corporal Wilson looks to Sergeant Jordan and says, "Yeah Sarge, that's him alright."

All three troopers—Chase, Irving, and Walley—also respond semi-simultaneously, saying, "Yeah, Sarge, that's him, that's him."

Sergeant Shaw looks hard to the 7th Cavalry lieutenants, then to Sergeant Jordan and says, "Which one, Sergeant?"

"The lieutenant giving orders," says Sergeant Jordan.

Sergeant Shaw looks to Lieutenant Mitchell delegating tasks to his men, as Lieutenant Mitchell now looks over to the 9th Cavalry with a hardened posture. Staring at the 9th, he taps a trooper on his arm to get his attention, as he says, "Hartigan."

Trooper Hartigan turns his head, showing a very hardened frontier look, as he looks to where Lieutenant Mitchell is staring.

Lieutenant Mitchell turns and looks to Trooper Hartigan and says, "They sure all look alike, don't they." He turns back, staring at the Buffalo Soldiers and says, "I can't tell one from another."

"What do you want from a bunch of mud turtles," says Trooper Hartigan.

Lieutenant Mitchell chuckles as he looks to the 7th Cavalry Hounds, motioning to the Hounds, Trooper

Hartigan, three other lieutenants, one non-commissioned officer, and one trooper to follow him over to the Buffalo Soldiers, preparing for the race.

The 7th Cavalry Hounds who are participating in the race are also weaponless, as Lieutenant Mitchell approaches with his men following, stopping in front of the Buffalo Soldiers and saying, "How you all boys doin' today?"

Then Trooper Hartigan says, "Think you're gonna beat the 7th Cavalry...hum, tar babies?"

Trooper Hartigan, Lieutenant Mitchell, and his men laugh with one another as the Buffalo Soldiers give a reluctant smile back at them, then continue with their preparations. Trooper Hartigan tries again to get their goat by saying, "Don't worry boys, we ain't gonna beat you porch monkeys that bad!"

The 7th Cavalry detachment laughs again, as Lieutenant Mitchell looks to the Buffalo Soldiers, and studies Sergeant Jordan, Corporal Wilson, and Troopers Chase, Irving, and Walley—all of whom are ignoring him. Lieutenant Mitchell thinks to himself that he recognizes some of them as he looks to Sergeant Jordan and says, "Where do I know you boys from?" Lieutenant Mitchell thinks again, then looks to Sergeant Jordan, saying, "Wait...I know where. Aren't you all boys from—the Santa Fe Depot, where I got my commission?"

"Yeah, we were there," says Sergeant Jordan.

Lieutenant Mitchell snubs and chuckles as he says, "Are you as good on a mount as you think you are on foot?"

"They ain't any good. Shoot, my pappy and I use to coon hunt for you runaways all the time. Heck, you porch monkeys...you all the same...catch ya' within miles of our place," says Trooper Hartigan.

Sergeant Jordan stands, just feet away from Trooper Hartigan, and so does the rest of the Buffalo Soldiers, including Major Henry. Sergeant Jordan, with a pointed look, smiles, looks at Trooper Hartigan face to face and says, "Trooper, I ran away from the plantation in Tennessee. I won my freedom. Lets see how well you do today!"

Trooper Hartigan looks to Lieutenant Mitchell for help as Lieutenant Mitchell looks at Sergeant Jordan with the look of disrespect and says, "No problem, NIGGER!"

The 9th Cavalry, which heard this, moves towards Lieutenant Mitchell. Major Henry has heard all he wants to hear. Stepping in front of Sergeant Jordan and the 9th Cavalry, confronting Lieutenant Mitchell and Trooper Hartigan, he says, "Wait a damn minute Lieutenant...why don't you two grow up! You want to race, then it's a race you'll get, but don't call my men names!"

Lieutenant Mitchell looks at Major Henry and says, "What's wrong? You and your nigger boys can't take a little school house funnin', Major?"

Major Henry, with a pointed expression, looks at Lieutenant Mitchell and says, "Just because this is a game between our regiments, 'Lieutenant,' doesn't mean—" Major Henry steps into Lieutenant Mitchell's face, nose-to-nose, and says, "You can forget your 'rank,' 'Lieutenant'!"

Lieutenant Mitchell climbs into his shell, along with Trooper Hartigan, as Scout Robinson calls out to the crowd, "Lookouts, mount, take positions. Hares, start line."

Lieutenant Mitchell, Trooper Hartigan, and the Hounds are backing away from Major Henry and Sergeant Jordan, knowing they just got roped and hog-tied by Major Henry. They walk back to their staging area with their tails between their legs.

Ten lookouts from the 9th Cavalry and ten lookouts from the 7th Cavalry have already mounted their mounts and are spurring them out to their positions along the race-trail.

Sergeant Jordan, Major Henry, and Trooper Chase walk to the start-line as Scout Robinson holds up a piece of yellow cloth, looks at the contestants, and says, "The trail is marked with cloth." He drops the cloth then says, "Ninth Cavalry Hares stay on trail, if leave trail...lose. Seventh Cavalry Hounds, start fifteen minutes later. If in sight of Hares, take shortcuts, but when not in sight, must return nearest trail. First Hare or Hound back, wins race. Questions?"

The 9th Cavalry Hares shake their heads no and look to Scout Robinson as he examines his pocket watch, points the start gun in the air, and fires. Sergeant Jordan, Major Henry, and Trooper Chase take off like jackrabbits towards the Wichita Mountains and Medicine Bluff Gorge with the Hare fans cheering them off.

Several miles away from Fort Sill, yellow cloth markers wave in the breeze, tied to stakes placed in the ground, across the open hilly plains of Indian Territory marking the race trail as far as the eye can see. Lookouts, sitting on their mounts, are sporadically stationed on hilltops, in valleys, off the trail. Most are out of sight as the Buffalo Soldiers run from yellow cloth to yellow cloth.

Sergeant Jordan leads Trooper Chase by several yards, and Trooper Chase leads Major Henry by twenty yards. A gunshot is heard in the far distance as Major Henry—running and breathing hard—looks at Sergeant Jordan, who is ahead of him, running to the next yellow cloth. He says, "They started, Sergeant."

Sergeant Jordan looks back and shouts to Major Henry saying, "I heard, sir."

Sergeant Jordan is leading the Hares around, over, and through scrub brush, towards a yellow marker that is tied to a tree at the bend of the Medicine Bluff Creek gorge.

As Sergeant Jordan reaches the yellow cloth, he stops and looks to the marker tied to the tree in front of him, then down into the river gorge, and to the steep cliff before him. Sergeant Jordan quickly looks in both directions, then along the rim of the gorge to his left as he searches for the next marker. Sergeant Jordan and the Hares search for the yellow cloth, when in the distance they see a lookout that is watching them. Sergeant Jordan puts his hands over the top of his eyes, backs up, looks out, then stops as he sees a yellow cloth staked to the edge of the rim, several hundred yards along the edge of the gorge, downriver. "This way!" shouts Sergeant Jordan as he leads the Hares running towards the yellow cloth.

As the Hares run along the rim towards the yellow-marker, Trooper Chase shouts, "Sarge, down there!" Trooper Chase points to another marker that is staked in the riverbed, far up ahead, just below the yellow marker they are running towards.

As the Hares reach the marker on the rim, they begin searching for a way down the cliff. Trooper Chase quickly points and shouts, "Sarge, over there!" Sergeant Jordan looks at Trooper Chase, who is pointing to a way down and says, "I see it, Trooper." Sergeant Jordan runs to the spot Trooper Chase pointed to, and begins climbing down the side of the gorge. Trooper Chase and Major Henry follow.

As they reach the riverbed, they run back upriver through scattered trees and bushes towards another yellow cloth that is tied on a tree in the riverbed. Then they run further upriver, to another marker that's staked in the ground, under a large bush at the bend in the river gorge. When they reach the marker at the bend, they see another yellow marker further upriver, staked in the water on their side of the riverbank, before they see, on the other side of the river, another yellow cloth staked in the water, upriver.

Sergeant Jordan takes off running with Trooper Chase and Major Henry following. As the Hares reach the yellow cloth staked in the water, Sergeant Jordan runs into the river, with Trooper Chase and Major Henry following, creating waves of splashes.

The water is cold as the Hares shiver: "Burr." "Errr." "Burr."

After entering the slow-moving river, they begin wading their way upriver through the deep water towards the yellow marker on the other side, indicating where to climb out of the river. Sergeant Jordan, wading his way towards the marker, says, "Do you see any yellow near the cliffs, where to climb up?"

Major Henry points to a landslide area in the steep cliffs and says, "Yeah—the marker is over there. That's where we climb up Medicine Bluff Gorge."

Just as Major Henry spoke, Lieutenant Mitchell yells, "There they are! This way!" Lieutenant Mitchell is on top of the gorge, where the Hares first saw the river.

Major Henry wades his way across the river, looks back, then up, and spots Lieutenant Mitchell running along the rim of the river gorge towards them, trying to keep the Hares in sight through tall trees that line the riverbank, and tall bushes that line the river gorge rim.

Major Henry then turns and yells to Sergeant Jordan, "Go Sergeant! Go! Go!"

Sergeant Jordan and the Hares quicken their pace through the river to the yellow marker, as Lieutenant Mitchell, with the Hounds following, runs along the edge of the cliff, keeping the Hares in sight, looking for a place to climb down.

Sergeant Jordan is first to reach the yellow marker on

the riverbank, with his comrades following, running out of the water, to the other marker in the hollow. Sergeant Jordan then begins climbing into the semi-steep cut in the cliff, making his way up as if it were child's play, with Trooper Chase and Major Henry flanking both sides of him.

Lieutenant Mitchell reaches the other side of the gorge across from the Hares. He begins running along the edge of the cliff, back and forth, several yards one way, then several more yards the other way, looking for a way down the steep cliff, trying to keep the Hares in sight. As Lieutenant Mitchell runs, he passes a possible way down. When he sees it, he puts on the brakes, causing some of the Hounds to run into the back of him, knocking him down—BOOM! CRASH!

Lieutenant Mitchell looks to the Hounds angrily, "Damn you, watch where you're goin'." Lieutenant Mitchell gets back up and double-times to the spot, and begins climbing down the side of the gorge, with his Hounds following. Halfway down, Trooper Hartigan clumsily trips, falls, and comically knocks Lieutenant Mitchell down, causing both to tumble towards the bottom of the river gorge.

Trooper Chase hears the commotion, stops, turns, and—seeing Lieutenant Mitchell and Trooper Hartigan tumbling to the bottom—says, "Hey...look at the mighty Seventh."

Major Henry looks to Trooper Chase and says, "Get going, Trooper!"

"Yes, sir." Trooper Chase turns and scrambles up the cliff.

On the other side of the gorge, the Hounds make their way down the cliff to aid their comrades. As the Hounds reach Lieutenant Mitchell, lying on his back, they help him to his feet, looking dazed, suffering only a bruised ego. He looks to Trooper Hartigan on his knees, still trying to figure out what happened as Lieutenant Mitchell shouts, "Get up, you idiot, get up, get movin'! Get across the river..." Lieutenant Mitchell points to the Hares saying, "While we can still see them, before they get up and over the bluff!"

Lieutenant Mitchell staggers towards the river as the Hounds help Trooper Hartigan to his feet. Trooper Hartigan staggers forward as the Hounds catch and pass Lieutenant Mitchell, running into the river and kicking up water as they pursue the Hares.

Lieutenant Mitchell yells to the Hounds as he runs into the water saying, "Don't let 'em out of your sight!"

The Hares are almost at the top of the gorge, as Sergeant Jordan, Trooper Chase, and Major Henry make their way over the top, disappearing.

Lieutenant Mitchell looks to the disappearing Hares and yells out, "Damn it!"

Later, the Hares are running through a valley surrounded by hills. Major Henry is running behind Trooper Chase by several yards, and Trooper Chase is trailing Sergeant Jordan by ten yards, as Trooper Chase shouts to Sergeant Jordan, "Hey Sarge, we've been here almost six months; everything's been calm. There's been no calls for patrols for trouble. This is what I call keeping the peace, Sarge."

"Trooper, Indian Territory will open for settlement in several years. Land-grabbers are already staking out claims, which is illegal—they have been found by several troops, arrested and removed from Indian land. So you'll get your chance of keeping the peace soon, Trooper," says Major Henry, who is running behind him.

Trooper Chase respectfully says, "Yes, sir... Sir?"

"Yes, Trooper."

"Sir, they call them Boomers."

"You're right, Trooper Chase, thank you," says Major

Henry respectfully.

The Hares are following the yellow markers back towards the river gorge, where the cliffs are red clay and sandy, sloping downwards. Sergeant Jordan sees a yellow marker, stops, then runs to the edge of the gorge, sees another yellow marker below, sits down and slides on his butt to the riverbed below him as the Hares follow.

As they reach the bottom, they run to the river and to another marker, where the river is wider and shallower. They plow through the thigh-high water, splashing all the way, to reach the other side of the river, and as they reach the riverbank they are dripping wet. The Hares then run to the embankment, where another yellow cloth is staked in the ground, and begin crawling and climbing up the red clay sand embankment to the yellow marker above, sliding backwards occasionally.

Being wet has caused the red clay and sand to stick to them and as they reach the top of the cliffs and begin running, they look like red sand-people.

Fifteen minutes later, most of the red sand has fallen off the Hares as Sergeant Jordan, Trooper Chase, and Major Henry run along the marked trail towards Fort Sill in the distance. Smoke wafts in the air from the garrison, as spectators and fans of the 9th and 7th Cavalry stand at the finish line in a festive mood, watching the Hares run towards the garrison.

The 9th's fans begin cheering the Hares on as Sergeant Jordan turns and begins running backwards, towards the garrison, looking to the Hounds in the far distance. Sergeant Jordan, seeing the Hounds have no chance, turns back around and begins running forward again towards the garrison.

Minutes later, the fans applaud and cheer as the Hares cross the imaginary boundary of the garrison, then the finish line, while Scout Robinson fires the gun, signaling the end of the race. Mrs. Henry and Henry Junior run and hug Major Henry, as Trooper Brown pats him on the back.

Trooper Chase has swept a very pretty young colored woman with a yellow ribbon tied in her hair off her feet, with a real frontier kiss—clay, sand, sweat and all.

Sergeant Jordan is getting handshakes and pats on the back from the 9th.

The ragtime band strikes up "The Swallowtail," and the 7th Cavalry's fans begin cheering as Lieutenant Mitchell and the Hounds come staggering in, and cross the finish line, with Trooper Hartigan following.

The Hares look to the Hounds and then back to their fans as Scout Robinson looks to Sergeant Jordan taking in the jubilation and says, "Good job, Sergeant."

"Thank you, Robinson," says Sergeant Jordan.

Sergeant Shaw, smiling, walks up to Sergeant Jordan and says, "Very good, very good," as they both hug.

Trooper Chase stops kissing the young lady, looks to the sky, smells the air and rolls his eyes back in his head as he looks to Sergeant Jordan shaking Sergeant Shaw's hand, and says, "Sarge, you smell that?"

"All the way here, Trooper," says Sergeant Jordan.

Corporal Scott is talking with Mrs. Henry, who is holding Major Henry's hand as Sergeant Jordan looks to Major Henry and says, "Sir, like to get somethin' to eat?"

"Sure thing Sergeant," says Major Henry as he looks to Henry Junior and says, "Henry Junior, ready for some good smoked meat?"

"Yes, father."

Major Henry looks at Mrs. Henry finishing her conversation with Corporal Scott, and begins walking with

Mrs. Henry, holding her hand. Sergeants Jordan and Shaw, Corporal Wilson, Troopers Chase, Irving, Walley, Corporals Dorch and Scott, and Scout Robinson walk to the smoky pits, smiling and having a good time. The rest of the 9th Cavalry follows, licking their chops, followed by spectators, and the 7th Cavalry Hounds, dusting themselves off.

Half an hour later, smoke wafts in the air from the fire pits. They're filled with sides of beef and lamb, spread across iron slats. Everyone is having a festive time, celebrating the day's events, especially eating the wood-cooked meat, which just about falls of the bone.

The 9th Cavalry is gathered together in their groups as the 7th Cavalry is in theirs.

Henry Junior runs with other children, playing games as Major Henry and Mrs. Henry walk along the perimeter of the festivities, holding hands and talking with each other. Mrs. Henry says, "You and your men were marvelous, dear."

"Thank you my sweet. I was hoping to come in second with my men...though..." He chuckles and says, "Physically, the colored is of a better spirit than I."

Mrs. Henry looks to Lieutenant Mitchell, who is walking towards them and says, "Guy, here comes that horrible officer who was disrespectful to you this morning."

Major Henry looks to Lieutenant Mitchell approaching as Mrs. Henry looks back to Major Henry and says, "If you can call him an officer...I don't want to be in his presence, Guy. I'll go look for Henry Junior."

Mrs. Henry kisses Major Henry on the cheek quickly, and walks off before Lieutenant Mitchell reaches their location.

Lieutenant Mitchell reluctantly knows his place now, but he is still arrogant in his own way when he stops where Major Henry is standing, and looks to Major Henry who is somewhat ignoring him as he says, "Sir, is that your wife?"

"...Yes it is, Lieutenant."

"Very beautiful if I may say so, sir."

"Thank you Lieu—"

Interrupting, Lieutenant Mitchell says, "Sir, you and your men performed well."

Major Henry pointedly says, "I'll pass on your compliments to my men Lieutenant. Lieutenant...?"

"Lieutenant Mitchell, sir. Sir, I met your men several years back when I got my commission."

"So you said, Lieutenant Mitchell," says Major Henry pointedly. He looks to Lieutenant Mitchell and says, "Lieutenant, your actions before the race were unbecoming of an officer—"

Lieutenant Mitchell interrupts Major Henry again with a somewhat evil disposition. Out of earshot of everyone else, he says, "Sir, I joined the Army to kill Injuns, to avenge Custer, not to bow to any of those tar—"

Major Henry interrupts, saying, "That's why you joined, Lieutenant—to avenge Custer? You are a United States Soldier, a soldier of peace. Not a soldier of revenge!"

"I'm a soldier of war, Major. Those Injuns declared war on the United States, and I'm just carryin' out my orders!"

"Orders yes, revenge, no, Lieutenant!"

"Excuse me, sir," says Trooper Chase, walking up with his young lady friend holding his arm.

Lieutenant Mitchell looks to Trooper Chase and his lady friend with disregard as he looks back to Major Henry and says, "Sir, I'll let you get back to your...party."

Lieutenant Mitchell salutes Major Henry, makes an about-face, and walks away as Trooper Chase looks at

Major Henry and says, "Sir, Sergeant Jordan said you needed relief."

Major Henry laughs and says, "Yes, thank you Trooper Chase. Where is Sergeant Jordan?" Trooper Chase points to Sergeants Jordan and Shaw standing next to Mrs. Henry, Henry Junior, Trooper Brown and Scout Robinson who are waving to him. Major Henry looks to Trooper Chase and says, "Thank you Trooper Chase for saving the day."

Trooper Chase salutes Major Henry, who returns the salute, then walks towards Sergeant Jordan and his family. As Major Henry walks away, Troopers Irving and Walley walk up to Trooper Chase who is talking with his lady friend, "...I'll see you later," says Trooper Chase.

Trooper Chase's lady friend kisses him on the cheek and walks away, as Trooper Walley says, "Chase, what was that about with the lieutenant and the major?"

"Sarge said that lieutenant was a big pain for the major, so he sent me to rescue him. Sarge said the lieutenant would leave, if I stood by the major."

"I'm sure glad he's not in our command. It would be real hell."

"You ain't just a whistlin' Dixie, Walley."

Scout Robinson walks up and greets Trooper Chase and says, "Good race, Trooper."

"Thanks Robinson—hey, Robinson, the major said some Boomers are starting to stake claims to Indian Territory and cavalry troops arrested them."

"Yes, startin' already, Indian land not for sale...maybe many years before white fathers in Washington sell Indian Territory."

"Shoot...Chase, Robinson said many years. We can still just sit back and retire," says Trooper Irving.

"Wait, white man will come soon, like grasshoppers, in search of land...we will have plenty to do. As you say, already reports of cavalry troops, arrestin' Boomers, takin' 'em back to Arkansas and Kansas," says Scout Robinson.

"Robinson," says Trooper Walley, "What happens to the Boomers when they take them to Arkansas and Kansas?"

"Fined hundred dollars, given their guns back, to try again."

"Well until then my friends...we can sit back and enjoy life," says Trooper Irving.

They walk back into the festivities, arm in arm.

Three years later at Fort Sill, Major Henry is sitting at his desk writing a letter. The date on the letter reads, "Twenty-one, May, eighteen-eighty-five" and is addressed to "Congressional Committee, Washington, D.C." Major Henry is writing the last part of the letter, which reads: "I cannot stress enough, the importance of non-commissioned officers to the Troop, and I would gladly be the first to take a cut in pay, so non-commissioned officers can be rightfully compensated for their duties in the regiment."

Then Major Henry signs the letter, folds it, puts it in a pre-prepared envelope, seals it, looks to the adjutant, and says, "Adjutant, take this letter into town, see that it gets mailed right away."

The adjutant walks over to Major Henry, snaps to attention, takes the letter, puts on his Capi and walks out the open front door, past the sentry.

Moments later, the adjutant mounts his mount that's just outside of the Command Office and spurs his mount past the garrison library, where Troopers Chase, Irving, and Walley are gathered on the porch.

Trooper Chase is sitting in a chair, reading the newspaper to Troopers Irving and Walley, both of whom are sitting on a bench. "This is the latest Omaha Progress," says Trooper Chase, "It says, Sitting Bull to join Buffalo Bill Cody's Wild West Show next month."

"Wow, think of being in a show like that," says Trooper Walley.

"Sure would be somethin', wouldn't it," says Trooper Chase.

"It sure would beat dealin' with these Boomers all over the place every time we turn around," says Trooper Irving.

"Shoot, you're right about that Irving, we haven't been enjoyin' life much, chasin' white people off Indian Territory...bein' disrespected while tryin' to do our job," says Trooper Walley.

Trooper Chase looks back to the newspaper as he says, "The Boomers are gettin' a lot of attention, look at this." He shows the newspaper to his comrades and begins to read: "President Grover Cleveland warns Boomers to stay off Indian Territory, he's issuin' orders to Federal Troops to—"

Trooper Chase stops reading as he and his comrades look to Scout Robinson riding in hard and fast, stopping at the Command Office, dismounting, hurrying to the front door. He knocks on the doorjamb, and then enters, passing the sentry.

Trooper Chase looks to his comrades and says, "Well my friends, looks like we're back in the saddle again."

Trooper Chase stands and folds the newspaper as Major Henry comes out of the Command Office with urgency. He shouts to the bugler, "Bugler, sound 'Boots and Saddles.' K Troop and scouts."

The bugler sounds his call as Troopers Chase, Irving and Walley hurry to the stables with most of the garrison responding to the call.

Fifteen minutes later, in Fort Sill's stable, five Seminole Indian scouts and forty soldiers from K Troop are saddling their mounts quickly.

Sergeants Jordan and Shaw, Scout Robinson, and Lieutenant Matthias W. Day walk into the stables, as Corporal Wilson looks to K Troop and says, "Attention!"

"At-ease," says Lieutenant Day.

Lieutenant Day is twenty-eight years old, white, and has a boyish look. He graduated from West Point, but wasn't a great scholar, and received an alarming number of demerits for mischievous offenses. Lieutenant Day is shy, but daring. He received the Medal of Honor several years ago.

K Troop continues with preparations for duty, looking up occasionally to Lieutenant Day, as Sergeant Jordan says, "Gentlemen, this is Lieutenant Day. He will lead K Troop to arrest and escort the intruders from Indian Territory. The lieutenant will say a few words, then Robinson will fill you in on the details."

Sergeant Jordan looks to Lieutenant Day and says, "Sir."

"Afternoon gentlemen," says Lieutenant Day, looking to his men as they respond simultaneously saying, "Good afternoon, sir."

He says, "It's a pleasure to be in your presence. Colonel Hatch sends his regards, and says he hopes to return to the regiment soon." He looks to Scout Robinson and says, "Scout."

Scout Robinson steps forward and says, "Many Boomers, cross border, I Troop, arrest intruders, Cimarron River." He looks to Sergeant Jordan then says, "Sergeant."

"Gentlemen, there are reports that William Couch has taken over since their leader Captain Payne died last year. They have boasted...no nigger this time...will take them back alive. Gentlemen, I want your military best in the field. No matter what is said or done, you will obey the lieutenant's orders to the T—understood!"

"Yes, Sarge," shouts K Troop simultaneously.

"That's it gentlemen, parade ground as soon as you mount up, twenty days' rations," says Sergeant Jordan.

K Troop goes back to saddling up as Trooper Irving looks to his comrades and says, "Here we go again."

Several days later, a bright spring day, as two columns of K Troop, five Indian scouts and several supply wagons, ride and roll along the rolling plains of Indian Territory.

The 9th's guidon flag, K Troop blows in the breeze, when in the distance, the soldiers begin to hear a methodical faint drumbeat—BOOM, BOOM, BOOM—resembling a human heartbeat.

Sergeant Jordan turns and looks to Sergeant Shaw and says, "You hear that comin' from up ahead, Sergeant?"

"Yeah, Indian drum sounds like, never heard that drumbeat before."

The soldiers are looking for the location of the sound as they ride along, and then, in the far distance, they begin to see over one hundred Cheyenne Indians, dressed in colorful ceremonial clothing.

The men are wearing long muslin and leather-fringed shirts. The women are wearing beautiful fringed leather dresses, all decorated on both sides with colorful, bird-like, and Indian hieroglyphic symbols. The Cheyenne are chanting, holding hands, and dancing in a large turning circle around a single denuded tree, staring in the direction they're moving.

As the 9th Cavalry nears, they can see the Cheyenne have a desperate and exasperated look to them. Some are pulled along because of sheer exhaustion; however, when the soldiers approach the Cheyenne, the drumbeat stops, as does the chanting and dancing. The Cheyenne look to the Buffalo Soldiers with bewilderment, as if in a trance.

The soldiers look to the Cheyenne, as Lieutenant Day looks back to the columns and says, "Scout Robinson."

Scout Robinson spurs his mount to the front of the troop in between Lieutenant Day and Sergeant Jordan.

"Robinson, what kind of ceremony are they performing?"

"Don't know, several tribes, start dancin', beginnin' of year. New spiritual ceremony...don't know meaning."

As the last soldiers ride pass the Cheyenne, the Cheyenne come out of their trance, and stop staring at the soldiers riding away. The Cheyenne look to each other as the drumbeat begins, resuming their ritual, as if the soldiers were never there.

Trooper Chase looks to Sergeant Jordan ahead of him and says, "Sarge, permission to sing."

"Yes trooper, go ahead," says Sergeant Jordan.

Trooper Chase begins singing "Amazing Grace" in the background as Trooper Irving looks to Trooper Walley, then back to the Indians dancing and says, "Walley, did you see how those Indians were lookin' at us...like we're—"

"We're ghosts," says Trooper Walley.

"Yeah, kinda," says Trooper Irving.

K Troop is about a half a mile from the Cheyenne, riding along with Trooper Irving still looking back to the dancers in the distance.

Trooper Walley is looking around the territory, then looks to Trooper Irving and says, "Lee, over ten years ago about this time, I came through this territory. There were bison as far as you could see—and now...not a one."

Trooper Irving says, "Chase said the other day, buffalo hunters killed off most the herds, couple years ago, ain't that true Chase?"

Trooper Chase stops singing and looks back to Trooper Irving and says, "Yeah, there was an article in the newspaper. Said Buffalo Bill Cody and other hunters, killed off the buffalo, trying to keep the renegades from leaving the reservations."

Trooper Chase goes back to singing "Amazing Grace" as Trooper Walley looks out to the territory and says, "It's a shame; that's a beautiful animal."

Several days later, in the afternoon in Indian Territory, K Troop rides along a trail, through a grove of trees, when they come upon an old type-set poster with weathered edges, nailed to a tree.

Lieutenant Day holds his hand in the air and calls his orders, softly, "Troop, *hooo*."

The columns come to a stop as Lieutenant Day, Sergeants Jordan, Shaw, and the front of the columns look to the poster titled:

"Oklahoma and Busted"
"…We had teams and wagons and plenty to eat,
We're loaded with flour and canned goods and meat,
And a jolly lot of good fellows together;
The only drawback, General Pope and the weather.
We found, when we struck the promised land,
The soil neither good nor the climate bland;
But worse than rain or cold or sleet,
Was the cavalry force we had to meet;
And as if to add to cold and grief and shame,
We fellows who went under Captain Payne,
Had to surrender to a troop of "niggers."
Without once daring to pull our triggers."

After reading the poster, Lieutenant Day calls his orders, "Forward, *hooo*."

K Troop spurs their mounts on, with each trooper looking to the poster as they ride by the tattered paper.

The next day, numerous wagons dot the landscape, with several cooking and debris fires burning along the Cimarron River, as two hundred Boomers—men and women—go about building their halfway-completed town. Women are washing clothes. Men are chopping trees, building the town, and plowing the land as children go about playing.

Scout Robinson is mounted, and looking through a grove of trees at the Boomers as Sergeant Jordan says softly, "Sir, that's the most I've ever seen."

Sergeant Shaw says softly, "There only use to be, maybe...up to fifty or so...never this many."

Lieutenant Day and Corporal Wilson are also looking through the trees, with K Troop mounted several yards behind them, as Scout Robinson looks at Lieutenant Day and says softly, "Been here a while, well hidden...in trees...smoke give them away."

Lieutenant Day looks to Scout Robinson and says softly, "Good scouting, Robinson," then he looks to Sergeant Jordan and says, "Sergeant, I want ten of your best men to accompany you, I, Sergeant Shaw, Corporal Wilson and Scout Robinson across the river to their encampment. Spread the rest of the troop along the tree line here"—Lieutenant Day points to the tree line—"and to their left flank, keeping out of sight. We will proceed across the river to their encampment. There, you'll give a signal on my command for the rest of the troop to come up to their side of the river, with carbines drawn at the ready. This will give us a show of force, and a good disbursement along their perimeter, in case of any trouble."

"Yes, sir," says Sergeant Jordan softly as he looks to Corporal Wilson next to him and softly says, "Corporal Wilson, you heard the orders, give me a ten-man detail. Tell Corporals Scott and Dorch that they will remain with the unit once we cross the river, I'll raise my hat in the air—that will be the signal to come forward with carbines at the ready."

"Yes, Sarge."

Corporal Wilson slowly turns his mount and rides back to the troop, as Lieutenant Day looks to his group and says, "Once we reach their encampment gentlemen, I will order the work halted. Sergeant Jordan, when I say the word, halted, that's when you will give the signal for the troop to move up."

"Yes, sir."

Corporal Wilson rides back with Troopers Chase, Irving, Walley, two other troopers, and five Seminole Indian scouts.

Lieutenant Day draws his carbine, as does Sergeants Jordan and Shaw, and the rest of K Troop.

Several Boomers' dogs begin barking from across the river at the trees where the Buffalo Soldiers are hiding. This alerts the Boomers to the presence of something or someone there, causing some Boomers to grab their weapons.

Lieutenant Day looks to his men and says, "Ready gentlemen."

Sergeants Jordan and Shaw, Corporal Wilson, and Scout Robinson nod their heads yes, as Lieutenant Day calls his orders: "Let's go."

Lieutenant Day spurs his mount forward as Sergeants Jordan and Shaw, Corporal Wilson, Scout Robinson and the ten-soldier detail follow. The rest of K Troop disburses to their positions in the trees, keeping out of sight.

Lieutenant Day rides past the trees into the open with Sergeant Jordan to his right and Sergeant Shaw to his left. Scout Robinson and Corporal Wilson divide to both sides, forming a V shape, and the ten-man detail fills in the rears, carbines at the ready.

Lieutenant Day and the detail kick up splashes of water as they gallop across the river. The Boomers, who weren't looking towards the barking dogs, are now grabbing their weapons, looking to the soldiers crossing the river to confront them.

All the Boomers have stopped working as the women gather their children quickly when Lieutenant Day and the detail reach the riverbank on the Boomers' side.

The Boomers' dogs are going really crazy, barking at the soldiers' mounts, as the soldiers ride side-by-side, entering the Boomers' encampment.

Lieutenant Day calls his orders, "Troop...ho."

The detachment of soldiers comes to a stop, with the dogs still barking and now trying to nip the hoofs of the soldiers' mounts, as Lieutenant Day yells to the Boomers, "Quiet these dogs and call them back. Who's in charge?"

William L. Couch, a tall thin man, in his late forties, with a salt-and-pepper beard and hair, whistles to the barking dogs, calling them back. Some Boomers are tying them to trees. As Couch steps forward with an ax in hand, he looks to Lieutenant Day and says, "I am...who be you, soldier boy?"

"I'm Lieutenant Matthias H. Day, 9th Regiment, K Troop, U.S. Cavalry. You are trespassing on Indian Territory. You must pack up your belongings and go back to the Kansas border."

"Well Lieutenant, my name is William L. Couch. And who's goin' to make us pack up our belongings—soldier boy! You and your little...half-breed Injuns, and nigger soldiers?" Couch laughs, as do most the Boomers. Lieutenant Day, with a serious look to Couch, says, "Sir, I'm ordering all work halted!" Sergeant Jordan takes off his campaign hat and raises it in the air.

Across the river, the bushes begin to shake and the ground begins to rumble, as K Troop gallops through the trees and into the open. K Troop is majestic splashing through the river and riding onto the riverbank, coming to a stop in front of the Boomers' encampment. They surround the Boomers' perimeter along the river, with their carbines at the ready, as the Boomers' dogs really go crazy.

Lieutenant Day looks to the Boomers and shouts, "Drop your weapons, back away from them, and pack up your belongings!"

The Boomers that picked up weapons begin lying them down, some hesitantly, as they look at the soldiers, then begin backing away—even though the Boomer men outnumber the soldiers, three to one. Some of the Boomers that laid their weapons down just stand there and look to the soldiers with contempt.

Lieutenant Day sees resistance on their faces as he calls to Sergeant Jordan, "Sergeant Jordan, take the detail and start helping these nice people pack up their belongings."

"Yes, sir, detail, dismount...and help these nice people pack up their belongings."

Sergeant Jordan, Corporal Wilson, Troopers Chase, Irving and Walley, two other troopers, Scout Robinson, and the five Seminole scouts, holster their carbines, and dismount with two troopers holding their reins. The soldiers begin gathering the Boomers' equipment, tools and supplies, loading them in wagons, as the Boomers stand around, watching the soldiers going about their task.

Trooper Irving, who has already gathered some tools in one hand, stoops down to pick up a shovel lying on the ground with his other hand. As he grabs onto the end of the shovel, a large boot steps on the handle in the middle, painfully pinning Trooper Irving's hand against the ground. This causes Trooper Irving to drop the other tools he's collected in his other hand, grabbing the handle and crying out, "Sarge!"

Everyone looks to Trooper Irving in pain, as a big and tall, really ugly Boomer looks down at him and puts more of his weight on the handle, which prevents Trooper Irving from picking it up or regaining his hand.

All the Boomers begin chuckling and laughing as Couch looks to Trooper Irving and says, "You see nigger, Mr. Thompson there, he don't like nobody touchin' his tools—especially a nigger."

All the Boomers are really laughing now as Boomer Thompson just stands there with a big grin on his face, while Trooper Irving tries to dislodge his hand.

The Buffalo Soldiers' faces begin to show tension as their mounts start moving nervously, but still under the control of their masters.

All the Boomers begin laughing at Trooper Irving, pointing their fingers at him, having a good time of it, as Lieutenant Day looks to Couch and angrily says, "Mr. Couch, order your man to back away from the trooper!"

"Now why should I do that for, soldier boy! I told you, Thompson there, just don't like nobody touchin' his tools—especially niggers!"

Lieutenant Day looks to Trooper Irving, then nods his head to Sergeant Shaw, who is mounted next to him.

Sergeant Shaw looks to Trooper Irving and says, "Trooper Irving, free yourself!"

Trooper Irving, with his pinned hand, wraps his fingers

around the handle, then grabs the shovel with his free hand, stands, pries the shovel off the ground, knocking big Boomer Thompson off balance, and backwards several yards. As Boomer Thompson regains his balance, he charges towards Trooper Irving like a wild bull, tackling him to the ground hard.

At this point, Couch swings at Sergeant Jordan, who ducks, then raises back up, coldcocks Couch on the jaw, sending him back like a giant pine tree falling to the ground, out cold.

A midget Boomer then jumps on Sergeant Jordan's back, somewhat comically, causing Sergeant Jordan to spin around, trying to throw the Boomer off, as he shouts, "Get this son of a bitch off my back!"

Trooper Chase runs to Sergeant Jordan's aid, grabbing the Boomer from behind by his britches, and pulling the Boomer off, tearing Sergeant Jordan's shirt.

An all-out fistfight ensues as Boomers either begin swinging at or tackling the soldiers that are on foot, causing the soldiers to defend themselves. Sergeant Jordan is tackled and Trooper Chase is swung at, and the Boomers who are not involved begin cheering on their comrades who are fighting the soldiers.

The mounted Buffalo Soldiers, see the Boomers cheering, then begin cheering for their comrades, still keeping one eye on the Boomers. The soldiers on the ground are holding there own as tables, benches, tents, and anything else in the path of the brawl, are being destroyed. The soldiers begin to gain the upper hand as some of the cheering Boomers begin moving towards their weapons when Lieutenant Day yells to the Boomers, "Halt where you are, stay away from those weapons gentlemen!"

The Boomers slow their pace, but still inch their way to towards their weapons as Lieutenant Day calls his orders,

"K Troop, take aim, cock your weapons!"

The soldiers, mounted, smartly aim their carbines at the Boomers moving towards their weapons, cocking their hammers back—CLANK, CLICK, CLANK. The Boomers—hearing the hammers cock—stop in their tracks as the soldiers fighting the Boomers have subdued most of them, except for a few, who still put up a fight.

Sergeant Jordan is tying Couch's hands together as he lies on the ground dazed.

Trooper Irving, with a few scratches on his face, has gagged and tied Thompson's hands and feet together well enough as if he is ready to be shipped off to market. Thompson has a bloody nose, the beginning of a black eye, and he is still struggling, as Trooper Irving massages his soar hand.

Several Boomers whom Lieutenant Day had told to stop moving towards their weapons begin inching their way towards their rifles again, stopping within arm's reach of them. Lieutenant Day looks at them somewhat nervously, but seriously, and yells to the Boomers, "I meant what I said, back away from those weapons gentlemen, or I'll order my men to fire upon you!"

The Boomers begin to reach for their rifles as Lieutenant Day panics. He yells his orders, "Troop fire!"

The soldiers don't fire. All the Boomers stop in their tracks as one begins to wet his pants.

Sergeant's Jordan and Shaw, with urgency written on their faces, look to Lieutenant Day, then to their men as some of the mounted troopers look at Sergeant's Jordan and Shaw, and Lieutenant Day with skepticism. Other mounted troopers are keeping a carbine sight on the Boomers that were reaching for their rifles.

Lieutenant Day regains his senses, spurs his mount in front of the mounted soldiers, holds his hands high in the air and yells, "Halt! Halt! Don't fire! Don't fire!"

All the Boomers look to the soldiers, still aiming their carbines at the Boomers that were reaching for their weapons. The soldiers aiming their weapons slowly begin bringing their carbines back to the ready as most of the Boomer women and children cower.

All the Boomers have realized just how close they and their comrades came to being shot by U. S. Cavalry troops. Some of the Boomer women run towards their men who attacked the soldiers as the soldiers begin tying their hands together.

Sergeant Jordan looks to Lieutenant Day, who is still looking a little shaky, then he looks and points to the Boomer women running towards their men as he shouts to the Seminole scouts, "Scouts, stop those women!"

Scout Robinson and the five scouts run and block the women—holding their arms out, preventing them from passing.

Lieutenant Day, a little shaky still, rides back to Sergeant Shaw, stops his mount, turns, then looks to Sergeant Jordan, who is finishing tying Couch's hands, and says, "Sergeant, collect their weapons, finish securing the prisoners, pack up their belongings, load the intruders in their wagons, take a head count..." Then he looks at the log buildings and says, "Torch these structures!"

"Yes, sir," says Sergeant Jordan as he looks at his men and says, "Corporal Dorch, dismount your men, collect weapons, pack up these people's stuff. Corporal Wilson, take a head count, secure the prisoners in the wagons. Corporal Scott—burn 'em down!"

The soldiers dismount and go about their tasks.

Boomer Thompson is still struggling, and trying to talk through his gagged mouth, as Trooper Irving and Scout Robinson grab him by the arms, and pull him

192

along—dragging his feet towards the wagons.

The Boomers that didn't attack the soldiers, slowly begin helping the soldiers pack up their belongings. Meanwhile, the soldiers mounted keep watch.

Some of the soldiers have minor scratches on their faces. Their uniforms are dirty and torn, compared to some of the Boomers, who have badly torn clothes, bloody noses, and blackened eyes.

Sergeant Jordan and his men are walking their prisoners by the arm, some reluctantly, towards the prisoner wagon.

As Sergeant Jordan reaches the prisoner wagon with Couch, Couch stops short, and shouts, "I'm not goin' anywhere, nigger!"

Sergeant Jordan, still holding Couch's arm, says to him with an attitude, "Boy, don't let me put another hurtin' on ya."

Lieutenant Day looks at Couch with a disgusted look, then looks at Sergeant Jordan and pointedly says, "Sergeant, gag that man, and if any person refuses to climb in the wagons, tie them to the rear. They either can walk or be dragged all the way to Fort Smith!"

"Yes, sir," says Sergeant Jordan smartly as he looks to another trooper close by and says, "Trooper, hold this prisoner."

The trooper hurries over to Sergeant Jordan, grabs Couch's arms as Sergeant Jordan takes off his paisley as Couch says, "Go to hell nigger, I'm not goin' no…!" Sergeant Jordan has gagged Couch's mouth, as he still tries to resist.

Trooper Walley, standing in back of the prisoners' designated open wagon, whistles to Sergeant Jordan and throws one end of a rope to him as Trooper Walley ties his end of the rope to the prisoner's wagon. Sergeant Jordan, with help from the trooper, ties Couch's hands to the rope. Couch struggles.

Fires begin to burn in the Boomers' town as Corporal Scott and his men set the town ablaze.

Trooper Irving, Scout Robinson, and another trooper lift a hog-tied, struggling Boomer Thompson onto the wagon with help from the troopers onboard.

Smoke wafts in the air as Lieutenant Day and Sergeant Shaw watch their men load the rest of the prisoners and Boomers into their wagons, who watch their town burn down.

A week later at Fort Sill. It's another beautiful spring day. Lieutenant Day, Sergeants Jordan and Shaw, Corporal Wilson, and the rest of K Troop ride across the imaginary boundary of the garrison. Dusty and dirty, wearing their same torn uniforms, they are in high spirits.

Garrison soldiers and several laundresses go about their tasks as Major Henry stands several yards in front of the Command Office, watching K Troop ride towards the stables.

Major Henry cups his hands over his mouth and shouts, "Lieutenant Day, before you go to the stables, come to the Command Office, bring Sergeant Jordan and Sergeant Shaw."

"Yes, sir," says Lieutenant Day.

Major Henry turns and walks back to the Command Office as Lieutenant Day looks at Sergeants Jordan and Shaw, saying, "Sergeants, accompany me to the Command Office." Then he looks back to K Troop and says, "Corporal Wilson, Scout Robinson, take the troop to the stables."

"Yes, sir," says Corporal Wilson and Scout Robinson simultaneously.

Lieutenant Day, Sergeants Jordan and Shaw then spur their mounts out of formation towards the Command Office, as K Troop rides towards the stables.

Moments later, Lieutenant Day, Sergeants Jordan and Shaw walk pass the sentry as Lieutenant Day knocks on the doorjamb and Major Henry says from within, "Enter." Lieutenant Day, Sergeants Jordan and Shaw walk through the door opening into the Command Office.

They stop several feet inside at attention, then salute.
Major Henry and Colonel Hatch are standing several feet in front of them with the adjutant sitting at his desk as Colonel Hatch says, at-ease.

Sergeant Jordan is standing to Lieutenant Day's left, and Sergeant Shaw is standing to his right as all three move from attention to at-ease when Sergeant Shaw looks at Colonel Hatch with surprise and says, "Sir, are you back with the regiment from marksmanship instruction?"

"No Sergeant Shaw, I'm still instructing. I'm just here on official business."

Major Henry looks at Sergeant Jordan, to his dirty and torn uniform, then he looks at Sergeant Shaw, then to Lieutenant Day and says, "Lieutenant, I see by the looks of your men, you had some difficulties."

"Uh, yes, sir. We found two hundred and nine intruders settling on the north side of the Cimarron River."

"That's the most we've ever seen," says Colonel Hatch.

"That's what Sergeants Jordan and Shaw said, sir," says Lieutenant Day.

"Continue Lieutenant," says Colonel Hatch.

"Sir, expecting trouble, I took fifteen men to their encampment, dispersing the other men along their perimeter, out of sight. Once we reached their encampment, we realized that some of the intruders were armed. I ordered all work halted. The intruders began laughing. I then determined the intruders were not going to cooperate, therefore, I had Sergeant Jordan signal for the rest of K Troop to come forward, to show a sign of force. Once K Troop was in position, I ordered the intruders to drop their weapons, then I ordered Sergeant Jordan and his men to dismount and pack up their belongings...when the intruders started using profanity, and several attacked the men, including Sergeant Jordan..." Lieutenant Day becomes a little nervous as he then says, "...causing the men to defend themselves...when—"

"When we finally got the upper hand sir," says Sergeant Jordan interrupting.

Lieutenant Day is caught off guard by Sergeant Jordan's interruption as everyone looks at Sergeant Jordan with surprise. Lieutenant Day also looks to Sergeant Jordan, who winks at him, then looks back to the officers and continues with his report as he says, "...Uh...uh...yes, thank you Sergeant." Lieutenant Day becomes confident again as he says, "The men subdued the attackers and we arrested them. One had to be bound and put in the wagon and another refused to cooperate, therefore, I had him gagged and leashed to the wagon forcing him to walk. I ordered their structures torched, and then we took them to Fort Smith..." Lieutenant Day becomes disgusted as he says, "...where they were fined, given their guns back, and freed."

"Very thorough report Lieutenant, and I'm sorry for your frustrations in trying to carry out your duties," says Colonel Hatch.

"Thank you, sir. I'll have a full written report on the major's desk by first light tomorrow, sir."

"Very well Lieutenant," says Colonel Hatch as he looks

at the sergeants and says, "Sergeants, I believe Major Henry has some good news for the regiment."

Sergeants Jordan and Shaw look to Major Henry with expectation, as he walks to his desk and retrieves a military envelope.

He then pulls a letter from the envelope, looks at the sergeants as he smiles and walks back to the group looking to them saying, "Well gentlemen, the Army has finally recognized the true reward the regiment well deserves. Gentlemen, the Ninth's Regimental Headquarters is transferring to Fort McKinney, Nebraska Frontier."

Sergeants Jordan and Shaw are surprised by the news, as Sergeant Shaw, elated, looks at the officers and says, "That's wonderful news, sirs."

Sergeant Jordan, with a happy look, turns and looks to Sergeant Shaw and says, "Wait till the men hear this."

Colonel Hatch somewhat disappointedly, says, "I'm sorry I'm not joining you gentlemen."

Sergeants Jordan and Shaw look to Colonel Hatch with concern as Sergeant Jordan says, "Sir, when will you finish your assignment at the Department of the Missouri?"

"Couple more years, Sergeant. Something else Major Henry didn't tell you...with the Ninth's transfer, I'll be transferring to the Department of the Platte to continue marksmanship instruction."

"Sir, seems like after you improved the regiment's marksmanship, the Army snatched you up faster than you can wink your eye," says Sergeant Shaw.

"Yes they did Sergeant. Hopefully I'll be back with the regiment in another two years or so."

"We look for your return, sir," says Sergeant Jordan.

Sergeant Shaw says, "Sir, when are we due to transfer?"

"One month, Sergeant," says Colonel Hatch.

One month later at Fort Sill. It's early morning, pouring down rain, as lightning flashes across the sky, and the loud crack of thunder is heard.

The regiment is mounted, with 169 soldiers, all wearing their yellow-lined, blue overcoats, preparing to leave for their new garrison as water drips from their trail hats.

Guidons identify each troop—K is first, followed by I, D, and F—as they are lined up in formation, by a column of twos in back of the American flag.

The 24th Infantry guidon is mounted on the first of ten supply wagons, which are dispersed throughout the columns, with the teamsters making last-minute preparations on their wagons for the trail. Major Henry, Sergeants Jordan and Shaw, Corporal Wilson, Troopers Chase, Irving, Walley, Corporals Dorch and Scott, and the adjutant are in place with their comrades.

Scout Robinson is talking to Sergeants Jordan and Shaw in the background as Major Henry looks to Lieutenant Day and says, "Lieutenant...it's been a pleasure."

"Yes it has, sir. Sir, it's a lousy day for traveling. You don't want to wait till it clears?"

"No Lieutenant, we have to be there in nine days." Major Henry looks to the sky as rain hits him in the face and says, "This storm has already delayed us a week."

"Yes, sir. At least your wife and son are back in Washington by now, where it's more comfortable and dry, sir," says Lieutenant Day.

"Yeah, I miss my wife and son already, Lieutenant. Hopefully they'll join me in several months..."

Major Henry looks back at the sky then says, "Well, we better get on the trail before we get waterlogged sitting here."

Major Henry looks to the regiment as Lieutenant Day looks to Sergeant Jordan and Sergeant Shaw, saying, "Sergeants, it's also been a true pleasure..." Then he looks to Sergeant Jordan and says, "Sergeant, I'd have you and your men in my ranks any day."

"Thank you, sir."

Sergeant Jordan smiles to Lieutenant Day and salutes as Major Henry looks to the columns, then to the bugler and says, "Bugler, sound forward."

The bugler sounds his call as Major Henry calls his orders, "Forward, *hooo.*"

As Major Henry calls his orders, the Buffalo Soldiers wave and bid a farewell to Scout Robinson and Lieutenant Day, to the other garrison soldiers, and to the laundresses staying out of the rain undercover near the buildings. Sergeant Jordan looks to Scout Robinson and says, "See ya, Robinson."

Scout Robinson salutes Sergeant Jordan and the soldiers as they ride towards the garrison's imaginary boundary and into the rain-soaked territory with Lieutenant Day, Scout Robinson and the rest of the garrison watching their departure.

Act III
To the Rescue

Several days later, the rain is subsiding as the long columns of the 9th Cavalry regiment ride over the rolling hills, and along the rain-soaked wooded frontier just east of the Rocky Mountains. In the gray cloudy weather, the raindrops, which adhere to the giant trees and the green foliage, glisten all around them.

The soldiers are at-ease as Trooper Walley pulls the collar of his overcoat tight around his neck, trying to keep the water out. He looks to the sky, then to his comrades and says, "I'm sure glad it stopped rainin'." He shakes the water off his hat then says, "It's been rainin' for three days straight since we left Sill."

"Walley, I don't care if it rained all the way there. After all that hard duty...fifteen-plus years, I'll take this rain any day. Shoot, and with that extra money we just got, we can sit back and enjoy life now, it's gonna make retirement mighty sweet," says Trooper Irving.

They ride on a few more paces as Trooper Chase looks to his comrades and says, "Augustus, Lee...you know that was real nice of Perry leaving his money to us like that."

"Yeah, Chase," says Trooper Walley. "After supper last night, that sure was a real surprise when Sarge gave us that letter he got from Washington D.C. last week—five years after Perry died."

"You know the government Augustus—slow as molasses," says Trooper Chase.

Trooper Irving is thinking to himself, then says, "The will said, one hundred, seventy five dollars. That's a little over a year's pay."

"Irving, I would rather have Perry alive than his money any day. He was a good man, and so was Guy," says Trooper Walley.

"You right about that Augustus," says Trooper Chase.

Trooper Irving and his comrades agree with one another as the rain begins to fall again—hard—and several rifle shots echo in the distance, with BANG! BANG! BANG!

The soldiers look in the direction the shots came from as a very faint methodical drumbeat emanates—the sound surrounds them. Some of the soldiers look at one another to see if their comrades hear what they hear. Others look to the trees, the sky, then for the origin of the sound around them, trying to figure out where the sound is coming from.

Then, a very faint ghostly image of Sioux Indians dressed in colorful ceremonial clothing, dancing in a very large circle around a single denuded tree, appears high above the soldiers in the sky - the phantom image that they cannot see.

Sergeant Jordan looks at Sergeant Shaw and says, "You hear that?"

"Yeah, where is it comin' from? Sounds like it's all around us," says Sergeant Shaw.

"Sounds like that drumbeat we heard back in Indian

Territory, when we were evictin' that last group of intruders," says Sergeant Jordan.

"We don't know where that drumbeat is coming from Sergeant, but we do know the direction those shots came from," says Major Henry as he looks at Sergeant Jordan and says, "Sergeant Jordan, we'll take K Troop to check out the rifle fire."

"Yes, sir."

Sergeant Jordan turns his mount around and gallops back through the columns where the supply wagons begin. When Sergeant Jordan reaches the wagons, he stops his mount, looks at Corporal Jackson who is mounted and says, "Corporal Jackson, we'll take K Troop and check out those shots. Follow our trail. If you hear more gunfire, bring your men and D Troop. Have the Twenty-fourth circle the wagons and await further orders along with F Troop."

"Yes, Sarge, but what about that drumbeat we all hear?"

"No idea, Corporal."

Corporal Jackson nods his head, turning his mount around, and calls Sergeant Jordan's orders as Sergeant Jordan turns his mount back around and gallops to the front of the columns.

As he nears the front, Major Henry looks at him, then calls his orders, "K Troop...at a gallop, ho."

Major Henry, Sergeant Shaw, and K Troop spur their mounts ahead, galloping, as Sergeant Jordan gallops to his position in the column, while the rest of the troops, I, D and F, remain behind, riding on.

Several minutes later, the rain, the drumbeat, and ghostly image continues, as the regiment gallops along an open grassy area. Major Henry sees a man sitting on his

horse holding a Winchester rifle across his lap. Major
Henry points to the man, veering K Troop towards him.

As the columns near the man, Major Henry calls his
orders, "Troop...ho."

The columns come to a stop in front of a white rancher,
in his fifties, wearing a six-shooter and a big rancher's hat.
He looks at the soldiers with surprise, wearing the biggest
smile you've ever seen.

The rancher tilts his hat back, with the rain hitting him
in the face, as he says, "Well howdy soldiers...I'll be fit to
be tied...I've heard of you darkie soldiers before, but I
never thought I would ever see one of ya—much less this
many."

The rancher looks down the line of soldiers as Major
Henry says, "I'm Major Henry, Ninth United States
Cavalry, K Troop. What's your name, sir?"

"Griffin...V. Griffin," he then motions with his hand to
a hill and says, "I own the ranch just over that ridge."

"We heard rifle shots Mr. Griffin," says Major Henry
as he then looks around to the faint drumbeat's location
and says, "And do you know where that drumbeat is
coming from?"

"No, Major, been hearing it now, from time to time, for
about a half a year. Seems to come from all directions."
Then Rancher Griffin points to a grove of trees and says,
"Yeah, just them pesky wolves. I took a couple shots,
missed. They've been attacking my livestock."

"Wolves, you say, Mr. Griffin—one moment, sir."

Rancher Griffin looks to Major Henry, as Major Henry
looks to Sergeant Jordan and says, "Sergeant Jordan...is it
Trooper Chase, who's been using the library, helping the
troops with their reading?"

"Yes, sir. Reads newspaper and books almost every
day since you had the library built, sir."

Major Henry looks to his men and calls out, "Trooper Chase, front and center!"

Trooper Chase is surprised that Major Henry called his name as he looks at his comrades, then spurs his mount forward with his comrades looking at him. Trooper Chase reaches the front of the columns, and brings his mount to a stop in front of Major Henry. He salutes and says, "Yes, sir."

"Trooper Chase," says Major Henry, as he motions with his hand to Rancher Griffin. "This is Mr. Griffin. He's having trouble with wolves attacking his herds. Do you have any information regarding the predator, Trooper?"

"Yes, sir."

"Please tell Mr. Griffin what you know Trooper Chase."

"Yes, sir," says Trooper Chase, as he looks to Rancher Griffin and says, "Sir, the wolves' natural pray, the bison, have almost been wiped out by government-paid hunters with the intent to take away the Indians' food, shelter and tools, keeping them on the reservations. They are probably very hungry, and look to your herds for food. If you put dogs out that might discourage them a little, sir."

Rancher Griffin looks at Trooper Chase, amazed that this colored soldier can speak well, and is knowledgeable. Trooper Chase's comrades also look at him proudly as Major Henry proudly says, "Thank you Trooper Chase, very good report, you can return to the ranks."

"Yes, sir."

Trooper Chase salutes and spurs his mount back to his position in the columns as the rest of the 9th Regiment, D, I, and F Troops, with the 24th Infantry's wagons, come riding and rolling into the clearing. Rancher Griffin is overwhelmed as he looks to the regiment in the distance. He wipes his eyes thinking his vision is blurred by the rain as he looks at Major Henry and says, "Wow, how many of the colored are there, Major?"

"There are four units Mr. Griffin: The Ninth and Tenth Cavalry, the Twenty-fourth and Twenty-fifth Infantry. About one fourth of the western frontier Army is colored, Mr. Griffin." Major Henry then looks to the weather and says, "We should get on our way Mr. Griffin, I hope that information will help you with your problem."

"Why, why I think so, Major, thank you."

"Good day, sir," says Major Henry as he looks to the regiment approaching and says, "Bugler, sound forward."

The bugler sounds his call as K Troop spurs their mounts forward. The rest of the regiment follows. The soldiers look at Rancher Griffin as he looks at them riding past him, then he sees the contingent of wagons approaching, rolling along through the mud, and shouts, "Well if that don't beat all!"

Rancher Griffin watches the soldiers riding off as the drumbeat and ghostly image fade away.

Nine days later, a beautiful blue sky dominates the view as the 9th Cavalry, K, I, D, and F Troops' guidons are fluttering in the breeze as they ride into a very large clearing, looking a little tattered from the trail and weather.

They are in sight of their new garrison, Fort McKinney. It stands in the middle of the clearing and is just like the other garrisons they have been stationed at: there are no walls, fences, or gates. Only a wooded forest is the garrison's perimeter, one mile out. Brick, rock, and wood buildings, with a corral and stables, ring the far half of the garrison's boundary line.

On the opposite side of the garrison, closest to the approaching soldiers, smoke hangs in the air from several Sioux Indian campfires, and from their many lodges and tepees, that dot the outside perimeter of the clearing, forming the outside imaginary boundary line of the garrison.

The soldiers are halfway through the clearing, looking at their new home, when a tall, broad-shouldered man perched atop a jet-black mount gallops out from the corral, towards the soldiers. The rider gallops through the garrison and crosses the imaginary boundary, through the Sioux encampment. Major Henry surveys the rider and then calls his orders, "Troop, *hooo.*"

The two columns halt as the rider approaches. The broad-shouldered rider stops his mount in front of the soldiers, looks at Major Henry, and salutes. "Major Henry?" he says with a deep voice.

"Yes, I'm Major Henry."

"Welcome to Fort McKinney, sir. I have a letter for you," says the broad-shouldered rider in his deep voice. The rider pulls a letter from his coat pocket and hands it to Major Henry. "I'm Frank Grouard, Chief of Scouts and messenger for the northern territory."

Scout Grouard is truly an awesome-looking frontiersman, almost six feet tall. He is thirty-five years old, reportedly a colored and Sioux Indian half-breed with jet-black curly hair and a well-trimmed bushy mustache. He speaks good English, wears fringe buckskin clothing, a frontier hat with an Indian Scout Cross Arrows insignia pinned on top, a six-shooter, and buck knife.

Major Henry looks to the letter, elated, and says, "Ah, my beautiful wife."

Major Henry unbuttons his shirt, puts the letter inside, re-buttons his shirt, then looks to Scout Grouard and says, "Thank you—oh, I'm sorry," says Major Henry as he motions with his hand and says, "This is Sergeant Jordan and Sergeant Shaw."

"It's a pleasure," says Sergeant Jordan.

"Same here," says Sergeant Shaw.

"Welcome," says Scout Grouard as he looks to Major Henry and says, "May I accompany you to the garrison, sir?"

Major Henry smiles and says, "Yes Grouard, please do."

Scout Grouard spurs his mount around to the outside of Major Henry, as Major Henry looks at the bugler and says, "Bugler, sound forward."

The bugler sounds his call as the regiment spurs their mounts at a walk towards the garrison.

Major Henry, Sergeants Jordan and Shaw look to Scout Grouard as Major Henry says, "So Grouard, I haven't been in Lakota Sioux Territory in a while, tell me about the territory, and yourself, I don't put much faith in all that government material I get, and things I hear—never quite hear or read it right. Nothing like getting it from the person that knows."

Scout Grouard is a little taken aback by Major Henry's straight forwardness as he says, "Well, sir...Sioux are quiet, some livin' on the reservation," he points to the village and says, "Some are here. Sitting Bull tourin' with Buffalo Bill Cody in Wild West Show, other than that, it's quiet."

"What about yourself Grouard," says Major Henry.

"As I said, I'm Chief of Scouts and messenger."

"No, no—like, where you from? How much experience have you had? I like knowing about my men, Grouard."

"Yes, sir...I believe I was born in Texas...worked as a teamster from Montana to California and back a couple of times...rode for the Pony Express for a spell."

"Speak any Indian languages, Grouard?"

"Yeah, lived with Sioux for a bit..."

As the soldiers approach the Sioux village, they begin to ride into a light haze, which hangs in the air from the smoke.

When the soldiers enter the village, they see very few ponies, and watch Sioux men and women try to use tools made from wood and other items, which just don't work like the bone of the bison. Some women stir soup in big black iron pots suspended over open fires as children run and play around an old broken dilapidated plow that lays on its side among the weeds in a patch of farmland.

Most of the Sioux Indians' expressions are somewhat despondent or sickly, but the looks on their faces change, and show amazement, when they look to the colored soldiers. They begin staring at them and murmuring to one another, with the murmuring spreading throughout their village.

Some of the Sioux come out of their lodges and tepees, looking to the soldiers as Scout Grouard says, "They are curious about the soldiers, Major. They have not seen dark-skinned bluecoats before. I told them, you were comin', so they wouldn't be scared—some say, they heard of the 'dark-skin bluecoats,' that fight like buffalo when cornered."

Major Henry smiles, looks to both sergeants, and says, "I guess your fame precedes you." He then turns back to Scout Grouard and says, "Well, not only are they good fighting soldiers, Grouard, they're good soldiers period. Everything you heard, regarding their bravery and gallantry, is true."

The soldiers ride a few more paces as Scout Grouard looks to Major Henry and says, "Sir...there's a reason I rode out to meet you."

"Yes Grouard, what's the reason?"

"Sir, if we can stop here, you, I and the sergeants, sir—we can talk."

Major Henry looks at Scout Grouard, and sees the seriousness written on his face, as he turns and calls his orders, "Troop, *hooo*."

The soldiers and wagons come to a stop as Major Henry looks around, then looks at Sergeants Jordan and Shaw, saying, "Sergeants, have the other sergeants and corporals get the men settled in their new home, then meet me and Scout Grouard—" Major Henry looks around again, then points to a tree. "...Over there by that tree on the knoll."

Sergeants Jordan and Shaw say simultaneously, "Yes, sir."

Major Henry then looks to Scout Grouard and says, "Follow me, Grouard."

Sergeants Jordan and Shaw salute, then look to Major Henry and Scout Grouard spurring their mounts towards the tree as Sergeant Jordan turns and looks to Sergeant Shaw and says, "I'll get the men. You get the wagons?"

"Sure thin'."

Sergeant Shaw turns and gallops his mount back to the wagons, calling his orders as Sergeant Jordan turns his mount around and spurs his mount back along the columns calling his orders, saying, "All sergeants and corporals...take your men to the garrison, take care of your mounts, find your barracks, get settled in...let's get at it."

The Sioux look at the soldiers and the wagons as they begin moving across the garrison's imaginary boundary in organized chaos as both sergeants spur their mounts to where Major Henry and Scout Grouard sit on their mounts.

Moments later, Sergeants Jordan and Shaw arrive at the knoll, where Major Henry and Scout Grouard are talking, facing the Sioux village. Scout Grouard is saying, "...You see Sioux, they're lost people, have no place to go, no hope..."

Then the faint methodical drumbeat begins again and at the same time the ghostly image reappears high above them. Sergeant Jordan looks at Major Henry and then at Sergeant Shaw while looking for the origin of the sound as he says, "There it goes again."

Major Henry looks to Scout Grouard and says, "Grouard, you've been hearing that drumbeat?"

"Just recently, sir, six moons ago."

They look around the area, at each other, then at the Sioux village.

The Sioux are oblivious to the drumbeat as some Sioux stare to the soldiers in the garrison going about their duties, and then they look at the soldiers on the knoll, as the others, just stare into oblivion.

Scout Grouard looks at Major Henry, then to the sergeants and says, "These Sioux, out of place in these surroundings. Indian agents cheat them every month of government rations...get only enough for half-month. If they are to live like white men, the Indians must have tools, livestock, wagons, like white man...or they leave reservation."

"I know, Grouard," says Major Henry. "We had the same problem in New Mexico. Indian agents selling off Indian cattle and rations for profit." Major Henry looks around then at Scout Grouard and says, "The last time I was in this territory Grouard, the Sioux were proud people, the great overlords of this land..." He turns and looks to the Sioux encampment and says, "But now, look at them—they're disarmed, dismounted; their culture as they knew it—has disappeared."

Major Henry looks back at Scout Grouard, as the drumbeat and ghostly image fade away. Everyone looks around for the sound's source as Major Henry says, "The sound stopped."

"Yeah," says Sergeant Jordan, as Major Henry looks to Scout Grouard and says, "Grouard, there's not much we can do at this point, except keep the peace. I'll inform Colonel Hatch of what you've told me. He's a friend who's heard this story many times, and he tries to put pressure on Washington to get rid of those scoundrel agents."

Sergeant Shaw looks at Major Henry and says, "Sir, if they don't do somethin' quick, these people...are gonna die off."

"I know, Sergeant, we can only do what we can do as soldiers."

"Yes, sir," says Sergeant Shaw.

Then Major Henry looks at Scout Grouard and says, "Grouard, Colonel Hatch said General Crook wouldn't trade you for a third of his men."

"General Crook is a good man, like Colonel Hatch I hear—" With a surprised look, Scout Grouard says, "Then you already know about me."

"Yes Grouard," says Major Henry, "Like I said, I like to hear it straight from the people who know."

Four years later at Fort McKinney there are fewer lodges and tepees surrounding the boundary of the garrison. Local townspeople, laundresses, and miners are dressed in their Sunday best, standing on the perimeter of the parade ground, facing the garrison flagpole in the middle. The parade ground is virtually full with the 9th Cavalry Regiment, the 10th Cavalry, the 24th and 25th Infantry, and other regiments, all represented by their regiments' flags, standing at parade-rest in formation.

Over eight hundred soldiers, officers, and enlisted men are wearing their dress uniforms. All of K Troop is present, looking a little bit older, including the 9th Cavalry Band standing in the front rows of soldiers. They are listening to the colored chaplain, Captain Henry Vinton Plummer, speaking in front of the garrison flagpole. Chaplain Plummer is forty years old, born a slave, tall, slender and wears a full beard. With help from Frederick Douglas, he went to West Point and graduated.

Chaplain Plummer is delivering the final words of his memorial sermon, saying, "...and on this day, twenty-second, April, eighteen eighty-nine, with this memorial service, we say good-bye to our beloved departed Colonel, Edward Hatch...Amen."

The bugler begins playing "Taps" with a little bit of rhythm, as Sergeant Jordan, standing next to Major Henry, calls his orders: "Ninth Cavalry regiment, and all regiments...Attention!"

The soldiers snap to attention with military precision as Sergeant Jordan then says, "Salute!"

All the soldiers salute and the civilians put their right hand over their hearts, facing the American flag, which is flying in the breeze. As "Taps" concludes, Sergeant Jordan and Major Henry drop their salute, as does the entire garrison.

Sergeant Jordan and Major Henry make an about-face, as Sergeant Jordan looks at the soldiers and says, "At-ease."

All the troops move from attention to at-ease as Sergeant Jordan then says, "Gentlemen, Major Henry has given the Ninth Cavalry—except sentries—the day off in memory of Colonel Hatch. Dismissed."

Upon hearing the word "dismissed," some soldiers hold their heads low. Other soldiers and the civilian mourners begin dispersing, with K Troop gathering around Major Henry. Walking up to Major Henry is Sergeants Jordan and Shaw, Corporal Wilson, Troopers Chase, Irving and Walley, along with Lieutenant Day. Walking up behind them is Sergeant Major Brown, Corporals Dorch, Scott, and Jackson, followed by Scout Grouard, lighting a cigar.

Sergeant Jordan is a true soldier, however briefly he's finding it a little difficult to handle the death of his beloved colonel as he looks to Major Henry and says, "It's...a shame, sir...the colonel, like yourself...was a good man, very few and hard to come by, sir."

"Thank you, Sergeant...and yes he was a good man."

"Hey Sarge, tell us how the colonel died again," says Trooper Walley.

"He was racin' a wagon...horse playin' around I believe, it turned over on top of him and dragged him a ways...then he died a month later."

Major Henry looks to Trooper Walley and says, "He probably died from bleeding internally Trooper, from the wagon falling on him."

Chaplain Plummer finishes talking with some other soldiers, then walks towards K Troop, and as he approaches, Major Henry looks to him and says, "Very good sermon Chaplain Plummer."

"Thank you Major, thank you."

Chaplain Plummer then turns to the soldiers and says, "He was a great man, it's too bad the Army never gave him the recognition he well deserved."

"Chaplain Plummer, please make sure he gets a good headstone," says Sergeant Shaw.

"The very best there is, Sergeant."

The garrison adjutant pushes through the circle of soldiers and hands Major Henry a telegraph message. Major Henry unfolds the message, reads it, then looks to his men and says, "Gentlemen, this telegraph's from the Department...Indian land in Oklahoma Territory...just opened up for settlement. The Twenty-fifth Infantry is controlling the stampede of settlers."

214

Everyone looks at one another pondering whether this is good news or bad news. Trooper Walley looks at his comrades with a bit of excitement and says, "You hear that, Indian lands opened up—no more fightin'."

"Yeah, now we can sit back until we retire," says Trooper Irving.

"I don't know about all that sittin' back Lee. We had it easy for a couple of years now—somethin' tells me—the next couple is going to be the calm before the storm," says Trooper Chase.

Scout Grouard looks to the soldiers. "Trooper Chase is right. Look," he says, pointing to the Sioux village. "Very few tepees outside garrison now...they go to reservation, council with medicine men...there's a feelin' among Sioux, some new power...something to do with a religion from the west, no one talks."

"Scout Grouard, I believe I saw the Kiowa perform the ceremony recently, something I've never seen before. I watched them from a distance, singing and dancing in a large circle...for at least four hours...they never once halted their dancing," says Chaplain Plummer.

Sergeant Jordan thinks a moment, then says, "That sounds like the Cheyenne we saw in Oklahoma Territory years back, dancin' in a large circle around a bare tree."

Major Henry looks to his men and says, "Well gentlemen, the last time I looked, dancing and religion is not against the law, and as long as the Sioux stay on the reservations, they're not breaking the law."

Four months later in K Troop barracks, Corporals Wilson, Dorch, Jackson and Scott, Troopers Irving, Walley, and several other soldiers are gathered around listening to

Trooper Chase, sitting on the edge of his bunk, reading the newspaper aloud to his comrades, saying, "Last week, August third, the Great Sioux Nation was broken into small reservations. Sitting Bull, comin' out of the council, was asked by a reporter, 'How do the Indians feel about selling their land.' Sitting Bull shouted to the reporter... 'Indians...there are no more Indians left but me!'"

Trooper Walley walks to the barracks' window and looks out, then shouts with urgency saying, "Hey, come look at this! What's left of the whole Sioux village is packed up and movin' out."

All the soldiers rush to the windows and look out to the last of the Sioux Indians leaving an open space where their large encampment used to be.

Trooper Chase looks to Trooper Irving and says, "So much for rest, Lee."

Moments later, Sergeant Jordan and Scout Grouard are standing outside the barracks, watching the Sioux leave their village, with all of their belongings, walking northeast into the forest. The lucky ones, who have ponies, use them to pull the old and sick along on their travois.

Sergeant Jordan then looks at Scout Grouard and says, "Well, there goes the last of 'em."

"To the reservations, where there is very little food," says Scout Grouard.

"Yeah, yeah Grouard...lets tell Major Henry the last is headin' out."

Moments later, in the Command Office, Sergeant Shaw and the adjutant are sitting at their desks, listening to Sergeant Jordan.

Sergeant Jordan and Scout Grouard are at parade-rest, talking to Major Henry, who is sitting at his desk. "The last of the Sioux have left, sir," says Sergeant Jordan.

"Grouard," says Major Henry, "Has the cut in the telegraph line been found?"

"Not yet, sir. It's hard to see the leather they tie in between the cut wire. It takes time to find, sir."

"Yeah, I know...Grouard, I want you to take this message to Colonel Forsyth at Fort Custer," says Major Henry.

"Yes, sir."

Major Henry begins writing his message on a piece of paper, speaking his words out to himself. "All Sioux have left village adjacent to garrison. Heading northeast...awaiting further instructions from the Department. Have not found cut in telegraph line."

Scout Grouard walks to Major Henry's desk just as he finishes writing the message. Major Henry folds the message, and hands it to Scout Grouard. Scout Grouard looks to Major Henry and says, "Sir, may I stop in Sheridan on the way back for cigars?"

"No problem Grouard, just make sure that message gets to Colonel Forsyth within four days."

"Yes, sir, thank you, sir."

Scout Grouard salutes, makes an about-face, and exits the Command Office as Major Henry looks to both sergeants and says, "This doesn't look good, sergeants."

A week later, Scout Grouard rides through the torch-lit streets of Sheridan, Wyoming. The town is lively with the usual Saturday night revelry of the Wild West. There are no colored folks for hundreds of miles. Several white cowboys walking in the street fire their guns into the air, and the sound of BANG! BANG! BANG! rings out. Other cowboys walking, sitting, or standing on the porches of the town's buildings, stare at Scout Grouard, who is riding by them.

Two cowboys come out of the Sheridan Inn saloon fighting into the streets ahead of Scout Grouard. One tackles the other to the ground as Scout Grouard approaches. He looks at the cowboys tussling in front of him, then he looks at the saloon, where he hears a piano playing, hollering, and whooping coming from inside. He turns his mount towards the direction of the saloon, stops in front of the hitching-rail, dismounts, and ties his mount to the rail.

A few cowboys standing on the porch surrounding the outside of the saloon, wearing unfriendly looks, survey the big man towering above most of them. Scout Grouard is unaffected by the stares as he steps up onto the wood porch, looking at both sides of the saloon, then into the saloon itself, as he walks through the double swinging doors.

The doors shut behind Scout Grouard as he steps into the noisy, smoky, crowded saloon, stopping just a few feet inside. Scout Grouard also towers almost over everyone standing in the saloon, as several patrons near the double swinging doors stop their conversations and stare at Scout Grouard, who's scanning the room. Some cowboys from outside the saloon walk to the swing doors, stop and also gaze at Scout Grouard over the top of the doors.

Inside the saloon, Scout Grouard looks to the bar, where several patrons are conversing with one another. He begins making his way to the bar, passing patrons, as several dance-hall girls give him the, "Hey, big guy" look. Scout Grouard tips his hat to them, expressionless, as he makes his way to the far right side of the bar, stopping and looking at the bartender serving patrons at the other end. Scout Grouard raises his arm and signals the bartender for service. The bartender looks at Scout Grouard and acknowledges him rudely with a fast wave of his arm, then turning back to his patrons.

Scout Grouard then turns, knowing he'll get served one day, and faces the room with Wild West entertainment: piano player, poker games, roulette wheel, and dance-hall girls. He begins to overhear a conversation just to his right.

Scout Grouard turns his head and looks to a shoulder-length, semi-wavy white-haired man wearing an expensive all-white cowboy suit, a white hat and holster, with two pearl-handle guns, one on each side. The man's back is to Scout Grouard as the man says, "...and ya should of seen the buffalo we killed, carcasses as far as ya could see. Couple of days later, it stunk so bad, an Injun Chief—I think they called him Yellow Hand—why he came up to me makin' a fuss about the buffalo, and asked who I was. I told him my name is Buffalo Bill Cody...he then pulled his huntin' knife, pokin' at the hide and meat tryin' to show me somethin'..."

Scout Grouard looks at Buffalo Bill with a hard stare and says, "Then what did you do?"

Unaware who asked the question or how close Scout Grouard is to him, Buffalo Bill begins chuckling, turning towards Scout Grouard saying, "I shot him and scalped..." Buffalo Bill slows and stops talking as he turns into the face of Scout Grouard. Scout Grouard has taken off his cavalry hat so Buffalo Bill is now just about nose-to-nose and toe-to-toe with him. Buffalo Bill is almost frozen in place as the piano player slows and stops playing.

The entire saloon now quiets to a murmur as the bartender shouts from the other end saying, "Hey, take the trouble outside!"

Scout Grouard does not move or take his eyes from Buffalo Bill, as the bartender approaches and Scout

Grouard says, "There's not goin' to be any trouble bartender—unless, Mr. Cody here starts it. Give me a half dozen of your best cigars."

The room burst with murmur over Scout Grouard's statement to the bartender. Still nose-to-nose, Scout Grouard begins talking to Buffalo Bill with a soft, hard, firm-pointed voice, that only Buffalo Bill can hear. No one else can hear over the murmuring and chatter of the room, as he says, "You not so tough...you say you killed buffalo...leave their rotten carcasses to rot in the sun and wind...you think you're tough, you killed Yellow Hand, a good friend of mine, for nothin'! Let's see how tough you are—here and now!"

Scout Grouard means business. He stares right into Buffalo Bill's eyes, daring him to say or do anything. Buffalo Bill, the showman frontiersman he is, knows he's met his match, that he is standing toe-to-toe with a real frontiersman. Buffalo Bill begins to sweat, then he blinks and turns his head as the bartender says, "Here's your cigars Mister, half a bit."

The room goes into a high murmur again, as Scout Grouard, still staring down Buffalo Bill, reaches into his pocket, pulls out one bit without looking, and tosses it onto the bar. Scout Grouard then snubs Buffalo Bill, turns to the bar, and looks to the bartender, then says, "Keep the change." He grabs his hat, puts it on, takes his cigars off the bar, and puts them inside his fringed coat pocket. He looks back to Buffalo Bill, who is still looking away.

Scout Grouard turns and walks out, with the crowd looking at him. Then the crowd turns back to look at Buffalo Bill.

One year later, November 1, 1890. Snow flurries fall over lodges and tepees dotting the partially snow-capped landscape of Porcupine Village, Pine Ridge Indian Reservation. It's cold, and winter is setting in as two hundred Sioux Indians, looking very despondent, with very few tools and weapons, go about their tough task of survival.

A Sioux Indian rides into the village on his pony, wearing a large fur coat, looking at the despondent people. He rides up to a tepee with bird symbols and Indian hieroglyphics painted on the buffalo hide. The Indian stops his pony, then dismounts by bringing his right leg up and over the pony's head, sliding off the back of the animal onto the ground, as a Sioux brave takes his pony. The Sioux Indian stands in front of the tepee and calls out in Sioux language, saying, "Big Foot."

"Short Bull, I've been expecting you...come," says Big Foot, speaking broken English from inside the tepee. Short Bull splits the opening of the tepee with his hand and enters.

Short Bull has a chiseled jaw, a short stocky build, medium lips, long black hair, almond-shaped eyes, and speaks broken English. He walks through the tepee opening, stopping at a small fire burning in a dug-out pit in the center of the tepee floor, with animal hides lining the area around the fire ring. Several Indian bundles line the perimeter of the tepee, with a Winchester rifle, bow and arrow lying on top.

Short Bull then looks to Big Foot, who is in his thirties. He is thin, his eyes are dark, his hair black and long, parted down the middle into two long braids, which are wrapped with leather hide. The braids protrude down the front of his chest on both sides of his neck.

Big Foot doesn't look as despondent as his people, but he coughs as he stands, then walks around the fire and greets Short Bull, saying, "Long time my friend."

"Yes...yes it's been...I bring good news."

"I know—but first, smoke peace pipe," says Big Foot.

Big Foot motions with his hand to the center of the tepee. Short Bull walks to the far side of the fire ring, facing the flap of the tepee, then he crosses his legs and sits down.

Big Foot walks to one of his bundles, coughing several times. He retrieves a pipe and a leather pouch from the bundle, walks to the fire ring, crosses his legs, and sits. He opens the pouch, brings out a pinch of peace herb and puts it in the pipe. He then reaches into the fire pit, brings out a twig on fire and lights the herb in the pipe. After taking his puff, he passes the pipe to Short Bull.

Short Bull takes his puff, exhales, then looks to Big Foot and says, "You, your people, are poor, sickly, starving...I bring good news...hope, from the Paiute Medicine Man Wovoka." He motions with his hand and says, "From where the sun lays, far to the west."

"Yes, I hear, Sitting Bull's people at Standin' Rock look to this medicine man and dance. This what medicine man say do? Tell me what this dance means...Messiah, come?"

Short Bull smiles and says, "Yes, next spring—all things return good."

Big Foot looks to Short Bull with a curious look and says, "Tell me what Medicine Man Wovoka said."

"Wovoka says, make 'sacred hoop' around tree, cut branches...all Indians must dance, everywhere, keep on dancing. Pretty soon next spring, when new green come back, Great Spirit come. He bring back all game of every kind. The game be thick everywhere. All dead Indians come back and live again. They all be strong just like young men, be young again."

"I hear...Sitting Bull don't believe, dead come back alive."

"At first, but now he do believe."

"Tell me more," says Big Foot.

"When Great Spirit comes this way, then all the Indians go to mountains, high up away from whites. Wasichus can't hurt Indians then. Then while Indians way up high, big flood comes like water and all white people die, get drowned. After that, water go away and then nobody but Indians everywhere. Wovoka tell Indians to send word to all Indians to keep up dancing and the good time will come. Indians who don't dance, who don't believe in this word, will grow little. Some of them will be turned into wood and be burned in fire. Wovoka says, you must not hurt anybody or do harm to anyone. You must not fight. Do right always...the Messiah will bring the new earth."

"I hear Indian agents call for soldiers...soldiers come to reservations, to stop the dancing, scare people. What we do?"

"All Indians wear *sacred garments*." Short Bull opens his coat, revealing his shirt, as he says, "Like this, magic symbols...protect...no harm come to us. Not even the bullets of the bluecoats' guns...can go through *Ghost Shirts*."

Several nights later, in the wintry night air, a loud drumbeat emanates from Porcupine Village, sounding like a giant heartbeat as a brilliant huge bonfire rages, highlighting a denuded tree, in the middle of a very large turning circle of Sioux Indians, holding hands, dancing and chanting. Over seven hundred dancing Sioux Indians are dressed in their very colorful hieroglyphic animal-hide clothing. They are wearing no coats, and most are not wearing any headwear.

The dancers have carved a path through the snow-covered ground to bare earth as the heat from the bonfire has virtually melted the snow within the circle. The Sioux are exhausted. They have been dancing all day, non-stop. More men drop in their tracks than women from exhaustion as the women endure the marathon better than the men. Some men and women weep and wail, others laugh with happiness, while others appear to be hallucinating.

Many more Sioux watch, sitting on blankets, while others help their fallen comrades from the circle as the dancers continue chanting their song in Sioux language, "Father, Great Spirit, behold us! Our nation is in despair. The new earth you promised, you have shown us. Let the nation also behold it."

In an office, a wood sign hangs on the wall with the words inscribed, "Pine Ridge Indian Reservation - South Dakota - Indian Agent Office." The calendar hanging on the wall is turned to the date November 10, 1890.

Snow is falling outside the frosty window with a patchy snowy background as a man warms his hands over a wood stove in the middle of the room. This is Indian Agent James McLaughlin. He is forty years old, with salt-and-pepper hair, a thick mustache, and a thin goatee. He is wearing a black Western suit, with a black derby hat, and he is a very crafty man.

Another man walks to the stove with a log to stoke the fire. This is Indian Agent Dr. D.F. Royer. At thirty years old, he is clean cut, wears typical Western clothes, and is inexperienced.

He opens the door of the stove and puts the log inside as Agent McLaughlin says, "The agent before you, Gallagher—he noticed this dancin', and how it was spreadin' like a wild prairie fire."

"Mr. McLaughlin, I've only been here a week. I've noticed, they're not doing any work, children aren't in school and the trading post is empty. I don't understand these...these Indians dancing, instead of doing work...from sunrise, to way past sunset without halting their performance."

"Yes Dr. Royer, their excitement is very intense, they dance until they drop. This daily performance, with very little food, has made them subjects for the madhouse. I've notified Indian Affairs last week of what I've just told you, and I got a telegraph the other day." With disappointment, Agent McLaughlin says, "And for whatever God sake reasons, Indian Affairs is sendin' an agent by the name of...McGillycuddy in three weeks to look into the matter."

Dr. Royer looks at Mr. McLaughlin nervously and says, "Mr. McLaughlin, I heard one of them yesterday, talking to another Sioux Indian, saying they believe their clothes will stop bullets and their dead will return!"

"I heard the same from Sittin' Bull's people. He's our main problem doctor, but once I get rid of him, the rest will be easy, we should be able to quiet 'em."

Five days later, it's a clear cold day, as a drumbeat emanates loudly from Porcupine Village. Sitting atop his horse on a hill, watching from a short distance, is Agent Royer, dressed from head to toe in fur, looking to the Sioux Indians performing their dance, wearing no winter clothing.

The drumbeat continues as Agent Royer spurs his horse forward, down the hill, through the ankle-deep snow, towards the dancers, coming to within feet of them before stopping his horse.

The Sioux dancers and non-dancers alike don't look at

him as he dismounts and grabs a Sioux woman dancer, physically trying to stop her from dancing. He might as well have grabbed a locomotive with his bare hands trying to stop it as she pulls away. He grabs another woman dancer. She pulls away too. He grabs a man dancer and as with the women, he pulls away.

The dancers Agent Royer tries to stop pull away from him with ease as he begins walking along side of them, going from dancer to dancer, yelling at them saying, "You must stop, go back to work, send your children to school, go back to work—"

Agent Royer is interrupted by Big Foot's coughs as he walks up to Agent Royer, stopping in front of him. He looks to Agent Royer and says, "Why you try and stop my people? They are hungry and sick. They dance to bring better days."

"Better days!" Agent Royer says, irately, adding, "You can't bring better days by dancing! Food and medical supplies are coming!"

"You and the White Father...feed us more lies than food...we cannot eat lies!"

Big Foot turns and walks away, leaving Agent Royer with his mouth wide open, still looking at Big Foot. He then looks to the turning circle of Sioux, as the Sioux look forward and skyward, chanting and singing. Some talk to the sky, while others cry and weep aloud...

Agent Royer is back in his office, nervous and shaking, sitting at the telegraph key, transmitting a message he's prepared. The date on the message is, November 15, 1890. It's addressed to "Commissioner of Indian Affairs, T. J. Morgan."

"Indians are dancing in the snow and are wild and crazy. I have fully informed you that employees and government property at this agency have no protection and are at the mercy of these dancers. Why delay with further investigations!"

As he nears the end of the message, he speaks the words he is telegraphing: "We need more protection, and we need it now! The leaders should be arrested and confined in some Military Post until the matter is quieted, and this should be done at once!"

Several days later, back at Fort McKinney, in a room where the walls are lined with shelves and filled with books, a soldier walks to a shelf, and picks out a book. He turns and walks by a potbelly stove, and a sign that hangs on the wall nearby with the inscribed words, "Colonel Hatch Library."

Some soldiers are sitting at tables reading, while others are teaching their comrades how to read. Troopers Chase, Irving, Walley, and three other troopers are also sitting at a table near the front door, reading different items.

Trooper Walley is reading an "Army and Navy Journal" as he quietly says to his comrades, "Hey, look at this picture."

He turns the book around and shows the picture he's talking about to his comrades when Trooper Chase says, "Yeah, that's the Statue of Liberty in New York. France gave it to us, about four years ago." Trooper Chase turns the book around and looks at the front cover then says, "Yeah, this is an old Journal Augustus...eighty-six, October."

"I know Chase, since you taught me to read, I went back to these old books...I wanted to see what these pictures have been sayin' all along—they say she looks green."

"She's made out of copper and when it weathers it turns

turquoise green," says Trooper Chase.

Corporal Wilson walks into the library and calls to his men quietly saying, "Troopers, new winter issue just arrived. Quartermaster is gettin' ready to hand out the issue now, be the first in line."

"Thanks, Corporal, we're on our way," says Trooper Chase quietly.

Corporal Wilson exits the library as Trooper Walley looks to his comrades preparing to leave and says, "It's about time we're gettin' some new winter clothing. Four years in the north, it's cold out there."

The soldiers are excited about getting their new winter clothing. They close their books and rise from their chairs, putting on their overcoats, pushing their chairs back under the table. Trooper Walley says, "Too bad I and F Troop went to Fort Robinson the other day. They're probably not gettin' the good issue we're gettin'."

A trooper walks to the potbelly stove, opens the door and puts a log inside, as Trooper Chase and his comrades take their material to the book return box, deposit their books, then exit.

Moments later, outside the Quartermaster's Office, it's clear and cold, and a light snow lies over just about everything. All of K Troop is in line, ahead of the other garrison soldiers, standing behind the first of many covered wagons. They are looking to the garrison adjutant and a corporal, who are standing at the rear of one of the wagons, on its platform, with several large open crates.

Major Henry is watching Sergeants Jordan and Shaw, taking care of distribution paperwork, sitting at a desk, at the front of the line. Sergeant Shaw then looks to the adjutant and the corporal, and says, "All right, start passin' 'em out."

The adjutant reaches into the crate and brings out what appears to be a giant black furry rug bound with a rope. He hands the furry thing to the corporal, who then tosses it to Corporal Wilson, who's first in line. Corporal Wilson catches the semi-heavy giant furry item with both arms as the adjutant reaches into another crate, brings out two other small black furry items, and tosses them on top of Corporal Wilson's furry thing.

Trooper Irving, standing behind Corporal Wilson, looks over Corporal Wilson's shoulder as he is about to leave. He looks at the furry things in his arms, then holding his nose, he looks to Sergeant Jordan and says, "Sarge, what's that?"

Sergeant Jordan begins to chuckle as he says, "That there, Trooper, is a buffalo hide—your new winter coat, gloves and cap."

Corporal Wilson walks away holding his face from the hide, as Trooper Irving says aloud, "Pee-yew, it smells!"

"Sorry, Trooper, can't help the smell, it should wear off soon. That coat, gloves and cap, they will keep you warm this winter," says Major Henry.

The corporal on the wagon tosses Trooper Irving's buffalo coat, then his gloves and cap to him. He catches the coat as the gloves and cap land on top. He takes one sniff of the fur and holds his face as far away as possible, as Sergeant Jordan says, "Let's keep it movin' Trooper, we got several hundred to hand out."

Trooper Irving walks away, holding his face away from the fur, as Trooper Chase and Walley and the rest of the garrison step up to receive theirs.

Days later, back at the Indian Agent Office, Agent Royer is writing down a message that's coming across the telegraph wire: "November 20, 1890, Indian Bureau, Washington. To all Indian Agents. Telegraph names of the fomenters of disturbances to bureau in Washington."

As the telegraph stops, Agent Royer begins writing on a piece of paper, saying aloud, "Sitting Bull, Kicking Bear, Short Bull and Big Foot." He then begins telegraphing his message, checking off the names as he goes.

Later that day in Chicago, Army Headquarters, it's the picture of organized chaos as secretaries, adjutants, many officers and enlisted men (no colored, only white), go about their daily duties. An adjutant rushes out of an enter-office room, walking towards two large glass doors that separate the larger room from the building. He pushes the right door open, and walks down a long nearly deserted hallway to an open door on the right side, which leads to a private office. The adjutant stops at attention at the doorway, holding a military telegraph in his hand.

A sentry stands to the left side of the doorway as the adjutant makes a right-face, knocks on the doorjamb, and hears a voice echoing from inside saying, "Enter."

The adjutant walks through the doorway towards a cluttered desk and stops in front of the desk. Facing him is the back of a black, high-back chair in back of the desk, and protruding from the top of the chair back is a white-haired man, sitting, looking out the window. The man turns his chair around to reveal the promoted Brigadier General Nelson A. Miles, who looks a lot older with his handlebar mustache. He looks pensively at the adjutant. He's not a friend to the Sioux Indian, and is diabolical in his efforts to eradicate them.

The adjutant salutes and hands General Miles a telegraph. General Miles takes the telegraph, reads it, then looks to the adjutant and says, "Adjutant, telegraph Brigadier General Brooke at the Department of the

Platte..." General Miles gets up from his chair and walks to the military map of the territory that is sitting on an easel. The adjutant takes out a pencil and paper from his inside jacket pocket, and turns to General Miles, as General Miles says, "Have Brooke order out—" He looks to the map skillfully and says, "First, Second, Fifth, Sixth, Eighth, and Ninth Cavalry units, with two companies of infantry to be stationed at the rail and telegraph lines, south and west of Pine Ridge. "And I want the rest to surround the reservations." General Miles thinks for a moment then says, "delay sending the ninth's message." Then with a sinister look he says, "Adjutant, resend the other message I gave you regarding the Seventh...mark this part secret: You gentlemen will be first in the area, you need to be clear about what we're doing here...be professional, don't screw it up...you have the names...the word is green!"

Then General Miles looks at the adjutant and says, "Send those messages right away...then burn them!"

The adjutant folds the message and puts it in his pocket, salutes, makes an about-face and exits the office.

Several days later, a light snow falls over the agency grounds of Pine Ridge Indian Reservation. Protruding from the middle of the grounds are several tall pine trees, with two log buildings somewhat evenly dispersed around them.

Many Sibley tents and troop guidons dot the landscape surrounding the outside perimeters of the buildings, as the area bustles with soldiers and equipment. There are no colored soldiers; however, there are many white soldiers at work. The soldiers scurry, moving mounts, Gatling guns, Hotchkiss cannons and wagons, causing the equipment to carve many muddy paths through the snow-covered ground.

A sign hangs over the front porch of the main building

231

with the words inscribed, "Pine Ridge Indian Reservation - Indian Agent Office."

Standing on the porch, under the sign, is Agent Royer. He is standing next to General John R. Brooke. He's forty-five years old, has gray hair, a yes-sir man, and is giving orders to a lieutenant.

Lieutenant Sestak, a young ambitious lieutenant who follows orders to a T, is taking orders from General Brooke, who says, "Lieutenant, I want two troops to be placed along the telegraph lines to keep them from being cut. After you get through with that assignment, come back—I got more for you."

"Yes, sir," says Lieutenant Sestak.

Lieutenant Sestak salutes, then turns and walks to his mount, mounts and rides off to perform his duties as Agent Royer says, "General, what do you intend to do?"

"I'm declaring the reservations a Military Zone, Dr. Royer. In a couple of weeks, I'll have about nine thousand troops surrounding nine hundred square miles of Pine Ridge, Standing Rock and Rosebud Agencies. At that time we will round them up and take them to the railroad, so they can be transported to Oklahoma Territory."

A look of accomplishment and satisfaction is written on Agent Royer's face.

General Brooke takes a container out of his jacket pocket, removes a match, and strikes it, holding it under a telegraph message, setting it on fire.

The next day at Porcupine Village, some Sioux families are in a panic. They are packing up what possessions they have before leaving. Some that have already packed are headed north with weapons in hand through the snow, while others without weapons are headed south. Many other grief-stricken Sioux are standing around Short Bull listening to him talk with Big Foot, squatting outside his tepee.

Big Foot coughs as Short Bull says, "Many soldiers come, try to stop us...they cannot!"

Big Foot coughs then says, "Some say the soldiers will kill us all, if we keep dancin', that's why my people go."

"Big Foot wear *sacred shirts*...they'll stop the bluecoats' bullets! Tell your people."

Big Foot coughs, then looks to his people and says, "My people that don't believe go to Stronghold, Badlands, prepare to fight, others go to agents' office, scared."

"Big Foot, you must dance, keep on dancin'...Messiah come...all new things come!"

"Short Bull, I take my people to Cherry Creek, soldiers not find us there. There, we will dance."

"I'll go Standing Rock. Council with Kicking Bear and Sitting Bull...I'll tell them where you go."

Big Foot tries to stand as several Sioux help him to his feet. Short Bull steps up to Big Foot. They both hug each other, then the same Sioux who helped Big Foot up, helps him squat back down.

Short Bull hops on his pony's back as Big Foot calls out to his people in Sioux language saying, "Come my people..."

The next night, at Fort McKinney's assembly hall, all of K Troop and many other 9th Cavalry soldiers are gathered in their dress uniforms, enjoying a festive candlelit dinner party.

A fire crackles in a large stone fireplace with a canvas banner stretched across the front wall of the hall with the word, "CONGRATULATIONS." K Troop's guidon hangs just below the banner, in back of a podium, which is positioned several yards in front. Major Henry is sitting not far from the podium, talking with other officers and non-commissioned officers.

The hall is full of conversation as Major Henry looks around the hall, then looks to the table where he is sitting and says, "Excuse me, gentlemen." The soldiers at the table rise, as Major Henry rises, taking a large military envelope with him, making his way to the podium. As he reaches the podium, he lays the envelope on top, then looks out to the assembly, and with a proud look, he calls to the room saying, "Attention everyone. Attention everyone..."

The entire room quiets down as Major Henry reaches into the envelope and brings out a document. He reads the document briefly to himself and looks around the room proudly. Then he looks back inside of the envelope, and pulls out a military medal from inside.

He looks back to the assembly proudly and says, "Thank you. Tonight, the twenty-forth of November—it's a special night. It's a night that has a special meaning, a meaning of spirit and gallantry. Tonight, the United States Army and the Ninth Cavalry are happy and very proud, to present, for his actions, in the face of the enemy at Fort Tularosa—Sergeant George Jordan with the Medal of Honor..."

Everyone stands and gives an excited ovation to Sergeant Jordan as Major Henry waves for him to come up to the podium. Sergeant Jordan stands, from a table in the middle of the room, receiving even more applause as he makes his way towards the podium.

Major Henry holds his hands in the air to quiet the room, and as the crowd quiets, he says, "Please hold your ovations on this next introduction until I finish with the presentation, thank you."

Major Henry looks at approaching Sergeant Jordan then back to the document before retrieving another medal and a military certificate from the envelope and says, "I'm also honored and proud to present, the Medal of Honor for his actions, in the face of the enemy, at Carrizo Canyon—First Sergeant Thomas Shaw, and the Certificate of Merit to Sergeant George Jordan for his actions also in that campaign."

Again, the entire room bursts forward with cheers for both Sergeants, as Sergeant Shaw stands and makes his way to the podium.

As Sergeant Jordan nears the podium, he marches to the left side of Major Henry, becoming parallel with him. He stops at attention, making an about-face, then faces the audience, once again standing at attention.

Sergeant Shaw is now making his way to the podium. He marches to the right side of Major Henry, also becoming parallel, stopping at attention, making an about-face facing the audience, standing at attention.

Major Henry holds his hands in the air again, to quiet the soldiers, who are still cheering. The soldiers settle in their excitement as Major Henry makes a left-face, looks to Sergeant Jordan, and says, "Sergeant Jordan, front and center."

Sergeant Jordan makes a right-face, steps one step closer to Major Henry, and stops at attention, staring straight at Major Henry. Major Henry is holding Sergeant Jordan's Medal, as he reaches out and pins it on the left side of his dress uniform blouse, then takes the military certificate off the top of the podium and hands the certificate to Sergeant Jordan in his left hand. Major Henry smiles at Sergeant Jordan and shakes his right hand. Sergeant Jordan then takes one step back and salutes Major Henry. Major Henry returns the salute as Sergeant Jordan makes a left-face, looking back to the audience, standing at attention.

Major Henry then makes an about-face, and says, "Sergeant Shaw, front and center."

Sergeant Shaw makes a left-face, steps one step closer to Major Henry and stops. Major Henry then pins Sergeant Shaw's medal on the left side of his dress uniform blouse, and smiles at him as he shakes his hand. Sergeant Shaw takes one step back and salutes Major Henry, then he makes a right-face, looking back to the audience, standing at attention.

Major Henry then looks to both sergeants and says, "Congratulations, Sergeants."

Both sergeants turn to Major Henry, salute, then simultaneously say, "Thank you, sir."

Sergeant Jordan and Sergeant Shaw then make their turns and march back to their tables as their comrades give them a standing ovation.

The garrison adjutant rushes into the hall and looks to Major Henry, then rushes to him with urgency. When he reaches Major Henry, he hands him a telegraph message. Major Henry unfolds the telegraph, reads it, then looks to the adjutant and says, "Thank you, Adjutant."

Some of the assembly has quieted down looking at Major Henry and the adjutant as the adjutant salutes, makes an about-face, and walks towards his comrades in the hall.

Major Henry holds up his hands in the air to quiet the last of the conversations as he says, "Gentlemen, gentlemen..." The room quiets again as Major Henry looks to them and says, "I've just received orders for K and D troops to proceed to Pine Ridge Indian Reservation, South Dakota."

He looks to both sergeants while giving his orders saying, "Sergeants, rations for thirty days, as much ammunition the men and wagons can carry. Have the troops ready first light."

Sergeants Jordan and Shaw stand at their tables, salute Major Henry, and simultaneously say, "Yes, sir."

Sergeant Jordan looks to his men and calls out his orders, "Quartermaster, report to Sergeant Shaw, Corporals..."

The next day, at Fort McKinney, it's a clear cold frosty morning, with the wind gusts blowing snow flurries through the air. Old Glory on the garrison flagpole is flying forty-three stars and is being whipped by the winds.

Long icicles hang from garrison buildings as snow and ice cover everything else. The American flag and the 9th Cavalry's, K and D Troops' guidons blow in the chilly gusty wind from their positions in the columns. Ninety-nine Buffalo Soldiers sit on their mounts, in a column of twos. There are forty-eight soldiers in K Troop at the front of the columns, and fifty-one soldiers in D Troop to the rear. Fifteen supply wagons are situated in the middle of the columns, driven by the 24th Infantry, with the lead wagon flying its guidon.

Their bodies are wrapped in their buffalo coats that easily cover them from the bridge of their nose past their feet and stirrups. With their mount reins disappearing into the sleeves of their coats, not even their fur-covered hands are revealed. Their coats have very large collars, which are pulled up around the back of their necks and cover the lower part of their faces. Their buffalo caps cover them from the top of their heads to just below their brow line, with the flaps of the caps pulled down over their ears and under their coat collars.

Their faces barely show through their fur collars, and as they breathe through their mouths and noses, the condensation from their breath makes them look like the animal they are named after.

Sergeants Jordan and Shaw ride into their positions in the columns along with several other sergeants and corporals as Major Henry looks to his men, then calls his orders, "Troops...forward *hooo.*"

The Buffalo Soldiers spur their mounts forward as both beast and human inhale and exhale the cold, chilly winter air.

The next day, it's clear as the chilly howling wind blows in the northern territory. Two very long columns of cavalry soldiers and wagons make their way in the distance, tromping across the vast open wilderness of the snowy frontier, near what appears to be a frozen river.

The American flag and the 7th Cavalry's regimental flag wave in the breeze from the front of the columns, along with seven guidons, which are dispersed throughout the columns of more than seven hundred soldiers riding at-ease. Some are dressed in their blue yellow lined overcoats and others in their buffalo coats, fur gloves and caps making their way through the knee-deep snow. Most of the soldiers are bundled up with their coat collars pulled around their faces keeping them out of the frost-biting wind.

Riding behind the American flag, leading the left column, is Major S. M. Whitside, a yes-sir man. He's riding next to Colonel James W. Forsyth, riding outside the left column, an ex-paper-shuffling adjutant, who's office job, before being assign to the territory recently, made poor preparation for Indian warfare.

They are talking to each other over the howling wind, somewhat ahead of the columns, as Major Whitside says, "...This is your first field assignment Colonel, I sure hope you and the general know what you're doing?"

"We do, Major...and are you clear on your orders?"

"Yes, sir...but..."

Colonel Forsyth looks at Major Whitside quickly with a hard look and softly shouts, "Major, there are no buts!"

Colonel Forsyth turns and looks to his men quickly to see if anyone is listening, then he looks back at Major Whitside with seriousness written on his face, riding closer to him, saying, "Brooke's orders from General Miles are clear! Once we get the signal...hunt down those murderous savages that are off the reservation...kill 'em."

Major Whitside looks to Colonel Forsyth with concern and says, "You just can't kill them in cold blood like that Colonel!"

"They killed Custer, didn't they...Major!"

Lieutenant Mitchell is riding in the left column, behind Major Whitside. He is wearing his blue yellow lined overcoat. His blonde hair is a lot longer, tied in a ponytail protruding from under his cap, not the usual military haircut. Trooper Hartigan is riding to his right, in the right column wearing his buffalo fur. They are both pretending not to be listening to the colonel and major's conversation over the howling wind.

After hearing what Colonel Forsyth just said, Trooper Hartigan rides closer to Lieutenant Mitchell, and softly shouts, "You hear that, you're gonna get your chance to kill you some Sioux, Lieutenant, 'the ones that killed Custer.'"

Lieutenant Mitchell looks to Trooper Hartigan with a doubtful look and says, "Yeah, I knew somethin' was a comin' when that telegraph arrived the other night. Then they said, we're movin' out first..."

Trooper Hartigan interrupts Lieutenant Mitchell and says, "What's wrong Howard, you not havin' second thoughts now, are ya? You said Custer is your hero."

Lieutenant Mitchell becomes determined, but still a little doubtful as he says, "He is, was—I just wonder why they haven't said nothin' to us directly. They only said, we're goin' to Pine Ridge...wherever that is?"

Trooper Hartigan senses Lieutenant Mitchell is a little scared and begins to play with him as he says, "You sure you're not scared Howard. You haven't been in the field yet. Ever since they made you an office-boy adjutant...stuck you in with the colonel...you haven't gottin' out of the garrison to see any action, but you're gonna get some now."

As they ride on, Trooper Hartigan returns to his position in the columns, as Lieutenant Mitchell looks on with skepticism.

A couple of weeks later, in Indian Agent Royer's office, the date on the calendar reads December 9, 1890. The view, through the window behind Agent Royer's desk, is now snow-laden. Soldiers tread about through the deep snow.

Agent Royer is sitting at his desk looking to Indian Agent Dr. Valentine McGillycuddy, a bookworm type, with a meek and mild disposition, who is putting on his coat. He is finishing his conversation with Agent Royer, saying, "...They call it Ghost Dancing, Agent Royer, to bring back their dead. You should let the dance continue—"

Agent Royer interrupts Dr. McGillycuddy, shouting at him. "Let the dance continue! McLaughlin and I are trying to stop them from dancing. That's why we sent for troops."

"Yes, the coming of the troops has frightened the Indians," says Dr. McGillycuddy. He looks to Agent Royer with a pointed look and then says, "If the Seventh-day Adventists prepared their ascension robes for the second coming of the savior, the United States Army is not put in motion to prevent them...! Why should not the Indians have the same privilege?"

Agent Royer looks at Dr. McGillycuddy, who is putting

on his hat and gloves, with a that's-not-what-I-wanted-to-hear expression on his face. Agent Royer then turns in his chair and looks out the window.

Dr. McGillycuddy walks towards the front door, stops, turns looking back to Agent Royer, and says, "If the soldiers remain, Agent Royer—trouble is sure to come!"

Dr. McGillycuddy turns, opens the door and exits, closing the door behind him with Agent Royer turning in his chair and looking to the closing door.

The next day in the Northern Territory it's very cold and overcast, with no wind, as K and D Troops' faces now show through their buffalo coats, revealing they have been out on the trail for a couple of weeks. Patches of small icicles hang in clusters from their fur coats and caps as they ride two by two, at-ease through the snow.

They begin passing a herd of buffalo that is searching for grass under the snow with their snouts. The soldiers themselves look like buffalo riding on their mounts, with their buffalo caps covering their heads, and coats pulled tightly around their necks and body, keeping their body-heat in. The reins from their mounts disappear within their sleeves as their mounts tromp through the snow, making way for the wagons, which follow behind them.

Trooper Walley looks at one of the buffalo that seems to be looking at him as he says, "Don't look *at me*—it wasn't my idea to turn your cousin into a coat."

All the soldiers around him laugh and chuckle as Trooper Chase says, "Augustus, what makes you think that coat was his cousin?"

Trooper Walley says, "They all look alike don't they?"

Everyone around the conversation laughs and chuckles again with condensation spewing out from their mouths.

Major Henry looks back at his men laughing, then

looks to Sergeant Jordan and says, "It's amazing Sergeant."

"What's that, sir?"

"The men are always in good spirits Sergeant, no matter what the conditions may be."

"They are proud to be in your command, sir," says Sergeant Jordan.

"I'm proud to have them in my command Sergeant." Major Henry then stands in his stirrups and looks ahead to what appears to be a frozen river they're approaching.

Sergeant Jordan also stands and looks to the river, then looks at Major Henry and says, "I hope the ice is thick enough so we can cross the river up ahead sir."

Sergeant Shaw says, "This weather has already slowed us a week, sir. If we cannot cross the river at this point...it's gonna take us another week to make Pine Ridge.

"I know, Sergeant—but I have a trick up my sleeve that might only delay us by one day crossing here." As the soldiers approach the frozen river, Major Henry calls his orders, "Troop *hooo*."

The soldiers come to a stop as Major Henry looks at both sergeants and says, "Sergeants, dismount, bring a rope and follow me."

Sergeant Shaw looks at Sergeant Jordan, who is grabbing his rope, then all three dismount into the knee-high snow, with two troopers spurring their mounts forward, stopping to the side of Sergeant Jordan, dismounting, and taking their mount's reins.

Major Henry and the sergeants then walk, tromping through the snow towards the river and as they move forward, their buffalo coats drag behind them. When Major Henry reaches the riverbank, where the snow is not as deep, he stops, then takes off his coat and gloves, then hands them to Sergeant Shaw. He takes one end of the rope from Sergeant Jordan, ties it around his waist, and carefully begins clearing away the snow from the riverbank with his boot, revealing the edge of the frozen river. Major Henry kicks the ice with the heel of his boot, causing some ice to chip away as he then steps carefully out onto the ice. Sergeant Jordan is holding the other end of Major Henry's lifeline as he carefully steps out a little further, and further, stopping, kicking the ice again with the heel of his boot, first soft then harder.

Major Henry then steps out a little further, kicks the ice again, then senses it's not thick enough as he calls to both sergeants saying, "We're going to have to make this ice thicker for the mounts and wagons to cross. Sergeants: bucket brigade—toss water, beginning at this spot here, then all the way across to the other side. We'll build the ice, make it thicker, it's cold enough," then he points down river and says, "Break a hole in the ice, about forty yards, get your water there. Then have some troopers gather fire wood so the troopers can warm and dry themselves."

"Yes, sir," says Sergeants Jordan and Shaw simultaneously.

Major Henry takes his coat from Sergeant Shaw as Sergeants Jordan and Shaw salute, turn, and bark their orders to their men.

Sergeant Jordan says, "Bucket brigade, give me thirty men, K Troop and two troopers gather firewood and get a fire goin'..."

"Return brigade, give me thirty men, D Troop," says Sergeant Shaw.

The soldiers from K and D Troops dismount as other soldiers hold their mounts' reins.

K Troop soldiers begin retrieving buckets from the first wagon as Sergeant Jordan says, "Corporal Wilson, break a hole in the ice, there." Sergeant Jordan points to a spot downriver on the ice, then says, "String your men along the river edge with buckets, from there to this point and thicken the ice here, and all the way across—and be careful."

"Bucket retrieval brigade, in position, sir," says Sergeant Shaw looking at Major Henry.

Corporal Wilson, Dorch and Scott, and other corporals call out Sergeant Jordans' and Shaws' orders to their troopers. D Troop lines up along the river edge in back of their bucket brigade comrades as Corporal Wilson begins breaking a hole in the ice with a pick. When Corporal Wilson breaks through the ice, Trooper Chase walks up with a bucket and dunks his bucket in the river and passes it down the line of soldiers.

As the bucket of water nears the end of the line where Major Henry is standing, he takes the bucket of water from the trooper and tosses the water onto the ice. Then he looks to the last trooper in line and says, "Just like that, trooper, many times, all the way across."

Major Henry hands the bucket to a trooper in the bucket retrieval line, as new buckets of water continue coming fourth. The same trooper takes the next bucket of water and tosses the water onto the ice, as Major Henry then takes the empty bucket from the trooper and tosses it to a trooper standing in the return line.

Five days later, the sound of wailing is heard coming from Big Foot's village at Cherry Creek as more than five hundred Sioux Indians are in a state of hysteria. Many are quickly packing what belongings they still have and are leaving, while other Sioux Indians walk into the village sobbing. The Sioux that are leaving are quickly walking north through the snow, while some, who are lucky to have a pony, ride off towards the north, all with weapons in hand. Other Sioux, mostly children, old women and men, are wailing in large groups, while others—old women, men, nursing mothers, and children—stand in a circle around Big Foot and Short Bull.

Big Foot coughs a lot more. He really looks sick. He is sitting by a campfire with blankets wrapped around his shoulders as Short Bull angrily says, "...Bull Head shot Sitting Bull in chest, then Red Tomahawk shot him in back of head." Then Short Bull becomes sad and says, "The Wasichus...turn our people against us now."

Big Foot coughs as he says, "There's nothin' left of our nation Short Bull...Sitting Bull's people still come in...look." Big Foot points to some of Sitting Bull's people, who are trickling into his village. They all look very despondent. Big Foot coughs again and says, "They are lost and scared...my people scared...believe soldiers will come and kill all of us now. We must go back to reservation, show peace."

"No go reservation, come with us, to Stronghold in Badlands...time to fight, our *Ghost Shirts* protect us!"

"No more fight Short Bull, tired..." Big Foot coughs again and again, as he says, "Go to reservation." Big Foot attempts to stand as several of his people help him to his feet. They walk him to an old, rickety, uncovered, spring-less wagon that's hitched to a pony. Big Foot climbs onto the wagon with help from his people and lies down. An old woman known to the band as Old Woman and a young nursing mother called Little Deer, cover him with many blankets as he coughs.

At the same time, at Pine Ridge Indian Reservation agency grounds, it's a cold gray day. Mass hysteria is also rampaging through the agency. The Sioux that had come back and encamped there are quickly gathering what possessions they have, and begin packing north, stampeding away from the agency.

The soldiers on the agency grounds make no attempt at stopping the Sioux as they stand there looking at the Sioux with amazement. When the Sioux come near the white soldiers, they veer away from them.

General Brooke is watching from a window in Agent Royer's office. He then turns around and begins yelling at someone inside.

Inside Agent Royer's office, General Brooke is walking away from the window, yelling at Agent Royer, who is sitting at the telegraph desk. As General Brooke walks behind Agent Royer, he says, "...I don't care who's at fault! Are you ready Dr. Royer to write this message!"

Nervously, Agent Royer says, "...Yes."

"The date is, fifteen, December, 1890. McLaughlin...Sitting Bull dead. Band headed east to Rosebud to join Big Foot...Sioux at agency, stampeding north towards Badlands...7th and the other troops still have not arrived...await further orders."

As Agent Royer finishes writing General Brooke's message, he puts his ink pin in the pen well holder and begins working the telegraph key nervously. He is transmitting General Brooke's message. As he works the telegraph key, he turns around, looks to General Brooke saying, "Where are the rest of your troops? The troops you have here are not enough to control this!"

"Don't worry Dr. Royer, the 7th Cavalry will be here any day now. The snow is the worst I've seen in this territory. It's slowed them down—probably five days or so." General Brooke looks worried as he looks to the telegraph message on the telegraph desk next to Agent Royer. As Agent Royer finishes transmitting, General Brooke says, "Dr. Royer, hand me Mr. McLaughlin's telegraph."

General Brooke walks over to Agent Royer and takes

the telegraph message from him, then reaches in his jacket pocket and brings out the container of matches. General Brooke retrieves one match, strikes it, then sets the telegraph on fire, letting it fall to the floor, turning into carbon. Agent Royer watches the dying flame.

Later that day at Army Headquarters in Chicago, in General Miles' office, the adjutant stands in front of General Miles' desk, holding a pencil and paper in hand, ready to take notes. General Miles is sitting in his chair at his desk, reading a telegraph message as he angrily shouts, "Damn it...the Seventh was suppose to be there by now!"

He looks to the adjutant and says, "Telegraph General Brooke, I want the noose tightened around the agency! Round up all Indians, prepare for rail shipment...tell him the word is still green. I'm on the first train, should arrive Pine Ridge, seven days. That's it, Adjutant."

The adjutant salutes, begins to leave then stops as General Miles says, "Adjutant...after you send it...burn it!"

The adjutant salutes again, then exits.

Nine days later, it's early morning on the agency grounds of Pine Ridge Indian Reservation. Snow covers everything. The grounds are devoid of Indians except for Indian police and scouts. Amid a large contingency of cavalry wagons, dismounted soldiers, colored and white, stand at-ease by their mounts in uniform groups.

Colored soldiers are segregated from the white soldiers, except for the Buffalo Soldiers' officers. The 9th Cavalry's guidons, K, D, I, and F, are positioned within the ranks of the colored troops, as the 6th Cavalry's guidons are positioned within theirs.

There are many Crow Indian police walking around and standing guard under the agency sign. Sergeant Jordan and the troops are standing by their mounts at at-ease as General Brooke stares out the window of Agent Royer's office at them.

Inside the office, General Brooke turns from the window, walks over to the calendar on the wall, stopping in front of it, then looks at the calendar and says, "This is the twenty-forth of December, gentlemen." General Brooke then looks to Major Henry and the lieutenant from the 6th Cavalry, both whom are standing at parade-rest, watching him as he walks from the calendar on the wall to the territorial map sitting on an easel. General Brooke stops at the territorial map, looks, then points to the map and says, "These are the three Indian agencies, Standing Rock, Rosebud, and Pine Ridge, where you are now." Major Henry and the lieutenant are watching General Brooke point to the map as he turns and looks at them and says, "Gentlemen, we are already a week behind schedule. I've declared these agencies a military zone. Your orders are to bring Big Foot and Sitting Bull's people to this agency, and prepare them for transportation to the railroad. Major, I want you to take the Ninth...to the northwest here"—he points to the location on the territorial map—"to the Badlands. Lieutenant, take the Sixth to the southwest and scout here, hundred or so miles west of White Clay." He then turns to the officers and says, "Three weeks' rations, gentlemen."

Major Henry looks to the territory map, points to it and says, "Sir, I see the other troop flags in the north and all points south, what about the east and northeast?"

"When Colonel Forsyth arrives, Major, he'll scout to the east. He has the largest contingency of soldiers, he'll be able to cover that territory. Dismissed."

Later that night, in the northern territory, at White River, several bright campfires burn in the cold night air, sending sparks high aloft as the 9th Cavalry soldiers go about their duties preparing for the evening, and keeping warm by the fires. The 9th's guidons, K, D, I, and F, are staked next to the American flag in the snow, fluttering in the breeze, just outside the main fire ring. Many Sibley tents dot the landscape. The 24th's guidon also flutters from the lead supply wagon that borders the encampment.

Major Henry, Sergeants Jordan and Shaw, Corporals Wilson, Dorch, Scott, and Jackson, Troopers Chase, Irving, and Walley, and other soldiers—colored enlisted and white officers—are gathered around one of the campfires. Major Henry looks from his territorial map to Sergeants Jordan and Shaw, saying, "...We made twenty-five miles to the White River today. By tomorrow night, we should be able to make another twenty-five miles to the Badlands."

Sergeant Shaw looks at the regiment and says, "Now that I and F Troop are back with us, we'll have more men to comb the Badlands."

Sergeant Jordan then looks to the night sky, and at a bright star as he looks to Major Henry and says, "Sir."

"Yes Sergeant."

"Merry Christmas, sir."

Major Henry looks at Sergeant Jordan, smiles and says, "Merry Christmas Sergeant."

Everyone begins wishing their comrades "Merry Christmas" as Trooper Chase looks to Sergeant Jordan and says, "Sarge, permission to sing?"

"Sure thin', Trooper."

Trooper Chase walks to a log lying by the fire, puts one foot up on it, and begins to sing, "Si...lent night, Ho...ly night, all is calm, all is bright, round yon Virgin Mother and child..."

The fire crackles and sparks fly into the air as Trooper Chase continues singing.

In Agent Royer's office late that night, Lieutenant Sestak is standing near General Brooke, who is angry and yelling at Colonel Forsyth, and Major Whitside, who is standing in front of him shouting, "...The Ninth and Sixth left early this morning, the other units left yesterday, you were suppose to be here a week ago scouting for those savages! The Indian agent right now is trying to find Sitting Bull's band in the area where you are suppose to be...what the hell took you two so long—and I don't want to hear it was the weather!"

Colonel Forsyth looks to General Brooke and sheepishly says, "No, sir...it was a river we came across, we couldn't find thick ice for a hundred miles or so."

"You let thin 'ice' jeopardize this!" shouts General Brooke angrily. "My own wife knows how to thicken thin ice, you damn idiot! What kind of military man are you anyway, Colonel!" General Brooke shakes his head, then calms down, pulling his pocket watch from his overcoat pocket and looking at the time. He then walks to the calendar and flips the page revealing the new date as he says, "All right, gentlemen...I want you to take the Seventh and Battery E, First Artillery with two Hotchkiss cannons and Gatling gun. Scout to the northeast, towards, Wounded Knee. That's where you should find the Indian agent, Dr. Royer, who is searching for them." General Brooke points to Lieutenant Sestak and says, "Take Lieutenant Sestak with you. Your orders are green. Merry Christmas, gentlemen."

General Brooke turns, walks to a desk, pulls the top drawer open, and retrieves a bottle of whiskey and a shot glass. He begins pouring the whiskey nervously into the glass as Colonel Forsyth and Major Whitside look at one another, then to General Brooke, who is downing his shot, then pouring another...

Early morning, it's snowing and bitter cold in the Badlands of the Northern Territory as the 9th Cavalry, wearing their buffalo coats, gloves, and caps, are riding on their mounts tromping through the snow.

As the soldiers ride a ways, they begin to hear the methodical drumbeat again. Major Henry looks to Sergeant Jordan and says, "You hear that Sergeant?"

"Yes, sir," says Sergeant Jordan as he sniffs the air. "Wood burning also."

Sergeant Shaw says, "That's the same drumbeat we've been hearin', except it sounds like it's comin' from up ahead this time. That telegraph we got from Grouard, before we left...said he had found out what the meanin' was, said he would explain when he got back."

Looking around, Sergeant Jordan says, "Too bad he didn't make it back in time before we left, so he could of told us."

As the soldiers ride on, they begin coming across several wondering Sioux Indians, walking aimlessly north through the snow, disarmed, dismounted, frightened and looking very despondent.

The drumbeat continues as Major Henry, Sergeants Jordan and Shaw begin calling to them simultaneously, with Major Henry saying, "Go back to the reservation. Help is there. Go back to the reservation..."

Sergeant Jordan says, "Go back, there's food, and shelter—go back. Food and shelter..."

Sergeant Shaw is saying, "Food, shelter, go back, food, shelter..."

Some of the Sioux look to the Buffalo Soldiers with awe, while others appear as if walking zombies. As the soldiers ride along, the drumbeat becomes louder and louder, then they begin to hear chanting as they near the source. The soldiers begin to ride into a fog-like atmosphere. Then, they come upon what appear to be several hundred Sioux Indians, dancing and singing around a large fire and a denuded tree, wearing only their *Ghost Shirts* and bare necessities—no winter clothing.

As the Buffalo Soldiers approach, the drumbeat and dancing stop, and the Sioux Indians look at the soldiers with awe.

Major Henry looks at the helpless Sioux, then says to both sergeants, "After we find Big Foot and Sitting Bull's people, we'll come back for them."

"These poor people, they really look bad off, sir," says Sergeant Shaw.

"I believe you would call this a culture breakdown, Sergeant," says Major Henry as he holds his hand in the air and calls his orders, "Troop *hooo*."

The soldiers come to a stop as the Sioux begin backing away from the soldiers with awe written in their eyes.

Major Henry looks at the Sioux, then calls out, "Big Foot...Big Foot...Big Foot!" Then Major Henry looks to one of the dancers and says, "We look for Big Foot."

It's very quiet, you could hear a pin drop in the snow, if it wasn't for the soldiers' mounts breathing and snorting. The soldiers look to the Sioux, looking for Big Foot, as the Sioux look to the soldiers with more awe, saying nothing.

The Sioux Indian who Major Henry addressed says nothing. He stares into space as Sergeant Jordan looks at Major Henry saying, "I don't see anyone that matches his description, sir."

"No, you're right, Sergeant. We'll keep searching north, deeper into the Badlands." Major Henry then looks to his men and says, "Troop...forward *hooo*."

The 9th Cavalry spurs their mounts off as the Sioux look at them. When the soldiers are a distance away, the drumbeat begins and the Sioux begin dancing and singing their chant.

Three days later, it's a cold morning as snow falls on a medium-sized cavalry encampment, which is ensconced by a snowy landscape of sloping hills. Smoke wafts in the air from the many stove and heater pipes protruding from the top of the cavalry tents, which dot the landscape. Several campfires also burn on both sides of the crooked river gulch, called Wounded Knee Creek.

The 7th Cavalry's guidons are staked throughout the encampment as snow covers just about everything, except for where the soldiers' fires burn. Soldiers are busy with their morning duties as Colonel Forsyth stands in front of his tent, pointing to a territorial map sitting on an easel. His tent is on one side of the gulch, in the middle of the encampment, with the American and regimental flags staked in the ground next to it. Colonel Forsyth is briefing Major Whitside, Lieutenants Mitchell and Sestak, plus several other officers, saying, "Today is the twenty-eight of December gentlemen. We've been out here for three days now, and no sign of those Sioux anywhere! Damn it, General Brooke is not going to get in my tail feathers again! Whitside, we'll split up, take your men, north, scout Porcupine Creek, take half of Battery E and Gatling gun."

Major Whitside says, "What do I do if I find them?"

"Disarm them...send a messenger to me. I'll do the same. I'll scout northeast of here; the plan is the same, if you find them, bring them back here to Wounded Knee—disarmed. Oh, one other item." He looks at a message in his hand, then says, "The other units should be here by afternoon."

Lieutenant Sestak and the other officers salute Colonel Forsyth, then make an about-face and begin calling orders to their men as Lieutenant Mitchell stays behind, looks to Colonel Forsyth and says, "Sir...uh, do you think we'll see action?"

"I sure hope s——" Colonel Forsyth stops, catches himself, then says, "...not, son. You better get ready Lieutenant, we're pullin' out of here in about"—he looks to his pocket watch—"thirty minutes."

Lieutenant Mitchell salutes and makes an about-face, with an expression of, "office work wasn't such a bad job after all."

Later in the morning, south of Porcupine Village, it's very cold as snow flurries drift in the air, with dark storm clouds looming above. A long line of Sioux Indians tromps through the snow with several ponies and wagons dispersed in their long column. The leading open wagon trails behind the leading Sioux on foot by several yards.

In the wagon, Big Foot lays wrapped in blankets from his eyes to his toes. His eyes look very ill as he shivers under the blankets on the moving wagon. Old Woman and Little Deer, holding her baby, accompany him.

He is surrounded by both his and Sitting Bull's band. They are making their way through the snow, mostly on foot. There are more than 150 old men over the age of forty, and more than 200 women, mostly all old. Some nursing mothers, about forty young children and babies, are also present. This group comprises approximately four hundred desperate and disillusioned nomadic people. They are making their journey at the onset of a very cold and cruel hard winter.

They virtually have nothing left, but their eyes to cry with.

As they tiredly make their way through the snow, a 14-year-old Sioux Indian, Black Wolf—who appears to be the only young Indian left in the world—is walking next to another wagon. He is trading an animal fur skin with an elder, for a beautiful Winchester rifle. He looks to the rifle, then to the elder, and in broken English says, "This good huntin' rifle...good trade. My uncle Sitting Bull...would be proud."

Black Wolf holds the rifle with both hands in the air and looks to the sky to show thanks as he continues walking.

Early that afternoon, Agent Royer and two Crow Indian policemen are sitting on their horses, south of Porcupine Village, on top of a knoll, waving their hands to Major Whitside and his approaching cavalry detachment.

Four guidons blow in the breeze from the 7th Cavalry detachment, B, I, and G Troop, including Battery E, First Artillery and its guidon, which is at the rear of the columns. There are more than four hundred soldiers, three cavalry wagons, a Hotchkiss cannon and the Gatling gun that compose the brigade.

Lieutenant Sestak sees Agent Royer and the Indian police waving as he shouts out saying, "Indian police, and what looks to be the Indian agent signaling ahead, sir."

"I see them, thank you, Lieutenant," says Major Whitside as he looks at Lieutenant Sestak, then to his men and says, "Lieutenant, stay with the troop. Detail: at a gallop, *hooo*."

Nineteen 7th Cavalry soldiers of B Troop spur their mounts off through the snow towards Agent Royer and the Indian police.

Moments later, Major Whitside and his detachment ride

to the top of the knoll and stop, as Agent Royer excitedly greets Major Whitside, saying, "I'm Dr. Royer Indian Agent Pine Ridge." He then points to Big Foot's band in the distance and says, "There they are!"

Major Whitside looks to Big Foot's band headed towards them and says, "I'm Major Whitside." He then looks at Agent Royer and says, "Thank you Agent Royer, we'll take over from here."

Major Whitside turns back and waves his arm to Lieutenant Sestak. Lieutenant Sestak starts the 7th Cavalry galloping towards the knoll, with wagons, Hotchkiss cannon and Gatling gun following.

Major Whitside then looks to his detail and calls his orders, "Detail', forward *hooo*." Major Whitside spurs his mount towards Big Foot's band with his detail and B Troop's guidon following, as Agent Royer and the Indian police ride away in the opposite direction.

Several of Big Foot's people point to Major Whitside and the soldiers galloping towards them as a cold howling wind begins to blow. Big Foot hears his people talking about the approaching soldiers as he tries to sit up with help from Old Woman, who is watching the soldiers galloping towards them. Big Foot removes the blanket with one hand, revealing a bloodstained blanket, and his other hand, that's holding a partially frozen bloody handkerchief to his nose and mouth.

He removes the handkerchief, revealing his bloodstained nose. Then as he looks to Old Woman seated beside him, Big Foot whispers to her with a raspy voice in broken English, "Get white cloth, put on stick." He coughs again, spitting up blood in the handkerchief, as several drops of blood drip from his nose. Big Foot spits up blood into the handkerchief and says, "...Tie to wagon...show peace." Big Foot coughs again, falling back down on the wagon bed, deathly ill. He puts the handkerchief back over his nose and mouth as Little Deer covers him with blankets.

Old Woman brings out a piece of white cloth from one of their Indian bundles then she reaches to a bundle of firewood, pulling a stick from that bundle. Then, Old Woman tears the white cloth in half, tying a piece to one end of the stick, before tying the stick with the other piece of cloth to the wagon seat. The wagon now displays the white flag of truce, which is whipping in the wind, as Major Whitside and his nineteen soldiers stop their mounts, several yards before Big Foot's band. At the same time, Big Foot's band comes to a stop.

Some of Big Foot's people are from Sitting Bull's band. These members are especially fearful of these soldiers, because some of these old men and women were at Little Bighorn on that fateful day, fourteen years ago; thus, they cower in the presence of the 7th Cavalry.

Major Whitside looks at the Sioux, then says, "I'm Major Whitside, Seventh Cavalry. I'm looking for Big Foot, Medicine Man. I have orders for his arrest."

Big Foot, wrapped in blankets, barely sits up from the wagon with help from Old Woman. As he looks at Major Whitside, he raises his hand to show he is Big Foot.

Major Whitside sees Big Foot's hand in the air, and with a couple of his officers, they spur their mounts forward to Big Foot's wagon, stopping in front of the wagon.

Major Whitside then looks at Big Foot and says, "Big Foot." Big Foot nods his head yes as Major Whitside says, "Big Foot, I'm Major Whitside, Seventh Cavalry. I have orders for your arrest and to take you and your band back to Pine Ridge."

Big Foot removes the blanket from his face, revealing the blood-soaked frozen handkerchief he is holding to his nose and mouth. He then removes the frozen handkerchief from his face as blood begins to drip from his nose. As he begins to cough, he spits more blood into the handkerchief. The sight of the blood on Big Foot's face shocks and somewhat horrifies Major Whitside and his officers.

Big Foot then looks at Major Whitside and barely says, "I was takin'...my people to Pine Ridge...for safety...they think you bluecoats...will hurt them."

"Big Foot, as long as you and your people cooperate, nothing will happen. I have orders to disarm you and your people."

Big Foot coughs and then says, "My people have few weapons for huntin' Major...we have no food."

"I'm sorry Big Foot. Orders are orders."

Major Whitside then looks back at Lieutenant Sestak who is riding up and stopping with the rest of the detachment, as Major Whitside calls his orders, "Lieutenant, send the messenger to Colonel Forsyth, inform him we located Big Foot, we are disarming them and will make camp...Wounded Knee. Then Lieutenant—start disarming these people."

Lieutenant Sestak looks at the messenger near him and says, "You heard the major's orders. Get going."

The messenger turns his mount and rides off as Lieutenant Sestak points to several of his men, signaling them to pan out through the Sioux positions. A small detail, with Lieutenant Sestak at the lead, trot their mounts forward, towards the cowering, despondent Sioux.

Big Foot coughs, then looking at his people, exhaustively says, "Give soldiers weapons...they won't hurt us."

The Sioux cowering pass the word through the band as

Lieutenant Sestak stops his mount, and watches his soldiers riding through the Sioux positions, confiscating all weapons they can find.

When the soldiers come near Black Wolf, he hides his new rifle under his coat.

Lieutenant Sestak looks at his detail sweeping through the Sioux positions collecting very few weapons as he then spurs his mount back to Major Whitside. When Lieutenant Sestak reaches Major Whitside, he stops his mount in front of him, and says, "Weapons being collected, sir."

Major Whitside looks at Big Foot and says, "Big Foot, we will make camp at Wounded Knee Creek tonight, and head out for Pine Ridge tomorrow." Major Whitside then looks at Lieutenant Sestak and says, "Lieutenant, have my hospital wagon brought up for Big Foot." Lieutenant Sestak spurs his mount back in the ranks as Major Whitside looks back at Big Foot and says, "I think my hospital wagon will be a little more comfortable than that spring-less open wagon you're riding on."

Big Foot plops back down on the wagon bed, coughing, as Old Woman covers him.

Major Whitside's covered hospital wagon rolls up. A corporal is driving. An Army doctor sits beside him, as Lieutenant Sestak rides alongside the wagon.

The hospital wagon stops next to Big Foot's wagon as Major Whitside looks to Lieutenant Sestak and says, "Lieutenant, have your men help the doc carry Big Foot into the hospital wagon, then while we're on the march, have your men ride, left and right flank of their perimeters, weapons at the ready..." Major Whitside then turns to his men, barking his orders: "B and I Troop will lead the captives with weapons at the ready, G Troop and Battery E will bring up the rear, weapons at the ready!"

Lieutenant Sestak, the doctor and several soldiers

dismount and carry Big Foot off his wagon, as all the other soldiers hurry to their positions per Major Whitside's orders.

Later that day, it's turning twilight in the northern territory of the Badlands as a light snow falls on the 9th Cavalry. They are wearing their buffalo coats, gloves, and caps, and are headed back to their encampment, riding in two mounted columns. They are retracing their tracks from this morning's trek, skirting the Badland's rocky cliffs.

A ray of sun breaks through the stormy dark clouds, and shines on the soldiers. There's a lot of oohs and ahs coming from the soldiers as Trooper Walley softly shouts out, "Wow, now would you take a look at that...ain't that pretty."

The ray of sun disappears as fast as it came as Sergeant Shaw turns in his saddle and looking at Corporal Wilson says, "Corporal, pass the word, keep it down, be at the ready."

Corporal Wilson turns in his saddle and passes Sergeant Shaw's orders on as Sergeant Shaw looks at Sergeant Jordan turning his eyes towards the canyon cliffs, with his head basically pointed straight ahead. Then Sergeant Shaw looks at Major Henry, whose eyes are also looking at the cliffs.

As Sergeant Jordan rides along a few more paces, still pretending not to be looking towards the cliffs, he says, "They're still there, sir...watchin'...not pointin' weapons at us, just watchin'."

Major Henry says, "What do you make of it, Sergeant?"

"I don't rightly know, sir...don't seem to be threatenin' any."

"Sergeant, we'll post extra sentries tonight and take to

the highlands first thing tomorrow morning."

"Yes, sir," says Sergeant Jordan.

Meanwhile, it's twilight and snowing at the 7th Cavalry encampment, as Major Whitside's columns crawl over the last rise, and begin descending the slopes towards Chankpe Opi Wakpale, Wounded Knee Creek. Major Whitside with the guidons positioned in the ranks, leads B and I Troops, followed by Big Foot's band, with the hospital wagon in the middle, then G Troop, followed by Battery E, the Hotchkiss cannon and Gatling gun, all troopers with weapons at the ready.

Lieutenant Sestak's men are riding the perimeters as a wintry dusk settles in the encampment. The wind blows, breaking branch limbs from trees, causing a cracking popping sound in the frigid air, and with the wind howling, it creates a supernatural atmosphere. The 7th Cavalry escorts the Sioux Indians through the nearly deserted, but now enlarged cavalry encampment. The regimental flag is staked in the distance by Colonel Forsyth's tent. Sentries walk their post as the 7th Cavalry heads down into Wounded Knee Creek with their captives.

Major Whitside looks at the encampment, then at Lieutenant Sestak and says, "I see the other units of Colonel Forsyth's arrived looking for Big Foot," he then proudly says, "However, we were the ones who found him. Lieutenant, we'll take a head count before they settle in."

"Yes, sir," says Lieutenant Sestak.

The wind howls and the snow falls as they descend into Wounded Knee Creek.

Later that evening, in the valley of Wounded Knee Creek, periodic gusts of wind blow snow horizontally through the Sioux encampment. Several campfires throw sparks into the air.

In the center of the encampment, the defeated nomadic Sioux Indians stand in three long segregated lines—men, women, and children—all of whom are guarded by sentries. Positioned in the men's line, Big Foot barely stands. He is being aided and supported by members of his band as the soldiers perform their duties, including the securing the Sioux encampment.

Several yards in front of the segregated Sioux, Lieutenant Sestak sits at a table, facing the three lines. Major Whitside is standing next to him, looking over his shoulder, with several other officers. Lieutenant Sestak looks at the last Sioux Indian to be counted, a Sioux man standing in front of the table, as Lieutenant Sestak says, "You can go." The Sioux man turns from the table and walks back to the men's line. Lieutenant Sestak writes on a tablet and quickly counts to himself as he then looks and points to his writing, saying aloud, "One hundred twenty-nine men over the age of eighteen...one hundred ninety-nine women and forty children."

"Very good...Lieutenant, station extra sentries around their encampment and our perimeters with Battery E. Pass out rations and get them settled in for the night. If they don't have shelter, pitch tents for them," says Major Whitside.

"Yes, sir," says Lieutenant Sestak as he salutes, then barks out his orders: "Quartermaster, start passing out rations..."

Lieutenant Sestak continues to bark out orders, as the doctor walks up to Major Whitside and says, "He has a severe case of pneumonia, Major. He may not make it...not much I can do for him here, except make him comfortable."

"Doc, have a separate tent set up for him with a heater."

"Yes, sir," says the doctor as he salutes Major Whitside, makes an about-face, and marches off.

Later that night in Wounded Knee Creek, the wind has died down, but it's still snowing. Numerous tepees and Sibley tents dot the landscape of the virtually quiet Sioux encampment.

Sentries are dispersed throughout the encampment, with two sentries standing just outside one of the tents. Old Woman flips the flap of the tent back where the two sentries stand. She walks out of the tent, returns the flap, looks at one of the sentries and says, "I have to pee."

The sentry motions with his carbine to the back of the tent. Old Woman walks in the direction the sentry pointed, with the sentry following. Old Woman goes behind a bush, squats as the sentry keeps one eye on her.

Moments later, in the 7th Cavalry encampment, above Wounded Knee Creek, Major Whitside and several officers are standing by one of several campfires, warming themselves, looking down onto the Sioux encampment, then looking across the ravine at the other half of the 7th Cavalry encampment.

A sentry whistles, and softly shouts, "Colonel Forsyth and officers, comin' in."

Major Whitside is standing by the campfire as he looks at Colonel Forsyth, who is riding in with Lieutenant Mitchell—now looking more confident. Five other officers accompany them.

Colonel Forsyth stops his mount, dismounts, looks at Lieutenant Mitchell, and says, "Lieutenant, take the gentlemen to my tent. I'll be there shortly."

"Yes, sir," says Lieutenant Mitchell. Lieutenant Mitchell salutes, then spurs his mount forward, leading the other officers away.

Colonel Forsyth then walks with his mount towards the fire where Major Whitside stands warming himself.

Major Whitside and the other officers salute Colonel Forsyth as he approaches the fire while removing his fur gloves. Colonel Forsyth stops at the fire, returns their salute, and begins warming his hands as he looks at the officers standing around the fire. "Gentlemen, if you would excuse yourselves, I need to speak to the major," he says.

The officer's salute and walk away as Colonel Forsyth warms his hands, looks at Major Whitside, and says, "Good fire Major—and congratulations on the capture."

Major Whitside proudly says, "Thank you, Colonel."

Colonel Forsyth says, "I received a message from General Brooke. He has more than nine thousand troops on the perimeter of the agencies. They'll start bringing in the rest soon. We'll take Big Foot and his band to the Union Pacific Railroad to be transferred to military prison in Omaha in the morning."

"Colonel, he's got pneumonia. He should go to a hospital. Doc said he's pretty bad off."

"Did you hear me, Major...I said we have orders—period! Did you disarm them?"

"Yes, sir."

"We'll make double sure in the morning...Major. I want more sentries posted around the perimeters and position my Hotchkiss cannon and the Gatling on this side of the creek."

"Yes, sir."

Major Whitside salutes and makes an about-face, and marches off.

Later that night, the frigid wind begins to blow in the 7th Cavalry encampment above Wounded Knee Creek, as a quiet party atmosphere flows through the air. Several lantern-lit canvas tents show the shadows of soldiers within, who are pouring drinks in their shot glasses, then downing their fill.

Some soldiers are warming themselves by campfires, while other soldiers are having a good time in and around the cavalry encampment, going from tent to tent, including Trooper Hartigan, who appears to be a little drunk, and is standing outside one of the tents.

The American and the 7th's Regimental flags flutter in the breeze outside Colonel Forsyth's tent. Two sentries stand guard on both sides. The tent flap is flipped back as several officers walk out, and Lieutenant Mitchell enters.

Inside Colonel Forsyth's tent, Lieutenant Mitchell closes the flap behind him as he turns and sees the officers he escorted to the colonel's tent earlier in the evening. They are standing or sitting towards the rear. Also in the tent is Lieutenant Sestak, who greets Lieutenant Mitchell with a nod of his head.

Then Colonel Forsyth looks to Lieutenant Mitchell and says, "Uh, Lieutenant, good to have you. Did you get a chance to introduce yourself to these fine gentlemen?"

"No, sir."

"I'm sorry Lieutenant, I didn't have a chance to when you caught up to us."

Colonel Forsyth begins indicating with his hand as he says, "These are some of the finest officers in the U.S. Cavalry, and their men are as equal to ours. I'm sure you saw their added units when we rode up?"

"Uh, yes, sir."

"Here, let me introduce you." Colonel Forsyth looks to the officers and says, "This is Godfrey, Moylan, Varnum, Wallace and Edgerly."

Each officer shakes Lieutenant Mitchell's hand as they

are introduced, then Colonel Forsyth looks at Lieutenant Mitchell and says, "And this is Lieutenant Mitchell...Lieutenant, these gentlemen were at...Little Bighorn, that day."

A warm feeling comes over Lieutenant Mitchell, and a surprise expression develops on his face.

Colonel Forsyth walks up to a small keg sitting on a table. He stops in front picking up several shot glasses that sit alongside the keg, and begins pouring whiskey into the glasses. Colonel Forsyth begins passing out the spirits as he looks to his comrades and says, "Gentlemen, this is the first time the regiment has been together as a unit...since that horrible day..." he then proudly looks at his party, holding his glass in the air and says, "A toast."

They all raise their glasses as Colonel Forsyth looks around at the group and says, "A toast to green...Sitting Bull's death, and the capture of Big Foot...and those murderous savages."

They all raise their glasses higher and cheer, "Here! Here! Here!"

Moments later, in the Sioux encampment, inside the Sibley tent where Big Foot is imprisoned, sounds of the 7th Cavalry encampment above emanate within. Campfires blaze in the encampment, causing the shadows of the sentries standing guard outside the tent to be projected within by one of the campfires.

Big Foot is barely breathing and resting on a buffalo skin next to a cavalry heater and lantern. He is covered with blankets and he is being tended to by Little Deer as Old Woman, sitting next to him, sobs.

Some of the other old men and women have gathered inside the tent near their spiritual leader. They also cry and weep softly, as sobbing Old Woman kneeling next to Big

Foot says, "I see more soldiers come."

Big Foot coughs as he says, "They sound like many."

"They drunk with firewater...can hear them...they will kill us, it's in their hearts...they know who we are," says Old Woman.

Big Foot takes his free hand and pats her softly on her leg to reassure her as he coughs.

Early morning the next day, it's just turned light in the Badlands of the Northern Territory. It's not snowing, but it's dark and overcast as a periodic gust of wind blows.

Corporal Wilson, Troopers Chase, Irving, and Walley, and some other troopers are climbing in around the cliffs of the Badlands. Corporal Wilson looks down and shouts to Sergeant Jordan mounted below, "They're gone, Sarge. No trace of 'em."

"All right, Corporal, come on down," shouts Sergeant Jordan.

Corporal Wilson and the troopers begin making their way down the cliffs as Sergeant Jordan looks at Major Henry and says, "Sir, they were probably the ones that came in last night lookin' for food...poor souls...they sure were hungry, the way they put away that grub."

Sergeant Shaw says, "Yeah, and before we sent them back to Pine Ridge, they said Big Foot was east of Pine Ridge."

"I know Sergeant, however, General Brooke said Colonel Forsyth would search to the east. I did send word with the detail taking the Sioux back to Pine Ridge. We'll keep searching northwest, until we hear differently," says Major Henry.

The sergeants look at Major Henry with an expression of "orders are orders."

That same morning in the Sioux encampment at Wounded Knee Creek, it's been sunlight for an hour. The snow has stopped; however, dark clouds loom above as sentries stand on the perimeters of the encampment. Many Sioux, ravenous, are wolfing down and finishing the rations they've been given by the soldiers: hardtack and coffee.

A bugle call is heard, "To muster by your troop."

The Sioux look at the high ground above them, to the 7th Cavalry encampment on both sides of the gulch, seeing that the numerous guidons that dotted the landscape earlier are now being carried by soldiers to their positions. A great portion of more than a thousand 7th Cavalry soldiers are scrambling to the guidons on foot and mounted, surrounding the Sioux encampment with weapons in hand.

The Sioux women are now cowering and weeping as they see on both sides of the creek, the soldiers moving into positions, the Hotchkiss cannons and Gatling gun, now poised to rake the creek.

They then look to Colonel Forsyth, riding up on his mount, stopping next to the Hotchkiss cannon and Gatling gun on his side of the hill. He is looking through his field glasses, looking down at them, with the American and regimental flag staked in the ground next to him.

On the hill, above the Sioux encampment, periodic gusts of wind blow as Colonel Forsyth sits mounted, looking through his field glasses, to the quarter-mile-long Sioux encampment stretched out below him. He then trains his field glasses across the gulch, looking at Major Whitside and Lieutenant Sestak, who are getting into their positions.

He then takes the field glasses from his eyes and looks at Moylan, Wallace, and Edgerly, on his side of the gulch, with their men, getting into their final positions. Colonel Forsyth then looks at Lieutenant Mitchell, who now seems to have the spirit of the 7th Cavalry in him, and says, "Rations sufficiently passed out Lieutenant?"

"Yes, sir," says Lieutenant Mitchell smartly.

Colonel Forsyth then looks back through his field glasses and says, "Whitside, Godfrey, Varnum are in their positions." He removes the glasses, looks at Lieutenant Mitchell and says, "Lieutenant Sestak will join you in the Sioux encampment. Lieutenant...form the detail."

Lieutenant Mitchell salutes, then looks at his men and calls his orders, "Search detail—form up, column of sevens."

The guidon trooper quickly positions himself with the 7th Cavalry, B Troop guidon, as seventy soldiers, in Lieutenant Mitchell's detail, hurry into their formations: forty-nine on foot, twenty-one on mounts.

Trooper Hartigan, who is a little hung over, walks up to Lieutenant Mitchell, gives a sloppy salute, showing little respect as he says, "Uh, Lieutenant...forgettin' about someone, someone who's suppose to protect you?"

Lieutenant Mitchell looks at Trooper Hartigan as Colonel Forsyth looks at Trooper Hartigan and says, "Don't worry son, the lieutenant won't need any protection," as he looks at the Hotchkiss cannon and then says, "These Hotchkiss cannons, I hear, can fire one round a second—and are up to several miles effective..." Colonel Forsyth rides over to where Trooper Hartigan stands, leans down out of his saddle to Trooper Hartigan, and says, "Trooper, the lieutenant is getting ready to lead one of Custer's troops into the middle of those Indians down there. You want to join the lieutenant, Trooper, so you can get some real experience in dealing with these people?"

Trooper Hartigan delighted says, "Yes, sir!"

Colonel Forsyth looks at Lieutenant Mitchell and says, "You got you another man, Lieutenant."

Trooper Hartigan looks at Colonel Forsyth and says, "Thank you, sir."

Lieutenant Mitchell turns and marches towards the detail, stops, turns around, looks back at Trooper Hartigan and says, "Let's get goin', Trooper."

Lieutenant Mitchell turns back and continues towards the front of the search detail formation, with Trooper Hartigan following and calling to Lieutenant Mitchell, saying, "See, you gonna be alright...I see that talk I had with you has given you a new look, Lieutenant."

"Yeah, I appreciate what you said, remindin' me about Custer...and what they did to him. Besides, we're gonna have a little funnin' with them, uh...nothin' can happen, they already been disarmed." Lieutenant Mitchell smiles, and takes the outside lead position of his detail.

Trooper Hartigan looks at a trooper in the front of the formation closest to Lieutenant Mitchell and with a bully attitude says, "Get to the back!" The trooper cowers out of formation, relinquishing it to Trooper Hartigan, who is getting his second wind from his night of drinking.

Lieutenant Mitchell looks at the last man in his detail falling in as he calls his orders: "Detail...forward, march! Your left, your left, your left right left, your left..." Lieutenant Mitchell marches his detail down into the Sioux encampment as the frigid wind begins to blow.

Five minutes later, the soldiers march into the Sioux encampment where the Sioux nervously congregate close to one another as Lieutenant Mitchell calls his orders, "Troop...*hooo.*" The detail of soldiers comes to a stop, "one two" as Lieutenant Sestak rides into the encampment from the other side with his detail saying, "Detail...halt."

Lieutenant Mitchell looks at Lieutenant Sestak, then to the Sioux, showing no mercy as he shouts to their encampment saying, "My name is Lieutenant Mitchell...Seventh Cavalry...I want all men in the center of the camp! Sentries, bring Big Foot out of the Sibley and place him in the center."

The wind begins to blow a little harder as the Sioux men that understood nervously begin moving into the center of their encampment, while other Sioux tell their comrades who didn't understand.

The men slowly congregate in the center as several sentries carry Big Foot out of the tent with Old Woman and Little Deer, who is nursing, following behind them. They lay Big Foot in the center of camp, revealing the bloody handkerchief he is still holding to his face. Big Foot is barely breathing as some of the older Sioux men gather around him, sitting in a circle, as Old Woman covers him with blankets.

The Sioux women and children huddle, not far away, in a large group, weeping, as Lieutenant Mitchell looks at the Sioux, then looks at his detail, saying, "Search detail...look for any kind of weapons...break formation, ho..."

Lieutenant Sestak and several other officers stay with Lieutenant Mitchell as the search detail breaks formation, with the mounted soldiers riding to the outer parts of the encampment. The soldiers on foot move throughout the beginning of the encampment, going from tepee to tepee and tent to tent.

Trooper Hartigan and the other soldiers begin throwing the Sioux's personal bundles out of the lodges. Some fall apart as they hit the snowy, muddy ground outside. The Sioux women and children begin weeping as other items of theirs are thrown into the center of the encampment.

Trooper Hartigan is enjoying his superior status over

the Sioux, along with the other soldiers, as Lieutenant Mitchell shouts to the Sioux saying, "I have orders to disarm you and transport you to the Union railroad."

Some Sioux women begin crying, fearing the worst, as Big Foot is too ill to even know what Lieutenant Mitchell just said.

The soldiers go from tepees to tents, collecting tepee stake-pegs, axes, knifes, a couple bows, a few arrows and spears, putting the weapons in a pile in the center of the encampment. The mounted soldiers come riding back, with several old rifles and other items, dumping them into the pile of confiscated weapons.

Lieutenant Mitchell, seeing that his detail is coming up with nothing else, looks up to Colonel Forsyth, who is now dismounted, standing by the Hotchkiss cannon on the hill, looking through his field glasses. Lieutenant Mitchell cups his hands over his mouth and yells to Colonel Forsyth above him saying, "Sir, this is all we can find," as he points to the pile of weapons.

Soldiers pass his message up the hill to Colonel Forsyth who is looking through his field glasses. Colonel Forsyth takes the glasses from his eyes as he yells back to Lieutenant Mitchell below him, saying, "Lieutenant, search their belongings and persons...remove any unnecessary garments!" The soldiers pass Colonel Forsyth's message back down the hill to Lieutenant Mitchell, as Lieutenant Mitchell turns to his detail and says, "Start searchin' their bundles and line 'em up—search their bodies."

The soldiers are clearly out-numbered by the Sioux as the wind begins blowing harder. The soldiers begin tearing through the Sioux's bundles, throwing the last of the Sioux's earthly possessions into the blowing cold wind. Other soldiers begin rousting the men and women up from sitting, taking off their blankets, coats and any other cover they may have on, revealing their *Ghost Shirts*.

Some of the Sioux begin to show their anger and displeasure on their faces. Yellow Bird, a middle-aged warrior, takes off his blanket, revealing his *Ghost Shirt*. The wind blows harder, tree limbs begin snapping and breaking in the frigid air as Yellow Bird begins dancing and singing in Sioux language, the ghost chant, in the near-blizzard wind, saying, "The *sacred garments* protect you...the bullets will not go towards you...the prairie is large and the bullets will not go towards you..."

Lieutenant Mitchell looks at Yellow Bird, then shouts to Lieutenant Sestak, saying, "That's the dance Colonel Forsyth was talkin' about last night...I wonder what it means?"

Other Sioux begin joining Yellow Bird in their ritual, The *Ghost Dance*, as Trooper Hartigan shouts out to Lieutenant Mitchell saying, "Hey Lieutenant...this one's not cooperatin'!" Trooper Hartigan is struggling with Black Wolf for his blanket that covers him. Black Wolf pulls away from Trooper Hartigan and begins dancing and chanting, holding his blanket around him, as Trooper Hartigan yells at him saying, "Come back here Injun!" Trooper Hartigan runs to Black Wolf, grabbing his blanket, yanking it off him, revealing Black Wolf's new rifle hidden underneath, and his *Ghost Shirt*, as the wind begins to die down.

Black Wolf then holds the rifle high in the air with both hands as he dances. Trooper Hartigan runs and grabs the rifle, causing both to struggle for the weapon. Black Wolf looks to the heavens, then looks and shouts at Trooper Hartigan in broken English saying, "Shirt protect me...this mine, I paid for...not fair, you pay me for rifle, mine! Your bullets can't hurt me!"

Trooper Hartigan says, "Give me that rifle you damn Injun!"

They struggle more and more for the rifle, with both their hands near the trigger guard. Trooper Hartigan and Black Wolf pull at the rifle, bringing the rifle down, near their torsos, pulling back and forth, bringing their bodies close together, barrel pointing in the air above their heads—BANG! It goes off.

All of a sudden, the sound of gun, rifle and cannon fire escalates instantly: BANG! BANG! BOOM!

Trooper Hartigan and Black Wolf continue to struggle over the rifle as the indiscriminate weapon fire from above begins to take its toll. The rounds from the Hotchkiss cannons hit the ground, exploding, killing Sioux and 7th Cavalry soldiers alike. Tepees and tents begin to shred, as the Gatling gun goes to work, BANG! BANG! BANG!

A soldier runs for cover when he is hit in the back by a Hotchkiss round, tearing a hole through his chest, spattering blood and chest cavity remains against a tepee. In the chaos, the Sioux scramble to the center, and around their encampment, grabbing what weapons they can find, theirs or the soldiers'.

The soldiers in the encampment are dodging their own fire from above as they pull their revolvers and carbines, and begin shooting Sioux men, women, and children indiscriminately.

Black Wolf, still struggling with Trooper Hartigan, is shot two times in the back by a soldier in the encampment. Old Woman, who was taking care of Big Foot, walks through the chaos with a knife, and stabs the soldier in the back, who just shot Black Wolf. She then is shot several times by Trooper Hartigan, with the Winchester rifle.

The weapon fire from above is indiscriminate as Trooper Hartigan is riddled with Gatling gunfire—BANG! BANG! BANG!

Half an hour later, black powder smoke fills the valley below, with most of the soldiers on the hillsides still firing their weapons, and the Gatling gun still firing its deadly burst of lead.

The Hotchkiss cannon next to Colonel Forsyth and across the gulch fires, BOOM, BOOM, BOOM, as Colonel Forsyth looks through the haze and smoke through his field glasses, trying to see the deadly hits falling further up the creek. He yells out, "Keep firing! Keep firing! Second detail, mount your mounts!"

At the agency grounds of Pine Ridge Indian Reservation, the sky is dark with clouds, and the frigid wind blows, as bedlam runs rampant. In the far distance, a very faint sound of weapon fire is heard, sounding like a major battle is occurring.

The thousands of Sioux Indians that where pushed into the surrounding area from General Miles' military action are now stampeding away to the north. Soldiers are trying to stop them, just short of firing their weapons. There are too many Sioux to stop as the soldiers wrestle with the ones they can catch.

General Brooke is standing on the porch of the agency office looking at two Crow Indian scouts mounted on their mounts, starting to ride off. He shouts, "Find out...get word back right away!"

The scouts acknowledge as they spur their mounts off towards the sounds of the weapon fire, passing a detachment of eight white soldiers leading a military coach with a jet black mount tethered to the rear, followed by another eight white soldiers, mounted. The coach stops near the front of the agency as the coach door opens right away. General Miles steps out, looking at the panicking, fleeting Sioux, then at the faint sounds of a lot of weapon fire in the far distance. He then looks at General Brooke, standing in front of the agency, looking somewhat uncomfortable as he yells, "What the hell is going on, Brooke!"

General Brooke submissively says, "I don't know yet, sir. About an hour ago, we started hearing a lot of gun and small cannon fire off in the distance...then about ten minutes ago, several wandering Sioux rode in yelling to the ones that came in...then all hell broke lose...they started stampeding out of here."

"No shit, General! Get those Indians rounded up and back here...we're trying to ship them to the railroad. Damn it, I should of been here seven days ago and this wouldn't be happening...Damn weather!" General Brooke looks to General Miles quizzically as General Miles looks at the agency area, where most the Sioux have left, then to the distant weapon fire, as he looks at General Brooke and says, "Sounds like a lot of shootin' goin' on. Who's in that direction, Brooke?"

"Sir, that's coming from the, northeast...the Seventh, Forsyth and Whitside...like you said."

Back at Wounded Knee Creek, the air is thick with black-powder smoke in the Sioux encampment. The onslaught of Hotchkiss cannons, Gatling gun, rifle, and pistol fire has torn the Sioux encampment apart. Tepees and tents are shredded; bodies and partial bodies of Sioux Indians and 7th Cavalry soldiers lay dead everywhere. Big Foot lays on his back, dead, partly frozen, shot several times in the chest. His forearms are extended into the air, his fingers are contorted, with his blood staining the snow red beneath him.

Moments later, in the 7th Cavalry encampment above, periodic gusts of wind blow as Colonel Forsyth stands, looking through his field glasses, several miles up the creek gulch. He watches his men combing the creek valley, picking off Sioux Indians, wherever they can find them.

In the Sioux encampment, and further up the creek bed, indiscriminate killing is taking place. It's more hand-to-hand combat, with some gunfire coming from the 7th Cavalry soldiers that are mounted.

A Sioux man comes from behind the last tepee, and throws a spear at a soldier on his mount, spearing him dead in the back, mid-torso. Another soldier, mounted, comes riding from behind the Sioux man, and shoots him dead in the back of the head, dropping him where he stood.

Soldiers on foot and mounted whoop, yell, and holler, as they chase more than one hundred Sioux Indians up the creek, weaponless, out of their encampment, taking shots—at men, women, and children, who are running away, dropping the victims where they were.

Further up the creek, two women and a child are hiding behind some large bushes, weeping and crying softly as they are shot—BANG, BANG, BANG—from behind by two 7th Cavalry soldiers riding down on them. They spur their mounts and head towards the creek bed, whooping it up.

Further up the creek, a Sioux boy, Black Elk, lays wounded and motionless in the muddy snow, watching the soldiers massacre his people, shooting them like they were buffalo on the prairie.

Later in the afternoon, the same day, a heavy snow begins to fall over the 9th Cavalry, returning from combing the Badlands in the Northern Territory. They have been out now for four days in extreme winter conditions. Their faces show the battering of the cold, but they are still in good spirits in their buffalo coats, gloves and caps as they head

277

back to camp.

The Buffalo Soldiers are escorting nineteen Sioux Indian prisoners on mounts. Their hands are untied. Sergeant Jordan is riding with several guards, on their left perimeter, outside the column of prisoners.

Sergeant Jordan then spurs his mount forward, plowing through the snow, back to his position in the columns, and as he returns to his position, he looks to Major Henry and Sergeant Shaw saying, "Any more snow, they'll find us this sprin'."

"You're right about that, Sergeant," says Major Henry.

Sergeant Shaw says, "Sir, what are they gonna do with the Sioux, once we turn them over?"

"Probably send the children back east to schools and the adults to some camp in the south."

"It don't seem right to break up families like that, sir," says Sergeant Shaw.

"No Sergeant, it's not right, however, we're military men, paid to do what we're told."

"Yes, sir," says Sergeant Shaw.

As the 9th Cavalry rides on, the snow covers them, making them look like woolly animals riding mounts as Trooper Irving looks at Trooper Walley and says, "We must of ridden thirty miles today through this snow—day before that, another thirty. I'm startin' to feel like a snowman."

"You are starting to look like a snow-animal," says Trooper Chase.

Everyone around them laughs.

Several hours later, in Indian Agent Royer's office, the sound of weapon fire has dissipated somewhat in the distance and replaced by the wind beating against the log building as General Miles paces back and forth smoking a cigar, and General Brooke downs another shot of whiskey.

General Miles stops pacing, looks at the calendar on the wall, then turns to face General Brooke and says, "This is the twenty-ninth of December, Brooke..."

General Brooke stops talking, when all of a sudden they hear a rider, riding in fast, coming to a stop outside the office. General Brooke rushes to the window, looks out, and sees the beginning blizzard conditions. Then with a surprised look, he sees Lieutenant Sestak, who appears as if he has been in a war sitting on his mount, wavering. He dismounts, almost falling off his mount, stumbling exhaustively past two Indian sentries standing in front of the steps, leading to the office porch platform.

Lieutenant Sestak then barely walks up the steps, across the platform to the front door, where another sentry stands. He knocks on the door, as General Brooke looks to the door and says, "Enter!"

The sentry opens the door and Lieutenant Sestak stumbles in, stops, barely standing at attention, and salutes exhaustively. He's bleeding from the forehead, his overcoat is badly torn with bloodstains on the yellow lining and surrounding cuts on his right arm and left leg. His uniform is also bloody, dirty, and tattered.

General Brooke says, "What in the hell happen to you, Lieutenant?!"

Lieutenant Sestak says exhaustively, "Medical supplies...we need medical supplies...take back to Wounded Knee...sir. Many soldiers...Indians killed and wounded...sir. Big Foot dead, Wallace dead, Sioux on trail, ambushing other units...sir."

General Miles looks to General Brooke with an angry, disgusted look and says, "Brooke, I want to talk to you—outside!"

Lieutenant Sestak stays at a wavering attention as General Miles grabs General Brooke by the arm, and pulls him towards the front door.

Periodic gusts of wind blow snow horizontally with sporadic gunfire still heard in the far distance as General Miles closes the front door behind him. He pulls General Brooke by the arm, along the porch and past the office window, when they hear a KA-PLUNK from inside. They both stop and look back through the window and see Lieutenant Sestak passed out on the floor as General Miles looks at General Brooke and says, "Let him sleep it off!" General Miles again pulls General Brooke by the arm to the end of the porch, where he believes no one will hear his anger over the intermittent howling wind, as General Miles says, "Damn it Brooke, none of our soldiers were suppose to get hurt..."

The agency sentries are pretending not to be listening, as several other soldiers gather, looking at General Miles shouting at General Brooke over the gusting wind noise.

General Miles quickly looks at the sentries and soldiers gathering as he stops shouting at General Brooke, then looks at the soldiers and shouts, "Carry on!" The sentries quickly turn back around, and the soldiers scurry away through the snow as General Miles looks around the agency and senses that something isn't right with their plans. He then looks at General Brooke, who is cowering a little, either from General Miles' lashing, the whiskey, or both, as General Miles says, "Brooke, green is not good...send an urgent message to Major Henry...come at once, Pine Ridge Agency...Big Foot killed, bedlam now Pine Ridge. Need your assistance immediately...Urgent."

An hour later, in Wounded Knee Creek, several miles up-creek from the Sioux's encampment, a light snow swirls above the creek. In the creek, there's no wind, so the warm gunpowder smoke now mixes with the cold air, creating a thick fog-like atmosphere that settles several feet off the ground in the gulch.

Periodic sounds of intermittent Gatling gun and Hotchkiss cannon-fire continues from above several miles back, as a 7th Cavalry officer walks along the snowy, muddy creek through the fog, up from the encampment with his Sharps rifle by his side. His overcoat is shredded in the back from his earlier encounters as he pokes at the Sioux bodies lying about with his rifle, checking to see if they move, as he walks along the creek.

After checking several bodies, the officer stops in his tracks and suddenly points his rifle when he sees a Sioux woman moving and apparently breathing several yards in front of him. She is lying on the side of the muddy creek in a fetal position, facing him. She is partially wrapped with a blanket around her mid-torso, nestled in some tall brown creek grass. Part of her head has been blown away. She still appears to be alive, breathing, as her upper-torso moves under the blanket.

The officer begins walking towards her, nervously pointing his rifle, ready to shoot at a moment's notice.

The officer is Lieutenant Mitchell, with his ponytail tucked under his campaign hat. He has a deep cut across his left cheek. His face is pretty well beat up. His overcoat is torn in the front revealing his bloody uniform. He walks slowly towards the woman, talking to himself, barely moving his bloody bruised lips, he mutters, "You couldn't possibly be...alive...by the looks of your head?" Lieutenant Mitchell's eyes widen. He's shaking, scared, as he approaches the Sioux woman. When he reaches the body, he stops, and slowly pokes the woman's shoulder with his rifle barrel. Nothing happens. He pokes again, nothing, but the mid-torso keeps convulsing as if she is breathing.

Lieutenant Mitchell is really puzzled as he takes his rifle, snags the blanket with the front barrel sight, and pulls the blanket off her. Lieutenant Mitchell is horrified by what he sees. It's Little Deer, and her baby, who is nursing from her breast.

Lieutenant Mitchell has seen it all now as he begins to upchuck his last meal, and the meal before that, if any...

Later that night, it's blizzard conditions, as the wind swirls and howls in the Badlands of the Northern Territory. Sparks from several campfires blow horizontally in the wind as several soldiers try to stay warm, standing upwind of the flames and sparks in their buffalo coats, fur gloves and caps.

Other soldiers scurry, getting ready to bed down for the night, in their warm tents. It was a long day. They're tired, as several lantern-lit tents go dark.

At one of the tents where a sentry stands guard, Sergeant Jordan flips the flap open, somewhat stooping down he walks out into the blowing snow, then flips the tent flap back. Pulling his coat tight around him, he looks back and shouts, "Good night, sir."

From inside the tent, Major Henry shouts, "Good night, Sergeant."

Sergeant Jordan nods to the sentry standing outside Major Henry's tent, then walks away in the howling, blowing blizzard.

Inside Major Henry's tent, several minutes later, Major Henry is opening up his logbook, sitting on his cot by a wood stove and lantern. The weather swirls around his tent, and as the wind whips the canvas, it causes the canvas to create snapping sounds. Major Henry begins writing in the book, "29, December, 1890, Rode fifty miles, captured nineteen hostiles, brought back to main camp Harney Springs, Badlands—Blizzard conditions—Will search further north to"—

Major Henry stops writing as a sentry yells out, "Messenger! Messenger ridin' in! Messenger ridin' in!"

Major Henry hears the sentry's shouts, closes the log book, stands, then puts on his overcoat, walks to the tent flap, pushes it open, bends down and walks out, standing upright, closing the flap behind him in the howling wind.

Major Henry pulls his overcoat tight around him as the intense blizzard blows. He then looks at the sentry standing outside his tent and says, "Sentry, dismissed, get out of this weather."

The sentry salutes as Major Henry watches the messenger, who is riding up to one of the fires, shouting out, "Major Henry...Major Henry." Several soldiers standing by the campfire point to Major Henry, who is making his way through the blowing snow and howling wind walking towards them.

As Major Henry nears the campfire, he looks to the mounted messenger and shouts over the howling wind, "I'm Major Henry."

The messenger dismounts, looks at approaching Major Henry. The messenger salutes, as Major Henry returns the salute and the messenger says, "Urgent message for you, sir."

Major Henry takes the message and begins reading. As he reads the message, he quickly looks to the messenger, then back at the message again, before shouting with urgency, "Bugler! Bugler! Bugler! Sound 'Boots and Saddles'...'Boots and Saddles'...we're pulling out!"

The soldiers around the fire hurry to their task as the bugler comes out of his tent, in his long johns, bugle in hand, then realizes how cold it is outside his tent. He quickly puts the bugle to his lips and sounds Major Henry's orders, quickly, over the howling wind. Its organized chaos as soldiers hurry out of their tents, double-timing like ants, to follow the orders sounded on the bugle.

Sergeants Jordan and Shaw hurry out of their tent in the freezing cold, pulling up their britches, putting on their coats. They look at the bugler finishing his bugle call, then look and run to Major Henry standing by the campfire. As they reach Major Henry, Sergeant Jordan says, "Sir, what's wrong?"

"Urgent message from Pine Ridge, we're going back, Big Foot is dead and there's bedlam there now. Sergeants, we don't have time to wait for the wagons, pack what you can carry on your mounts.

"Yes, sir," say Sergeants Jordan and Shaw simultaneously.

The wind howls as Sergeants Jordan and Shaw salute. Major Henry returns the salute. Then Sergeant Shaw turns and double-times back to the center of camp calling his orders, as Sergeant Jordan turns and shouts his orders, "D Troop will stay with the Twenty-fourth, until the wagons are packed, then escort them back to the agency. Corporal Wilson! Corporal Wilson!"

The tents and the camp are already being broken down, as Corporal Wilson makes his way through the organized chaos to Sergeant Jordan. When he reaches Sergeant Jordan, he looks at him barking out orders to his men, then Sergeant Jordan looks at Corporal Wilson and says, "Corporal, we just got an urgent message to return to the agency...you have the most experience of the soldiers here. I'm goin' to leave you with D Troop, Captain Loud to lead the wagons back to Pine Ridge."

"Yes, Sarge."

Corporal Wilson turns and runs to perform his duties as Sergeant Jordan continues barking out his orders.

That night, a full blizzard rages at the Pine Ridge Indian Reservation agency grounds. The howling wind blows snow in and around the few tepees and tents that are pitched in the middle of the Army encampment, and into the faces of the sentries standing guard in their buffalo coats and caps, with their carbines at the ready.

Sporadic gunfire is still heard in the distance as snow also blows into the faces of Colonel Forsyth and Major Whitside and the rest of the 7th Cavalry riding into the agency grounds with their dead and wounded, their weapons at the ready. Colonel Forsyth and Major Whitside have no battle blemishes, unlike Lieutenant Mitchell, who looks pretty beaten up. His uniform is tattered and he doesn't look like he feels quiet soldiery at this point. Neither do the other soldiers who were in the encampment and survived the massacre.

Colonel Forsyth looks at his troops, holds his glove-covered hand in the air, and calls his orders, "Troop *hooo*." The soldiers and wagons halt as Colonel Forsyth looks at Major Whitside and says, "Major, get the men settled in on the north perimeter...take care of the men that need medical attention." He then indicates with his finger to an area on the agency grounds and then says, "Place the dead over there—post extra sentries, dismissed."

Major Whitside shouts to the columns over the howling blizzard, "Lieutenant Mitchell."

Lieutenant Mitchell spurs his mount forward as Colonel Forsyth spurs his mount to the agency office.

Moments later in Agent Royer's office, General Miles is warming his hands by the stove as General Brooke nervously downs another shot of whiskey.

General Miles looks to his pocket watch, then to Colonel Forsyth, who is closing the door behind him. General Miles shouts at Colonel Forsyth angrily saying, "It's past midnight Colonel...took you long enough to get back here," then he says pointedly, "We heard the engagement!"

Colonel Forsyth has stopped in his tracks with a surprised expression on his face. Looking to General Miles, he says, "I didn't know you were coming to the reservation General?" And then with even a more dumbfounded expression he adds, "You heard?"

General Miles shouts, "Yes we heard you damn idiot...you were only fourteen miles away...you were suppose to be further out, so no one could hear...this has caused a delay in our plans Colonel! The Sioux that came in stampeded out of here. Trains are waitin', and all because we heard!"

"Sorry, sir," says Colonel Forsyth sheepishly. He then says, "Uh, what took us so long? We were taking rifle fire all the way back—"

Several gun shots ring out in the near distance, interrupting Colonel Forsyth, as General Miles looks at him and sarcastically says, "Yeah, we can hear that too—what the hell happened out there, Colonel!"

General Brooke pours another drink and shoots it down as General Miles shouts at Colonel Forsyth, saying, "And none of our men were suppose to get hurt, and especially our officers...damn it...Colonel!"

"...Uh, uh...I don't know what happened, sir. There was a shot, and the next I knew...all hell broke loose below...I couldn't leave my men unprotected. I ordered my men above to fire...however some of our men in their encampment were in the way."

"In the way! Where in the hell did you learn your military tactics from Colonel! You get your men to safety first." General Miles begins pacing, then says, "Well...we did take care of green!" He stops pacing, looks to Colonel Forsyth, and angrily says, "Didn't we Colonel!"

"...Uh, uh, yes, sir," says Colonel Forsyth.

"I know Wallace is dead...where's Edgerly, Godfrey, Moylan and Varnum?"

"They took their wounded and dead back to their garrisons, sir."

"All right Colonel, it will just be you. Right now, you have several thousand Sioux running around out there, loose, and not where they're suppose to be." He then looks at Colonel Forsyth and shouts pointedly, "On the damn train!" General Miles calms down and says, "I sent a messenger to Major Henry, not knowing what to expect from you...but they won't be back for several days, at the earliest in this weather...that should give you enough time, so let's see if you can give the Seventh the name it deserves, by combing this reservation and getting those damn Sioux on the train—understood, Colonel!"

"Yes, sir."

General Brooke pours another shot and downs it as General Miles looks at General Brooke and says, "Where's the bottle, General?"

Moments later, the wind blows and howls. It's bitter cold in the Badlands of the Northern Territory. The 9th Cavalry, K, I, and F Troops are making their way on their mounts, at a force-march, through the bitter cold darkness and the blinding blizzard. They are wrapped from their spurs to their eyes in their furry buffalo coats, gloves and caps, and as the snow blows horizontally, it gathers in the slots they made between their coat collars and caps, which they peer through.

As the soldiers ride a few paces, Major Henry shouts to Sergeant Jordan over the howling wind, saying, "We got out of their fast Sergeant."

"Yes, sir. I believe the men are excited about being needed, sir."

As they continue to ride along, Trooper Walley clears the snow from his eyes, looks and shouts to Trooper Irving over the wind howls: "So much for your relaxin' Irving."

Trooper Irving takes some snow that has collected around his saddle, makes a snowball and throws it at Trooper Walley, who deflects it.

Then Trooper Walley looks at Trooper Chase and shouts, "Hey, Chase, where you reckon we're goin' in such a hurry this time of night in this weather. Think we're gonna see some fightin?"

"Maybe, I heard we're going back to the agency. Must be a lot of trouble to bring us out, as you said, in this weather."

"Oh well, I was gettin' bored anyway," says, Trooper Irving.

The blizzard blows as the 9th Cavalry dredges through the snow, towards Pine Ridge.

The next day, it's early morning and the blizzard has dissipated while being replaced by light snow that falls over the freshly laid snow from the storm. Nine miles away from the agency grounds, a mason mission sits at the end of a long curved, snow-covered, wide-mouth box canyon. Several yards in back of the mission, smoke begins to rise from the back of a medium-size wood structure. From the back of the now burning structure, two Sioux Indians appear weaponless, tromping through the knee-deep snow towards the front of the mission, then begin crossing the front yard of the mason church.

The two Sioux Indians stop in the middle of the yard and look at a weathered rectangular wood plaque that is partially buried in the snow in front of them. One of the Sioux picks up the plaque, inspects it, then throws it several yards in front of them, where it lands face up, revealing two words inscribed into the wood: "Drexel Mission."

The two Sioux Indians examine the plaque, and then look down the long part of the canyon, which curves towards the opening, hiding it from view. The canyon cliffs and rocks on both sides are covered with snow and seemingly move at times.

The two Sioux Indians begin tromping through the snow again, past the mission, until they reach the side of the canyon, where they begin climbing up into the cliffs. The two Indians climb over rocks, through crevasses, making their way up the cliffs, when they stop almost halfway up.

They look around when one of the snow-covered rocks stands, dropping the snow off its surface, revealing a Sioux warrior hiding under his blanket, holding a Winchester rifle. He reaches down to the ground, picks up two blankets, and hands them to the two Sioux standing in front of him as another snow-covered rock stands. It contains another Sioux warrior, who hands bows, arrows, and rifles to the two Sioux.

The two warriors then re-cover themselves with their blankets, and squat back down, as the other two Sioux begin covering them with snow, blending them in with the canyon. After the two Sioux finish covering their comrades, they continue climbing up the cliffs as the other camouflaged Sioux within the box canyon begin settling into their positions.

This is the remains of the Great Sioux Nation. They are

covered with blankets and snow, and as the light snow falls, it creates a whiteout condition, blending over one thousand Sioux Indians who have lost everything, into the canyon configuration. They have positioned themselves behind rocks, crevasses of the canyon and the high cliffs, with every weapon available to them, rifles, pistols, bows and arrows, spears, knifes, boulders, and rocks.

In Agent Royer's office that same morning, very few gunshots are heard in the distance, as Agent Royer looks out the window while General Brooke sits at a desk, finishing writing a letter. As General Brooke folds the letter, he looks to the calendar and says, "This is the 30th of December Dr. Royer, one more day to a new year and a fresh start."

Agent Royer turns, looks at General Brooke and says, "Good job General, in taking care of the problem. You think anyone will know?"

"All anyone needs to know Dr. Royer is that they fired first." General Brooke then rises, looks at Agent Royer, and says, "I'll be lifting the military zone probably next week, after we round up the rest."

General Brooke then walks to the stove, stops, and begins warming his hands as sounds of rushing footsteps are heard on the porch coming towards the front door.

There's an urgent knock on the door.

"Enter," says General Brooke.

They look at Lieutenant Sestak, who quickly walks through the front door, looking a little better, bandages covering most of his wounds. He looks at General Brooke with urgency, saying, "Smoke...smoke west of here, sir."

General Brooke and Agent Royer hurry past Lieutenant Sestak, out the front door, looking at the horizon.

As General Brooke and Agent Royer exit the office, Lieutenant Sestak follows behind them, pointing in the direction of the dark smoke, in the far distance through the light snowfall.

Agent Royer then looks at General Brooke and says, "That looks like the Drexel Mission, in White Clay Canyon. It's about nine miles from here. The Mission's been deserted now...for a month or so, since the trouble started. It's made of stone, must be the wood shed in back. Couldn't be anything else burning in this weather."

Lieutenant Sestak looks at General Brooke and says, "General, the Sixth was in that area, however, they went back to their garrison. Should I wake General Miles?"

"No!" says General Brooke excitedly as he then says, "I'm not going to wake General Miles for a little old smoke Lieutenant, and besides— " General Brooke calms down, and is a little embarrassed as he says, "He doesn't know how to handle his liquor. This should be something easy for the Seventh. They're scouting to the southwest today anyways. Lieutenant, ride over to Colonel Forsyth's camp...tell him to check out the smoke...you join his command."

Lieutenant Sestak quickly looks at General Brooke with a doubtful expression and says, "Sir, are you sure...you want me to join his command?"

"What did I say, Lieutenant!"

"Yes, sir."

Lieutenant Sestak salutes, and makes an about-face with an expression of "Lord, please help me" as he marches off.

An hour later, a few gun shots still echo in the distance as a light snow falls on the 9th Cavalry that is riding into the agency grounds, carbines at the ready. Their uniforms look weather-beaten, but their spirits are high.

They begin to pass 7th Cavalry sentries, who are guarding a few Sioux Indians that are sitting near military tents in the center of the agency as other 7th Cavalry soldiers dig graves and go about their tasks.

Major Henry and the troops look to the graves, then Major Henry looks at both sergeants and says, "Looks like some soldiers died, Sergeants. Sergeants, dismount the troops once in camp, unsaddle their mounts, get them fed and watered, then get the men something to eat, let them get a few winks. I'll go to the agency office, see what happened and where we are needed."

Sergeants Jordan and Shaw simultaneously say, "Yes, sir."

Sergeants Jordan and Shaw call their orders as Major Henry rides to the agency office.

Moments later, in Agent Royer's office, Agent Royer looks at Major Henry pensively. Major Henry is standing at parade-rest as General Brooke sits at a desk, looking like he has had no sleep. General Brooke downs a shot of whiskey, then looks at Major Henry and says, "They fired first, Major. The next thing Forsyth knew, his men were in the middle."

"That's a shame, sir...that anybody had to die," says Major Henry.

"Uh, yes it is, Major. Major, you got back here awfully fast in that blizzard. General Miles wasn't expecting you for another day or so."

"General Miles' message said urgent. I commanded a force-march, considering the message, sir."

"Well...General Miles thought things were getting out of hand, but the situation has calmed itself. Most of the regiments have returned to their garrisons. Colonel Forsyth is combing the reservation as we speak, bringing in the hostiles. We won't need you or your men at this point, so get some rest, Major."

"Yes, sir. Sir, we saw some smoke coming from the west."

"Yes, Colonel Forsyth will investigate. Major, just have your men get some rest. Dismissed Major."

"Yes, sir," says Major Henry.

Major Henry salutes, makes an about-face, and exits through the front door.

It's still snowing. Gunshots sporadically ring in the far distance as Major Henry exits the office, unties his reins, mounts his mount, and then rides towards the 9th's American flag, and its guidons, K, I, and F.

Most the snow on the ground where the 9th Cavalry are camped has been cleared away. Some soldiers are sprawled under trees, on their bedrolls against their saddles, wrapped in buffalo coats; their heads are covered with their fur caps. Others are resting or standing near campfires eating hardtack and dried beef.

Major Henry stops his mount at the guidons and dismounts as a soldier takes his reins. He then walks to the campfire where Sergeant Jordan is standing as Sergeant Jordan looks at Major Henry approaching and says, "Well, sir?"

"Tell the men to get some rest Sergeant."

"Yes, sir."

Sergeant Jordan salutes, then looks at his men as Sergeant Shaw looks to Major Henry and says, "Sir, what was that smoke we saw?"

"Don't know Sergeant. The Seventh will scout the area."

Major Henry begins to warm himself by the fire as Sergeant Jordan has finished giving orders to his men, picking up his buffalo coat, sitting down on his bedroll, then lying against his saddle, covering himself with the coat. Just as he sighs with relaxation, Sergeant Jordan tilts his head to his right side, and looks out to a rider, riding fast through the *snow*, into the agency grounds. Sergeant Jordan sits up quickly and says, "That looks like Corporal Wilson?"

Everyone looks at the rider as Sergeant Shaw says, "That's Wilson alright...you can tell by the hat...must be trouble."

Major Henry, Sergeants Jordan and Shaw, Troopers Chase, Irving and Walley, and other soldiers who are awake, stand, then begin shaking their comrades who just fell asleep as they look at Corporal Wilson, who is riding in fast. Corporal Wilson rides towards the guidons and Major Henry, slowing then stopping his mount in front of them. Corporal Wilson turns his mount sideways. He's almost out of breath as he looks at Major Henry, Sergeants Jordan and Shaw with urgency saying, "Supply wagons are being attacked about seven miles back!"

"'Boots and Saddles'! 'Boots and Saddles'!" shouts Major Henry as he then looks at both sergeants and says, "Sergeants! I'm going to inform General Brooke. Have my mount re-saddled. Get the men ready."

Major Henry runs to the agency office as Sergeants Jordan and Sergeant Shaw call their orders. All the soldiers hop to, putting the campfires out, grabbing their saddles, carbines, gun belts, coats and everything else they have out.

One hour later, on a snow-covered prairie, no gunshots are heard. It's quiet, almost too quiet as a light snow falls. Colonel Forsyth, Major Whitside, Lieutenants Mitchell and Sestak, ride side-by-side, four abreast, going to investigate the smoke at Drexel Mission.

Lieutenant Sestak has a bandage across his forehead,

and several others under his uniform. Lieutenant Mitchell has a black eye. A bandage crosses his left cheek. He has bruised lips, and his bushy and frayed ponytail protrudes from the back of his campaign hat. Both Lieutenants are still wearing their tattered uniforms under their overcoats, as are the other wounded soldiers who were involved at Wounded Knee. They are leading two very large columns of the 7th Cavalry over several hundred soldiers, with their regimental flag and guidons dispersed among the ranks. As the 7th Cavalry approaches the canyon, about a mile out, white smoke trails high into the cold air, deep from within the canyon. Major Whitside looks at Colonel Forsyth and says, "Sir, send out scouts?"

"No need Major...we're just going to see what's burning, besides—the Sioux are pretty much whipped."

Major Whitside says, "But, sir—"

Colonel Forsyth interrupts Major Whitside as he says, "Major! I said...no need."

"Yes, sir."

Major Whitside now shows contempt on his face, and as they ride on a few more paces, Colonel Forsyth looks at Major Whitside and then spitefully says, "Major, since you're so concerned...you and Lieutenant Mitchell ride up to the mouth of the canyon and take a look."

"Yes, sir," says Major Whitside, as he looks at Lieutenant Mitchell and then says, "Come on Lieutenant." Major Whitside and Lieutenant Mitchell spur their mounts out of formation towards the canyon.

Moments later, on the outskirts of White Clay Canyon, Major Whitside and Lieutenant Mitchell are galloping their mounts towards the canyon mouth. Major Whitside turns and looks at Lieutenant Mitchell and says, "You're lucky to be alive, Lieutenant."

"What was he thinkin' when he started firin' down on us like that, Major!"

"You know Lieutenant, like yourself...he's an ex-paper pusher. He doesn't know the first thing about military tactics. That's why they chose him to undertake this mission—if anything went wrong, they'd blame him."

Meanwhile, seven miles northwest from the agency grounds, Corporal Wilson is leading Major Henry, Sergeants Jordan and Shaw, and two columns of one hundred and fifty Buffalo Soldiers spurring their mounts as fast as they will go through the snow to rescue the wagons. The sounds of their mounts breathing hard is now replaced by sounds of sporadic gunfire up ahead of the columns.

Major Henry looks at his men, then the bugler and says, "Draw weapons...bugler, prepare to sound the CHARGE!"

The soldiers bring their carbines and revolvers out of their holsters to the ready. Major Henry looks at the bugler and shouts, "Bugler, sound CHARGE!"

The bugler trumpets his call, as Major Henry shouts, "CHARGE!"

Corporal Wilson is in the lead, followed by Major Henry, Sergeants Jordan and Shaw, and the rest of the 9th Cavalry, K, I, and F Troops, charging through the snow. Corporal Wilson, riding in front of Major Henry, shouts, "Yah...yah...yah, yah, yah...!"

Major Henry shouts, "Yah...ha, yah...ha...!"

Sergeants Jordan and Shaw, spurring their mounts, simultaneously shout, "Get on...get on...get on, yah yah, yah...!"

Trooper Chase and the soldiers alternate their chants, "Yah... Yah...yah, yah, yah...!"

As the 9th Cavalry approaches the besieged wagons, the Sioux Indians look at the hollering Buffalo Soldiers riding at them. They stop shooting at the wagons, and begin disappearing into the wilderness. Major Henry slows the pace of the soldiers as he sees the Sioux disappearing into the woods, then he looks at Sergeant Jordan and says, "Sergeant, send a group of men and see if you can catch them."

"Yes, sir. Troopers Chase, Irving, Walley, get after 'em with a detail!"

Troopers Chase, Irving and Walley wave to several of their comrades, signaling them to follow. The detail of K Troop spurs their mounts out of formation and pursue the marauding Sioux.

Major Henry then looks at his men and calls his orders, "Troop...ho."

Major Henry, Sergeants Jordan and Shaw, and the other troops of the 9th Cavalry come to a stop in front of the wagons. Major Henry looks at the detail riding off after the Sioux, then he looks at the lead supply wagon, whose mounts have been shot dead as he then shouts, "Captain Loud, Captain Loud, you and your men alright?"

From behind the lead wagon, Captain Loud peeks his head up, looks at Major Henry mounted, and says, "Yeah, yeah." He then turns and looks at his men and says, "I think so." He looks at Major Henry and says, "Thanks Henry...thanks a lot, that sure was close...boy, I didn't think we could of lasted much longer. Major, I want to especially thank that corporal of yours."

Corporal Wilson is sitting proudly on his mount, showing some wear and tear from the task he just performed. Captain Loud looks at him and says, "We didn't think you made it, Corporal, the way they where shootin' at you when you rode out of here." He then looks at Major Henry and says, "Why, if he didn't reach you Major, we sure would of been goners."

Major Henry, sporting a proud look, glances from

Captain Loud to Corporal Wilson and says, "I'll make sure I note that in his record, Captain." Then Major Henry turns back to Captain Loud and says, "However now, let's get you a team of mounts to pull that wagon."

Major Henry turns to Sergeant Shaw and says, "Sergeant, get two of the men's mounts and hitch them to the wagon. The men can ride with the wagon."

"Sir, the mounts are pretty tired. We should use four to pull the wagon," says Sergeant Shaw.

"Four it is, Sergeant. Send the other two troopers to another wagon, that will disperse the weight."

"Yes, sir."

Sergeant Shaw turns his mount around and looks at four troopers mounted in the columns.

Meanwhile, Major Whitside and Lieutenant Mitchell are back in formation as the two long columns of the 7th Cavalry are riding halfway into White Clay Canyon, looking at the Drexel Mission, which is ahead of them at the end of the canyon.

Some of the soldiers are looking at the canyon cliffs around them, searching for signs of movement; however, it's a virtual whiteout. Everything looks the same due to the falling snow.

When they near the end of the box canyon and the Drexel Mission, Colonel Forsyth calls his orders: "Troop, *hooo*." Colonel Forsyth, Major Whitside, and Lieutenants Mitchell and Sestak look at a small fire burning in the charred smoky remains of the woodshed in back of the mission.

Most of the soldiers' eyes are looking ahead to the shed, but some still look around the canyon as Colonel Forsyth looks at Major Whitside and says, "You see, Major, it's just a little fire, that's burned itself out almost."

Just as Colonel Forsyth finishes his statement, arrows come out of nowhere and find their marks, impaling the soldiers near the front of the columns in their backs; the soldiers at the end of the long columns also begin falling off their mounts—dead. The Regimental flag soldier falls from his mount dead, dropping the flag on the ground.

Within a couple blinks of an eye, the entire snowy canyon comes alive with Sioux Indians, who are inflicting vengeance from the heights above and from both sides of the canyon. The Sioux are shooting and throwing every weapon they have down onto the 7th Cavalry.

Colonel Forsyth, in shock, looks back at his men just in time to see his bugler fall off his mount with two arrows protruding from his torso. Colonel Forsyth looks at his other men being picked off, one by one, their blood staining the white snow beneath them, as he cries out with panic, "Dismount! Take cover! Take cover! *Take cover!*"

Colonel Forsyth, Major Whitside, Lieutenants Mitchell and Sestak, and some of the soldiers towards the front of the columns quickly dismount, taking ammunition and weapons, hightailing it to the mission.

Many other soldiers, further back in the ranks, seek cover quickly, behind their mounts. Others tromp through the snow, finding cover in indentations and crevasses on the canyon floor. Bullets hit all around the retreating soldiers as they run or spur their mounts for cover, returning fire above them and across the canyon to the other cliffs.

Three soldiers, one carrying the American flag near the front of the columns, spur their mounts back towards the entrance of the canyon, getting out of harm's way, returning fire into the canyon cliffs on both sides of them. As the three soldiers race through the canyon, they maneuver around their living and dead comrades, and their mounts. When they near the mouth of the canyon, their mounts are shot from underneath them, causing the three soldiers and the American flag to tumble onto the snow-covered ground, hard. The soldiers get up, dazed. All three are shot several times. They fall to the ground—dead.

The soldiers that took defensive positions on the canyon floor are trying to duck the rain of lead bullets, flying arrows, whizzing and zinging by them, hitting the snow and rocks, creating sounds of whiz and thud.

Some of the Sioux Indians begin rolling boulders and throwing rocks down from the heights of the canyon onto the soldiers, hitting or crushing some, while flushing other soldiers out into the open, who become good targets and are soon picked off.

The soldiers are pinned down and do not have good positions in the crevasses, which are low and near to the canyon floor. They cry out to each other for help as they are picked off from the opposite side of the canyon, one by one, especially when they show themselves, trying to return fire above them, to both sides.

Near the mission, a spear is thrown by a Sioux warrior, from midway up the canyon bluff, landing, spearing the 7th Cavalry's regimental flag on the ground, dead center.

From the mission, Colonel Forsyth, Major Whitside, Lieutenants Mitchell and Sestak, and other officers and enlisted men that made it to the church, return fire, when the bullets don't ricochet off the stone mission.

In the Drexel Mission the door is partially open as the sounds of war echo inside, with some bullets penetrating the wood door, and ricocheting off the walls.

Colonel Forsyth, Major Whitside, Lieutenants Mitchell and Sestak, and other officers and enlisted men that made it to the mission return fire when they can. Colonel Forsyth—with fear written in his eyes—waits for a loll in the enemy fire, peeks around the door and looks for a target. He fires a round from his revolver, and retreats back to safety, shouting to Major Whitside, who is standing near a window, saying, "Major, did anybody get out for help?"

Major Whitside—with a disgusted look on his face—looks at Colonel Forsyth and says, "I don't think so, Colonel!" Major Whitside tracks a target with his carbine and fires a round out the window. Lieutenant Mitchell and the other soldiers follow suit.

Lieutenant Mitchell's face now shows apprehension, as Colonel Forsyth cries out, "We've got to try to get word out!"

Major Whitside angrily says, "How, sir? It's not possible...they have the high advantage. We're pinned down and surrounded! You try and get out of here...if you do...you're dead!"

"We're dead anyway!" says Lieutenant Mitchell. Lieutenant Mitchell reloads his carbine, returns fire out the window, turns back to safety, putting his back up against the stone wall, with bullets ricocheting off the windowsill near him.

The look of mental anguish shows on Lieutenant Mitchell as the faces of Colonel Forsyth and Major Whitside display skepticism. The 7th Cavalry is now besieged as Colonel Forsyth looks out at the canyon and sees more of his soldiers being picked off.

An hour later, a light snow still falls, as the 9th Cavalry with their American flag and guidons K, D, I and F waving in the slight breeze are escorting the supply wagons and a few captured Sioux Indians with their hands tied behind them.

They are riding through a snow-covered forest on their way back to Pine Ridge. Major Henry is riding outside in the command position as Sergeant Jordan rides beside him leading the first column. Beside him is Sergeant Shaw, who is leading the second column.

As they ride a few paces, Sergeant Shaw looks at Sergeant Jordan and says, "Sergeant, you have any idea what these Sioux captives were tryin' to tell us?"

"No, Sergeant—but they were lookin' at us very strangely though. Trooper Chase said when they rode up on 'em, they gave up, without a fight, puttin' down their rifles...said the Sioux looked to 'em like they were ghosts, or somethin'...like we saw before."

As the soldiers ride a few more paces, Sergeants Jordan and Shaw, and Major Henry, look, then listen, to the horizon in front of them, off to the south, to what appears to be faint sounds of a lot of gunfire—more than they've been hearing previously.

Sergeant Jordan then looks at both men and says, "You hear that?"

"Yeah, concentrated, not hit and miss. Sounds like a whole a lot of trouble goin' on in one area," says Sergeant Shaw.

"Yes it does, Sergeant. I think there's trouble as you say," says Major Henry as he then says with direct military professionalism, "Sergeant Shaw, have a small detail stay with the prisoners and wagons, tell Captain Loud to follow our trail..." He then looks at Sergeant Jordan and says, "Sergeant Jordan, send out a couple of men to scout ahead, then ride back and get the troops ready. We just might be able to resolve the trouble. That's it, Sergeants."

"Yes, sir," say Sergeants Jordan and Shaw simultaneously.

Sergeants Jordan and Shaw salute with Major Henry returning the salute. Sergeant Shaw turns and spurs his mount—galloping back along the columns—calling out orders:: "I Troop, give me a ten-man detail..."

Sergeant Jordan spurs his mount to Trooper Chase then says, "Trooper Chase, take Troopers Irving and Walley, scout out the gunfire."

"Yes, Sarge. Lee, Augustus...let's go," says Trooper Chase.

Troopers Chase, Irving, and Walley spur their mounts out of formation, plowing through the snow towards the gunfire.

Sergeant Jordan then spurs his mount to a trot, back along the columns, looking at the soldiers and calling out his orders, as the soldiers look at him saying, "Listen up men! As you can hear, somethins' happenin' up ahead. Trooper Chase just rode out to scout the gunfire. Check your equipment and make sure your weapons are loaded and ready. We don't know what we'll ride into—pass the word."

The soldiers begin passing the word, then checking their equipment and weapons, while their mounts are at a walk.

Major Henry looks to both sergeants riding to the rear along the columns calling out orders as he begins checking his weapons, carbine, and revolver. Major Henry then looks back at the 9th Cavalry Troops, and sees Sergeants Jordan and Shaw riding back towards the front of the columns, finishing checking their own weapons while riding at a gallop. Major Henry stands in his stirrups and looks forward as he calls his orders, "Troop...at a trot...ho!"

The 9th Cavalry takes its mounts from a walk to a trot as Sergeants Jordan and Shaw gallop their mounts back into their positions in the columns, at the lead, keeping pace. Major Henry looks at his sergeants, who are in their positions, as he stands back up in his stirrups and calls out his orders, "Troop...at a gallop...ho..." The 9th Cavalry goes from a trot to a gallop, plowing through the snow, following the troopers' tracks, leaving a small detail behind with the prisoners and wagons. Major Henry, Sergeants Jordan and Shaw, Corporals Wilson, Dorch, Scott, and Jackson, and the rest of the 9th Cavalry Buffalo Soldiers ride through the cut snow path made by Trooper Chase and the detail as they ride towards the sound of massive gunfire.

On the outskirts of White Clay Canyon, very little smoke emanates from deep within the canyon as the 9th Cavalry follows Trooper Chase's detachment tracks with steady gunfire reverberating from the hollow of the canyon ahead of them.

They're about one mile away from the canyon's entrance when they come across many cavalry mounts grazing and running wild on the open snow-covered prairie.

At the same time, they see the three troopers riding back to the columns at full stride through the snow as Sergeant Jordan looks at Major Henry and says, "Sir...it must be somethin' awful wrong. Cavalry mounts runnin' around lose, no mount holders." Then he looks at the three troopers riding back and says, "And the way the troopers are ridin' back here."

Major Henry says, "I'm afraid you're right Sergeant." Major Henry then stands in his stirrups and calls his orders, "Troop...ho."

The two columns come to a stop as the three troopers spur their mounts through the snow towards them. When the troopers reach the columns, they bring their mounts to a fast stop, throwing snow as Trooper Chase, breathing hard, looks at Major Henry with urgency and says, "Sir, a whole lot of Sioux Indians have a cavalry troop pinned down on the canyon floor...looks like they've lost a lot of men, sir."

Major Henry looks at the canyon quickly and says, "What's the Sioux's positions Trooper?"

"They're high in the cliffs. It's a box canyon. The cavalry troop is trapped, sir."

Major Henry then looks at Trooper Chase and says, "Is there another way in, Trooper?"

"Maybe, sir, on the west side, you may be able to ride down on your mount, the east side is a little steeper."

The sound of gunfire continues to emanate from the canyon as Major Henry looks back to the canyon, to the bluffs, the perimeters, then at Sergeant Jordan. He says, "Sergeant Jordan, inform Captain Wright, I'll take K Troop—mounted—and we will assault their west flank. He's to take I Troop—mounted—with colors and commit to a frontal assault through the canyon on the bugle call." Major Henry looks at the supply wagons and their escorts, all of which are plowing through the snow towards them in the distance, before addressing Sergeant Shaw with an order: "Sergeant Shaw, ride back and get Captain Loud; inform him and Captain Stedman to leave a small detail with the prisoners and wagons, then ride to the east flank of the canyon, dismount his men, spread them out along the cliffs, out of sight, provide cover fire and attack down the bluffs. Take the bugler with you. Tell Captain Loud that when he is in position, to sound the bugle. After you're done, join K Troop. That's all, Sergeants."

"Yes, sir," say Sergeants Jordan and Shaw simultaneously.

Sergeants Jordan and Shaw salute, and as Major Henry returns the salute, they turn their mounts back to the columns, following Major Henry's orders as Sergeant Shaw says, "Bugler follow me."

The bugler takes off from his position in the column as Sergeant Jordan turns his mount and looks at Corporal

Wilson and says, "Corporal Wilson, have K Troop form-up over there." He points to an area to the west, then says, "Column of nines."

Corporal Wilson calls out his orders, saying, "K Troop..." as Sergeant Jordan then spurs his mount back along the columns, stopping in front of Captain Wright. He says, "Captain Wright, Major Henry said commit I Troop to a frontal assault, mounted, with colors through the canyon on the bugle call."

Captain Wright calls his orders, leading I Troop, spurring their mounts forward, towards the mouth of the canyon on both sides, keeping out of sight.

Sergeant Shaw is passing Major Henry's orders along to Captain Stedman saying, "Captain Stedman, the major said take D and F Troop, ride to the east flank of the canyon, dismount out of sight, once in position, have the bugler sound the charge-call, provide cover fire and attack down the bluffs."

Captain Stedman turns and calls the orders as the soldiers and bugler begin organizing under the guidons. Sergeant Shaw rides off towards the supply wagons.

Moments later, a light snow continues to fall as the long line of K Troop rides side-by-side, riding up the west slope towards the top of the canyon bluffs, near the end of the canyon, where gunfire emanates from within the hollow.

Major Henry and Sergeant Jordan are to the right of the troops, all with their carbines at the ready. Some of the soldiers are crouching low in their saddles, pointing their rifles at the ridgeline, just in case the Sioux pop their heads up.

Major Henry and Sergeant Jordan then look at the many foot tracks in the snow, leading to the top of the canyon bluffs and around the perimeters. Sergeant Jordan looks at Major Henry and quietly says, "Sir, I wonder why the cavalry troop didn't send out scouts... They would of seen all these tracks, and wouldn't of rode into what looks to be a trap."

Quietly, Major Henry says, "You're right Sergeant, I don't know why?" Gunfire continues to emanate from the canyon as Major Henry holds his carbine in the air, stopping the troops fifty yards from the ridge. Major Henry then looks at Sergeant Jordan and quietly says, "Sergeant, have the men spread out along the cliff, in intervals of ten yards."

"Yes, sir."

Sergeant Jordan turns to his left, looks at Corporal Wilson and quietly says, "Corporal, pass the word on my signal, intervals of ten yards."

"Yes Sarge."

Corporal Wilson turns to his left and passes the word to Trooper Chase, who passes the orders to Trooper Irving, who turns to Trooper Walley, and so on, down the line of soldiers till the orders reach the last man.

All the soldiers look at Sergeant Jordan now as he looks at them, raising his hand in the air, then bringing his hand down fast. The soldiers turn their mounts left, spurring their mounts to their new positions. Sergeant Jordan then looks down the embankment at Sergeant Shaw spurring his mount up the snowy hill towards them. Sergeant Jordan takes off his campaign hat, waves to Sergeant Shaw, and quietly says, "Come on."

As Sergeant Shaw continues spurring his mount up the hill towards them, Sergeant Jordan looks at K Troop in position, then to Major Henry and says, "Ready, sir, except for Sergeant Shaw who is riding in now."

Major Henry looks at Sergeant Shaw spurring his mount up the hill, and then he looks at his men as he backs his mount up. He looks at the quarter-mile-long line of Buffalo

Soldiers, with their carbines at the ready, sitting on their mounts, like proud gladiators awaiting battle.

Major Henry spurs his mount forward, back into his position, as Sergeant Shaw rides into his position, between Sergeant Jordan and Corporal Wilson.

Major Henry looks at both sergeants and quietly says, "All right Sergeants, we'll wait for the bugle call. Pass the word."

Moments later, in the Drexel Mission, several soldiers lay dead or seriously wounded as bullets continue to ricochet off the walls. Colonel Forsyth, Major Whitside, Lieutenants Mitchell and Sestak, and what remains of the 7th Cavalry soldiers inside the mission are returning fire when permitted.

Lieutenant Mitchell reloads, and aims his carbine out the window, trying to pick a target. He fires, then turns back to his safety position, looking into his ammunition bag. He cries out in despair, "Sirs...that's the last of my ammunition...pistol and carbine."

"I've only got one more round of carbine left myself," says Lieutenant Sestak.

After hearing what the soldiers just said, Major Whitside angrily looks to Colonel Forsyth, whose back is against the stone wall, looking down to the floor with a defeated look, and says, "Damn it, Colonel! If you would of listened to reason and put out scouts, and let me—"

Colonel Forsyth interrupts and wearily says, "Leave me alone Major."

Major Whitside looks at Lieutenant Sestak, and says, "Lieutenant, you'd better save that one for yourself...it won't be pretty." Major Whitside reaches into his ammunition bag, brings out a carbine round and tosses it towards Lieutenant Mitchell, hitting the floor at his feet.

Lieutenant Mitchell looks at Major Whitside, then to the round lying at his feet, and with a resolved look, he slowly stoops down and picks up the bullet off the floor. He opens the trapdoor of his carbine and inserts the round, then closes the trapdoor when the sound of a distant bugle charge-call is heard.

Lieutenant Mitchell stops, then looks up, thinking he is hearing things. Then he looks at Major Whitside as they all look to one another—are they hearing things, or are they really hearing the bugle?

The bugle charge-call, in addition to the sounds of soldiers yelling, is getting closer, louder, and echoing through the canyon as if a large army was surging upon their positions. The frequency of bullets ricocheting off the walls slows as the soldiers inside the mission keep their heads down, but begin to peer through the openings. The sounds of the bugle and the soldiers' yells coming from over the bluffs above them, and through the canyon, increase.

K Troop, hearing the bugler sounding the charge-call from the other side of the canyon bluffs, is shouting and hooting as their mounts dance.

Major Henry is holding his arm high up in the air, looking to his troops, as he brings his arm down, giving the signal for K Troop to begin spurring their mounts up the slope, to the top of the canyon ridge.

Meanwhile, most of the Sioux have taken their attention away from what's left of the besieged 7th Cavalry below them, hiding in notches and crevasses of the canyon and in the mission, and begin listening to the bugle charge-call and the sounds of soldiers echoing from all directions around them.

The Sioux are confused and unsure of which way to point their weapons, looking for signs of the cavalry, until they see the American flag and I Troop's guidon and troops rounding the bend, charging towards them in the far distance on the canyon floor.

The Sioux aim their weapons, preparing to fire, but stop when they hear, then look at the bugler on the east ridge, sounding the charge-call, and the long line of D and F Troops, and their guidons, standing on the ridge.

Some Sioux then train their rifles to the ridge. Carbine fire begins ricocheting around their positions. They look to the west ridge where the rifle fire is coming from, and see another long line of mounted soldiers: K Troop, 9th Cavalry, with their guidon blowing in the breeze.

The bugler continues sounding the charge-call, as K Troop surges down upon the Sioux's positions, with Sergeant Jordan calling to his men, "Don't hit 'em, unless fired upon. Push 'em out, push them out of the canyon...Get at 'em...yah, yah, yah!"

K Troop is spurring its mounts into action with zeal, down into the canyon, shooting at the ground, and over the heads of the Sioux Indians, causing them to leave their fortified snow-covered rock positions.

Most of the one thousand Sioux Indians are in full retreat because of the sure tenacity of the cavalry movement as other Sioux stop in their tracks and look at these dark-skinned bluecoats. Some of these Sioux have never seen or heard of a Buffalo Soldier before this encounter, and they just stand in their positions with a confused look on their faces.

The Sioux Indians near the entrance of the canyon are being routed to the middle of the canyon by I Troop, surging up, into some of the crevasses, forcing the Sioux down, onto the canyon floor. Many of them are running towards and past the mission.

D and F Troops keep a steady motivated carbine fire on their heels from above as some Sioux Indians stop in their tracks, and begin shooting at the soldiers all around them.

Trooper Irving is descending on his mount. One hand holds his reins while the other fires his service revolver at the heels of several retreating Sioux Indians as he is hit in the shoulder, and thrown off his mount.

Sergeant Shaw, upon seeing Trooper Irving shot and falling off his mount, looks to the Sioux who just shot him and fires a round—dead center in the Sioux's chest, causing him to fly backwards, then roll down to the canyon floor, dead.

At the same time in Drexel Mission, everyone is trying to get a better look at who is coming to their rescue.

Lieutenant Mitchell is peering up and out the window and sees K Troop surging their mounts down on the Sioux's positions on his side of the mission. He doesn't recognize any of them at first as he turns and looks at his comrades in the mission and with exhaustive jubilation, shouts out, "We're saved! We're saved! We're saved!" He then turns back to the window and looks out with a surprised expression and says, "Look at that...that's those colored boys. They comin' to save us...they're comin' to save us!"

In the mission, anyone who isn't too seriously wounded now clamors to any opening, keeping their heads down low, peering out at their oncoming rescuers, charging their foes from all positions.

The Sioux are making a hasty retreat towards the box-end of White Clay Canyon, passing the mission like a herd of stampeding ponies.

In the middle of the canyon, I Troop begins surrounding some of the Sioux Indians, taking their weapons and arresting them, while other Sioux Indians begin climbing up and over the bluffs at the end of the canyon, trying to escape the onslaught of soldiers. As the last remnants of the Sioux Indians pass the Mission, the occupants run out and begin rooting for their rescuers. Major Whitside, Lieutenant Sestak, and other soldiers cheer on the 9th Cavalry as Major Whitside says, "Go get 'em boys!"

Lieutenant Sestak yelling with jubilation says, "Go get 'em Ninth! YAHOO! We're saved! We're saved!"

Sergeant Shaw and K Troop spur their mounts by the mission in hot pursuit after the Sioux Indians as Colonel Forsyth stands at the bullet-riddled front door, looking to the Buffalo Soldiers routing the Sioux out of the canyon. He has a look that shows that he should of have died, instead of being saved. He surveys his regiment. About half are lying dead or wounded throughout the canyon.

Major Whitside walks over to Colonel Forsyth and pointedly says, "Colonel, I'm going to write a full report on your actions here today." He points to the dead and wounded and says, "Look—you got more than half of your regiment shot up!"

Colonel Forsyth looks at his soldiers. Most of them that aren't injured are helping their wounded comrades, or are cheering on the 9th Cavalry on foot and mounted, chasing the rest of the Sioux up and out of the canyon.

Some of the 7th Cavalry soldiers, and the ones that are not seriously wounded, run with elation to the Buffalo Soldiers who have stopped on their mounts, shaking their hands. Other 9th Cavalry soldiers who are dismounted, are converged upon by the 7th Cavalry soldiers with jubilant hand shakes, kisses on the cheek, hugs, while some, are just about kissing their feet!

Major Henry and Sergeant Jordan ride up to Major Whitside as Major Henry looks at Major Whitside and says, "Major, how in the hell did you get your men besieged like this?"

Major Whitside looks from Major Henry to the front door of the mission, then looks at Colonel Forsyth, who is standing there, as does Major Henry. Then Major Whitside, somewhat disgustedly, looks back at Major Henry and says, "Major...I'll have a full report by my return...however, right now, Major, I need help with my wounded."

Major Henry looks at Sergeant Jordan and says, "Sergeant, post guards around the canyon, have K Troop help with their wounded." He looks to the mission, then to Sergeant Jordan, and says, "We'll make the mission the infirmary."

"Yes, sir," says Sergeant Jordan as he smartly salutes, then turns his mount around, and looking at his men, says, "Corporal Wilson..."

Major Henry looks at Colonel Forsyth, who is collapsing at the front door. He quickly dismounts as he and Major Whitside run to Colonel Forsyth's aid. When they reach Colonel Forsyth, they pick him back up, standing him on his feet. Major Henry then looks around Colonel Forsyth's body, then at Major Whitside and says, "He's not wounded?"

"No, no he's not Major," says Major Whitside somewhat sarcastically.

"Let's get him inside," says Major Henry.

Major Whitside acknowledges with a nod of his head as both officers pick Colonel Forsyth up by the arms, and help him walk into the mission.

Inside the mission, Major Henry and Major Whitside

help Colonel Forsyth walk, holding him up by his arms, walking him to a bench, then sitting him down.

Major Whitside looks at the soldiers in the mission and says, "Water."

A soldier quickly brings a canteen of water to Major Whitside as other troopers lay buffalo coats on the benches and floor. Many wounded white soldiers are being brought into the mission, while very few wounded colored soldiers are brought in. The colored are carrying colored. Colored and white carrying white. All wounded soldiers are being laid on top of coats and covered with blankets. Major Henry is looking around the mission when he sees a lieutenant with long blonde wavy hair, tied into a frayed ponytail. The lieutenant is sitting alone on the top level of the steps that lead to the altar area. His uniform is tattered as he hangs his head low. Major Henry looks at the lieutenant as if he recognizes the long blonde hair. He then leaves Major Whitside, who is helping Colonel Forsyth drink from the canteen, and begins walking down the aisle to the steps leading to the lieutenant.

As Major Henry reaches the steps, he looks at the lieutenant and says, "Lieutenant...don't I know you?"

The lieutenant slowly lifts his head up; his eyelids hang low as he looks at Major Henry, thinking to himself that he recognizes Major Henry also, and with a dazed look says, "Yeah... Yeah, Major...I recognize you too…Hare and Hound race...I remember those two scars under your eyes."

Major Henry says, "You look bad, Lieutenant, do—"

Lieutenant Mitchell interrupts Major Henry and somewhat quietly says, "That damn fool..." Lieutenant Mitchell points to Colonel Forsyth and says, "Nearly got me killed...two times and..." Then he becomes distraught, and begins talking louder saying, "At that Wounded Knee place...none of us were suppose to get hurt Major, we had

314

Rescue at Pine Ridge

those Injuns surrounded...they were the only ones—"

Colonel Forsyth, looking at Lieutenant Mitchell, interrupts and shouts, "Lieutenant!"

Lieutenant Mitchell looks at Colonel Forsyth looking at him with a stern look on his face.

Major Henry looks to Colonel Forsyth also, then, turns back to Lieutenant Mitchell with intuitiveness. Major Henry puts one foot on the step in front of Lieutenant Mitchell, then bends down close to him and says, "Lieutenant, if I remember correctly...when I last saw you, I told you, we're soldiers of peace...nothing else..." Then Major Henry stands back upright, looks Lieutenant Mitchell over, and pointedly says, "By the looks of you, I think you know that now...war is not all the glory you thought it was...huh Lieutenant!"

Lieutenant Mitchell looks away from Major Henry, looking back down to the floor, as Major Henry turns from Lieutenant Mitchell and sees more wounded soldiers being brought through the front door of the mission. Major Henry then sees Sergeant Jordan and Corporal Wilson walking into the mission, followed by Troopers Chase and Walley assisting Trooper Irving to a bench with his wounded shoulder.

Corporal Scott walks in, looks at Sergeant Jordan and says, "Sarge, we're runnin' low on blankets."

Major Henry looks at Sergeant Jordan and says, "Sergeant, have a detail go back to the agency, at a gallop, report to General Miles only...on what happened here, and we need immediate assistance."

"Yes, sir. Corporal Scott."

"Yes Sarge."

"You and Corporal Dorch take a detail back to the agency, at a gallop. Inform General Miles only, Seventh Cavalry rescued, many dead and wounded...medical

315

supplies and wagons are needed immediately."

Corporal Scott snaps to attention, makes an about-face, walks out the front door as Sergeant Shaw walks past him, into the mission, looks at Major Henry and says, "All Sioux routed, about two hundred captured and taken prisoner, sir."

"Good job, Sergeant," says Major Henry.

Sergeant Jordan looks around the mission, then at Corporal Wilson and says, "Corporal Wilson." Sergeant Jordan then looks at and points to a long rolled-up canvas hanging above the front door with a rope hanging from one end, as he says, "Cut that canvas down. We can use it as cover."

Corporal Wilson takes his Bowie knife from its sheath. He then pulls on the rope that hangs at the end of the canvas.

The canvas unfurls with a plopping sound, getting every one's attention. All in the mission look at the canvas that contains the written words, "PEACE ON EARTH - GOOD WILL TO ALL MEN."

About a month later, two large columns of the 9th Cavalry, K, D, I, and F Troops, wearing their yellow-lined blue overcoats, are riding along a snow-covered trail, headed back to Fort McKinney. Snow flurries fall through the air around them.

K Troop is riding in their same positions as Major Henry looks at both sergeants and says, "It's almost the end of January, gentlemen, and we're finally going home."

Sergeant Jordan looks at Major Henry and says, "Sir, that's the first time I've ever seen a white troop give any appreciation to us."

"Sergeant, I believe it was scared into them," says

Major Henry as he chuckles.

Sergeant Jordan also chuckles as he says, "I think you're right about that, sir."

"Sir, if it wasn't for us, the Seventh would of been wiped out. The closest cavalry troops were hundreds of miles away," says Sergeant Shaw.

"That's exactly what my report will say, Sergeant."

Major Henry then turns in his saddle, looks at his men, who are in good cheer, riding at-ease, talking to one another as he looks at both sergeants and says, "They sure are happy. More than usual, Sergeants."

Sergeant Jordan turns in his saddle and looks back at the 9th Cavalry as quiet jubilation murmurs through the ranks. He turns back and looks at Major Henry and says, "Yes, sir...they're glad they're goin' home, and they know they did a good deed."

The columns ride on a few more paces, as Trooper Walley says to his comrades, "Wait till the folks back home hear the news...I helped save the Seventh Cavalry!"

Trooper Irving's arm is in a sling as he says, "You should of heard all the questions and things they were askin' me in the mission after you guys left—like where did you learn to ride and shoot like that?"

"Same old questions," says Trooper Walley, "They always want to know how we do things, but they never want to give us respect or the credit."

"There's one thing for sure", says Trooper Irving.

"What's that, Lee?" says Trooper Chase.

"That's the first time I've seen a whole lot of white men...glad to see a whole bunch of us colored," says Trooper Irving.

They all chuckle and laugh as Trooper Chase looks at his comrades and says, "Who would of ever thought...the Seventh Cavalry almost met the same fate again, fourteen years later, if it wasn't for us, the Ninth Cavalry."

A week later at Fort McKinney, regimental flags and guidons from detachments of all the Buffalo Soldiers' regiments blow in the breeze above the soldiers standing beneath them at parade-rest.

The 10th Cavalry, 24th and 25th Infantries, along with several miners and railroad men, are watching the 9th Cavalry ride across the imaginary line of Fort McKinney.

Scout Grouard is standing next to the adjutant, who is holding a newspaper. Both are standing on the Command Office porch, also looking at the 9th Cavalry that is riding into the garrison. Everyone in the garrison begins clapping their hands and cheering as the adjutant double-times off the porch, running towards Major Henry, holding the newspaper in his left hand. As the adjutant reaches Major Henry, he stops to one side of the columns and salutes. Major Henry returns the salute. Then, the adjutant begins keeping pace alongside Major Henry, while handing him the newspaper, pointing to the front headlines.

Major Henry reads the headlines, takes the newspaper and calls his orders quickly, "Troop, *hooo.*"

The troops come to a stop as Major Henry looks at Sergeants Jordan and Shaw, smiles, winks at them, then turns his mount and spurs his mount back in the columns. All eyes are on him. Major Henry stops his mount at Trooper Chase's position in the columns, looks at him, and says, "Trooper Chase, I believe your comrades would like to hear you read this. Everyone, everyone, circle around."

Major Henry waves his arms in the air as all of the two hundred Buffalo Soldiers spur their mounts into positions, making a very large circle around Major Henry and Trooper

Chase, filling in all the voids. Major Henry then hands Trooper Chase the newspaper and points to the headlines.

Trooper Chase begins to smile, and excitedly looks at his comrades and shouts, "Look at this guys, we, we...we made the front headlines of the Chicago Inter-Ocean Newspaper."

Sergeant Jordan stands in his stirrups and shouts to Trooper Chase, "What's it say Chase!"

Excitedly, Trooper Chase says, "The newspaper is dated, January 31, 1891—Ninth Cavalry, rescued Seventh Cavalry at Pine Ridge."

Trooper Chase is really excited, to where he almost can't comprehend what he's about to read, when Trooper Walley shouts to Trooper Chase saying, "Come Chase, what's it say?"

Again, Trooper Chase excitedly says, "It says here, half an hour more and the massacre of eighteen-seventy-six would have been repeated. But, at the critical moment...the valiant Buffalo Soldiers of K Troop, Ninth Cavalry attacked the Indians in the rear, and turned, annihilation into safety."

Several nights later in Fort McKinney's assembly hall there is a festive party. Everyone is dressed in their dress uniforms, and civilians are in their Sunday best.

Sergeant Major Brown is leading the cavalry band in playing "Down by the Riverside," with Trooper Chase singing.

A banner is strung across the front of the hall, hanging over the band, with the written words, "CONGRATULATIONS 9th CAVALRY – 'RESCUE AT PINE RIDGE' OF THE 7th CAVALRY - DECEMBER 30, 1890."

The 9th Cavalry is having a festive time as Sergeant

Shaw, Sergeant Jordan and Scout Grouard are sitting at a table talking. Sergeant Shaw looks at Scout Grouard and says, "...That's what that dancin' was about? To bring back their dead, bring new land...all white soldiers and people be washed away by a great flood."

Sergeant Jordan says, "That explains why the Indians looked to us the way they did."

"Yes, 'Ghost Dance,' not mentioned, colored people," says Scout Grouard.

The adjutant walks into the assembly hall, quickly looking around till he sees Major Henry, and walks towards him. As the adjutant reaches the table where Major Henry is seated, he smiles with a big grin and hands him a telegraph message.

Major Henry looks at the adjutant, then unfolds the message and begins to read. He then begins to smile as he looks back at the adjutant, then looks around the room at his men. Major Henry stands, then whistles to the room—quieting the band, Trooper Chase's singing, and the soldiers. Several tears well up in his eyes, and you could now hear a pin drop. Major Henry looks back to the telegraph, then to his men with a proud look, clearing his throat saying, "Gentlemen...I have just received orders...for K Troop, Ninth Cavalry and the cavalry band to represent the Ninth Regiment." He looks back to the telegraph, reads fast and excitedly saying, "...To transfer to Fort Myer, Arlington, Virginia, Presidential Parade and Burial Detail for accomplishments at Pine Ridge."

The entire room erupts into jubilation, as the band begins to play, "America" with Major Henry sitting back down with excited exhaustion.

Sergeants Jordan and Shaw, Corporals Wilson, Dorch, Scott, and Jackson, Troopers Chase, Irving, and Walley, and all of the 9th Cavalry soldiers are hugging one another and shaking hands.

After shaking Sergeant Shaw's hand, Sergeant Jordan turns and sees Major Henry. He salutes him. Happiness is written across his face as Major Henry stands, returning the salute, then shakes Sergeant Jordan's hand in true friendship.

Trooper Chase looks at Trooper Irving and says, "Lee, now we're going to finally get that rest you've been talking about all these years."

They smile to one another, shake hands, turn to the party and begin celebrating with their comrades.

Several months later in Washington, D.C., it's a beautiful spring day, as the Presidential Parade is in progress. Thousands of people of many ethnic backgrounds, mostly white and colored, line the street of Pennsylvania Avenue. They are waiting for the President of the United States—President Benjamin Harrison—and his parade carriage to reach their location.

Leading the parade is the 9th's United States Cavalry Color Guard mounted with forty-three stars on the Union Flag, proceeded by the 9th's United States Cavalry Band, with Sergeant Major Sammy Brown proudly leading his musicians who are playing "Hail to the Chief."

The 9th Cavalry, K Troop, Buffalo Soldiers are proceeding the band, riding on their beautiful black cavalry mounts, escorting the President of the United States in the middle of the regiment.

The beginning of the president's escort forms a "V" shape. Major Guy Henry is leading, center, with Sergeant George Jordan and Sergeant Thomas Shaw flanking to his left and right rear respectively. Corporal William O. Wilson and Trooper Henry Chase are riding outside of both their sergeants' flanks, with Troopers Lee Irving and Augustus Walley riding outside their flanks, skirting the crowd.

The president's carriage is in the middle of his escort and the other forty-three members of the 9th Cavalry Regiment, K Troop brings up the rear. They are behind the president riding forth in full glory.

As the parade moves down Pennsylvania Avenue, the crowd cheers and applauds. There is a colored teenager, Benjamin O. Davis. He is fourteen years old, and is standing with his grandmother in the crowd waving to the band, then to the Buffalo Soldiers and the president. As Sergeant Jordan approaches Benjamin's location, Benjamin looks at Sergeant Jordan and shouts, "Soldier! Soldier! Soldier!"

Sergeant Jordan hears Benjamin's shouts. He looks at him as Benjamin salutes. Sergeant Jordan smiles at Benjamin and returns his salute smartly, and just like Howard J. Mitchell, Benjamin O. Davis has just found his first hero.

Benjamin then turns to his grandmother somewhat excitedly saying, "I want to be a Buffalo Soldier, Grandma."

"One day, Benjamin, one day," says his grandmother.

THE END

Epilogue

The 9th Cavalry in a forced march, rode fifty miles back to the Pine Ridge Indian Reservation on the night of the December 29th 1890, in a full blizzard.

The Rescue of the famed 7th Cavalry, by the 9th Cavalry Buffalo Soldiers, was the most heroic valiant act of the Wild West frontier days by a United States Cavalry unit. This illustrates the true gallantry of the 9th Cavalry, K Troop and all the Buffalo Soldiers of that time.

Early 1891 United States flag - 43 Stars

In 1992, General Colin Powell gave a speech at the Buffalo Soldier Monument, dedicating the Buffalo Soldier Statue, in Leavenworth, Kansas, where he spoke of General Benjamin O. Davis, Sr.

General Benjamin O. Davis, Sr. File, 1940

General Benjamin O. Davis, Sr. France, August 8, 1944

Benjamin Oliver Davis, Sr., was born in 1877 in Washington, D.C. In 1899, after a year in the infantry during the Spanish-American War, Davis enlisted as a private in the regular Army. He served for two years in the Philippines and in 1901 he was commissioned a second lieutenant in the cavalry. In the following years, Davis served in various posts in the United States, until he was sent to Monrovia, Liberia, as military attaché, a post he held until 1912. Several times throughout his career he joined and rejoined the faculty of Wilberforce University in Ohio, teaching military science both there and at the

Tuskegee Institute in Alabama. During World War I, Davis was promoted to major and to full colonel in 1930. In 1940, President Franklin D. Roosevelt promoted Davis to brigadier general.

This made Benjamin O. Davis, Sr., the most senior member in the armed forces, and the first American of African heritage to become a general in the United States armed forces.

During World War II, Davis served as special adviser to the commander of the European theater and as assistant to the inspector general in Washington, D.C., in charge of a special section dealing with racial matters. In 1944, he persuaded the Army to try a limited form of integration. For these activities, he received the Distinguished Service Medal in 1944 and the Bronze Star in 1945. After serving fifty years, Davis finally retired from the armed forces in 1948. He died in 1970.

In 1997, the United States Post Office honored Benjamin O. Davis, Sr. with the issuance of a thirty-two-cent commemorative stamp where this information was ascertained.

Benjamin O. Davis, Sr.'s son, Benjamin O. Davis, Jr., commanded the famous Tuskegee Airmen.

"If you know your history, then you would know where you're coming from, then you wouldn't have to ask me, who the 'ack do you think I am."

—*Buffalo Soldier*; Bob Marley and N. G. Williams

Buffalo Soldier Monument, Leavenworth, Kansas

9th Cavalry Band in Santa Fe, New Mexico, 1880

APACHE INDIANS AND SIOUX INDIANS

Chief Victorio – Mescalero Apache

Nana – Mimbres Apache

*Geronimo –
Chiricahua Apache*

*Big Foot –
Mniconjou Sioux*

9TH CAVALRY OFFICERS

Colonel Edward Hatch

Captain Henry Carroll

Lieutenant Matthias W. Day

Major Guy V. Henry

329

Lieutenant Henry O. Flipper was the first colored man to graduate from the United States Military Academy at West Point—a class of 50 out of 76, majoring in engineering and surveying. Not one social word was spoken to Lieutenant Flipper during his four-year tenure. In 1881, he was brought up on trumped-up charges of embezzlement. In 1882, the charge was reduced to a lesser crime of "conduct unbecoming an officer and a gentleman" for dating a white woman, for which he was convicted. In 1976, a special Army commission reversed the dishonorable discharge, to honorable. In 1999, President William Jefferson Clinton gave a full pardon to Lieutenant Henry Ossian Flipper.

Second Lieutenant Henry Ossian Flipper

Lt. Flipper designed "Flippers' Ditch", to caused water to drain, running uphill to relieve the area of mosquitoes which caused malaria. Flippers' Ditch still exist today at Fort Sill, Oklahoma and was designated a National Historic Landmark in 1977.

The U.S. government legislated that colored chaplains were needed for the colored troops. In 1884 Chaplain Henry V. Plummer was assigned to the 9th Cavalry. On June 3, 1894, Chaplain Henry Plummer was brought up on two trumped-up charges of fraternization between an officer and enlisted men, and conduct unbecoming an officer and a gentleman. On November 2, 1894, Plummer's conviction was approved by the first Democratic president since the Civil War, Grover Cleveland. Today, the charge has still never been proven, and his conviction has not been overturned.

Chaplain Henry Vinton Plummer

25th Infantry, D Troop
Names unknown

Scout Frank Grouard was one of the most famous Chief of Scouts in the Northern Frontier, and was also commissioned as United States deputy marshal in Wyoming, April 4, 1892.

Frank Grouard, scout for the Third Cavalry

Chief of Scouts Frank Grouard

Corporal William O. Wilson, born in Hagerstown, Maryland, received the Medal of Honor on September 17, 1891, for gallantry in saving the cavalry wagons at Pine Ridge Indian Reservation, South Dakota, on December 30, 1890.

Corporal William O. Wilson Medal of Honor Winner

Corporal William Othello Wilson

Corporal Wilson's Medal of Honor was issued on September 17, 1891. Corporal Wilson was the last colored soldier to receive the Medal of Honor in the fight for the West. Corporal Wilson's story can be found in Frank Schubert's book, "Black Valor." Two current photos by Christopher Busta-Peck.

AUTHOR'S OPINION

It is the opinion of this author that the Ghost Dance was the American Indians' last chance of hope, keeping their nations alive. After their lives were changed by the intrusion/settlement of the whites from Europe, the American Indians sought any means necessary to hold their nations together, peaceful and non-peaceful. In the mid-1880's, the Great White Father brought the American Indian chiefs to Washington, D.C., to show the Great White Father's might, as a pacifier. Not only did the American Indian chiefs see the Great White Father's might, they also saw the Great White Father's religion. In their desperation for survival, they mixed their religion with the Great White Father's, creating the Ghost Dance.

NEVADA PAIUTE MEDICINE MAN –
JACK WILSON - WOVOKA

Young Jack Wilson

*Older Jack Wilson –
Wovoka*

GHOST DANCE

*National Archive Smithsonian Institution
Frederic Remington – 1890*

GHOST SHIRTS

Ghost Shirt
Nebraska Historical Society

Lakota Ghost Shirt
National Museum of
American Indians

MASSACRE AT WOUNDED KNEE

*Dead Sioux with mounted
7th Cavalry soldier*

The massacre of Wounded Knee

Big Foot lays dead and frozen as 7th Cavalry Soldiers observe

*Mass grave burial of the Sioux, Jan. 1, 1891
Nebraska Historical Society*

BLACK ELK

Sioux Ghost Dance, Forestier 1891

A quote taken from Black Elk, who witnessed the massacre of Wounded Knee as a child:

"I did not know then how much was ended. When I look back now from this high hill of my old age, I can still see the butchered women and children lying heaped and scattered all along the crooked gulch, as plain as when I saw them with eyes still young. And I can see that something else died there in the bloody mud, and was buried in the blizzard. A people's dream died there. It was a beautiful dream...the nation's hoop is broken and scattered. There is no center any longer, and the sacred tree is dead."

Black Elk

SITTING BULL

Sitting Bull

A quote from Sitting Bull:

"Indians...there are no more Indians left but me."

Chief Sitting Bull - Tatanka Iyotaka
Hunkpapa Sioux

REFERENCES

Black, Buckskin, and Blue - by Art T. Burton

Black Elk Speaks - by John G. Neihardt

The Black West - by William Loren Katz

Buffalo Soldier - by William Leckie

Buffalo Soldiers and Officers of the 9th Cavalry 1867-1898 - by Charles L. Kenner

Bury My Heart At Wounded Knee - by Dee Brown

Due Reward - by Chuck Barth

The Native Americans - An Illustrated History - by Alvin Joseph, Jr.

New Mexico Buffalo Soldiers 1866-1900 - by Monroe Lee Billington

COMMUNICATIONS / LETTERS / QUOTES

Quote – "They virtually have nothing left, but their eyes to cry with."

General Phillip Sheridan

Orders to Colonel James W. Forsyth
Dec. 28, 1890

"Disarm the Indians. Take every precaution to prevent their escape. If they choose to fight, destroy them."

General Nelson A. Miles

Hon. T. J. Morgan
Commissioner of Indian Affairs

Sir:

"...but I do feel it my duty to report the present 'craze' and nature of the excitement existing among the Sitting Bull faction of Indians over the expected Indian Millennium, the annihilation of the white man and supremacy of the Indian, which is looked for in the near future and promised by the Indian medicine men as not later than next spring, when the new grass begins to appear, and is know amongst the Sioux as the return of the ghosts..."

Major James McLaughlin
Indian Agent, Standing Rock Agency

Telegram to Washington, D.C.
Nov. 15, 1890

"Indians are dancing in the snow and are wild and crazy. I have fully informed you that the employees and the government property at this agency have no protection and are at the mercy of the Ghost Dancers. We need protection and we need it now."

Dr. Daniel F. Royer, Agent
Pine Ridge Agency

The Chicago Tribune
Nov. 16, 1890

"Settlers on the farms and ranches south of Mandan are fleeing their homes, believing that an Indian uprising is at hand. They urgently demand protection and many a farmhouse in North Dakota will soon be deserted unless the settlers receive some assurance that they will not be left to the mercy of the murderous redskins, who are now whetting their knives in anticipation of the moment when they begin their bloody work. The Indians are trading their horses and all other property for guns and ammunition."

Omaha World Herald
Dec. 1, 1890

"Mr. Royer seemed determined to believe that there would not be carnage. After a time it became apparent to me and to every Army officer and most are Old Indian fighters that Mr. Royer was trying to substantiate the fright which had caused him to call upon the troops. To hold his job Mr. Royer may succeed in aggravating these Indians into some sort of warlike demonstration, but it will be fighting against their will..."

The Aberdeen Saturday Pioneer, South Dakota
January 3, 1891

"The peculiar policy of the government in employing so weak and vacillating a person as General Miles to look after the uneasy Indians, has resulted in a terrible loss of blood to our soldiers, and a battle which, at its best, is disgrace to the war department. The Pioneer has before declared that our only safety depends upon the total extermination of the Indians. Having wronged them for centuries we had better, in order to protect our civilization, follow it up by one more wrong and wipe these untamed and untamable creatures from the face of the earth. In this lies future safety for our settlers and the soldiers who are under incompetent commands. Otherwise, we may expect future years to be as full of trouble with the redskins as those have been in the past."

Edited by: L. Frank Baum, creator of the fairy tale book; "The Wonderful Wizard of Oz", later becoming, "The Wizard of Oz".

Trooper Augustus Walley received the Medal of Honor on October 1, 1890 for his actions at Cuchillo Negro Mountains, New Mexico.

THE LAST WORD:

This epic story is also dedicated to all past American Indians—all Nations, and to all past Buffalo Soldiers who have gone before us.

Erich Martin Hicks

CPSIA information can be obtained at www.ICGtesting.com
Printed in the USA
LVOW120155191211

260055LV00001B/161/P